Silver Lining

Book One of the MANIPULATORS SERIES

by

C. Martin

Silver Lining
Copyright © 2015 Crystal Martin

Edited and Formatted by:
Pam Berehulke
Bulletproof Editing

Cover by:
Collin McWebb
McWebb Designs

Print Edition

Table of Contents

For Brent, my rock

Chapter 1

"It's time. I have to tell Violet that her father will be coming for her soon."

My stepfather's voice drifted up over the balcony from the living room as I abruptly halted at the top of the stairs, my heart seizing at his words. I took a step back toward my bedroom and leaned against the wall as I listened.

"No," my stepbrother said in a low voice. "You can't tell her yet. She's too young. Can't it wait?" Vick sounded strained and urgent, so unlike his usual calm and laid-back self.

I covered my mouth with the palm of my hand to keep from breathing too loudly. What did he mean? How could my father be coming for me—he was dead! What a weird thing for my stepdad to say; I didn't understand at all. And I didn't want to go anywhere. This was my home, my life. It was all I knew.

"Vick, I just want you to know what's going on. You know I don't have much say in the matter. Since her mother died, Violet's had a tough time, and the last thing I want to do is upset her or scare her. Look, the hospital called, and I'm needed in the cardiac unit. Keep this between you and me for right now," my stepdad said with a ring of finality in his voice. "See you tonight." His heavy footsteps crossed the floor.

When I heard the front door close behind him, I ran down the steps two at a time. My stepfather was gone, but Vick was still sitting on the couch.

"Vick! Who's coming for me? I don't understand." Confused and a little desperate, I dropped to my knees in front of him so we could be eye to eye, and was shocked at his expression. His face was anguished yet his eyes were vacant, as if he didn't really see me.

"Vick!" I waved my hand in front of his face. Nothing.

Trying to get his attention, I grabbed his hands, but was instantly dizzy. I shut my eyes, swallowing to fight the wave of nausea that swept through my body.

1

Then everything went black.

• • •

"Vi, are you okay?"

When I opened my eyes, I found myself lying flat on the floor as Vick leaned over me, shaking my shoulders. He let out a relieved breath as I sat up, then stared at me, his eyes wide.

"Violet, you scared the shit out of me! You passed out right in front of me."

I shook my head slowly, trying to make sense of it all, then frowned. "I-I had a horrible dream."

Little did I know, it wasn't a dream at all.

Chapter 2

One month later

Sitting in third period AP History class was usually the highlight of my day, which proved just how crappy my life was. Not only did my secret boyfriend sit where I could admire his gorgeous profile, but I happened to love the section we were currently studying.

Mr. Prickler paced in front of the class, his hands folded primly behind his back. "What president supervised the excavation of a Native American burial mound on his land in Virginia in 1784?" he asked in a nasal monotone. He stopped behind the lectern, the fluorescent overhead light reflecting off his bald pate as he waited for a volunteer, but no one raised their hand.

"All right, Miss Vancourt," he finally said with a sigh. "I know you know this one."

I groaned inside, cringing at the attention being drawn to me. "Thomas Jefferson," I answered politely.

A few dirty looks came my way, especially from JP Miller, who sat in front of me. "Little Miss Know-it-all," he mumbled under his breath.

Embarrassed, I adjusted my ever-present sunglasses, making sure they concealed my eyes, and sank a little lower in my seat.

"Mr. Miller, would you like to answer the next question?" Mr. Prickler asked over his shoulder as he wrote on the chalkboard.

"No, sir. Sorry, sir," JP responded quickly.

I bit my lip to keep from smiling, pleased that he got busted, but not wanting to provoke a reaction. It would only draw more attention to me, and that was the last thing I wanted. Being considered one of the few "have-nots" in a school full of "haves" was hard enough, even though my family wasn't poor, just not disgustingly rich. The fact that I wasn't originally a local, not born into one of the well-heeled area families with their strange customs and expectations even though my family had lived here for years, set me apart even more. So I tried to keep my head down and fly under the radar as much as possible.

Seated at the front of the classroom, Adam Price flirted with his girlfriend, Olivia. She was his "public" girlfriend, the only one anyone would know of. When he touched her hand and she giggled, it made my stomach churn and my mood go south. Normally he wouldn't display affection like that in front of me, considering our own relationship over the past few months.

To me, Adam was more than the captain of the football team and student body president, he was the first boy to care about who I was as a person. He'd been one of my best friends for the longest time, but this summer our relationship had changed, had become something more.

To all the other girls, Adam was a catch, and Olivia had him ensnared. Their parents had pushed them together since birth, and that pressure had ensured it.

I mentally shrugged my shoulders, determined not to care. Adam glanced back my way for a second before returning his attention to the teacher. His blue eyes were shuttered, showing nothing of his feelings.

Better be careful, Adam, someone might have seen you look at the outcast, I thought sarcastically.

Adam's world was like a snow globe, perfect but insulated. And every day I was reminded that I was an outsider, able to see into his world, but not really be a part of it.

Coming back to school in the fall shouldn't have been hard, but it was. It should have been exciting, this being my junior year in high school, yet it was anything but. This summer had been a roller coaster, starting out on a huge high as Adam and I had developed feelings for each other, even though we shouldn't. Then my mother had been diagnosed with cancer, and weeks later had passed away, shocking all of us with the swiftness of her death.

I'd been reeling over the loss, completely devastated, until Adam had helped me pick up the pieces of my broken life. By the end of the summer, he and I had become incredibly close, having spent many hours talking about love and loss, our lives and what we wanted to do with them, and exploring our growing feelings for each other.

At least over the summer, his relationship with Olivia wasn't flaunted in my face. She'd been on an extended trip to Europe with her family, so she hadn't been around. But I'd barely been back to school a week and already felt like the Titanic, on a crash course toward disaster. The mundane lectures and tedious homework were suffocating me.

The sun that hovered in the brilliantly blue September sky outside the classroom window did nothing to improve my unreasonably antagonistic mood. It seemed that the great weather was rubbing off on everyone except me, because I was trapped in this hellhole with a ringside view of the perfect couple.

Annoyed at myself, I shook my head, clearing all thoughts of Olivia and Adam from my mind, and concentrated on Mr. Prickler for the remainder of the hour.

While I was switching out textbooks in my locker before lunch, someone bumped into my shoulder, knocking my books out of my hands. As I bent to pick them up, a pair of hands swept down and grabbed them for me. I straightened up and adjusted the hood of my sweatshirt only to come face-to-face with JP, and his gloating smile told me it wasn't an accident after all. He was such a jerk, always trying to get my attention.

I rolled my eyes. "JP, can I have my books back, please?"

He handed me one of the three, holding back the other two with a smug look on his face. "What are you doing for lunch?" he asked as he leaned his shoulder against the locker next to mine.

I filed the book into the top shelf of my locker as he handed me another one. "I'm meeting Callie for lunch."

"How about you two sit at our table?" JP cocked an eyebrow and gave me a wolfish grin.

"I don't think so." I shook my head slightly, confused because he'd never asked me to sit with him before. I wasn't accepted at his table; he sat with all the other popular kids.

Several kids frowned at me as they passed us in the hallway, probably because of JP standing there talking to me. I wasn't one of *them*, and they always made sure I knew it.

Frustrated, I sighed and gave JP a hard look. "Can I have my last book?"

He handed it over, then pushed off the lockers. "See ya later," he called over his shoulder as he left, the halls now close to empty.

I narrowed my eyes at his retreating form, then walked alone down the now-empty halls, taking my time meeting Callie for lunch. I was brown bagging it today, PB&J and a yogurt. She was at our usual table when I arrived, and I hurried to sit across from her.

"Hey," I said as I sat down and pulled out my sandwich.

Callie was drinking lemonade, her idea of lunch. She had some issues with food. Since she was too picky to eat cafeteria food and too lazy to pack anything, she usually resorted to chugging lemonade while I ate.

"Hi." Her green eyes sparkled as her gaze swept over me. "Take your shades off, Violet. Your eyes are gorgeous, you shouldn't hide them." She uncapped her bottle and took a long swig.

My eyes were an unusual shade of gray, as piercing as silver, I'd been told. No one else I knew had eyes like mine, which made me different. It wasn't as if I'd been trying to hide them by wearing sunglasses all the time; I just had an issue with forced conformity. The fact that I could hide behind them was an added benefit; they were my own personal armor I put on every day. But for Callie's sake, I took the shades off.

As usual, she reached over and did me the unwelcome favor of tugging my sweatshirt's hood off my head, allowing my untamable auburn curls to spill out over my shoulders, so different from the dark brown hair she had pulled back into a sleek and fashionable pony.

"Was that necessary?" I complained, glancing self-consciously at Adam's table to find him watching me, his expression thoughtful.

His best guy friend was sitting next to him. JP gave me an assessing look from across the room and I turned away, focusing my attention back on mangling my sandwich.

Ignore them. That would be the logical thing to do, but I couldn't help myself. I had to have one more glimpse of Adam. He had draped his arm around Olivia and was grinning as he whispered in her ear. She smiled and tossed back her blond hair; it bounced in a disgustingly perky way with every movement.

"Yes, it was necessary," Callie said, her voice drawing my attention back to her wide, serious eyes. She scrunched up her nose before taking another sip of lemonade.

"All right, I've lost my appetite," I said unhappily.

Callie gave me a fierce look, her eyebrows drawing together over her pixy-like nose.

Uh-oh, I knew that look. It was the one she always gave me when she was going to say something she thought I needed to hear. My best friend was outspoken and stubborn, and even though I wouldn't always like what she had to say, she was determined to say it anyway.

"Here's a piece of advice," she said emphatically, flashing me a bright white smile.

I played with my hair, twisting a strand around my forefinger and slowly untwining it as I regarded her with apprehension. "Okay?"

"Let it go. Adam was a nice distraction for the summer, but you knew this would happen. Don't give him the opportunity to play you both. That would be every guy's dream." She nodded at me with a knowing look, and then took another long drink of lemonade.

"You're probably right," I said, smiling wistfully.

She leaned over and patted my hand. "I know I am."

I stole another glance and watched Adam give Olivia a kiss. Served me right for looking.

The truth was, I longed to be Olivia. She knew Adam was hers, and there wasn't a thing that I could do about it. It was the way things were here. Frustrated, I tossed the remainder of my sandwich into the brown paper sack, and left the yogurt untouched.

"All right, I'm going to jet." Before Callie could argue with me, I yanked my hood up, shoved on my sunglasses, and beelined for the

7

exit. Looking down at the floor like I normally do, I ran into a hard, muscular body just as I was going to push open the doors.

When I glanced up, JP was staring me down. He adjusted the sunglasses perched on top of his close-cropped blond hair, and then rested his hand against the door behind him, blocking my way. He jerked his chin up a notch in that tough-guy gesture that looked a lot better in the movies, and looked down at me with a challenge in his gaze.

"I was really hoping you were going to sit by me at lunch. I'm hurt that you didn't." His lips curved into a mock pout, his penetrating blue gaze boring into mine.

"I'm sure you'll live, JP. Please move."

It took all my strength to force myself to say the words nicely. I pointed at his chest, then poked it roughly when he didn't respond, gesturing for him to get the hell out of the way.

"You. Move." I spoke the words slowly; who knew if a caveman like JP could comprehend the concept? And why on earth was I suddenly his next female target?

"You'll come to realize soon enough that I'm all you've ever dreamed of." He snatched my hand and held it against his chest. "Next time, why don't you stand a little closer?" He winked at me and his lips curved into a sly grin.

"Ugh, JP. Let go!" I yanked my hand out of his grasp, sidestepped around him, and pushed through the cafeteria doors. His laughter echoed down the hallway, mocking me, and I didn't stop until I was safely in my next class.

• • •

After school, I made my way to the Prices' house; I worked there after school for spending money. Adam's dad, Alex, had hired me as a favor to my stepdad. Even though my stepfather's position as a cardiac surgeon ensured that he could afford to buy me anything I wanted, he and my mom had firmly believed that I had to learn responsibility. I wanted to work outside and wasn't bothered by getting dirty, and my sarcastic personality didn't exactly make me a good fit for a cashier or waitress position at the local diner, so Dad found me a job taking care of the Prices' grounds last year.

Adam's family's house was an impressive three-story brick home with a two-car attached garage and a separate three-car detached garage. It boggled my mind that they needed so much garage space. Seriously, how many cars could three people need?

Today I was scheduled to feed the goldfish in the pond and weed the garden. When I arrived, Adam's BMW was in the driveway. I pulled up next to it, unable to resist comparing his ride to mine. Although I didn't drive a hunk of junk, my Mustang was nothing compared to a Bimmer, underscoring once again the differences between us.

Silently, I prayed I wouldn't run into him. Summer was over and reality had set in. The truth was that Adam and I ran in two completely different social circles. There was also the little issue that had been hanging over our heads like a storm cloud all summer: his impending engagement to Olivia Melbourne.

Were they a little young to be getting engaged? Of course they were. Anywhere but here, that is. This little town's movers and shakers were an insular group, determined to keep their money close and their bloodlines "pure." They'd been arranging marriages for their children for the last several generations, and always announced the engagements right after high school graduation.

As for me, I thought the practice was archaic and barbaric, especially since it had put a serious crimp in my own love life.

The sun shone fiercely in the blue sky, its rays heating my skin as they washed over me. It had turned out to be a beautiful day in spite of the way I was feeling. I jogged across the wide expanse of lawn and hoped not to be noticed, my feet sinking into the plush green grass with every step.

When I reached the beautiful brick edifice the Prices ridiculously referred to as a "shed," I knelt down and moved the tiny blue pot of daisies on the ground next to the door to grab the key hidden underneath.

Once inside, I flipped on the light switch, revealing an organized collection of any tool I'd need to tend to the yard. I surveyed the bottom shelf, grabbed the goldfish food, and emptied some into a sandwich baggie. Glancing over my shoulder as I strode toward the pond, I noticed the deck was empty. Anyone on Adam's deck at the back of the mansion would have a perfect view of the pond below. It wouldn't be long before Adam realized I was here.

When I was standing at the edge of the pond a few minutes later, tossing food to the goldfish, I felt his presence behind me. Looking down, I saw his shadow on the grass.

"Adam," I said curtly. "What do you want?"

I glanced back at him just as he placed his hands on my shoulders, and stiffened against the warmth that seeped through my T-shirt. It was nice to have his hands on me, but I refused to give in to his touch.

"It's hot out here, isn't it?" He ran a hand through his tousled dark hair and gave me a mischievous, up-to-no-good smile. "You should take a break, cool off a bit."

His smile grew more devious and his dark blue eyes seemed to glow with intent. My heart sped up from that look . . . his dangerously sexy, you're-so-hot look that made my knees weak and all thoughts fly right out of my head.

"Adam, what do you—"

My words were cut off as he wrapped his arms around my waist and leaped full force, tackling me into the pond. In that split second before we hit the water, I was thankful my sweatshirt and sunglasses were safely on the grass.

The water was cool as it enveloped me. We broke the surface simultaneously with me still in his arms. I wiped the water from my face and he shook his head, spraying me with water from his hair. With one arm wrapped around his neck, I swiped a hank of dripping hair from my eyes and couldn't help but notice that even sopping wet, how incredibly good looking he was.

"Now, doesn't that feel good?" His lips curved upward and at that moment I wanted to kiss him, but I decided to play hard to get instead.

"I'm sorry, but you must have me mistaken for someone else," I said with a frown. "I don't like pond scum." I struggled to my feet in the murky water, pulling a long piece of slimy green muck from my hair and tossing it away. "It doesn't really do anything for my appearance."

I wanted to be angry with him, but all the animosity I'd harbored had vanished. Droplets of water dotted his handsome face. His deep-set blue eyes looked like two beautiful gems that pierced me with a tenderness I couldn't describe. The attraction that danced in the air between us was electrically charged as he reached up to push aside a piece of wet hair from my cheek.

"You look good enough to drink," he whispered as he cupped my face, his thumb gently stroking as he wiped water from my lips.

I swallowed, uncomfortable with his nearness and the intimacy of his touch. *Did I hear him correctly?*

Adam's lips parted and he leaned his head toward me, his gaze focused on my lips. He slid his fingers back, curving behind my neck and drawing me forward. My skin prickled and I froze for a second, shocked at the realization that he was going to kiss me.

The lip-lock I'd witnessed earlier between Olivia and Adam pushed its way to the forefront of my thoughts, and all desire to kiss him withered instantly. Desperate to divert his plan of action, I tangled my fingers into his dark hair and pushed with all my might until his head was underwater, then swiftly began kicking for the shoreline.

The weight of my waterlogged clothing hindered my quick getaway, and I didn't get as much of a head start as I had hoped. A hand clasped my shoulder just as I began pulling my dripping-wet body up onto the grass. I groaned and squeezed my eyes shut.

"What was that for?" Adam asked.

I twisted around, my elbow resting on the grass while the rest of me was still submerged like a mermaid, and came face-to-face with him. He didn't look angry, just bewildered, and since I shared the same lack of communication skills with my stepfather, I just shrugged my shoulders and crawled clumsily onto the bank. He quickly followed suit, springing out of the pond easily, and I envied him for his effortless grace of movement.

"How was your first week of school?" Adam asked as he plopped down on the ground, his voice low and his expression wary.

I sat down in the grass and leaned forward, wringing the water from my hair as he sprawled out next to me, propped up attentively on one elbow.

"The usual," I said as I began wringing out my shirt in a similar fashion.

His hair dripped like a wet mop, water droplets cascading down his cheeks. I tentatively reached out to catch a drop with my finger, allowing myself to caress his soft skin. He closed his eyes briefly at my touch. Unnerved, I pulled back quickly.

Adam tilted his head, giving me an appraising look. "Missing your mom? If you want to talk about it, I'm here." He squinted at me in the bright sunlight and combed a hand through his wet hair.

"Thank you," I said softly and averted my gaze. My heart ached just thinking about my mother; her loss was still so raw for me. "I don't feel like talking about it right now, though."

"Do you want a towel?" His gaze roamed over my body, causing my cheeks to flush.

"No." I shook my head. "I should probably be going." I glanced down at my soaked clothing before turning back to his eyes, which I'd always believed were his best feature.

"But you didn't weed the garden." He seared me with a look that said he wasn't ready for me to leave just yet.

"Adam, I'm all wet and I need to go home and change. What I didn't finish today I'll finish tomorrow." All that was partly true, but the real reason was that my stomach was a ball of nerves.

"I understand." The corners of his mouth lifted in a small smile. "I just want to spend more time with you. Come here." He reached over and stroked a finger down my forearm, sending shivers throughout my body. "My arms feel empty without you in them."

And just like that, Adam made my heart pinch. It always amazed me how easily he could share his feelings with me; most guys couldn't do that. It was too bad he wouldn't do that in public.

"That's because they *are* empty," I said, pointing out the obvious. My eyebrows knitted together in frustration. When we were alone, he was so open, so vulnerable, and so very different from his

12

confident, tightly controlled public persona. As much as I wanted to see what might happen next, I knew I should go.

"You can be such a smartass," he said, smirking at me. "That was meant to be charming."

I grabbed my sweatshirt off the grass and thrust my sunglasses on my face, refusing to let him see just how unsettled he made me feel.

"I'm sorry," I said, my tone sharper than I'd intended. "I just don't understand why you won't just break up with Olivia. You obviously don't like her. I think it's stupid that your parents think they can tell you who to marry. People shouldn't get married because their parents insist on it," I said, then added softly, "They should get married because they're in love."

"Violet," Adam said with a sigh. "When my dad and his friends started their business, they made a lot of money. They just want to make sure their investment is protected, to be sure it stays in the family, you know that. It's the way things have always been. Why can't you understand that?"

I let out a little snort. "The saying that money doesn't buy love rings a little truer, doesn't it?" I didn't wait for him to respond. "Now that I'm soaked, I need to go home and get cleaned up. Maybe next time you'll think about that before tackling me into the pond." I stood up and muttered an evasive, "See ya later."

Adam's mouth dropped open as if he was going to protest, but I took off at a sprint toward my car before he could say a word, water squishing out of my sneakers with each step.

He didn't follow.

• • •

After changing clothes, I wasn't in the mood for dinner and it was still a little early, so I decided to go down to the park to relax and do some reading. The park was right next to the lake, and had some gorgeous views. It was pretty and serene; a place I loved to go for some quiet time.

When I got to the park, I grabbed my backpack and made my way down a brick path that wove in and out of maple and evergreen trees, its edges dotted with flowers and shrubs. When I reached the

13

end, I pulled a light blanket from my backpack and laid it out on the grass inside a small grove of trees. There was just enough room for myself and one other person, which unfortunately reminded me of Adam because he used to come here with me.

I leaned back on the blanket and enjoyed the beautiful scenic view of the lake. The sun shimmered as it reflected off the water, making me think of diamonds floating on the sea. I was fond of this particular spot; this place always had a calming effect on me, and many memories had been made here. Adam used to lie on the blanket with me, drawing pictures on my back. He'd make me try to guess what he was drawing, and nine times out of ten it ended in a tickle fight.

I smiled to myself as I pulled out my book from my backpack and turned to my stomach, propping myself up on my elbows so I could read. Moments later I was still on the same page, my focus blurring as tears filled my eyes when thoughts of my mom kept intruding.

We'd been so close, my mom and me. She'd had a tough time of it after my father had been killed in a car accident when I was little, although I didn't remember much from those years. My earliest memories revolved around the year I was five, when Mom married Dr. David Williams. Dr. Williams had a son who was nine at the time, and Vick had turned out to be a terrific stepbrother, never minding when I'd tagged along after him and his friends.

We'd been happy together, the four of us, and before long I'd started calling Dr. Williams "Dad" and Vick had called my mother "Mom." Everything had been great until Mom had started having these weird pains back in June. She'd gone to the doctor, spent a week or so having tests run, and the results changed our lives forever.

Cancer is a heartless bitch. It took my mom from me in a matter of weeks, and turned my life upside down. When Mom died in August, I felt as if my own life were over. I cried for days, and was barely able to get through the funeral. Then I'd worried about what would happen to me, since I was technically an orphan now, but Dad had assured me that things would be fine.

14

Vick and Callie had been there for me, which helped a lot. But Adam had been my rock during that time, but now that school had started again he was always with Olivia. Just when I'd started getting my feet back under me, it felt as though the rug were pulled out from under me yet again.

I must have dozed off because I jerked when my phone beeped in my pocket, signaling that a text message awaited me. I fumbled for it, still half asleep, and closed the book I'd been reading, that unfortunately was stained with a little bit of drool. I made a face at it, madder at myself more than anything for falling asleep in the first place.

The text was from Adam, and my heart skipped a beat just at the sight of his name.

Adam: What are you up to?

Me: In the park reading.

My fingers flew over the screen as I typed out my sentence. I almost typed *at our spot*, but caught myself and backspaced over the letters.

Adam: Want some company? I can be there in five.

What? I panicked, not wanting to see him right now.

Me: Sorry, just leaving.

I sent the message quickly. Grabbing my book, I shoved it along with the blanket into my backpack and gave one last glance at the calming water that sparkled as it quietly lapped the shoreline, then started up the walkway toward my car. My phone beeped again.

Adam: Too late.

Great. Trying to put off the inevitable, I slowed my pace on the path, dillydallying along the way. People at the marina were putting their boats away for the night. The breeze was cool but I wasn't chilled; the anticipation of facing off with Adam had my body heated. I knew he wasn't happy with me after the way I left him earlier, and I shouldn't have been surprised that he had tracked me down.

15

I took a deep breath as I rounded the bend, and there he was leaning against my car, the only obstruction I had to my quick getaway. I had left my sweatshirt and sunglasses on the passenger seat, which I regretted immensely.

My gaze traveled over him as I took in his orange tee, khaki shorts, and sandals. He looked good. God, he always looked good, I thought. Even in the early evening light that was slowly fading, I could see he wasn't smiling. His posture was stiff, his arms crossed in front of his chest.

I walked past him without so much as a hello and circled the rear of the car, while he went around the front and ended up blocking my path anyway.

"Adam," I said, disheartened. I pressed the UNLOCK button on my key fob and opened my door so I could toss the backpack into the backseat. He was standing so close I could feel the heat from his body, smell the scent that was so uniquely him. He smelled good, like fresh autumn leaves. "What are you doing here?" I said casually.

"I feel like I got the brush-off earlier today." He ran his hand through his hair in frustration. When I didn't respond, he said, "I know I haven't seen you much this week. With school starting up and people popping in and out after school . . ." His voice trailed off. "I just want to spend some time with you, you know. Violet?"

My mind was elsewhere. I mean, I heard him, but didn't concentrate on his words too closely. I didn't really know what to say, and avoidance always worked best for me. Rather than answer him, I gazed over his shoulder at the setting sun and the mosaic of colors it created in the sky. It was breathtaking.

"Violet, will you at least look at me when I'm talking to you?"

I peeked up at him through my lashes. Adam was almost a head taller than me. The world he was a part of was the world I defied. It wasn't normal for people like us to be in a relationship, especially when one was already committed to someone else, even if it wasn't by choice. If pushed, I'd have to admit that the fact that we weren't supposed to be together played a large part in our attraction in the beginning of our relationship.

"I miss you," he said softly, and pulled me into a gentle embrace.

16

I was stiff in his arms, unwilling to relax, but with the heat radiating off him and his intoxicating scent, I slowly found myself melting into his hug and my insides turning to mush. My anger slipped away, replaced by a soft tenderness for him. I let the breath I'd been holding escape my lips. This wasn't how I had envisioned my evening turning out.

Adam sighed as I settled comfortably within his arms. Was it a sigh of relief? A sigh of despair? I didn't know.

He snuggled me closer, then dropped his voice low as he asked, "Why did you blow me off earlier?"

I could feel his warm breath in my hair as he kissed the top of my head, before pulling away so he could study my face, making it very difficult to lie. Where were my sunglasses when I needed them? Oh yeah; they were in the car.

"Adam, I'm not your girlfriend." My voice was a little shaky, even though I tried my best to keep it steady, with no evidence of emotion reaching my face. I was good at masking my feelings; at least, I thought so anyway.

His jaw ticked, revealing the first glimmer of anger. Yep, I fooled him.

"I told you titles don't mean a damn thing to me."

"I know you said that," I said, struggling not to raise my voice. Despite taking a calming breath, I could feel my temper rising, gaining momentum. "It's just hard to watch you with Olivia every day. And quite frankly, I shouldn't have to."

I had to go before I lost my composure. Tears had formed and were brimming my lashes, threatening to overflow. I quickly reached up and gave him a kiss on the cheek; his skin was soft under my lips, his fragrance intoxicating. I had the urge to let my lips linger there longer than they should, but I fought it.

"Good-bye, Adam," I said. As I went to get in my Mustang, he grabbed my elbow, pulling me to a stop.

"Violet." The pure anguish in his voice tugged at me and I turned my gaze on him, silver to blue. I halted, waiting for him to continue. He opened his mouth, whatever he wanted to say on the tip of his tongue, and then closed it with a sigh of defeat, his words lost to him.

I took this as my cue to leave. After yanking my arm from his grasp, I whirled and hastily jumped in my car, then drove away. It was the second time I had walked away from him that day. When I glanced in my rearview mirror, I could see his face darken with pure frustration.

A few seconds later, he was nothing but a silhouette fading into the coming darkness.

Chapter 3

During first period the next day, I began compiling a list of why Adam and I should or shouldn't be together.

I started with the "pro" column. *He has a good heart, I like the way he makes me feel, and he's easy on the eyes.*

Next came the "cons." *Different peer groups, he has a girlfriend his parents chose for him, our relationship is secret.*

I tapped my pencil on the desk as I studied the list again. My reasons for not being with him outnumbered my reasons to be with him, since being easy on the eyes wasn't a good enough reason to be with someone. My mom had drilled that into my head as soon as I started liking boys.

It was times like these that I really missed my mom. If she were still alive, we'd be able to talk this out together over cups of hot chocolate at the kitchen island after I came home from school. And at that thought, my eyes began to prick, so I sniffed hard and forced myself to focus on the list.

By the end of first period, I wasn't any closer to deciding if I should quit seeing him, or if I should just go all in and pursue something more. It was as if I were making a huge wager at a gambling table and everything counted on the flip of the next card.

Cards. A light bulb had gone off in my head; I knew what I was going to do. I could see everything with so much clarity.

I met Callie at her locker before lunch, and as we walked toward the cafeteria, I began to fill her in on yesterday's events. "Adam tackled me into the pond yesterday. I think he was trying to be romantic," I said, smiling at the thought.

Callie rolled her eyes. "Weird. I think 'trying' is the key word. When does he not think he's being romantic? Oh, that's right—"

I elbowed her ribs for her to shut up as JP and Adam veered in front of us from a hall to the right. Adam's eyes lingered on me seconds longer than they should have, and he looked troubled. I purposefully slowed my pace, not wanting to get too close to them. It would be hard to keep my eyes from seeking Adam out.

When the guys walked on ahead out of earshot, Callie frowned at me. "Violet, look. I get it, he's hot. But you should really find another hot guy to crush on and ASAP." She hitched her book bag a little higher on her shoulder, then said, "I'm seeing Henry today after school. We're going downtown to see a movie. He has a friend," she added, and widened her eyes at me hopefully. "I could definitely hook you up."

Callie's relationship with Henry was an arranged one. Her parents had set it up for her just like Adam's parents set up his with Olivia. I didn't understand it and I didn't really care to. She was my bestie, and I knew that she would never say anything to anyone about Adam and me. I trusted her with my life.

I shook my head and ducked my chin so I could look at her over the top of my sunglasses. "Sorry, no can do. Work after school, remember? Oh, and I'm so not interested in Henry's friend, no offense. But you and Henry go on and have fun," I said with a wink.

She laughed at me and shook her head. We made our way through the cafeteria and when we reached our usual table, we sat across from each other. Callie actually had a granola bar today with her lemonade, which surprised me, and I had my usual.

"Hey, can I ask you something?" I asked, not waiting for her to answer. "There's a place in Marquette I want to check out. The lady reads tarot cards and tells fortunes, among other things."

Callie looked at me like I had lost it, her eyes growing huge. "You can't be serious."

Her face looked so bewildered, I nearly choked on my sandwich from laughing so hard. "Actually, I am, but hear me out. I just want to know if I'm wasting my time with him."

"What about your job?" she said, looking purposefully at the boy in question.

I followed her gaze. Adam wasn't sitting with Olivia today; JP had all his attention. Relief washed through me, but it was short lived. As if sensing me, JP turned his head and gave me a little wink.

20

When my mouth dropped open, a grin spread across his handsome face.

Annoyed, I turned back to Callie. "I'm going to do it tomorrow. It's Saturday and I was kind of hoping you would come with?" I gave her my poutiest I-need-my-best-friend look. It had never failed me before, and it didn't fail me now.

She rolled her eyes at me and scrunched up her nose, mulling over her options. "Okay, what are friends for? It will give me a good chuckle at the very least," she said as she grinned back at me.

• • •

I decided I'd head to Adam's right after school to weed their expansive flower garden. I didn't expect him to be there because he had a football game tonight. My participation in school activities was on an as-needed basis, and I was definitely not needed at a stupid football game.

When I pulled up at the Prices', I was surprised to see Adam's BMW there, as well as a couple of other cars pulled alongside it. I was pretty sure that the Lexus was JP's and the Maserati belonged to Olivia.

I frowned, annoyed that Adam was home. Well, at least he would be too preoccupied with his visitors to hassle me today, which was a bonus, so I went to work in the garden with a lighter spring in my step.

I was singing softly to myself when a shadow fell over me. I looked up, expecting to see Adam, and my frown returned when I saw JP standing there.

"What do you want?" I demanded, standing up so I could face him while wiping my hands on my jeans. I wasn't in the mood for his bullshit today.

JP's blue eyes stared at me with calculation. "You have a bit of dirt right . . . here," he said, thumbing my cheek with a soft caress that contradicted everything I knew about him. When I jerked away and glared at him, he said, "Don't worry, the look suits you. It's sexy." He let the last word roll off his tongue.

I scowled at him and he gave a low chuckle, crawling under my skin like he always did.

21

"Don't touch me," I snapped at him. "I don't care if I'm dirty. I'm working. Maybe you wouldn't know what that is since you haven't worked a single day in your life." I glared at him, hands on my hips.

He gave me a mischievous smile, then turned without a word and sauntered away, whistling off-key under his breath.

Damn it. I kicked the ground with the toe of my shoe and then knelt down, digging furiously at the weeds that dared invade the Prices' perfect garden. I'd let JP succeed in riling me, which was exactly what he wanted. One minute he was asking me to sit with him at lunch, and the next minute he was infuriating me.

Adam came out onto his deck, a look of concern flickering across his handsome face. Then Olivia appeared at his side, and without missing a beat, he casually wrapped his arm around her. I turned away, not wanting to be reminded of how perfect they looked together. Unfortunately that glimpse of them was burned into my mind.

"JP," Adam called out uneasily. "What are you doing?"

I shoved the trowel into the dirt and sneaked a peek over my shoulder.

"Just talking with Violet," JP said innocently as he strolled back toward the deck.

Seething, I gritted my teeth to keep my mouth shut. No need to cause more trouble by bringing JP into the mix. I went back to work and ignored the rest of their conversation.

When I was finished, the garden was immaculate but I was a small disaster, covered in dirt and sweat. Instead of going home to eat dinner with my stepfather and stepbrother, I went straight into mowing the lawn. One less thing for me to do on a different day.

It was nearly nine by the time I was finished, and the sun was just beginning to set while I hurried through the motions of putting the riding mower away. Over the summer, my normal routine would be to jump on the hammock and close my eyes until Adam came home.

But things were different now, and I wasn't sure if he was even going to come home tonight, which was fine by me. I focused my attention on the hammock swaying in the soft breeze, walked over, and climbed in to relax for a few minutes. Once settled in, I hung one grass-covered sneaker over the edge, moving it back and forth to set the hammock swinging.

The roar of an engine startled me out of my relaxed state. I touched my chest where my heart was beating, trying to catch my breath. Forgetting I was on the hammock, I rolled over and almost ended up on the ground. I hated the fact that I was anxious and excited to see him. It was hard denying since I had purposefully waited around just to see if Adam would show up like he always had before.

"Violet!" He jogged over to where I was now sitting and took me into his arms, catching me off guard. "We won!" he said as he lifted me up and spun me around.

Instinctively, I wrapped my arms around his neck and hung on for dear life. He had obviously showered and changed out of his football uniform, wearing jeans and a white T-shirt. His skin was warm against mine, contrasting with the coolness of the damp tendrils of his hair. His good mood was contagious and I smiled, even though I couldn't have cared less whether we won the game.

"I'm happy for you," I said as he put me down. Seeming reluctant to let me go, he kept his hands on my waist, leaving me no choice but to rest my hands on his forearms, unsure of where else to put them.

"Hey, the garden looks great. Did you cut the grass?" He squinted as he surveyed the landscaping more closely under the remaining light of the setting sun.

"Yeah, I won't be back until Monday now."

His brows drew together at my words, his lips setting into a grim line while his jaw flexed.

"Look, I'm sorry about yesterday," I said, speaking rapidly before I lost my nerve. "I didn't mean for things to get so heated between us." I peeked up at him. "I wasn't sure if you were coming home after the game or not."

He slowly blew out a breath, then asked, "Do you have any plans?" The hope in his expression combined with the way his thick lashes framed those blue eyes of his made my heart beat faster.

Before I could stop myself, I giggled. "At this moment?"

"Yes, at this moment." Adam's lips curved upward in a small smile. "I'm glad you find me funny," he said dryly.

My face burned, and I could picture the embarrassing pink stain that must be spreading across my cheeks.

"I'm sorry, Adam, but I'm dirty and sweaty. I just want to go home and take a shower." I pulled my gaze from his and focused my attention on my hands that lay on his arms, taking slow breaths in an effort to relax the ball of nerves forming in my stomach.

"For the record," he said, brushing the back of his fingers against my cheek in a slow caress. "I think you look beautiful." His fingers left a warm trail, making my stomach clench. He leaned down, drawing his lips so close to mine I could feel the warmth of his breath against them.

"Sit down with me for a little bit?" He pulled me the short distance to the hammock and sat down, tucking me securely under his arm and close to his body.

"Just a little bit, okay?"

He nodded, his expression thoughtful as he kicked his feet against the ground, causing the hammock to sway. We lay there quietly for a while, swinging slowly back and forth as the sun finished setting and darkness fell.

As I lay my head on his chest, breathing in the smell of fresh-cut grass, I heard a car churning up gravel in his driveway, and our private little moment was interrupted. Adam sighed and pulled away from me.

I folded my arms over my stomach, frustration overtaking my nervousness, and rolled my eyes at him. "I'm so tired of being in the dark."

I wasn't sure if Adam understood that I didn't mean it literally. The exciting part of our hidden relationship was over. It seemed that every time we got close, he pulled away from me, a little further each time. The secrets and the lies were becoming a burden, and the close, intimate moments we used to experience seemed few and far between. I jumped up and turned to stalk away, and he trailed me toward my car.

"If you're not coming here till Monday, can I see you before then? You know, when you're all cleaned up?"

Glancing at him, I saw him smiling in his shy way, and my heart melted like butter. "I'm not sure," I mused aloud. "Why don't you send me a text?" I peeked over at him as we walked, a little dizzy from the attraction I constantly experienced around him.

"Why," he said sharply. "So it's easier to blow me off?"

Insects hummed in the darkness around us as I searched for a response. We were almost to my car, the gravel crunching under our footsteps. I glanced around, wondering who had driven up. There were no other cars in the driveway, but Adam didn't seem curious, so I pushed the thought out of my head.

"Here's an idea, why don't you go do something with Olivia? I'm sure she's free," I said flatly. I'd wanted a little more sarcasm behind the words, but I was too exhausted to muster any.

"Listen, Violet." He grabbed my arm, gently pulling me back from my car, and turning me toward him. "I can see Olivia anytime I want, but I'd rather see you. I'd pick seeing you over her any day of the week." His voice was low and sincere, but his relationship with Olivia lingered between us. Always lurking, always the elephant in the room.

Adam leaned down and kissed me with a sudden urgency, his soft lips slowly molding to mine with a gentleness that instantly made me feel hot and dizzy. My knees were weak so I clutched his shirt, and his arms went around me, holding me to him as if I were the most precious thing in the world.

His fingers tangled in my hair as our lips moved in a slow dance, and I relaxed in the comfort of his embrace. Our lips pressed together, touching, exploring, and I let all my inhibitions fly right out of me as my fingers wove through the damp, silky locks at his nape. I wanted this kiss just as much as he did.

My emotions were at war with my brain, and in the back of my mind I thought I heard a soft *click*. But Adam's lips demanding mine soon made me forget all about the strange sound.

We reluctantly parted. My breath came quickly and my face was warm. He laced his fingers with mine and looked down at the ground, obviously with something on his mind, but I wasn't in the mood to push him tonight. Maybe I just didn't want to know.

"I have to go. It's getting late," I said reluctantly.

I was still bothered by the strange clicking noise. Adam hadn't seemed to notice it so I didn't bring it up to him, but what was it? I let my eyes wander to the full moon, which had a pale yellow halo. It was eerie, straight out of a horror flick. Amused at my own imaginings, I looked down at his strong, square hands and silently wished it could always be this way.

He flashed me his sexiest smile and said, "See you tomorrow," his eyebrows raised in expectation of my usual response.

I swallowed a lump forming in my throat, reluctant for the moment to end. Surrendering to the inevitable, I gave him a chaste kiss on those gorgeous lips and said, "Not if I see you first!" in a voice much more cheerful than I felt. Then I got in my car and headed home.

That night in bed I tossed and turned, hoping that tomorrow would be the day I got the answer I was looking for.

Chapter 4

Saturday morning I rose even earlier than I normally would have for school and spent an hour on the treadmill, trying to burn the extra nerves out of my system. I was excited about meeting with the psychic, and the possibility of getting answers. The possibility that this person might be able to shed some light on my relationship with Adam was what made me so eager. The what ifs were what made life so exciting.

I blow-dried my hair and tried to brush my curls into submission with some smoothing gel. Peering into my reflection in the mirror, I sighed; at least the frizzy look was gone.

I practically sprinted back to my room and threw open my closet doors, grabbing the first outfit my eyes landed on, a purple V-neck hoodie sweater with dark jeans, and dressed as fast as possible. I grabbed a pair of black boots with purple laces and ran down the stairs, my hair bouncing on my shoulders.

I lifted my keys off the hook in the entryway and snatched my phone from my pocket to send Callie a text.

Me: On my way! You better be ready :)

"What's the rush?" My stepfather's voice boomed from the couch, and I skidded to a halt right before the door.

Making my way to the other end of the couch, I plopped down, knowing from what Dad said that he had something on his mind. I watched him set the paper between us and take a sip of his coffee, then adjust his glasses.

"Violet, I know with your mom being gone that life isn't easy. I'm at the hospital quite a bit, and there's not much I can do about that. But I miss her too, you know." He paused, crossing his leg over his knee, but not meeting my eyes. "Life is about changing and adapting to every situation you may find yourself in and making the best of it. Don't ever forget that, okay?" His nose twitched like he was going to sneeze, and he pulled one of the tissues from the box on the coffee table and rubbed his nose with it.

I frowned for a second. Dad could be cryptic at times; communication wasn't his strong suit, and expressing emotions was even tougher for him. Nodding slowly, I said, "Yeah, I understand. I'm doing better, though." My heart still hurt at the loss of my mom. But at least my eyes didn't well up with tears every time I thought of her, like they did a few weeks ago, so I guessed that meant I was making progress.

"How is school going?" He picked up his paper again and opened it, a clear signal that the conversation was coming to an end.

Relieved, I said, "It's great, Dad. I'll see ya later. I'm going to pick up Callie for some girl time."

"Have a good day, sweetie."

My Mustang was all polished and shiny black in the driveway, making me wish it were warmer so I could drive with the sunroof open. Callie's house was located on Lake Bluff, raised high on a cliff with a stunning view of the lake, which would have made a gorgeous painting if I had any artistic skill. Since it was still so early on a weekend morning and the traffic was light, I was able to shave five minutes off the usual fifteen-minute drive.

Callie was waiting outside for me and clambered in when I pulled to a stop, smiling from ear to ear. "I can't believe you're doing this," she exclaimed. Glancing at my outfit, she added, "Cute shirt."

She was wearing light jeans and an aqua-colored tee, which contrasted well with her green eyes. Her bubbly personality always boosted my mood, and I gave her a big grin.

"How was your date with Henry?" I asked as I backed out of her driveway. Callie and Henry went to the movies at least once a week, and every now and then I would tag along as the third wheel.

"Good. I still think that you should have met his friend," she said, giving me a pointed look. "He was sweet and funny."

"You know how I feel about this subject already." I glanced over at her with a little frown. "It's weird that your parents feel they have to protect their inheritance with arranged marriages between

28

their kids just because that's what their parents did. I know they make a ton of money, but we are in the twenty-first century," I said with an eye roll.

Callie ignored my complaint, which was her usual way to avoid conflict. "How long is the ride?" she asked as she reached over and flipped through stations on the radio.

I kept my eyes on the road. "It's in Marquette, so about an hour. Speaking of arranged marriages, how come JP doesn't have one? The one person who should have one, doesn't. I wish he would just leave me alone."

"Why? What did he do?"

I tapped my fingers to the beat of the music on the steering wheel. "He asked me to sit with him at lunch yesterday, and he sounded like he was actually serious. So what gives, why doesn't he have one?"

Callie shrugged. "His mom isn't from here, so she refused to go along with the custom. Apparently his father agreed, but I heard he wasn't happy about it. Oh, and there were an odd number of babies born that year, so it didn't really matter since there was no one to match him with."

My excitement level ensured that the drive seemed to take forever. We finally pulled in front of a quaint little shop with a sign that read RAMONA'S PLACE, flashing in red, white, and blue neon.

"I love the patriotic theme," I noted as we climbed out of the car. Callie nodded her agreement.

The bell hanging over the door clanged as we entered. It was dark inside the store, the only lighting from candles strategically placed throughout.

"I feel like I just stepped into Frankenstein's house," she muttered to me.

"Callie," I whispered with a reprimanding tone. "Someone might hear you."

There were rows of glass shelves everywhere and stacks of books, both old and new. I walked over to one and picked it up, *Magic for Beginners*. It seemed strange holding the book and I quickly set it down.

29

The place was so eerie it looked like someone had decorated for Halloween, complete with spiderwebs in the corners of the ceilings that looked real. A counter stood in front of a back wall where a purple curtain was hanging, hiding a doorway, I presumed, which piqued my curiosity. The music that played in the background was peculiar and the place looked desolate.

There was no one in sight, so Callie and I browsed around, checking out the displays. One held gems and unusual stones, some very pretty, but I couldn't tell what they would be used for. There was a wall covered with dried herbs hanging from hooks; I browsed the labels and hadn't heard of many of them. Shelves near the counter contained a bath and powder section, and what looked like dried flowers.

"Hello," I called out to no one in particular, wondering if there was an employee around. I glanced over to Callie, who was inspecting a display of animal feet that were made into key chains. She was fingering a bunny one with a horrified look on her face. Disgusted, she let it fall from her grasp and scurried over to me.

"Listen," Callie whispered. "I'm gonna have a panic attack if I don't get outta here. This place is really weirding me out. Do you mind if I wait in the car?"

I shrugged. "No, it's fine." I handed her my keys and watched her leave. The bell rang again, echoing throughout the shop.

I pivoted to walk back to the counter and jerked backward instinctively when I almost collided with a boy. *Holy crap!* I stumbled back another step and when I ran into something solid and sharp, I winced in pain. My hand immediately shot to my heart as if I could physically calm the racing with a soothing touch, and I closed my eyes in relief for a few seconds. I hadn't expected to have someone standing right in front of me.

"You scared me," I said accusingly as I opened my eyes. When I looked up, my lungs seized, unable to draw in a breath for a moment.

The boy's striking, deep-set silver eyes locked with mine, his unfriendly glare taking me by surprise. His full, expressive lips were set into a grim line, and I looked at them for a second too long before taking in his tousled blond locks with just a touch of auburn, which reminded me of the sun.

Chills ran down my spine when his gaze locked with mine, and despite his unfriendliness there was something that nagged at me. What was it? I bit my bottom lip, annoyed that there was something oddly familiar about him and I couldn't put my finger on it.

Suddenly it came to me and I gaped at him. I had never met anyone whose eyes looked like mine in my entire life. The seconds ticked by as his forehead creased and his eyes narrowed at me. Why wasn't he saying anything? He did work here, didn't he? My mind spun in a million different directions.

His body looked agile and lean beneath all the black he was wearing, and his jeans hung off his waist in a delicious way. I kept my eyes trained on him, unwilling to look away. He seemed to make my every nerve ending sing, and I just wanted to bask in his attention. My stomach did a little flip, but in a good way.

"Is there something I can help you with?" he finally asked, cool politeness winning out. His voice sounded bored, but his actions suggested otherwise as he watched me intently, putting me in the spotlight. "Are you okay?" He grabbed my arm, inspecting my torn sleeve. "There's no blood, so you didn't get cut."

I nodded my head stupidly, wondering why in the world I just couldn't say something. I took a step back, carefully avoiding the shelf I'd apparently backed into before.

The boy was incredibly handsome, and I was growing uncomfortable with the proximity between us. He let my arm drop and gave me a confused look, obviously waiting for me to say something. I swallowed a lump in my throat and realized I desperately needed a glass of water.

"Is Ramona here?" My voice cracked with anxiety.

He shot me an amused look and sauntered toward the back wall where the counter stood. I had no choice but to follow.

"Let me guess." His gaze roamed my body, scanning down and then back up as we walked.

He was obviously trying to make me nervous, and it worked like a charm. Heat instantly bloomed in my cheeks, and I knew I was turning a lovely shade of red. Thank goodness for the terrible lighting. I tried to act like I wasn't intimidated, but the smile that spread across his perfect face suggested he didn't buy it.

He stopped abruptly and turned so he was facing me, and I managed to stop just shy of hitting him, leaving nothing but a breath of space between us. "You're not our normal type of customer." He looked a little puzzled. "You don't seem like you would believe in this kind of thing. Surely this can't be about a guy, right? You're looking for help on a test, aren't you?"

I frowned at him and he smirked. "I'm right on the second one, huh?"

I clenched my fists to keep from hitting this annoyingly handsome boy.

"Ryder." A middle-aged woman had quietly stepped up behind him and placed a hand on his shoulder.

I tore my gaze from his to look at her. She was heavy-set, wearing loose-fitting tan pants and a blue sweatshirt. Her hair was dark red and curly, pulled back with a patriotic bandanna that allowed a few loose strands to hang down the sides of her round face. Her expression was friendly, and when she smiled at me, dimples appeared on both cheeks.

"What on earth do you have playing out here? This music is awful," she exclaimed, chuckling to herself. "Be kind to the girl. Now, honey, come on over here and let me take a look at you. I'm Ramona."

I walked over to the counter and accepted her outstretched hand. "I'm Violet Vancourt," I said and then added, "It's nice to meet you."

Ramona had a firm handshake and her skin was soft. Her presence was comforting, putting me instantly at ease. Perhaps it was the fragrance that surrounded her that was strangely familiar, something like lavender, which reminded me of my mother.

The thought of my mother brought a sudden pain in my chest. I winced inwardly, struggling not to show it.

"Violet, it's nice to meet you. That handsome fella over there is my nephew, Ryder."

I turned my gaze on him again. Ryder had moved to a corner behind the counter and was sitting on a tall stool with his feet propped up on the glass countertop. His eyes were downcast, his gaze fixed on the cell phone in his hands, probably texting based on the rapid thumb movement. His gaze flicked to mine momentarily before returning his focus to his phone.

"Let's get started on your reading. That's why you're here, right?" Ramona shut her eyes for a moment, and when she opened them again they were alight with excitement.

I nodded and glanced over at Ryder. He was still texting and didn't look my way. He was so gorgeous; no one should be that handsome.

She pulled the heavy purple curtain back so I could step through and it silently fell behind us, effectively shutting us off into another world. The room we entered was even darker than the first, despite the fact that the entire back wall was covered with mirrors. There was a chalky circle marked on the floor, surrounding a small table with a chair on each side. A large cream-colored candle stood in the middle of the table. The flame reflected luminously in the mirror.

I glanced at my reflection and was taken aback at what I saw. My eyes looked haunted. I wouldn't have recognized those eyes, had I not known they were mine. The air seemed mystically charged, affecting my perceptions, and my outward appearance was mysterious, even to me. The auburn curls that framed my heart-shaped face glowed with an unusual glint of red I'd never noticed before.

"Please sit," she said in a matter-of-fact tone. She took the chair across from me and I angled myself in the chair facing the mirrors. My hands began to sweat, and my stomach churned like an angry ocean.

"What kind of reading do you want?" she asked. She studied my eyes intently, as if she thought she could find the answer there.

"A tarot card reading." I wiped my hands on my jeans, trying to rid them of the moisture that tickled my palms.

"Hmm. Are you sure you don't want a palm reading instead?" she asked, tilting her head curiously as she maintained eye contact while shuffling an oversized deck of cards.

33

"No. I want the tarot card reading," I said firmly. After all, that was why I drove all the way here; there was no going back.

Ramona smiled reassuringly. "Okay." She shuffled the cards a final time with quick fingers, then lay them out in front of me. "Please cut the deck."

I reached out, my fingers trembling slightly, but I managed to pick up half the deck and set it on the table. She placed the cards that remained from the pile I'd picked from, on top of the half I had picked up.

"We'll do this two more times," she said, and I followed her instructions, going through the simple motions.

"Close your eyes and think about the question you want answered," Ramona said softly.

I took a deep breath as my eyelids fluttered shut, picturing Adam's teasing blue eyes.

Will Adam and I ever be together openly? That was the question I really wanted answered. Who wanted to be in a relationship with someone if you couldn't acknowledge that it even existed?

"Okay," she said excitedly as she flipped the first card over. "Hmm," she murmured as she leaned closer to get a better view. "This is the Three of Swords."

Instinctively, I leaned closer too and studied the card. There were three intricately designed swords piercing a beautiful blood-red heart. Clouds hung above the heart, and it looked as if rain were beating down on it.

"Hmm, that can't be good," I offered.

"Let's finish and then I'll explain," she said as she flipped the second card. "Ace of Cups."

This card pictured a hand holding what appeared to be a wineglass with a fountain of water spilling over both sides. A dove looked like as if it were flying into the cup.

I kept silent this time, although I was itching to ask questions. When I realized I was nervously tapping the table with my fingers, I jerked my hand back and tucked it under my thigh.

Ramona finally flipped the last card over. "This is the Knight of Swords."

I stared at the card that portrayed a black knight riding a white stallion with his sword poised in the air, like he was heading into battle.

"Okay, my dear. I can explain to you what the cards mean." Ramona glanced up at me. "But it's up to you to decipher what the significance is in relevance to your question."

She pointed to one card. "Let's start with the Ace of Cups. This card signifies the start of a new relationship. The relationship has the possibility to blossom into true love, but both people involved have to want it for this to happen."

I thought about Adam, and our relationship that had already started.

"A present relationship doesn't qualify," she said, answering my unspoken question.

Startled, I met her eyes that were alight with curiosity, then sighed out loud, confirming her suspicions. It was the first strike against Adam and me.

"The Three of Swords is a card of lessons. There are many types of lessons when it comes to the frailty of the human heart. Among these are rejection, grief, loneliness, disloyalty, heartbreak, and separation. It's not a good card. You have to be prepared for whatever lessons this card signifies." Ramona's voice softened. "If you're prepared, it may help soften the blow."

I felt sick. This was another card I didn't want to get.

She pointed to the last card. "The Knight of Swords will usually appear in the form of a person. The knight is fearless, and because of this courage he believes he's invincible. This can be both a fault and strength. A fault because no one is unbeatable, and a strength because he has the courage to go after what he believes in. He's a person that buries his emotions because he feels that he doesn't need to show them. Someone can break through their barrier if they try hard enough."

My shoulders sagged. "Wow, this is a lot to take in. I didn't really hear anything I expected to hear." Defeated, I couldn't hide the disappointment in my voice.

She stacked the cards back together as she watched me. "I assume your question was about a particular boy?" Her eyebrows rose as she looked at me expectantly.

I shrugged. "It was, but it seems like it's a lost cause."

Ramona smiled sadly as she patted my hand and set the cards aside. "I must cleanse the area before I see someone else. Ryder will get you a bill, my dear. Please keep in mind that the cards don't predict the future, only possible outcomes."

Numb, I stood up and pushed my way through the purple curtain, feeling overwhelmed.

"The reading didn't turn out too well, did it?" A smirk twisted Ryder's sexy lips as he watched me re-enter the shop. "You don't have to answer. It's all over your face."

He moved closer until he was standing right next to me. I crossed my arms and ran my hands over my biceps, unnerved that his very presence made my body grow warm and my skin tingle.

"You don't know anything about me," I said sharply.

His smirk disappeared, replaced by a frosty glare. I moved to the other side of the counter, digging in my purse to keep busy so I wouldn't have to look in his piercing silver eyes. I didn't like seeing myself in them.

He walked to the cash register. "That will be fifty dollars," he said abruptly.

I opened my wallet and pulled out a fifty-dollar bill. When I handed the bill to him, my fingers brushed his as I placed it in his palm, setting off a whirlwind around me. I took a sharp breath and gasped as a dizzying feeling began to pulse in my head, and bright-colored lights swirled around me. I tried to focus on Ryder, taking in his shocked expression as he stared at me.

I squeezed my eyes shut. Please stop, I silently begged. My hair whipped around me and I was dizzy, as if I was going to lose my footing. My eyes still shut, I reached out to grab anything that might right the sudden chaos that surrounded me, and found Ryder. I pulled myself to him, clutching him like a lifeline. His body was warm and his strong arms came around me, holding me securely. My chest hurt and my body craved oxygen. I gasped, drawing precious air into my lungs. How could I forget to breathe?

Just as I was beginning to think I might pass out, the dizzying feeling retreated from my muddled mind, leaving my thoughts crystal clear. The wind calmed and my hair finally settled into a tangled mess of curls. I let go of Ryder and touched my hands to my cheeks in wonder, then opened my eyes.

• • •

One minute I had been standing at the tarot reader's counter, paying for a reading that I didn't much like, and the next I was standing in my school's hallway outside the registration office. I looked down at my arm, searching for my purse, but I didn't have a purse, just my backpack. My mind whirled, trying to understand how I could be here when I knew I was just at Ramona's.

What the hell just happened? And where did Ryder go?

I didn't have time to ponder the thought further because the door to the registration office opened and a student walked out, a boy I recognized. I suddenly realized I was now wearing my sunglasses, so I reached up and snatched them off. The boy had blond hair with a touch of auburn, tousled just like I remembered. He had papers in one hand and a backpack over his shoulder, and was wearing dark jeans and a black tee. When he turned toward me, his silver eyes met mine, and a fleeting look of surprise crossed his face.

It was so strange. Everything seemed so real.

He sauntered right up to me and said, "So you're the one." His eyes were just as cold as I remembered them. He cocked his head to one side, as if I had confirmed something for him just by being here, and there was a touch of amusement in his tone.

I closed my eyes. *This can't be happening. Am I totally losing it?* His hand touched mine gently, and I opened my eyes to see him regarding me with an almost sympathetic look.

An electrical shock coursed through my body at his touch, brightly colored lights swirling around me once more, and I squeezed my eyes tightly against the dizzying feeling that shot through me.

Oh no, not again.

My hair whipped about and I twisted and turned, not knowing which way was up. I wrapped my arms around myself, willing it all to stop, wishing with all my might to be free of the sudden chaos that enveloped me. Then everything went black.

• • •

I opened my eyes. My head was on the counter—no wait; it was too soft and cozy for it to be the counter. It was so dark and my mind was still fuzzy, then I realized someone was holding me up. I pulled away and found myself on the floor in Ryder's arms, his gorgeous face looking down at me with curiosity.

"You were at my school," I said with wonder, the sudden memory of what had happened rushing back at me. His face was blank but his eyes still had a small trace of coldness that lingered there. "What happened?" I demanded angrily as I pulled myself to my feet.

"You passed out, and I caught you," he said, his eyes narrowed. "I should be asking *you* what happened." Ryder's tone had an implied meaning I didn't understand. His eyes were demanding, staring into mine, seeking answers that I didn't have. "Why you?" he murmured to himself.

"I have to go," I said quickly, then pushed out of his arms and started for the door.

"I'll be seeing you soon," he called out, his tone full of promise.

Butterflies immediately rushed into my stomach. I risked one last glance back before I pushed out the door. He was shrouded in darkness, his dark clothes blending in with his surroundings, and the flicker of the candlelight partially illuminated his face and one arm as he looked at me, a half smile playing on his lips.

I shoved my way through the door and was never so excited to see the sun before in my life. Shaking my head, I tried to clear my thoughts. Nothing like that had ever happened to me before, although . . . did it really happen? Or did I just pass out and have a strange dream?

I didn't want to think too hard on it as I headed to my Mustang and got in. Callie was hunched down in the passenger seat, texting furiously, and looked up at me when I slid into my seat.

"So, how was the freak show?" she asked with an amused smile.

"Adam and I are doomed," I said unhappily.

Callie sighed. "That bad, huh?"

"Pretty much." I sank back against the seat, suddenly feeling exhausted.

"That's only if you believe in that sort of thing," she reassured me.

"True," I conceded, shrugging my shoulders as I sped along the highway, heading back home.

Chapter 5

The next day, Callie and I decided to have lunch and hang out at Price's Stop-and-Shop, a diner and a touristy gift shop. Adam's dad owned it, along with a shopping mall, two car dealerships, a movie theater, a dry cleaners, several gas stations, and a large stake in the paper mill that had made their family and several others filthy rich. The diner has always been a favorite hot spot for our age group because it was a great locale, down at the marina and right in the middle of the park.

It was a beautiful day outside and we had just finished eating. I was pleasantly full, having opted for a Cobb salad over a burger and fries. Anything too greasy never sat right with me, causing me to balloon up and feel like I should walk around with a READY TO EXPLODE sign around my neck to give people fair warning. It was bad enough the smell of grease hung heavily in the air; I knew I was going to smell like a big french fry. Every time we ate there, the stench permeated my clothing and my hair, embedding in my pores. But my salad was good and Callie was pleased with her burger.

The best part about the place was the view, definitely eye candy for anyone who loved the water. The marina outside harbored everything from yachts to power boats to bass and sailing boats, lined up and bobbing in the clean and well-maintained docks.

The inside of the diner was small and had a long row of booths situated against windows facing the lake. A few tables were scattered throughout, and the focal point was a hand-carved wooden bar that served liquor and food near the front entrance. French doors opened to an outside wooden deck, where white twinkle lights snaked around the outer railing like a vine. Three large tables that could comfortably seat ten were set so anyone could eat and bask in the tranquility of Mother Nature.

Quite a few people I recognized from school were already gathered outside around the center table, laughing as they played

40

some game, and among them were JP, Olivia, and Adam. Callie and I were seated inside at a booth, waiting for Henry.

"So, when is Henry getting here?" I asked as I shredded my napkin left over from lunch.

"He should be here soon," she said, her eyes alight with excitement.

"Did you study for the chemistry test?" I put on a severe face, grilling her, even though I knew full well that she probably hadn't.

"Is that Monday?" Her eyes widened as realization dawned on her and she slapped her forehead, the sound echoing inside the quiet diner. "Crap! I do this every time, don't I?" She rolled her eyes in exasperation.

"Yep, you do." I smiled at her predictability. Callie had been my best friend for ages, so I knew her well. I loved this girl like my sister.

"I completely forgot," she said with a sigh. "This sucks! I won't be able to stay here for very long." She made a pouty face at me.

"What am I going to do with you?" I said, laughing at her forgetfulness. When Callie's pout turned to a frown, I assured her, "I'm laughing with you, not at you."

I glanced through the window at the kids outside, my eyes lingering on Adam. Olivia was wrapped around him like a cold lake breeze, every inch of her body touching him in some way.

Adam looked so good in his dark jeans and blue tee. He seemed . . . happy. They had some sort of card game going on and from the looks of it, JP was winning; his gloating expression confirming my suspicion. I frowned.

"What's that look on your face for?" Callie followed my line of sight. "Ah, I see."

Just then the brass bells on the door tinkled and we both turned to see Henry stroll in. Tall and lean, he was a decent-looking guy with short brown hair and light freckles dusting his nose. I couldn't help but feel a little resentment against him, since my friend was gypped out of the whole dating scene with their arranged marriage, but he was nice enough.

41

He slid in next to Callie and slipped an arm around her, his dark hair grazing her forehead as he leaned in and kissed her affectionately on the cheek. His feelings for Callie seemed genuine, but was it love? I couldn't be sure.

Henry looked over at me and grinned, greeting me with, "Hi, Shades." I rarely went anywhere without my sunglasses, so his nickname for me seemed to make sense to him.

"Hi, Henry," I said to be polite. My phone buzzed in my pocket, distracting me from their conversation. I slipped it out and Adam's name flashed across the screen.

Adam: Miss you. Want to meet up? I'm free.

My stomach tightened in response, a bundle of nerves gathering deep within. I instinctively looked over to where he sat with his friends outside. He was smiling and laughing, having a good old time. Olivia was still hanging all over him, being her usual clingy self.

I sighed, feeling the sting of his words deep in my chest. It didn't look like he was missing me, belying his words and giving them bite.

"Who is it?" Callie asked me in her sly, you-better-spill-everything-later kind of way.

"One guess." I had to be vague around Henry. If word got around what was really going on, Adam's whole future could be in jeopardy.

"I want to know," Henry chimed in, his eyes dancing as he leaned forward as if we were in a conspiracy.

"Fat chance, Henry. No way," I said teasingly. "It's just my stepdad. You know, the usual. What time will I be home later, that sort of thing."

The last thing I wanted was to let on that it was Adam. I pulled my phone close to my chest and texted him back.

Me: It doesn't look like you miss me! And from where I sit you look very busy. I don't even know how you can breathe with that troll hanging all over you!

Whoa, did I just come across as the jealous girlfriend? I reread the text quickly. Yes, I did. Shit.

Me: Never mind, I take that back. I don't care anymore!

"That's cool," Henry offered. "I can't believe your stepdad texts. My parents don't even know how." Callie gave him a smile as he nudged her gently with his shoulder.

"My stepdad is always too busy to pick up the phone and call," I said, shrugging my shoulders and rolling my eyes.

Callie started laughing at me. She knew I was lying about who the text was from.

The truth was I missed my stepdad almost as much as I missed my mom. He seemed to be distancing himself from me over the last few weeks, and I had this feeling whenever I was around him lately that there was something he wanted to say, but he never did.

I stood up and shoved my phone back in my pocket.

"Where are you going?" Callie asked, surprise flitting across her face.

"I'm going to walk home," I said casually.

"No, you're not!" she exclaimed, trying to push Henry out of the way, but he didn't budge.

"Henry just got here. You two have fun. Besides, it's nice out. I'll enjoy the walk." I leaned over and gave her a quick hug, then whispered, "Text me later."

Glancing out the window, I saw Adam disentangle himself from Olivia as he searched the surrounding area conspicuously. He stood up and walked toward the door that led inside the diner. Could he be any more obvious?

I left through the side door without another word, and didn't look back to see if Adam had spotted me.

I hadn't lied, the day was beautiful for being mid-September. The leaves were mostly still green, and the smell of fresh-cut grass lingered in the air as I walked through the park. I was half tempted to go to my favorite spot, but without a blanket or a good book, I didn't see any point to it.

My phone rang and I quickly grabbed it from my pocket. "Hey."

"Violet, it's me. Where are you?" Adam asked, his voice anxious.

"Aren't there people around? You probably shouldn't be calling me right now," I said, worrying that he might have been too obvious.

"Listen, Violet, I left them. Tell me where you are so I can pick you up."

"No, Adam. I don't want to talk right now."

When I reached the end of the path where the park ended and a neighborhood began, that was when I saw him, the guy from Ramona's place. He was unloading a moving truck parked next to the curb. Surely he wasn't moving here?

"I've got to go." I hung up on Adam as I came to a standstill ten feet from the back of the U-Haul.

I watched the boy's muscles bunch and move under the tight shirt he was wearing with every box he lifted and moved to the grass. He paused to wipe his forehead with a rag that was hanging out of his front pocket.

"Ryder?" I asked cautiously.

He turned slightly and sure enough, those piercing silver eyes stared me down for a second before he shuttered them and turned back to whatever he was doing. Unpacking? Working? He took another box out of the back and dropped it on the grass.

"What are you doing here?" I didn't mean for it to come out the way that it did, like an accusation. He was supposed to be in Marquette, wasn't he? I wasn't supposed to run into him again.

"What does it look like I'm doing?" he said curtly as he unloaded another box.

Surveying him from his golden-blond hair to his black tank and black jeans that were dusted with dirt and debris from all his hard work, I struggled to find something to say.

"Hauling boxes?" My voice sounded a little high-pitched.

I swallowed nervously as he squinted at me in the bright afternoon sunshine, and that look he gave me . . . oh my God, my heart tried to pound right out of my chest. I wasn't sure if it was the attraction I felt for him that unnerved me so, or the icy exterior he presented. Maybe it was both.

Ryder walked over to me, taking an extra step so he was invading my personal space. He was so close I could feel his warm breath on me, and I had the urge to take a step back. But I held my ground, not wanting to appear intimidated by this gorgeous boy.

He narrowed his eyes at me, then reached up and pulled my sunglasses off my face, careful not to come into contact with my skin, and casually tossed them to the lawn.

"Hey," I protested, and he gave me an answering smile, obviously pleased with himself.

"If you're going to stand there and have a conversation with me, then I'm at least going to look at you," he said matter-of-factly, like he had the right to do so.

"So you're either moving in or *working*?" My voice cracked and I silently prayed for the latter, but I wasn't quite sure why. My phone beeped in my pocket, signaling another message. I had forgotten all about Adam, and ignored it for the time being.

"I'm moving in," he said, all business once again. He grabbed a water bottle off the bumper and took a long swig from it.

I drank him in as he swallowed, as if I were the one in need of water. It looked like he was doing an Aquafina commercial. I remembered him being good looking, but with the sun beating down on his physique, it intensified the effect he had on me that much more. He seemed to glow with unearthly beauty.

"You're moving in there?" I pointed to the oversized white two-story house sitting high up on the lawn, majestic with a semi-circular front porch, tall white pillars supporting it on each side. It looked big enough to house a family of eight.

Ryder ignored me, and I fidgeted in the silence. "The for-sale sign is still up," I said, hating to point out the obvious. I guess I was just hoping that it wasn't true.

"I haven't had the chance to take it down yet," he replied bluntly as he hauled another box out of the back.

"Where are your parents? Shouldn't they be helping you?"

45

"It's just me and my dad's right-hand man. My parents aren't moving in just yet. Don't you know that curiosity killed the cat?" He smirked at me and my breath hitched. Wow, he was beautiful.

"Ever hear of nine lives?" I smiled at him, proud of my comeback. Wait—what was I doing flirting?

Ryder gave me a full brilliant smile. *He should smile more.* Then his brows drew together and in the blink of an eye, his expression was once again indifferent. He took another box and stacked it on the lawn with the others.

He glanced around as if he was looking for something or someone, then turned back to me, one eyebrow raised. "What are you doing here?"

I shifted nervously from one foot to the other, then shrugged and mumbled, "Escaping life."

He nodded at my response, then leaned against the side of the truck. "Come sit." He motioned at one of the boxes, his tone commanding.

I did as he said, eyeing him cautiously as I walked to the box and gingerly sat down, hoping the cardboard would take my weight.

"I know a little bit about trying to escape life," he said, then paused and locked his gaze with mine. "And trust me, it always catches up with you. You're better off to face things head-on." His voice had lowered, almost soft with concern, yet his face remained impassive.

That was damn good advice, I thought, captivated by him and unable to tear my gaze away. How could I have captured the attention of the most gorgeous boy I had ever laid eyes on? My chest was tight, making my breathing shallow. I tapped my fingers on my jeans as I rolled his words around in my mind.

He crossed his arms in front of his chest, his muscles flexing as he did, drawing my attention to them. When I looked back up, a small smile played on his lips. He was enjoying making me squirm. His eyes seemed to light up at my uneasiness.

"What happened between us?" I asked softly, almost embarrassed to bring it up. What if he thought I was crazy? "You know, back at Ramona's."

I watched him, my gaze unwavering, and his lips parted as he inhaled sharply. I heard a car pull up near us, but I was too enthralled with Ryder to care who it was.

His gaze flicked beyond me and his expression shuttered again.

"Friend of yours?" Ryder asked, gesturing toward the street.

It was as if he had released me from a trance. I glanced behind me and saw Adam get out of his BMW. Adam's eyes narrowed, his brow creasing as he looked at Ryder.

"Adam." I kept my voice even, going for a casual tone. "This is Ryder, a friend from Marquette." I gestured to the extremely hot guy in front of me.

Ryder's lips twisted with amusement, probably at my presumption of referring to him as "a friend." I silently prayed he wouldn't spill how we actually met.

Ryder waited patiently for Adam to come to him. I guess he was used to people coming to him, and not the other way around. Adam moved from the door of his BMW until he was in front of Ryder, grasping his outstretched hand.

"Nice to meet you." Ryder's tone was polite. "Ryder Essen." He gazed at Adam speculatively and narrowed his eyes.

"Adam Price." He gave Ryder a quick once-over, then asked, "Are you just moving to town?" in a tight voice. The tension in the air was palpable as Adam took a couple of steps back to stand close beside me. "Violet didn't tell me she had a friend moving here," he went on, glancing at me with a meaningful look.

Another glint of amusement flashed in Ryder's eyes, but I was the only one who seemed to notice. "It was a last-minute deal," he said, smirking at me. "I just hadn't had the chance to visit with Vi *alone*."

What was that supposed to mean?

"We have to be going," Adam said tersely. He gently tugged my arm, and I took a few steps with him before remembering why I was mad at him to begin with. His eagerness to get me away from my so-called friend was also annoying.

"No way, Adam. I told you, I'm walking home." I glared at him, annoyed with him all over again.

"Violet," Adam said in a low voice. "Can we talk about this later, in private?"

I could feel Ryder scrutinizing us. He had crossed his arms and was leaning against the back of the truck, taking in the show.

"Isn't that something you should do with your girlfriend?" I said sharply.

"Is this a lover's quarrel?" Ryder interrupted, seemingly entertained.

"No," Adam and I echoed in unison, although the tone of our voices probably suggested otherwise.

"We had a disagreement over what time I'm supposed to work over at his house," I lied. "I mean, I don't work for him," I said, gesturing to Adam. "I work for his dad." I shrugged. But the big question was . . . why did I care enough to explain myself to Ryder?

"Okay," Ryder said, giving me a mischievous smile. "By the way, Vi, I lost your number. Why don't you be an angel and call your phone from mine so I have it again." Tossing me his iPhone, he lifted his eyebrows as if daring me to challenge him.

I caught it easily. I didn't want to give him my number, but I *had* just said we were friends and Adam *was* standing right there. I swiftly typed the numbers and hit CALL. My phone started ringing in my pocket, and I pressed a button to silence it. Well, at least I'd have his number. I could always avoid his calls, I reasoned.

I tossed the phone back to Ryder a little harder than I should have. He grimaced as he caught it, then slipped it back in his jeans pocket. His silver gaze connected with me again, and I fidgeted under his scrutiny. Uncomfortable, I walked over to where my sunglasses lay in the grass, picked them up, and put them on. Immediate relief flooded my body, and I finally relaxed behind my shield to the world.

"See ya around," I said softly, giving a little wave to Ryder. He was staring intensely at me for some reason, why I didn't know. All I knew was I kind of liked it.

"Much sooner than you think." Ryder's tone was like silk, and once again I was a little wary.

I gave Adam a little wave, and said, "I'll talk to you some other time, Adam."

He looked like he was going to protest, and then thought better. Smart boy.

With that said, I turned my back on both boys and started the walk home. I heard Adam start his car and peel off in the other direction. I knew he was pissed, but the fact remained that he had no right to be.

· · ·

While I was on my bed listening to my iPod after dinner, my phone beeped, signaling I had a text message.

Callie: Hey, did Adam find you? He better be careful. Peeps are going to notice!

I shrugged. It wasn't my problem, was it?

Me: He did. I didn't give him the time of day. He's pissed. I did run into someone from Marquette that I met at Ramona's. Her nephew who just moved to town.

I wondered what she would say to that? Though I had a pretty good idea.

Callie: Hottie?!?!

Exactly what I thought she'd say.

Me: He's OK. Did you get the homework done?

I downplayed it just for fun. When she met him, she would definitely think "okay" was the understatement of the year.

Callie: Yeah I did but it wasn't fun. Speaking of fun, what are you doing Friday?

Me: No plans. Why?

Callie: Bonfire!

I could just picture her face lighting up. She always got excited over these stupid social events.

"Ugh." I sighed. Every year the seniors at our school put on a huge bonfire near Ardent's Field. All the classes were invited. It was

49

a fundraiser for the football team, to pay for new athletic equipment and travel expenses. Last year as a sophomore, I didn't attend. This year it seemed like I wasn't going to be able to avoid it since it was a social event that no one, who was normal, would miss. I usually refused to go to things like this, but for Callie's sake, I would, but reluctantly.

Me: OK, I'm in.

It was hard to force myself to type the words, and I actually cringed when I hit SEND.

Chapter 6

Mondays were never my favorite days. I arrived at school later than usual and the parking lot was full, so I got stuck with pretty crappy parking way in the back. I decided if I was stuck with crappy parking that I was going to use up at least two parking spaces, because I definitely didn't want to get door dents from some careless classmate. My stepdad wouldn't be happy with me if that happened.

I glanced at my watch and was annoyed to realize I was going to be late for my first period class. After grabbing my books from my locker, I veered off toward the registration office to get an excuse so I could be allowed into class late.

As I reached the registration office, the door opened and a student walked out. Standing at the counter was a boy that I recognized. I took my sunglasses off. He had tousled blond hair with a touch of auburn, which reminded me of the sun, and was wearing dark jeans and a black tee. He had papers in his hand and a backpack over one shoulder. When he turned, his silver eyes met mine and a fleeting look of surprise crossed his face, exactly as I saw it when I was back at Ramona's. A shiver washed over me.

Had I seen this before it actually happened? Was I going crazy?

Ryder walked right up to me. His eyes were just as cold as I remembered them. "There you are," he said, his voice low but with a touch of amusement in his tone.

I shook my head, thoroughly confused. How did I see this happening?

"You look pale." He scanned my features, his expression turning serious.

"I'm not feeling so good." I gestured at the paperwork in his hand. "Is that your class schedule?"

"It is." He stepped even closer, then handed it over for me to review.

I guess personal space didn't mean anything to him. He did, however, smell incredibly good, like soap and fresh air. As I glanced through his list of classes, his eyes burned into me.

"We have AP History together, third period." That ought to be interesting, especially with Adam and Olivia sharing the same class.

I looked up into his silver-gray eyes and my breath caught in my throat. I glanced down at my shades, which I still clutched in my hand.

His face was alight with amusement. "Vi, do you believe in destiny?"

He sounded like he was baiting me, and my stomach knotted in response. I wanted to wipe that smirk off his face. I knew that he knew something weird had transpired between us, but I wasn't ready to admit it yet. Let alone talk about it.

"No. I'm late." After all, ignorance was bliss, or so they said. For some reason, I really didn't want to talk about it. Besides, I really was late and needed to get going.

I glanced at the clock in the hall, surprised to see it was already ten after eight. "I'm outta here," I said, and pushed his class schedule up to his chest. His fingers brushed against mine when he took the paper from me.

Oh crap.

The now familiar electrical shock coursed through my veins as the brightly colored lights churned around me. I squeezed my eyes shut from the fuzzy feeling that enveloped my mind and pulsed through my body.

Oh no! Why does this keep happening to me?

My mind was churning, having a hard time stringing together a coherent thought. My hair whipped around me and I doubled over, or at least it seemed that way. My hands went to my head, trying to cradle it, willing it to all stop so I could be free of the sudden chaos that surrounded me. Then everything went still except for the ball of nerves in the pit of my stomach, twisting and turning, threatening to explode.

• • •

I resisted opening my eyes, finally giving in and lifting my eyelids with deliberate slowness. I wasn't in the hallway anymore, even though I knew without a doubt that Ryder and I had been there before he had touched my hand. I told him I didn't want to talk about what happened, so what did he do? Forced it to happen again! Whatever this was.

Darkness surrounded me except for the luminance of the flames licking the night sky. Smoke danced in the air, along with the sounds of loud music and people talking with animation. There were kegs of beer and red plastic cups, and bodies swaying in time to the music. Was I at a bonfire?

Reaching behind me, I touched bark against my back. I was leaning against a tree. Relieved to get my bearings, I inhaled a calming breath of fresh air mixed with a pungent tinge of smoke.

Several feet away, Ryder leaned casually against a tree watching me, his face blank, his eyes aloof. He took a long drink from his cup and then started toward me with purpose.

I turned my attention back to the flames, not happy about being here. What was he trying to prove by doing this again? I didn't know what was going on, but at that moment, I decided I didn't want any part of whatever this was. My confusion rapidly turned to firm resolve.

"You look confused." He startled me by leaning against the side of my tree, his shoulder nearly touching mine, so close I could feel the warmth of his body. It caused a shiver to run through me, he was so electrifying. The chemistry his nearness provoked inside me was enough to make me want to run far, far away.

The thought of sounding crazy terrified me. A moment ago, I was standing in the middle of the hallway with him. Not at a bonfire that wasn't supposed to happen until Friday!

"You're not crazy, you know." His face was indifferent, but his voice was surprisingly gentler than I'd heard before.

"No? Well, I feel crazy." I shrugged.

He moved in front of me, drawing my attention from the flames to his face. There was an imperceptible softness in those steely eyes, the same startling silver as mine. The kind of eyes that snared you,

53

captured your attention, that were hard to turn away from. I was quoting Adam on that last thought, but now I knew what he meant. I was completely mesmerized, but also curious as to why we shared the same unusual eye color. What did it all mean?

"Watch," he said, his tone commanding attention. He reached up and gently touched my cheek with the tips of his fingers, leaving an icy sensation in their wake. My heart rate sped up, and I wasn't quite sure if it was from the anticipation of what was coming, or because it was *him* touching me, igniting these outlandish sensations.

I heard an almost inaudible gasp from him at our contact, and was pleased. Here I'd thought I was the only one affected by it. Before the brightly colored lights took over my vision and forced me to close my eyes, I caught a glimpse of curiosity lingering in his.

My hair whipped around me and the dizzying feeling dominated my body, electrical awareness pulsing in my veins. I ignored the need to try to right myself, knowing that I wasn't really losing my footing. I concentrated, doing my best to ignore the sudden chaos that both surrounded and invaded me, knowing that it had to be almost over. Surely, it would end soon.

As soon as that idea filled my mind, the dizzying feeling slipped away and my hair settled haphazardly around my face, my auburn curls in disarray. The thrust of being jolted back to the now put me slightly off-balance, and my knees went weak. A light sweat covered my skin and my cheeks burned.

• • •

Ryder reached out a steadying hand to my shoulder, giving me just enough balance so I wouldn't topple over.

"That's progress. At least you didn't faint this time."

Trembling a little, I took a step backward, away from him. "Don't touch me," I said firmly.

Now I knew I wasn't crazy. Ryder knew; he knew everything. Why was this happening to me, to us? And why did it happen when we touched? I knew that Ryder had the answers, or at least, I thought he did. He seemed to know more about what had happened than he let on. At any rate, he didn't seem surprised or confused like I was.

I sidestepped around him, wanting to get to the safety of the office. Before I walked in, I looked up at the clock in the hall; it was still ten after eight. There had been no change in time. My mind whirled, questions spinning at the implications. No change in time. I froze with my back to him, realization dawning on me, then took a steadying breath to calm my nerves and lower my heart rate.

"See you in AP History," he said, and I could hear the amusement in his voice. Without looking at him, I could picture the smirk on his handsome face. He turned and walked away, his footsteps echoing down the hall as he left.

Struggling to keep my mouth from hanging open, I forced myself into the office to get my tardy slip with two words echoing in my mind.

Time travel.

• • •

All morning I dreaded history. With my shades on and my hood up, I felt less vulnerable. I hadn't talked to Adam at all the rest of the weekend. I was scheduled to work at his house tonight, though, and there would be no avoiding him there. I wasn't really looking forward to that either.

By the time I took my seat in third period, I was a ball of jumbled-up nerves. Class hadn't started yet and everyone was talking amongst themselves, their voices a discordant hum.

Adam's attention lingered on me as he walked in. I could tell from his posture that he was fighting the urge to come over to where I sat, but he diligently took his place next to Olivia at the front of the room.

A moment later Ryder walked in, and every girl cocked their heads simultaneously in his direction, drooling over him. He projected an air of confidence about him that no one seemed to question. His icy exterior was his barrier to the world, probably like my shades and hoodie was for me. When he spotted me in the back, he made his way over to where I sat, and took the seat next to me.

As I tried to ignore him, I heard a mumbled whisper, "Why is he sitting by her?" Out of the corner of my eye, I saw Ellen elbowing her friend, Heather, who in turn looked my way. Uncomfortable at their scrutiny, I pulled out my textbook and ducked my head, pretending to stare at it.

"Sitting next to me isn't good for your reputation," I said to him quietly without looking his way.

"I'll be the judge of that," he mumbled back.

Adam turned and glared at Ryder, jealousy written all over him, which caused me to smile.

So he finally knows how I feel with Olivia sitting next to him every day, I thought, and rolled my eyes.

"Vi," Ryder said softly as he leaned toward me. "You want me to explain now what happened between us? Or are you going to keep pretending that it didn't happen?"

I shrugged, knowing I was being childish, but didn't care.

"How about during lunch," he suggested.

I kept my eyes down. "I can't. I'm meeting Callie for lunch," I said, surprising myself with how calm I sounded. Just talking to him was upsetting my stomach, and my heart was racing. I felt like I couldn't catch my breath.

"Callie? That's your friend, right? I think I remember seeing her at my aunt's shop."

When I didn't reply, he tried again. "How about after school? You can come over to my house."

I was aware of all the eyes that were trained on us as our classmates eavesdropped on what he was saying to me. I received some shocked glances from jealous girls, but Adam's look was the one that nearly tore me to pieces. It was helplessness.

"I can't, I have to go to Ad—" I caught myself. There were too many people listening. "I have to work," I corrected quietly. I looked at Adam as I spoke and was thankful for my glass shield.

Ryder glanced from me to Adam, seeming to catch on quickly. "For your sake I hope you'll swing by after *your job,*" he said, "if you know what I mean."

For the first time since he'd sat down, I turned my head to look at him. His eyes were cold and hard, his expression deadly serious. Obviously he wasn't going to let me out of talking about this. He leaned forward and with careful fingers removed my sunglasses, snaring my gaze when my eyes were revealed.

Suddenly it was as if we were the only two people in the room. One look was all it took for a lump to form in my throat and leave me suddenly speechless.

He set my sunglasses on my desk. "I'll see you tonight then," he said, not giving me much of a choice.

"Okay," I said hesitantly. "I'll be there when I'm done with work."

Ryder smiled at me, not a quirky, arrogant, or smart-ass smirk, but a real smile that stilled my heart and made my mouth drop open slightly in shock. Then I remembered where I was and shut my mouth, embarrassed by my reaction to him and his charm.

"All right, ladies and gentlemen, listen up." Mr. Prickler called the class to order, and Adam was one of the last people to turn his attention to the teacher.

I slid my sunglasses back on, wanting to be out of the spotlight. Unfortunately that wouldn't happen anytime soon, especially since Ryder Essen was the hot new guy in school. Ryder's sudden friendship elevated me to a new level of interest with my classmates, and I didn't like it one damn bit.

When I walked out of the classroom, JP was lingering in the hallway. He walked toward me and I frowned, suddenly wary. JP never did anything without an ulterior motive, and I had no reason to expect anything less from him now. I tugged at my sweatshirt's hood and shifted my backpack to my other shoulder.

"Hello, Violet."

I ignored him as I walked to meet Callie at her locker. He followed in step with me.

"JP, what do you want?" I ground out, clenching my fists at my sides.

"A little bit of your precious time," he said as he pushed me into the boys' restroom while a couple of his buddies loitered outside the door.

I didn't bother fighting him on this. He was too strong and would just win anyway.

"No one comes in," he instructed one of his friends, a football player named Dylan.

I stood there, not wanting to touch anything. Based on the smell alone, the boys' restroom was far from clean. With toilet seats left up and toilet paper littering the floor, not to mention the unfamiliar and nasty urinals, it really made me want to yak.

"I have something to show you." He smiled at me with a vicious, wolf-like grin.

Uneasy, I waited while he fished around in his backpack for something. Whatever it was, it couldn't be good.

"JP, I don't have all day. Will you hurry it up? I'm supposed to meet Callie for lunch." The boy was senseless sometimes.

His hand finally emerged with an envelope that he handed to me with as much satisfaction as if he were handing over a ticket to a carnival ride.

"Take a look." His tone was taunting, causing my insides to squirm with apprehension.

I opened the plain white envelope, my heart thudding loudly in my chest, and pulled out a photo. The photo was of Adam and me . . . kissing. It was taken at night. I remembered the strange clicking sound I'd heard the night of our last kiss, and realization dawned on me. It was a camera click. JP had stolen our moment and frozen it in time.

My heart thudded as the realization hit me that my least favorite person had in his possession a very valuable piece of evidence that my relationship with Adam existed. We had done everything in our power to keep our relationship secret, yet this tangible proof of it was in JP's hands. What was he going to do with it? He was Adam's best friend, so why would he want to hurt him?

But he wouldn't want to hurt Adam, I realized. Just me.

"What do you want?" I asked him cautiously.

His leering smile grew wider. "It's simple, really," he said. "Break up with Adam and I'll forget the picture even exists." He frowned as he added, "You're not supposed to be with him, you know. You could ruin his future."

So that was it, I realized. JP thought he was protecting Adam or doing him a favor. "I don't understand why you care."

"You'll see. You have until the bonfire," JP said, gloating. "You can keep this picture as a memento. I have another copy." His predatory grin made me shrink away and take a step back.

There was a knot in my stomach and a lump in my throat that I couldn't swallow. "Break up with Adam. That's all you want?"

His eyes gleamed in triumph and he nodded. "I'll forget the whole thing ever happened," he assured me. "No offense, but I can't stand you being with him. You and Adam are really a world apart."

His hurtful tone stung me, but I tamped down my feelings. Apparently I was good enough for him to flirt with and torment, but not good enough for Adam. I slid the photo back into the envelope, then zipped it up into the front pocket of my backpack.

"What happens if I don't?" I said, crossing my arms in front of my chest.

JP looked at me dangerously. "I'll give *him* a reason to break up with *you*. Either way, you'll both be better off."

He laughed cruelly and before I could stop myself, I slapped him across the face. The cracking sound seemed to echo off the yellowing, graffiti-stained walls. His eyes widened a little in shock, then narrowed to a menacing glare as he grabbed both my hands and pinned them to the wall behind me, his face inches from mine.

"You have until the bonfire, don't forget." His voice was low as he released my hands and took a step back, allowing me to leave.

Shaken, I left the bathroom with JP close behind me. Dylan gave me a curious look as I stomped past the rest of JP's posse, still hanging around outside the bathroom.

I needed to talk with Callie, but stopped off at my locker first. I didn't want the picture on me, even if it was hidden in my backpack. With the picture safely locked away, I hurried to the lunchroom, weaving my way through all the people that were late to lunch.

When I entered the lunchroom, Callie wasn't at our usual table. I scanned the room and was shocked to finally find her at the popular kids' table with Henry, Adam, Olivia, JP, and . . . *Ryder*?

59

Ryder was laughing and talking away with the others, so different from the way he behaved with me. He actually looked like he was acting his age, and from the looks of it, he had won them all over.

I snorted and veered away from them.

"Vi!" Ryder called out.

I jerked to a stop, turning back to him to see everyone's attention trained on me, which gave me a sinking feeling in the pit of my stomach.

Callie smiled and waved at me as Henry sat next to her, grinning my way. JP had just slid into a seat with a sneer on his face; no surprise there. Adam's expression was shuttered as he sat next to Olivia. The other kids at the table were rather cool as they looked my way, except for Ryder. His expression was warm and friendly. When I didn't respond, he got up and strode purposefully over to me.

Still shaken from my confrontation with JP, I had no desire to be a part of the social gathering at the popular kids' table. I wasn't from one of the local families, and neither was Ryder. We didn't belong there.

"Vi, I saved a seat for you next to me." Ryder stared at me intently, trying to pierce the dark glass that shielded my eyes. "And I'm not taking no for an answer," he added. He took my arm, gently pulling me along with him to the table, but careful not to touch my hands. Not wanting to make a scene, I obligingly went with him.

Dylan had joined the table and sat across from JP as kids I didn't know very well picked up their trays and left. Maybe they all had somewhere else to be, but I had the sinking feeling that I was the reason they had cleared out so quickly. Ryder nudged me into a chair and sat close to me. Then he tugged down my hood and pulled off my sunglasses.

"Much better," he said. He ran his fingers through my hair, smoothing out my curls. "Beautiful," he whispered.

At his touch, I froze. He was gorgeous and intimidating, and while I always tried to hold my own, I really didn't know if I could keep up with this one. He had a strange pull on me that made me wary, plus he ran hot one minute and cold the next, confusing me.

60

"Violet," Olivia said. "Ryder tells us you two have a special connection." She leaned over the table toward me, giving me a sweet smile, her blue eyes wide with curiosity, but I didn't sense any animosity there.

Adam ran a hand through his hair, and I smiled inside; I knew it was a nervous habit of his. JP shifted in his seat, obviously uncomfortable with the attention I was getting.

"You could say that," I said, looking at Ryder's full lips, which twisted into a smirk. I found myself silently wondering if touching his lips would do the same thing as touching his hands. Annoyed at myself, I pushed the idea out of my head as he handed me a lemonade from his tray.

Olivia smiled warmly at me. "You two are perfect for each other. You both have the neatest eyes, and there seems to be chemistry between you two."

Little did she know just how close she was. For some reason her words caused my appetite to leave me, and I wasn't quite sure what to say.

"Thank you, Olivia," Ryder responded for me.

I nearly choked on my lemonade. "We aren't dating—" I began, but Ryder cut me off.

"Yet," he finished with a slight edge to his tone that only I seemed to pick up on.

I ran my gaze over his perfectly contoured face, from his high cheekbones to his strong, defined chin, and almost sighed aloud. He was completely charming and he knew it, which irritated me. I should be flattered by his attention, but I couldn't stop the strange apprehension I was feeling. He was handsome but he had a dangerous edge, that bad boy essence that made him exciting. And that excitement did strange things to my insides. I put my hand on my stomach, trying to calm myself down.

My phone buzzed in my pocket, and I pulled my gaze from his to glance at it. It was a text from Callie. I glanced at her and she smiled slyly at me.

> Callie: He's so hot! You failed to mention this very important detail!

When I read it, I giggled out loud. Ryder looked at me curiously, and I shoved the phone back into my pocket. "What?"

"So, as I was saying," Olivia said, "wouldn't it be fun to all meet up at the bonfire?" She looked at me and then at Callie.

Weird. Since when did we qualify as people she wanted to hang out with? I glanced at JP and was pleased that he looked less than enthusiastic.

I didn't like Olivia, for obvious reasons. After all, who liked the competition? I knew deep inside that Adam and I would have to part ways eventually; it was inevitable. It was just going to happen sooner rather than later, and JP would make sure of that. In the meantime, I could probably try to get along with Olivia.

"We can meet up Friday," I said reluctantly as Adam threw eye daggers at me.

"Do you want me to pick you up?" Ryder asked.

There was a flutter in the depths of my stomach. Must be nerves with everything that's going on, I reasoned with myself. It couldn't be because of the way he looked at me.

"Um, that would be awesome. Thanks." I smiled warmly at him, then said, "I'll catch up with you guys later." Adam's eyes followed as I rose to my feet, but he didn't say anything. I hadn't eaten anything for lunch, but I just couldn't stomach anything right now.

Ryder turned to me and said, "See you tonight," his voice all silk-wrapped steel.

"Sure," I said nonchalantly and hurried away from the table.

"Text me later!" Callie called after me. I gave her a swift nod of acknowledgment as I made my way toward the exit, reeling inside at all that had just happened.

Chapter 7

It was nearly four o'clock that afternoon by the time I arrived at Adam's. The sun's rays had disappeared behind a thick blanket of clouds, and I hoped it wasn't a hint of what was to come.

As I pulled up to the house, Adam's car was the only one in the drive, which was strange. Usually JP was over on Mondays. He was probably steering clear so I could use the time to break up with Adam.

I parked the Mustang and made my way to the garden, noting with satisfaction that it looked just as good as when I had left on Friday. Tackling the watering first, I hooked up the water hose and began spraying, taking my time to be sure that all the rows were well watered without being flooded. I always took pride in my work, it didn't matter what I did. If it was worth doing, it was worth doing well, my mom taught me.

"Hey." Adam's voice startled me and I jumped, spinning around and accidentally spraying him in the process.

Oops.

I frowned. "I'm so sorry, Adam, I didn't see you there."

"Can we talk," he asked, his blue eyes seeming unusually sad. He sprawled out on the grass and patted the spot next to him. His unruly dark hair glistened with water drops from the hose, and I had to resist the urge to wipe them away.

"Are your parents home?" I asked, concerned about being caught sitting on the job. He shook his head, so I carefully sat down, leaving a good two feet between us as a safety buffer.

Not sure what was on his mind, I asked hesitantly, "What's up?" We hadn't talked since Saturday, which was a long time for us to go without even a text message.

"Listen, I didn't know you were down at the lake when I texted you. I didn't want you to feel bad that I was hanging out with Olivia. I was thinking about you the whole time and just wanted to be with

63

you." He looked at me expectantly, those ocean-blue eyes trying to see right through me.

"Hmm, okay," I said, shrugging noncommittally.

"Violet, take the sunglasses off," he said a little forcefully.

"Fine," I bit out. I hastily took them off and threw them next to me on the grass.

"Your eyes are beautiful." He spoke softly as he scooted closer to me.

"Adam, I have to finish watering." I rose to my feet, feeling uncomfortable with his nearness. "I told Ryder I'd go to his house after I finished with work."

"You can't!" he exclaimed, rising to his feet. He wrapped me in his arms, pulling me close. "It'll drive me nuts to even imagine you alone with him. You know how I feel about you."

Uncomfortable, I looked away, not able to meet his gaze full on.

"Violet, look at me."

So I did. A couple of his wavy locks fell onto his forehead, and I sighed inside at the force of my feelings for him.

"Adam, you don't get a say in what I do anymore," I said quietly. The seriousness of his commitment to Olivia was always with us, even though neither of us usually spoke of it.

"It's time we quit playing games," I said sadly. "It's not fair to Olivia or to me. I deserve to be happy." Adam's face looked pained as the meaning of my words hit him, but I forced myself to continue. "I'm really sorry. Even if I didn't want to, I don't have a choice anymore."

"Violet, listen to me," he said, his voice low and sincere. "This isn't a game to me. I love you."

Those three powerful words stopped me dead, wrapping tight bands around my chest so that I couldn't even breathe. I shook my head, unable to believe what he'd said.

"You can't," I murmured, backing up to step out of his embrace. He quickly grabbed my arm, halting my retreat and keeping me close.

"But I do," he insisted. "I can't help the way I feel. I don't love her. I never did."

His gaze penetrated mine as my thoughts whirled. I felt close to him. Yes, that I was sure of. I enjoyed his company; I was sure of this too. But did I love him?

I couldn't answer that because it wasn't even a remote possibility in my mind. I probably would have fallen in love with him if we had continued down this road, but JP had set up a road block with a huge flashing sign that read DEAD END.

Adam's gorgeous eyes entreated me, seeking an answer I couldn't give, and his lips thinned in a frustrated straight line. So I did what I was really good at. I looked the other way, away from his pleading eyes, away from his perfectly tousled hair, away from the mouth I loved to kiss, and pulled my arm from his hand. He let his hand drop dejectedly, letting me slip from his fingers.

"Isn't there anything I can do to convince you that what we have is real," he asked, his voice soft, pleading.

"No," I said with stubborn resolve, surprised that I was able to distance myself from the situation and pretend it was someone else's life that was being messed up. It was the only way I knew to hold myself together and keep my emotions in check, even though I was shattered inside.

I turned my back on him and returned to spraying the garden. As if on cue, JP's car came rolling up the drive. Adam had no choice but to walk away.

"Hey, Violet," JP called out from the driveway, giving me a sexy grin that made me feel like spiders were crawling up my back.

I narrowed my eyes at him and continued doing my job, trying to shake off the feeling. As I worked, Adam and JP settled on the deck, part of their conversation floating to me on the afternoon breeze.

"You look like your favorite pet just died," JP said to Adam.

I stiffened, but didn't turn around to see the look on Adam's face. I knew I'd hurt him, and it hurt me too. I didn't need a reminder but that was JP, always rubbing it in.

"It's personal, JP." Adam sounded cold and distant.

"All right, man," JP said. "I'm just saying, snap out of it. You should be happy. I heard Olivia was ready to go all the way."

"What?" Adam's voice went up an octave on that one.

I might have done what JP wanted me to do, but I didn't have to stand here and listen to him talk about Adam having sex. It was just too much, especially considering how PG-13 our own relationship had been. Without thinking, I dropped the hose and ran for my car.

"Violet, you're not finished yet!" Adam yelled to me.

"I have an emergency," I called back over my shoulder. "Tell your dad I'll finish tomorrow."

Panicked, I jerked open the car door and jumped inside. I hesitated for a second as I tried to shove the key in the ignition, suddenly unsure where I should go. Then I remembered Ryder's invitation and turned the Mustang toward his house. At least he would take my mind off Adam.

• • •

When I pulled up to Ryder's house, I parked behind a brand new black Tahoe and wondered if it was his truck. At the foot of the stairs, I hesitated and looked up at the magnificent white house. The stairs were so pretty, made of marble so expensive I didn't even want to walk on them. I had to force myself to take that first step. When I reached the top, the front door opened before I could ring the bell, and an older man stood at the doorway in a black suit.

"Please come in," he said to me with acute politeness.

I stepped over the threshold and took stock of the man, assuming it was who Ryder had referred to as his father's right-hand man. To me, he looked more like a butler. He was in his forties and had dark brown hair with slight traces of gray. He was of medium build, but in great shape for someone over forty. I smiled at him and when he didn't smile back, I couldn't help but wonder if he knew how.

"If you come this way, I'll show you into the den."

"Okay." I shrugged, then bent over to take my shoes off.

"Please leave your shoes on," he instructed me.

66

I cringed as I walked across the beautiful tile in these shoes. After all, I'd just been doing yard work, and there was no guarantee my shoes were clean.

Stepping over the threshold onto the tiled floor, I followed him past the half wall partition separating the entryway from the sunken living area. Taking an immediate right followed by a short left, I found myself wandering into a dining area complete with chandelier and breakfast bar. The scent of ham tickled my nose and made my stomach rumble. Ham was my absolute favorite. The room's woodwork was old, an intricately carved mahogany. It was gorgeous.

I followed him past the kitchen and into a den that was furnished with a couch and a coffee table, and a huge flat-screen TV hung directly across from it on the wall. On the left was a wet bar with some stools.

"Ryder will be right with you." He walked over to the bar. "Can I make you a drink?" His bushy eyebrows pulled together, looking like a unibrow, and I swallowed to keep from laughing.

"No. That's okay," I said, standing there awkwardly.

"You're not thirsty?"

A smooth voice that I instantly recognized made me jump. I whirled around and there Ryder stood so close to me, his proximity was a little unsettling. His icy facade was firmly in place, his cold eyes taking me in and chilling me to the core.

"Ryder, do you always make it a habit to scare your guests?" I said breathlessly.

"Only ones I like." A smile barely broke the surface before it disappeared. His catlike eyes were quick to give me a once-over as he walked to the bar.

Without another word, the butler backed out of the room and closed the door behind him.

"How was work," Ryder asked, then picked up a two-liter of Diet Coke, holding it up for my approval.

"It was fine." I gave him a little nod, fidgeting under his glance. He took out two glasses and filled them with the ice and soda, then tucked a straw in one and pushed it my way.

"Thank you." I took a seat on a bar stool and wrapped my lips around the little green straw to take a small sip.

"Refreshing, huh?"

Annoyed at all the stalling, I said, "Listen, I'm not here for a social call. You wanted to talk, so let's talk."

Ryder studied me intently before speaking. "You put on a brave face and most of the time you are. But around me, you don't feel that way. I make you feel weak."

His statement made me shift in my seat. He was right on the money. I stared at him, unsure of how to respond, and noticed that his tousled hair was a little more wild than usual. Just looking at him made my breathing slow down, but my pulse raced. I opened my mouth to respond, but he cut me off.

"I make you nervous because you're drawn to me. You're afraid that it's beyond just mutual attraction, which scares you more than your worst fear and when we touch . . . something unexplainable happens. That inability to control the situation frightens you."

I stiffened, holding my tongue while the thoughts swirled in my head, unable to comprehend how he could be so dead-on. But the look he gave me said he already knew and I didn't have to say anything. He took another sip of his drink.

Finally, I found my voice. "All right. I'll play."

He raised his eyebrows at me, and I found myself lost in his gaze, noting how his thick black lashes framed the silver perfectly.

Breaking the spell, I slid my glass out of the way. When I looked back up, he was smirking at me.

"Want something to eat?" he asked, a half smile playing on his lips.

"No, I'm good," I said as I crossed my legs. As I reined in my emotions, questions began to form, and unable to stop myself, I shot them at him in rapid succession. "Why does it happen? When we touch, why does *that* happen? I mean, we were seeing the future, right? Where was everyone else?"

He nodded. "Yes, I believe it was us on Friday. I don't know where everyone else was. There somewhere, I would think." He

68

refilled our glasses and put mine in front of me. "Listen, Vi, I'm not going to lie to you."

He brought a book from under the counter and slid it over to me. The title, *Essen Family*, was embossed in the brown leather cover and pressed with silver.

I fingered it, noticing the leather bookmark with a tassel that hung over the deckled edges of the fragile yellowed pages. "How old is it?"

"It's old, going back to the seventeen hundreds. Every person with silver eyes in my family is listed in here, along with their powers. I don't think it's an accident that you moved here."

"Powers?" My voice squeaked as I stared at him, at first thinking maybe he was joking with me. But his expression was completely serious, and then I remembered what had happened between us. If I wasn't crazy and we actually time traveled, I supposed that would be considered a pretty awesome power to have.

"What exactly is it?" I asked as I glanced over at him. He seemed more open, as if his icy facade was slowly beginning to thaw. "Can I read it?"

"Every family should have a book, and each family belongs to a clan. Including yours," he said as he gave me a pointed look. "It's not like a normal book, it's more like a family tree, but with a lot more detail."

"Let me get this straight. You're trying to tell me that my family is part of a clan, and we have a book similar to the one you have?" I looked again at the fragile book and then up to Ryder's serious face.

He nodded, and his gaze focused on the straw he was using to push the ice around in his glass. "We're called Manipulators, Vi. From time to time, children born into particular families that have certain powers; it's been happening for centuries. Not everyone born into the families have powers, but some do. I know it doesn't sound real, since you haven't been raised the way you should have been, knowing from birth about your powers like the rest of us. You have no idea how to use or control your power. In fact, I'm not even supposed to be around you."

Before I could respond, he looked up at me, his expression sincere as he said, "I'd like to help you. If you wanted, we could maybe even experiment a little. What do you think?"

I frowned. "Why is it you're the one telling me this and not my parents?"

"Your stepfather probably doesn't know what you're capable of. And your mother . . ." Ryder's forehead creased as he shrugged his shoulders. He seemed worried.

My heart began pounding. "How could my mother not have told me the truth? Maybe she didn't know either." As I thought of my mom and the possibility that she could have kept something so huge from me, my eyes welled with tears.

Ryder swallowed and took a deep breath. "There's more."

Frustrated and embarrassed, I swiped away the tears that threatened to fall, then motioned for him to continue.

"I know who your real dad is. It's important that you trust me and don't ask any more questions. I'll help you any way I can. You're special, Vi, and it's not just your family and my family. There are many more clans out there with powers."

"Who he *is*? My real father is alive? How can that be? He died in a car accident when I was two!" I cried out. When Ryder gave me a sad look but said nothing, I leaned toward him and shrieked, "Why doesn't he want to see me? Where has he been all this time?"

My heart hammered inside my chest as my mind reeled. How could a parent who was alive not want to be a part of their child's life? And had my mom known he was still alive? Did she lie to me?

"I'm sorry, Vi. I honestly don't know." He reached under the bar and grabbed a tissue and handed it to me, then looked at me hopefully.

This was so much to take in, I was shaking. Ryder was obviously telling me the truth, no matter how hard the truth was to wrap my head around. There was so much I wanted to know—*needed* to know—that I didn't even know where to start. *My father is alive?* It boggled my mind.

Then I froze, remembering that odd dream I'd had about my stepdad telling Vick that my real father was coming for me. Could it be that it wasn't a dream at all, that I'd really heard that?

I looked at Ryder, considering the possibility, and came to the conclusion that yes, it probably did really happen and I'd just suppressed it. After all, my mom had died just a week or so before that, and I was an emotional wreck at the time.

But Ryder apparently had the answers to my questions, if not all of them, at least some of them. If I wanted to learn more about my real father and Manipulators and these so-called powers, Ryder was my best bet.

So I pulled myself together and gave him a halfhearted smile, and for the first time that night he actually smiled back. A real, honest-to-goodness, ear-to-ear smile that displayed his perfect white teeth.

I let out a sigh, then took a long swig of my drink and closed my eyes. I was starting to feel nauseated. *Probably information overload.*

"Are you all right? You look pale."

"Yeah, I just haven't eaten since breakfast. And with finding out my dad is alive and not dead like I thought he was all these years . . ." I shrugged. "I'm a little shaken."

"I can take care of that," he said quickly, then walked to the door and stuck his head into the hallway. "Xavier, will you bring in something for us to eat? Thanks."

I shook my head in amazement, realizing that Xavier must be a butler. Families like the Prices had lots of money and big houses, which required housekeepers and other staff, but a butler? It was like something out of an old movie.

Minutes later, Xavier knocked quietly at the door, then came in with a plate of nachos on a silver tray. He set out the nachos on the bar, along with napkins and silverware, then made a discreet exit.

As we helped ourselves to the nachos, I glanced over at Ryder and asked, "Can you tell me more about these clans?"

He ran a hand through his hair before resting his chin on his palm, leaning on his elbow. "Our powers are linked to our eye color,

71

believe it or not, and clans are differentiated by eye color. I belong to the Silvercrest Clan. Those with silver eyes, like us, use time travel to see future events, so all of our clan members have silver eyes."

I shook my head, trying to make sense of what he said. It all sounded ridiculous, like a sci-fi movie, and if I hadn't experienced it myself, I'd have never believed it. "How many clans are there?"

Ryder paused with a loaded nacho chip in midair. "Several. There are the ones with emerald eyes, violet eyes, amber eyes, blue eyes, and there's one clan made up of multis. Those have eyes of different colors, like one blue eye and one amber eye. The clans are supposed to be divided by their colors and powers so one clan doesn't have advantage over the others, but the multis—"

He stopped short with a shake of his head. "I'm sorry. This is a lot for you to take in."

"Wow, I guess so. Your parents . . . where are they? Why aren't they here?"

"They're in New York. I usually go to a school on a small island off of New York, so most parents live in the city to be close to the school." He bit into the chip he'd been holding.

My stomach started to growl at the aroma coming from the nachos, so I reached out to load up a chip of my own. It was delicious. As I chewed, I came up with my next question.

"Then what are you doing here?" *Could it be because of me?* The thought made my stomach do a little flip.

He reached for a napkin and wiped his mouth before giving me a little smirk. "Remember, I'm not supposed to be here, but I've known about you for a long while and I couldn't help myself." He then took another bite, chewing slowly.

I took another sip of my drink. I wasn't sure what to do with his admission, but I did like the way he looked at me.

Ryder suddenly seemed to find the nachos fascinating, and he poked around at them as he casually asked, "What's up with you and Adam?"

"Absolutely nothing," I said calmly, but inside, I was still shaken. I wasn't sure if it was from too much information or the mention of Adam. "Hey, these are great." I gestured to the plate, hoping to steer the conversation to something safer.

"Can I touch you?"

Chills instantly shot through me at his unexpected question. "Huh?" I dropped the chip I was holding back in the plate.

"I've been dying to try it again since you walked into my house." He wiped his hands on a napkin and stared intensely at me.

There was no way I wanted to go through that whirlwind thingy again. My head was spinning with everything I'd just learned, I'd had the day from hell earlier with the incident with JP and having to break up with Adam, and I was completely drained. I just wanted to go home and hole up in my bathroom with a hot bath and some tunes.

"No, I don't want to try it tonight. It's been a long day and I'm tired. I should probably be going, it's getting late." I stood up and pushed away from the bar stool quickly.

"Okay," he said reluctantly. "Do you want to get together tomorrow then?"

Amazed at how easily he gave in, I matched his easygoing tone and gave him a smile. "Sure. Why not? It would be nice to learn a little bit more about your lifestyle."

What was the worst that could happen, other than another psychedelic whirlwind trip down a wormhole together. Nothing to worry about, right?

Ryder walked me to the door. "See you at school," he called out as I walked down the marble stairs.

"See ya tomorrow." I gave him a distracted little wave as I hurried to my car. It was getting late, and I needed to hurry home.

• • •

When I walked into the house that evening, Vick was sitting on the couch in the living room. "A little late for a school night, don't you think?" His voice had an edge, and I stiffened a little, annoyed that he was keeping tabs on me.

"Dad made sure I stayed up to wait for you. He got called into work."

"I had a lot of stuff to take care of." I shrugged noncommittally, hoping that he would assume I meant at work so I didn't have to explain Ryder. My relationship with him was new and confusing, and I doubted my overprotective stepbrother would take that very well.

Vick's green eyes darkened to an olive color as he narrowed them, probably not buying it. He clicked the TV off and tossed the remote aside, then got to his feet.

Ignoring him, I took my shoes off and left them by the front door, then grabbed the smooth wooden banister to head upstairs.

"Vi, Adam called me."

I paused halfway up the stairs and looked back at him. His knowing expression confirmed that I was so busted.

"He said you had an emergency and had to leave abruptly, and that was a couple of hours ago. So my question to you is—where did you go that you didn't want me to know about?"

He crossed his arms over his chest and stared at me steadily. When I didn't answer right away, he raised an eyebrow as if to say, *Well?*

Ugh, I hated lying! It never occurred to me that Adam would actually call here to check up on me; I figured he would just send me a text. I pulled my phone out of my pocket and glanced at it quickly. I'd left it in silent mode, and sure enough, counting Adam and Callie I had several missed calls and five unanswered texts.

"I went to a friend's house," I said. After all, being vague wasn't lying, right?

"Callie's house?" Vick fired back at me quickly. "Oh, and before you dig yourself into a deeper hole, you should know that she called here too."

If he knew I wasn't at her house, then why was he grilling me like this? Sometimes Vick took the big brother thing a little too far.

"Vick, I was at a guy friend's house. His name is Ryder and no, I'm not dating him," I added, just to set the record straight. I knew that would be Vick's next question, and there wasn't any use in keeping anything from him.

74

His face softened a little. "Ryder who? I suppose Adam was jealous, huh?"

Stunned, I gave my stepbrother a bewildered look, and said slowly, "Ryder Essen, he just moved to the area." Not wanting to confirm or deny anything with regard to the other, I ventured, "And as for Adam, you know he's seeing Olivia."

"Oh, come on, Vi. Don't try to deny it. I'm your brother, remember? I can tell when you're lying." His face serious, Vick's lips were pursed as he studied me.

I shrugged. "Think what you want," I said stubbornly. Desperately wanting to change the subject, I went all-in for a diversion. "Did you know my real dad is alive?"

Vick visibly paled as he looked at me for a moment. "How do you know that?"

I rolled my eyes. "I consider you my brother, since I've grown up with you since I was little. How could you not tell me something so important?"

Saying nothing, Vick took a deep breath and looked away.

Tears welled in my eyes at his betrayal. When a couple of tears fell, cascading down my cheeks and leaving wet little trails, I spun on my heel and ran up the stairs two at a time.

"Violet! I'm so sorry."

Vick's voice carried up to me as I slammed my bedroom door and threw myself on my bed. Tears and anguish pouring out of me till I was nothing by a dry well. I thought about everything Ryder had told me, about having powers and my dad being alive and clans and such, and decided it was too much for me to think about right now. I'd talk to my stepdad and Vick about all this later, when I wasn't so emotional. They had a lot of explaining to do.

Remembering all my messages, I rolled over and grabbed my phone.

Adam: Did you leave because of what JP said? I'm not interested in sleeping with Olivia, just so you know. I want to be with you.

I could picture him as if he were standing there speaking to me; I knew him so well. Letting out a heavy sigh, I decided not to respond and clicked to the next message, also from Adam.

Adam: Violet, I don't like how things ended without really talking them through. Please call me.

Unbelievable. He just didn't get it. I was so frustrated and didn't want to discuss it anymore. My mind was made up, so I typed out a text that I hoped was clear enough.

Me: Sorry, Adam. There's nothing to talk about anymore.

I clicked SEND and buried my face in my pillow. After a moment of wallowing in self-pity, I rolled over and called Callie. She answered on the second ring.

"Hey, Violet!" Her voice was bubbling over with excitement.

"Okay, spill. What's so exciting?"

There was no way I could tell Callie about what Ryder had told me about our powers; she'd think I was completely nuts. My best bet right now was to go about my life as usual, so I pulled my backpack up from the floor and grabbed my history book, then flipped to the assigned chapter and bookmarked the spot I needed to read tonight.

"I'm just thrilled that you're finally accepted at the table," she said. "You're not an outcast anymore. I have Olivia in sixth period, and she was talking about how nice you and Ryder are."

I snorted. "The only thing that's changed in my life is Ryder, so my guess is he's the only reason they're tolerating me. If it was up to JP, I wouldn't even be allowed in the same room as Adam."

"Yeah, maybe," she said slowly. I could tell she was pondering what I had said.

Changing the subject, I dropped my big news. I was about to burst with everything I'd just learned, so figured it would be safe enough to tell Callie about my dad. "By the way, my dad isn't dead like I thought. He's alive somewhere." I screwed my eyes shut. "Oh, and JP shoved me into the bathroom today and showed me a picture of Adam kissing me."

"What? Oh my God, how do you feel? I can't believe your dad is alive." Callie was squealing so loudly, I had to pull the phone away from my ear a little.

"I don't know how to feel yet. I want to find him, but I have no idea where to even begin. And what if he doesn't want me?"

"Only an idiot wouldn't want you, Violet. And what's this about JP?"

I sighed. "I'm not sure how JP found out, but he knows about me and Adam. He said he'd give Adam a reason to break it off with me if I didn't break up with him first."

"Oh my God! What did you do? What did you say," she asked rapidly, like she always does when she gets excited.

"There wasn't anything I could do. He gave me the picture as a memento. So I broke up with Adam this evening, and afterward I ended up going to Ryder's house—"

"Whoa, slow down," she said. "How did Adam take it? Did you say *Ryder*?"

I sighed again. "Adam sent me a couple of texts. He doesn't understand why I don't want to see him anymore. And he said he loves me." I thought back to that moment and clenched the phone a little harder in my hand.

"Wow!"

"Tell me about it. As for Ryder, we're just friends."

Friends with special powers who belong to some freaky clan, I wanted to tell her. Callie was my bestie, but until I knew exactly what I was dealing with, I didn't want to tell her any more than I had to. It seemed safer that way.

"But there's potential," she said slowly, thinking out loud. "Yes, definite potential. I see it when he looks at you."

"Can you please stop playing matchmaker?" I said with exasperation. My plate was full enough as it was. The last thing I needed was pressure in that direction.

"All right," she said. "Wow, a lot has happened."

That was an understatement, I thought.

"Hey, I have to jet. I have the history chapter to read before tomorrow's quiz."

Callie giggled, back to her perky self again. "Okay, well, I'll see you tomorrow!"

I smiled as I disconnected the call, her bubbly personality rubbing off on me a little.

It had been such a stressful day, I decided to take a warm, relaxing bath before doing my homework. I grabbed my comfy red plush robe, my phone, and my ear buds, then headed to my bathroom.

As the tub filled with hot water, I added a generous sprinkle of fragrant bath salts, and placed my phone on a folded towel on the floor within reach. Stepping gingerly into the hot water, I eased in slowly, then closed my eyes and relaxed as my play list began. I was listening to Lady Antebellum when my phone beeped loudly midsong. I dried my hands and picked it up.

Ryder: What are you doing?

I rolled my eyes. Couldn't a girl get a little peace and quiet? I should have known better than to take my phone in the bathroom with me.

Me: Trying to take a quiet relaxing bath . . . but I keep getting interrupted.

I found myself smiling while I awaited his reply. The phone beeped immediately and I laughed out loud at his response, then sent one back.

Ryder: Nice! Wish I could be there.

Me: Typical guy response. See you tomorrow.

Ryder: Sounds good!

I tossed the phone down onto the towel, then submerged my whole body under the water and came up wiping my face. After my bath, I curled up in bed to read my history chapter.

Chapter 8

The next day I hurried to meet Callie at her locker. "Hey," I called to her. She flashed me her quirky smile as she filled her backpack with books.

"Hi." Her grin widened. Her brown hair was down and curled.

"Love your hair," I said as I repositioned my backpack onto my shoulder.

"Thanks, I had to get up at five in order to be here on time. You're so lucky you have natural curls," she said with a little whine.

I rolled my eyes mentally; leave it to Callie to turn a compliment into a complaint. "I don't always feel that lucky."

I spotted Ryder walking toward us. His expression cold and distant, he seemed to be watching me carefully, and I swallowed nervously. Today I was wearing blue sunglasses to match my blue hoodie. Ryder had made it clear he didn't like my hoodies and shades, but he couldn't make me change who I am.

"Hi, Vi. I think I could spot you anywhere." His tone was light and his face seemed relaxed.

Obscured by my sunglasses, my gaze wandered over his blue T-shirt that clung to his hard torso, all the way past the dark blue jeans that hung off his hips in that sexy way, knowing full well he couldn't see where my eyes roamed.

"I can assure you that the way I dress has nothing to do with you spotting me. Wait, that didn't come out right," I said quickly. "I meant I dress for your eyes only." My cheeks began to burn and I fumbled, sure I was turning a bright shade of pink. "I mean for *my* eyes only. I dress to suit *me*."

Callie covered her mouth, giggling at my Freudian slip.

"You're right," Ryder said seriously. "The way you dress has absolutely nothing to do with me finding you." He didn't even crack a smile.

Next to me, Callie chortled as Ryder and I stared each other down.

What was he trying to imply? My heart started to race. I couldn't take much more of him scorching me with all his intensity.

"Look, you guys match!" Callie exclaimed. "Wow, you really are perfect for each other." I turned to glare at her, but the sunglasses ruined the effect.

"Would you look at the time," I said. "I have to get to first period." I spun on my heel and began to speed-walk to my next class.

"See you later," Callie called after me.

"See you."

Initially I was annoyed to find Ryder keeping pace with me, but couldn't hold back the small smile that tugged at my lips. I was beginning to like running into him.

"What time do you want to get together today?" he asked, easily matching my hurried strides.

His question caught me off guard, so I hesitated. "I don't know. I'm supposed to work after school. I'm always so dirty afterward, I usually like to go home and shower right away."

"Then I'll come to your house when you're done," he said adamantly, not really giving me an option.

Ryder brushed against my side and my heart almost stopped. I took a deep breath, trying to calm my nerves.

"That's probably not a good idea. I happened to mention you to my stepbrother, and I don't want him getting the wrong impression about us."

We came to a stop outside my classroom and I leaned my back against the lockers. Ryder's lips curved into a slow, seductive smile.

"What kind of impression are you afraid he might get?"

His voice came out low and husky as he leaned over to whisper his question into my ear. I could feel his warm breath on my ear and my neck, causing my heart to hammer and my face to flush again. I took a shaky breath, inhaling his scent that smelled faintly of cinnamon, and swallowed the lump in my throat.

"You're too close," I whispered. "I can't think."

He chuckled quietly then pulled away, allowing me breathing room. I shook my head as I cleared my thoughts.

"My stepbrother is overprotective. I'll text you when I'm done, and if it's not too late we can figure something out."

The truth was that I didn't want to commit right now. These powers we supposedly had intrigued me, but power like that could be dangerous, and it worried me.

"All right, I'll see you at lunch." Ryder gave me a little wink as he turned and headed off toward his class.

I went into my classroom and took my seat in the back, impatiently waiting for the teacher to show up. All through class, I daydreamed, having a hard time concentrating on the lesson. By the end of the class, it took all my willpower not to run for the door. I just wanted to be done with this day.

Maybe I should quit my job, I thought, but then dismissed the idea as quickly as it came.

I was on my way to third period when Ryder suddenly appeared at my side. "Hello, Vi," he said smoothly, his voice low and sexy all at the same time. "Excited to see me?"

"I'm ecstatic. Can't you tell?" I gave him a flirty smile.

"Ouch." He smirked and put a hand across his heart as we came to a standstill outside our classroom.

Olivia and Adam strolled our way.

"Oh, you guys are so cute," she exclaimed. "Look, Adam, they're both wearing blue. They match. Why can't we do that?" she whined, tossing back her blond hair as she looked at him imploring. Her eyes shone with love; it looked like she really did care about him.

I glanced at Adam and noticed he looked beyond disturbed, his eyes were an angry ocean. Granted, he was probably still thinking about what had happened between us. I winced behind my shield of dark glass.

"We would be cute if we were a—" I began, as Ryder gave me a gentle push toward the door.

"Vi, we'd better get to our seats. Class is going to start."

He gripped my shoulders, and even through the thin cotton material of my hoodie, I could feel the electricity pulsing between us. A quiet hum that made me feel . . . alive. Ryder's hands only released me once my ass was firmly planted in my chair, taking the electric charge between us with him. I didn't hear Adam's comment, he responded too quietly. I didn't think he was happy, though.

I gave Ryder a disapproving glare, even though he couldn't see it because of my shades. He didn't have to make Adam jealous like that, especially when we were just friends. If you could even call it that.

"What?" he said innocently, although his face told me he knew exactly what I was thinking.

"You know what. Cut it out, okay?" How could he go from being charming to being so infuriating?

His full lips were rueful but his cold eyes seemed to be laughing at me. The contradictions made him unreadable. The slopes of his cheekbones made me want to reach over and trace them. The only thing that was certain was my growing attraction for him. I shook my head slightly, as if trying to deny my thoughts.

Ryder leaned over and said quietly, "Vi, you should know by now that I hate your sunglasses. I don't care that they coordinate with your outfit. Your eyes are like a book, but I can't read you with them on."

"Didn't you know that this book needs a key?" I said, quietly seething. "You have no right. You have a barrier too. Your barrier is just invisible to everyone else, but I see it."

I spoke softly too, trying to keep my voice under control. We were undoubtedly attracting the attention of at least half the class, and it irritated the hell out of me. My hands were clenched so tightly at my sides that my knuckles were turning white.

"Okay, Violet. Leave them on, for now. When we're alone, you're taking them off, though." His tone was sharp and firm, telling me that I probably wouldn't be able to reason with him later, but on the bright side, I could try.

Just then Mr. Prickler's cell phone rang. I couldn't hear what he was saying because everyone started chattering amongst themselves. When he ended the conversation and sat his phone on his desk, the socializing stopped abruptly.

He cleared his throat. "Our class is the next one to meet our new principal. So, students, line up and we'll walk down to the gym."

After a few moments of mumbled confusion and jostling for position, our class formed a line and followed Mr. Prickler down the hallway toward the gym. Ryder bumped my shoulder with his and gave me a warm smile as we brought up the rear.

"Don't you think it's weird that the principal is taking the time to call students out of their classes just to meet everyone?" I asked him. "I mean, I can totally see one assembly, but class by class seems like such a waste of time."

"It is strange," he agreed after a pause. He was texting on his phone, not really paying me any attention.

We walked in silence the rest of the way, but he stayed close to my side and I was fully aware of his body next to mine. He brushed against me now and then, which sent chills coursing through me. My heart raced, and I found myself wanting more.

Upon entering the gym, we could see there were twenty seats located near the front podium. A middle-aged woman stood next to the podium, her shoulders pulled back and her expression severe. She was wearing a flower-patterned dress with short sleeves, her brown hair in a tight bun. As we made our way to our seats, her eyes scanned us while she spoke to a short, blond-haired girl who had her back to me. We took our seats slowly.

When everyone was seated, the blond girl turned around and her gaze pinned Ryder instantly. I stifled a gasp when I saw her eyes; she was just like Ryder and me.

Ryder stiffened next to me and I looked at him with curiosity. Yes, he was definitely uncomfortable, his eyes trained unwaveringly on the new girl.

I tapped my foot restlessly while the principal waited for the talking to subside. I started to turn to him, but he nudged me to stay where I was.

The girl's gaze swept the crowd as well, but it always came back to land on Ryder. She seemed pretty darned delighted to see him, glowing like a little ball of sunshine. Her eyes narrowed as her gaze landed on me, no doubt sizing up her competition. I was the only person sitting next to Ryder as he had the aisle seat, and she examined me with curiosity.

The principal seemed to take notice too. "Hello, students. My name is Margaret Norman, and I'm your new principal. This is my daughter, Raeann. We're pleased to meet you. It is most unfortunate that your former principal left on such short notice. Unfortunately he had family business to attend to in a different state, and will not be returning. I'll be taking his place."

Her gaze swept over us all again, and came to land on me. "Young lady, please remove your sunglasses."

Everyone's attention turned on me. I rolled my eyes behind the polarized glass, annoyed that I was being singled out and didn't have a choice in the matter. With deliberate slowness, I pulled my shades off, and surprise flashed across her face. The expression was fleeting and she quickly composed herself.

"Happy?" I muttered as I put them in my backpack. Ryder elbowed me again, and I looked at him sharply.

"Thank you for all coming down and taking the time to meet us."

Principal Margaret continued her speech, her gaze drifting over all the students and every now and then lingering on me just a tad bit longer. The scrutiny was beginning to make me feel uncomfortable. Obviously she noticed that Ryder and I shared the same unusual eye color as her daughter, but why would that be a big deal? Unless they were from our clan?

All I knew is that I wanted them both to leave. I didn't like the way Raeann was drooling over Ryder; it was irritating. I frowned, shifting slightly in my chair.

Raeann's gaze didn't leave Ryder for more than a second. There was definitely something up with that. Did he know her, I wondered silently, and decided then and there that I was definitely going to find out.

During the principal's speech, her gaze kept going back to the two of us. Adam noticed and gave me a strange look. A moment later, the phone in my pocket vibrated from a text. I pulled it out and gave it a surreptitious glance.

Adam: What is up with her? Why are she and her daughter staring at you two? It's weird. Be careful, OK?

Something strange was definitely going on. Obviously I wasn't imagining things. There was no good reason for the principal and her daughter to be focusing on us, and my instant dislike for them got a brand new friend in the form of distrust.

Quickly sending a short "OK" back to Adam, I then focused my attention back to the principal.

"I hope you all know that my door is always open." The new principal smiled at everyone, but it didn't make its way to her eyes. She then stared at Ryder as she concluded, "Oh, and please make Raeann feel welcome here. I know you all will."

It was close to lunchtime by the time Principal Margaret's speech ended, so Mr. Prickler said we were dismissed. As the class dispersed, I didn't stray from Ryder's side. Strangely enough, I felt safe next to him, even though he seemed so secretive and I barely knew him.

"Ryder," I said in a low tone.

"Hmm?"

"Do you know the principal's daughter? I couldn't help but notice that Raeann's eyes never left you for more than a second during her mom's speech. She lit up like she's in love with you or something," I said as we walked.

Ryder didn't acknowledge me at first, staring straight ahead as if he were lost in his thoughts. Finally, he said, "They're from our clan. I'm not quite sure why they're here, though."

My mind was spinning with questions as I grabbed for Ryder's hand to get his attention so he would look at me. A jolt of electricity ran through me as my hand closed on his.

For crying out loud! I didn't mean to bring this on myself.

The instinct to stop him and talk to him had been too much, and I'd carelessly forgotten about what happened when our skin came into contact. The colored lights began to spin and the dizzy feeling hit me like a hurricane, fast and hard.

I squeezed my eyes shut as the colored lights swirled around us and my hair whipped in the wind, thinking desperately, *Please, hurry up. Please, hurry up.*

• • •

I opened my eyes to near darkness, the moonbeams weak in the starless, cloudy sky. The trees around me swayed menacingly in the wind, and low-hanging branches seemed to reach for me.

Wary, I took a step back and something hard poked my side. I turned to find a tall stone grave marker next to me. I took a few steps forward, hearing nothing but the wind's low howl and my footsteps crunching on the dead leaves. I squinted in the darkness to see more grave markers all around me, jutting out of the ground this way and that. It looked like an array of oversized chess pieces scattered on a grass chessboard, the graveyard their playing ground.

Walking at a slow but steady pace, I was making my way through the maze of headstones when I heard faint voices carrying their way to me on the breeze. I followed the soft sounds, the voices growing louder as I neared.

When I could make out what they were saying, I crouched and made myself small behind a headstone. I had completely forgotten that others couldn't see me or hear me when I traveled like this.

"Listen, Slade," a girl's voice said. "It's no secret that there's a lot to the book. The only way to truly know is by trial and error."

"Raeann, I told you! I'm not interested in experimenting with you."

It was Ryder's voice. Why did Raeann call him Slade? And why was he talking with her in this vision? From past experience, no one had been able to see or hear us, but this vision was different somehow.

"There isn't anyone else with the gift," I heard Raeann say.

86

"I don't care," Ryder replied, a cold finality in his tone. "Good-bye, Raeann."

"This isn't over!" Raeann shouted at him, then she ran through the graveyard, disappearing into the darkness.

When she was gone, I ran to Ryder. He was staring off into the distance after her with the Essen family book clutched in his hands.

"Ryder!" I said breathlessly. "Thank God you're here. I thought I ended up here by myself."

Relief washed through me at the realization that I hadn't traveled here alone. But Ryder ignored me and turned to walk away.

"Ryder, where are you going? Why were you meeting with her?"

Confused and a little desperate, I fell into step beside him, watching as he kept his focus on where he was going. Too busy paying attention to him, I walked right into a low marker, catching the brunt of the impact on my thigh and then losing my balance, toppling headfirst over it onto the ground and landing on my shoulder, arm, and head.

The air whooshed from me and I gasped as sharp pain suddenly hit me. My body throbbed from the hard fall I'd taken, and Ryder didn't even bother to stop to see if I was okay. *The jerk!*

I righted myself as quickly as I could, ignoring the pain in my thigh that protested as I stood up, and rushed to catch up to him. Every movement caused my head and body to ache and burn. My eyes had adjusted to the darkness and I spotted him quickly, thankful that he was relatively close. I sighed in relief and promised myself to pay more attention to my surroundings.

"Ryder!" I grabbed his arm, completely exasperated with him, and pulled with all my might. But my grip slipped down to his hand as he continued forward like I wasn't even clinging to him.

The touch of his cool skin in the night air sent a hot electrical charge churning through my body. I shut my eyes, squeezing them tight. Through my eyelids, I could see the colored lights bouncing.

• • •

It all stopped at once and I jolted awake, my whole body convulsing as I startled. It took my eyes a minute to focus after I opened them.

At first the light was blinding, but soon Ryder came into focus. He was leaning over me expectantly, and for once his expression wasn't cold but worried. I was still at school, but I was lying on a cot in the nurse's station, looking up at plain blue walls with the smell of disinfectant stinging my nose. My stomach churned with nausea.

"You're so pale." Ryder reached out without thinking to touch my cheek, then realizing he shouldn't touch my skin, went to pat the top of my head awkwardly.

"Why didn't you answer me," I demanded. "Why were you meeting with her?" My voice was hoarse and my pride a little wounded.

Ryder narrowed his eyebrows, concern wrinkling his forehead. "What are you talking about?" he said quietly. "Wait a minute. Did something happen to you when you touched me?"

It seemed like a silly question for him to ask me, so I ignored it. "How long was I out?"

"Fifteen minutes or so. What happened?"

I shut my eyes. "Just let me think."

So time moved when I was gone alone, but it hadn't moved at all when Ryder and I were cast into the future. That meant that what I had just seen must have been . . . the past.

A memory. Ryder's memory! Oh my God, I saw a memory!

Excitement bubbled up inside me until I realized if that were true, then he knew Raeann. The bubble of excitement burst just as quickly. Apparently the question I had in mind as I grabbed him earlier was answered by the memory I saw.

I opened my eyes. Ryder's unruly golden hair seemed to glow in the dim room. He pinned me with his silvery eyes, obviously not happy. Perched on the edge of my cot, he frowned and his jaw tightened.

"Do you know Raeann Norman?" I asked him point-blank. Given what I'd just seen, I was certain I knew the truth. The question was, would he be honest with me?

"Why do you ask? What happened to you?"

When he narrowed his eyes at me, I recognized his questions for what they were. Avoidance. I'd used it myself as a diversion in the past, and wasn't happy for someone else to use my own tricks on me.

"Don't answer a question with a question, Slade," I snapped back.

I didn't mean to use the name Raeann had called him, it just sort of rolled off my tongue from all the frustration building up inside me. His smoky gray eyes flashed with sudden surprise before melting into a full-force blizzard.

"How do you know that name?"

Ryder's voice was guarded and tight, barely containing his fury. Smoldering gray eyes seemed to scorch me, and I found it difficult to breathe with all the intensity radiating from him. It didn't matter what emotions played across his face. He could be angry or indifferent; it didn't matter. The boy was gorgeous no matter what.

I shifted uncomfortably on the cot and sat up. "I don't need to be here anymore."

Realizing I wasn't wearing my shades, I searched around me before remembering they were in my backpack. I spotted the blue pack on the floor near the closed door and scanned the room for a quick exit, but didn't find any. Ryder moved from his perch, allowing just enough room for me to sit up and stand, but he was clearly blocking the doorway with his muscular frame. I sighed aloud.

"Are you going to answer me," he demanded, his voice coldly in check. His gaze locked with mine, making me feel weak.

"You first," I insisted. "Do you know her?"

"She's a part of the clan, so of course I know who she is," he said carefully.

It was all I could do not to roll my eyes. I hated it when guys gave you enough in a roundabout way to answer the question, but still left you hanging. Having a brother meant I was very familiar with the tactic.

"I saw her call you Slade somewhere in the past."

"You were inside my head? Seeing a memory?" He seemed thoughtful as he leaned his whole body against the door frame. "Where did it take place?"

Gosh, he was persistent.

"I'm tired," I said, trying to stall, then relented when he shot me an answer-the-question look. "Damn. Okay, it took place in a cemetery. That's all I saw. You two were arguing. She wanted to experiment with the book."

I thought back to the Essen family book and my eyes widened as suddenly it dawned on me. "You knew what would happen when we touched back at Ramona's," I said, pointing my finger at his chest. "You knew I was coming, didn't you?"

If I sounded a little frantic, it was because I was. I was scared shitless. I didn't know a thing about Raeann, and I had no idea why she and her mother were here.

"I did," he admitted. "My aunt saw you coming, which is the reason I moved here. So we can figure out all this together."

"Listen, Ryder, I'm not going to be your little science experiment. I want my life back. Just the way it was before I touched you and everything changed!"

He grabbed my waist to hold me in check. It was probably the only safe place to grab me so we wouldn't have another vision of the future, or risk my seeing into his memories again.

"Listen to me," he said calmly. His voice was soothing and despite my anger, I began to calm down. "The ability to see someone's memories isn't discussed in the book. Maybe it's something new or evolved. It could help us, Vi. Don't you see?"

Ryder leaned his head close to mine, his gaze imploring. "We could try to see if you could do it again. We could even practice to see if maybe I could do it too. Seeing into the past can help us with the future."

He shoved his hand through his hair, excitement in his eyes as he began to pace in front of me. "Something about the way you touched me was different than before. It could be something little, but whatever it was, it brought you inside my head."

His arguments sounded reasonable. I could understand his wonder and excitement at what had just happened, but at the moment I didn't want any part of it.

He doesn't realize it's the question, I thought. The key to seeing someone's memories was asking a question. I didn't want him to know right yet how I did it, so I decided to keep that little nugget of information to myself. There was no way I was going to let him or anyone else try to get inside my head.

I snagged my backpack and said, "Sorry. I'm not up for it." I brushed his shoulder as I stepped around him.

He stood rooted to the spot and watched me leave. "This isn't over," he called after me.

I didn't turn around and felt a hundred times better as I walked out the door. My mind cleared, as if my brain had finally cleared the fog away. The pressure from Ryder was starting to get to me, and all I wanted was to get away from it. And him.

My phone buzzed in my pocket. "Oh my gosh!" I pulled it out and whipped it open. "Hello!" I practically screamed with irritation as I stalked through the empty halls, determined to call it a day and go home.

"What's wrong with you," my best friend asked me.

"Callie, thank goodness. If you were Adam calling, I was going to have a hysterical breakdown. I'm so tired of all the drama, and I'm physically sick from it all."

When Callie giggled at me, my cold anger and tension slipped away. "I so need some girl time," I said as a slow smile crept across my face.

"Okay, let's do it," she said enthusiastically. "I'll cut class. Let's go shopping. Face it, you could really use a new wardrobe."

"Hey, I take offense to that! What's wrong with hoodies and jeans?" I demanded half jokingly.

"Um, let's just say hoodies and jeans are outdated," she said, laughing. "Meet you in the parking lot in ten."

"All right, sounds good." I shoved my phone back into my pocket, already in a better mood.

Chapter 9

I didn't have to wait long for Callie to meet me at my Mustang in the school parking lot. We tried to keep our departure on the down low, since our absence wasn't exactly sanctioned by school administration.

"So," she said as she hopped in. "What's the drama?"

"The new principal called our class down to meet her and her daughter today during third period. She kept staring at Ryder and me the whole time, and it made me really uncomfortable." I shuddered at the memory.

Her green eyes widened. "What is up with that? Why were they paying so much attention to you and Ryder? I heard all about it from Adam and Olivia. Adam said it was really strange."

"I don't know," I said, feeling a little guilty. I hated lying to my BFF. I knew their interest had something to do with the uniqueness of our eyes and the special power that seemed connected with them, but I couldn't tell her that.

We went to several different shops in town, but finally hit pay dirt at both Vanity and Maurice's. While we were in Maurice's, Callie finally talked me into trying on a slim-fitting hooded sweater that highlighted my slender waistline.

"See, I told you they had stylish hoodies." She gave me a triumphant look as she threw more colors of the hoodies into our checkout pile. "Ooh, and this silver one will complement your eyes," she said as she ogled it.

"Okay. I think three is enough!" I frowned, giving Callie a you're-on-thin-ice look. She just laughed at me and shrugged.

"If you say so." She grinned from ear to ear, thoroughly pleased with herself.

I nodded and collected the items, putting them on my debit card. The shopping trip had turned out to be a success for us both. Callie was happy she got me to try something sort of new, and I was happy because my dark mood had completely vanished.

I glanced at my watch. "Oh crap." Callie gave me an alarmed look. "I have to go to Adam's house to work. I think I'm going to try to change my schedule a little bit. It was nice going there every day when we were sneaking around, but now that it's over . . ." I took a deep breath, trying to put my feelings into words. "I think it's overkill, ya know?"

Callie smiled at me encouragingly. "I'm glad you finally see the light."

I sighed. I knew she would be happy. "You know, he sounded like he really meant it when he said he loved me, but I know you're right. Even if he did . . . there's no way around his family's expectations."

"Nope, not unless he was going to break with tradition and risk being blackballed out of the family money."

"You know I think arranged marriages are stupid, right?" I asked as we threw our shopping bags into the backseat and then climbed into the car.

"Yeah, I know." She shrugged her shoulders. "It's just the way it's always been. I know pairing babies from birth sounds weird to an outsider, but our parents are just trying to protect their legacy. Gotta keep the money in the family, you know. The paper money," she joked.

We both cracked up laughing as I pulled into the school parking lot, which was nearly empty since school had already ended for the day. She gave me a hug before grabbing her shopping bags and heading to her own car.

Waving good-bye to Callie deflated my mood a little, since my next stop was Adam's house. It was time to make some changes to my work schedule.

• • •

When I arrived at the Prices' a little later, Adam's BMW was the only car in the drive. Since the garage doors were closed, I couldn't be sure if his dad was home or not, and it was Mr. Price that I really needed to talk to.

I went to the door and rang the bell, holding my breath until someone answered, and it seemed like an eternity before the door slowly opened. I let my breath out in a shaky whoosh when I realized that Adam had answered the door, and not his father.

He looked surprised. He shot a nervous glance behind him, and that was when I realized he thought I was there for him, and his dad was probably home.

"Hi, Adam," I said quickly. "Is your dad home?" A cheerful whistling sounded from somewhere inside, his dad's habit, which answered my question.

"Hi, Violet, fancy meeting you here," he said in a tight voice. "Why do you want to speak to him?"

Okay, so he was a little mad at me for breaking up with him, which was understandable. He searched my face, and behind his anger I thought I saw a little sadness.

"I just really need to talk to your dad," I said, keeping my voice low.

Adam shrugged and stepped out of the way so I could step inside, and called out, "Dad, Violet's here and wants to talk to you."

Movement sounded from the back of the house, and then his father's footsteps drew closer. Adam closed the door and stayed where he was, staring quietly at me, and at that moment I really wished that I could wear my sunglasses. But I'd never disrespect Mr. Price like that, and Adam knew it.

Mr. Price rounded the corner and put on a warm smile when he saw me standing in the hallway. Dressed in a nice gray suit and tie, his features and coloring resembled an older version of Adam.

He clapped his hand on Adam's shoulder as he said, "Hi there, Violet, how are you?"

"I'm good. Thank you for asking," I said as pleasantly as I could. "Mr. Price, would it be okay to cut back the amount of days I work here after school, and just extend the hours I put in on the other days? The work will still get done."

From the corner of my eye I could see Adam's mouth drop open partway to object. Then he must have thought better of it, because he pressed his lips together quickly.

His father cocked his head to the side and considered my request for a moment. Then he nodded and said, "You're a hard worker, Violet. You do as you see fit." He gave me another warm smile and walked away, pausing for a moment to add, "Tell David I say hi," referring to my stepfather.

"Thank you," I called out after him. Without a look at Adam, I made haste for the door and the freedom of being outside.

Adam followed me out of the house. "Why are you doing this, Violet? Are you trying to avoid me?"

"I don't know how that could be possible since I still work here. But at least the amount of time I have to see you will be cut in half."

I didn't want to be mean, but it was true. It would be so much easier on my heart if I could keep my distance from him. I hurried across the wide expanse of lawn, wishing that Adam would quit following and leave me alone.

"Violet." His tone made me hesitate and slow my steps. "Do you still have feelings for me?"

He grabbed my arm and tugged me into the shadows next to the shed, out of view from the house. He turned me so I was facing him and tilted my chin, forcing me to look up at him. His blue eyes bored into me, daring me to deny my feelings.

I sighed. "Adam, I just broke it off with you. The feelings I have for you aren't going to disappear overnight, you know that. So, yes, I do," I said softly. "But it doesn't mean anything. You're promised to someone else. It's a lost cause and we need to accept that. So it's best that you get over it too."

He narrowed his eyes angrily. "You don't just stop loving someone overnight," he said in a voice as cold as the shade that hid us. Then he grabbed me and his warm lips found mine in a hasty but sweet kiss.

It was wrong and I knew it, but I found myself returning the kiss. His lips moved softly against mine, then became urgent as the attraction that had always been between us took over. His arms wrapped around me, pulling me tighter against his body, his hand lingering at the small of my back.

A good-bye kiss, I thought, that's all this is.

We were both breathing rapidly when we parted. He gently pushed a few strands of my hair away from my face, running his gaze over my features as if he were trying to memorize them.

"Violet, this just feels so right," he said, giving me an additional kiss on my forehead. "I feel so empty without you."

Adam sounded so lost and sad, his eyes burning into me with need and grief so deep that I was forced to look away. I didn't want to feel sorry for him, feel guilty, because this was the way it had to be. Someone had to be the strong one, and it looked like it would have to be me.

"I really am sorry." It was the only thing I could muster up to say; he completely bewildered me. "I get your point, but it isn't going to change anything. We can't be together. You're still with Olivia and I'm still . . . alone," I finished quietly.

"Oh yeah, what about you and Ryder? Where does he fit into all this?" Adam raised his voice, his tone sharp.

Jealous much?

"We're just friends, but it shouldn't matter to you anyway." I hardened my heart and took a step back. "I need to get to work, and you should probably get back inside before your dad wonders where you are," I said to him firmly.

He leaned in for another kiss, but I stepped back, just out of his grasp. "We can't, Adam. That was our good-bye."

He looked miserable, but rather than argue, he wrapped me in a tight hug and kissed the top of my head.

"See you tomorrow," he said sadly.

I knew what he wanted me to say, so for old times' sake, I did. "Not if I see you first."

Then he turned and walked away. I watched him go, knowing that with the change in our relationship, it was probably the last time we were going to be able to say those lines to each other.

• • •

I arrived home around seven. When I walked in, the foyer light was on but no one was around from what I could see. Hearing faint male voices carrying up from the basement, I realized that Vick must have some friends over.

Good, I thought. I won't have to deal with him tonight.

I made my way to the kitchen and grabbed a piece of leftover pizza from a cardboard box in the fridge, along with a can of Coke, then found a plate for my pizza and headed upstairs. I was halfway up the stairs when there was a knock on the door.

"Geez Louise," I said aloud, then set the Coke and pizza on the last step and turned back around.

I opened the door to find Ryder standing there. He shifted his weight and ran a hand through his hair, seeming a little unsure of himself.

"Ryder," I said, raising my eyebrows in surprise. "What are you doing here?"

I crossed my arms in front of my chest, not knowing what else to do with them. He stepped forward and leaned nonchalantly on the door frame. I glanced down and noticed he had a satchel over his shoulder, and in it I could see part of the book.

"Can I come in?" he asked. "I'd like to talk with you." He seemed like he was trying, even though his expression could have said otherwise.

"Uh, yeah. Come on in," I said reluctantly.

I turned to go back up the stairs. "Close the door behind you, please." I grabbed my pizza and Coke and headed to my room, not checking to see if he was behind me. Once there, I tossed my plate onto the desk and set my Coke down. Motioning for him to sit at the desk in front of the window, I took a seat on my bed.

Ryder pulled out the chair and sat down, leaning forward to rest his forearms on his knees. "I was reading through the book and it says nothing about seeing someone's memories," he said, taking the small leather-bound book out of the satchel and setting it carefully down on my desk.

"It can't be coincidence that Raeann and her mother showed up here shortly after you did," I said. "Why do you think they followed you here?"

I took a seat on the rug with the book laid out in front of me. Ryder moved to sit down next to me, careful not to touch me.

"Unless they found out about you like I did?" He glanced at me uncertainly. "Other than that I'm not sure, but if we practice we may be able to figure it out."

He held his hand out to me, seeming so out of place sitting on the floor of my bedroom. His eyes dared me to take his hand, his body calling to mine with a low hum of energy that pulled me toward him.

I reached out hesitantly, then laced my fingers through his. Bracing myself for the inevitable, I was still taken aback by the jolt of electrical current that flowed through my body, and the swift onset of wind whipping around me. Buffeted back and forth, I felt like a dog with its head out the car window while speeding down the interstate.

Like I'd done before, I closed my eyes. In the midst of all the craziness, Ryder gave my hand a reassuring squeeze, his gentle affection sending a shiver of tingles coursing through my body. Then the chaos came to an abrupt halt.

Chapter 10

When I opened my eyes, I was outside again. It looked to be early evening, barely light out, and there was some event going on with people milling around. I didn't see Ryder, but assumed he would be around somewhere. Secretly, I worried that maybe I had traveled into one of his memories again, but then realized that this must be the bonfire we were going to on Friday. If I was back here again, it must be for a reason.

I searched the crowd, looking for Ryder, finally spotting him huddled with the "in" crowd around the bonfire. The fire cast an eerie glow on my peers, sending a chill to creep up my back. I strolled over to them and Ryder looked up, motioning for me to join him. Thank goodness I wasn't in this alone.

As I settled in next to him, I noticed that Adam, JP, Olivia, Raeann, Callie, and Henry were all gathered around the fire. It looked like JP and Raeann had already hit it off, talking quietly by themselves. Watching them for a moment, I got the feeling that JP really liked her, but Raeann was probably just playing him to get closer to Ryder.

"Aren't Ryder and Violet supposed to be here," she asked JP sweetly.

"I don't know why you'd care if Violet shows up," he said stiffly. "No one else does. Was she even invited?"

I narrowed my eyes at him and crossed my arms, letting out a little huff of annoyance. Ryder glanced at me, his mouth twitching like he was trying to hold back a smile. Feeling a little foolish, I realized I'd almost forgotten that we weren't really there.

"That's enough," Adam snapped, his eyes narrowing at JP.

"Yeah, quit being rude," Olivia said with a frown.

JP rolled his eyes. "Whatever."

I glanced at Ryder. He was taking it all in, his eyes moving back and forth as he followed the conversation. "If you ask me," he said,

"Adam's definitely got it bad for you. I can't believe I'm the only one who notices."

Damn, he's perceptive, I thought. Knowing he was trying to gauge my reaction but unable to help myself, it was hard not to be defensive.

"Hmm, I didn't notice." I still had the overwhelming feeling to protect Adam, even though we weren't together anymore.

Ryder raised his eyebrows in disbelief. "Interesting."

I folded my arms in front of me and frowned as the conversation continued around us.

"I was thinking about having a party," Raeann continued. "It's too early for a Halloween party, since it's still September, but I'd like to have a costume party anyway. Would you all like to come?"

"That sounds great!"

Of course JP was the first to chime in. He would agree to anything she said; he was already following her around like a little lap dog. I rolled my eyes.

"All right, I'm in," Adam said.

Olivia smiled at him and said, "Me too. It will be so much fun!"

"Please make sure that Ryder and Violet get an invite," Raeann said, saying my name with a hard edge and emphasizing the *T* in my name.

"Did you hear her tone?" I asked Ryder.

"Loud and clear."

"She absolutely hates my guts," I said. "Why do you think that is?"

"Isn't it obvious?" he asked, gazing at me with those intense platinum eyes.

"Isn't what obvious?" I looked away, feeling awkward under his scrutiny.

"You're beautiful, and you've seemed to . . ." He paused and appeared to consider what he was going to say before actually saying it. It seemed as though time were standing still as I waited.

I'm beautiful to him? The thought ricocheted inside my head, causing my heartbeat to pick up its pace. It seemed to grow wings and fly up into my throat, making it difficult to swallow back the nervousness I was feeling.

How could you respond to something like that? Ryder was just too gorgeous, too perfect, and despite the coldness that lingered in his eyes, there was something else hidden there, something gentle.

"You seemed to have captured my attention, and *that's* what makes her jealous of you."

He had chosen his words carefully, and his eyes seemed warmer somehow, even though I knew it wouldn't last. It never lasted. He was always quick to rebuild his wall, pulling it around him as the warmness faded and nothing but cold remained in its wake. I didn't understand how someone could live like that, trying to force feelings out of their life. It seemed exhausting to me, but the fact remained. He thought I was *beautiful*.

"Thank you, Ryder."

A warm sensation spread throughout my body, starting in my heart and traveling to every nerve ending. Boy, he could be charming when he wanted to be. It didn't help that he looked good enough to eat. That magnetic pull of his tugged at me but I resisted, deciding that a change of topic was in order.

"What is it we're supposed to be looking for, exactly? I mean, we found out she's going to throw a costume party. We know that she's hanging with JP. I just don't see how any of this can help us," I complained.

"You never know what can be important," he said, all business-like again. "Just keep a mental note of everything."

"Are *you* going to go to the costume party?" I asked him curiously.

He looked at me again, his face impassive. "If you go, I will."

I noted that he didn't ask me to go with him; he was just stating a simple fact.

"JP, can I speak with you in private?" Raeann cooed.

"Sure," he said, jumping up from the log they were sharing. He reached out a hand to help her up, his eyes lit up with excitement.

101

I couldn't help but snort a little as she looped her arm with his and they started walking off into the woods. JP probably thought she wanted to make out with him.

"This is our chance," I said to Ryder excitedly. "Let's follow them."

We tagged along, unworried that they would notice us. It was definitely neat to hear everything they were saying. I could get used to this fly-on-the-wall thing.

"JP, I get the feeling that you don't like Violet at all," she said to him.

"I wouldn't say I completely dislike her." He shrugged. "She's just never been a part of our group, and I don't know her very well," he lied.

"I don't know what to think of her yet," Raeann was saying. "Here's the thing. I need to get her away from Ryder for a little while. We have unfinished business and I can't have her in the way. She seems to be around him all the time. Can you help me out?" she asked quietly, fingering his shirt collar and pulling him in for a kiss that made me look away.

"I would really, really appreciate it," she continued when their kiss had ended.

"Sure. There's someone I know that can distract Violet." He smiled at her, apparently happy to do whatever she wanted. "I'll arrange it, but for when?"

"During my party."

"What if she doesn't come?" His eyebrows knit together with concern.

"She will." Raeann smiled smugly. "She won't be able to help herself."

I looked at Ryder. "Can we go back now? I'm getting tired."

He nodded, looking thoughtful, then reached over and caressed my fingers, gently joining his hand with mine.

• • •

The spinning of the whirlwind made me ill as we were returned to my room. It took me a minute to open my eyes after the vertigo

102

faded, and I realized that I was still in Ryder's arms. He was on the floor, leaning against the side of my bed with one of his knees bent, and I was snuggled against his chest, between his thighs.

All I could feel was the warmth of his body spreading to my own, and the sickness of being shifted back to reality gave way to butterflies in the depths of my stomach. I froze and held my breath, mortified at what I'd done. Oh God, why did I grab him like that?

There was really no good way to end this embrace. I knew I was going to feel more embarrassed if I tried to cling to him any longer, so I reluctantly pulled away, feeling like I should apologize for my actions.

He let his hands travel over my shoulders and down my shirt sleeves, avoiding my bare hands. I finally pulled from his grasp and nervously folded my hands together. His gaze remained on my hands for a moment, then moved up and locked on mine, his expression slightly confused. Mesmerized, I couldn't look away, held captive by his smoldering gray gaze.

"I shouldn't have done that," I said, "I'm sorry."

We sat on the floor, facing each other, and I still knelt between his thighs. He continued to look at me thoughtfully, not saying a word, which was driving me crazy.

"Violet?"

I jumped, startled at hearing my stepbrother's voice just outside my room, then a knock at my door.

"Shit," I said softly to Ryder then raised my voice. "One sec, Vick!"

I stood up quickly and practically ran to my walk-in closet and opened the door. "In here." I pointed for Ryder to get in.

His face broke into a sly grin as he got up and sauntered casually over to the closet, shaking his head. I knew he was secretly laughing at me, but at least the awkward moment was over.

"Violet!" Vick knocked on the door a little more forcefully.

"One sec!" I yelled, then hissed, "Will you hurry it up, Ryder?"

I waved him through impatiently. His amused eyes held me for a second longer than they should have, and when he smirked at me, I shut the closet door on his handsome face. Praying that Vick wouldn't be a jerk, I hurried to my bedroom door and opened it.

"Hey!" I said as I held the door open just enough to show my body.

Vick's narrowed eyes assessed me carefully. "Who are you talking to?" He pushed the door open wider, forcing me a step back as he surveyed the room suspiciously.

"No one. I was just singing to myself. Don't you have company over?" I asked pointedly.

"Um . . . yeah. I just had to grab something from my room, and I could have sworn I heard a conversation going on in here." Vick scanned the room again quickly, then shrugged.

"Nope, just me singing." I grinned innocently at him, which forced him to grin back.

"Okay, kiddo."

I watched him shuffle quickly back down the stairs and shut my door, letting out a huge sigh of relief.

"You can come out," I said quietly. Ryder emerged with an ear-to-ear grin that took my breath away.

"I'm not supposed to be up here, am I?" He raised his eyebrows and I giggled, thinking the whole situation was funny. "It's been a while since I've been in a closet," he said mysteriously.

"Oh, really. How many closets are we talking about?" I asked, giving him a brilliant smile.

He walked closer to me, invading my personal space and pinning me with a smoldering gaze. "A few."

I held my breath, suddenly realizing we weren't really talking about closets anymore.

"What about you?" he asked. "Any closets?"

His eyes were burning me with curiosity. No, we definitely were *not* talking about closets anymore.

"You have to breathe, Vi."

Oh, right. I sucked in a whiff of his spicy smell. *Mmm . . . mint.* Gosh, he smelled good.

He chuckled quietly, and I tore my gaze away from his.

104

"We're getting a little off track," I said hesitantly, sidestepping around him and heading back to the safety of my desk.

Once seated in my desk chair, it was easier to be more impersonal. "Okay, back to Raeann, she definitely wants to get you alone," I said, feeling a small stab of jealousy, which I pushed out of my thoughts instantly.

"I saw that," he said quietly. "That won't happen," he added, leaning over me and looking down at my notebook I had on the desk, where I was currently drawing small circles while we talked. It was a nervous habit of mine.

"You don't know JP. If JP says he'll find a way, he will," I said adamantly. I tapped the pencil on the desk a few times.

"Vi."

Ryder's tone made me gaze up at him, his face close to my own. Close enough to kiss. Wow, I did *not* just think that!

"I'm not intimidated by JP," he said with a small smile. "He could do his worst and it still wouldn't be enough to compete with me. So don't sweat it. We'll just go together."

He said it so simply. I wanted to ask if our going to the party together meant it was a date, but didn't want to bring up the possible complication. Although, it would be nice if it were a date. My skin flushed at the very idea, and my stomach did a little flip in nervous anticipation.

"Or what if we didn't go at all? What if we just decide to do something else?" I suggested, leaving the thought open-ended.

I pictured us walking along the beach, holding hands, and dancing under the star-lit sky. The sand beneath our bare feet would feel cool and soothing, and maybe we would go swimming down at the lake, or sneak up to the lighthouse—

"Vi, what are you thinking?"

His words jerked me back to reality from my little fantasy. I frowned when I realized that there was no way we could hold hands, because we couldn't touch without the synergistic effect of our touch.

"Oh, nothing." I focused my gaze on my notebook and drew a few more circles, not wanting to meet his gaze.

"We'll see. Avoiding the party may be better . . . but on the other hand, we could be somewhat prepared if we go. If we don't show up, she'll just find another way and we may not be so prepared."

I nodded; what he said made sense.

I was tired and knew I shouldn't, but I had a sudden impulse to move a lock of hair on his forehead and to think more about Ryder and Raeann's relationship. If I could travel into another memory, I might be able to shed some light on their relationship. It was driving me crazy and he'd been so secretive; I just couldn't help myself.

He didn't even have to know that I did it on purpose; maybe I could fool him. He was standing so close, I could feel the heat radiate off his body. I looked at his handsome face, admiring the curve of his cheekbone, his kissable lips, and then there were those intriguing eyes that gazed back at me and forced me to hold my breath. Yeah, I could do it.

I stood up and leaned toward him, reaching for his hair, and caught him off guard when I impulsively went in for a kiss instead of touching his forehead. He froze as I closed my eyes and thought about him and Raeann.

Ryder pressed his lips to mine, his arms instantly wrapping around me and pulling me flush with his body, unable to control the reaction we both felt. A warm tingling feeling coursed through my body, and my heart raced. I was excited and thrilled to be the aggressor for the first time, but I had no idea what I was doing. The sensations I was feeling were very new to me, and were so different from when I kissed Adam. If I'd known kissing could be like this . . .

The colored lights began flashing around us and the dizzying feeling swept over me. I melted into his warm embrace as he slowly gained control of our kiss and broke contact by trailing feather-light kisses from my mouth, down my jawline, to my neck.

All the muscles in my legs relaxed as I practically collapsed into his strong arms. He was breathing heavily, his nose in the crook of my neck as he supported my body weight. Entranced, I listened to his heartbeat and reveled in the rise and fall of his chest as we traveled.

・ ・ ・

When the dizziness faded, I couldn't feel Ryder with me anymore. My hair fell across my face, so I tentatively brushed it away and opened my eyes.

It was dark . . . very dark. I smiled giddily, reliving for a moment the best kiss I'd ever had in my entire life. It took a minute for my eyesight to adjust, but there was nothing but blackness. I moved carefully, unable to see anything. A light flickered in the distance, a fire in the middle of the darkness. I walked toward it slowly, knowing that I was inside of one of Ryder's memories.

My footsteps were nearly silent on the dirt path. I saw the silhouette of trees up ahead, illuminated by the glow of the fire a good distance away. Above me the sky was infinitely black, no moon and no stars. The closer I drew to the fire, the more I could make out. Ryder sat in one of two chairs near the blaze, the light from the flames flickering on his stoic face. The other chair was empty.

I came to a standstill behind the chair and gazed at Ryder, who was watching the fire. Did he know I was here? What kind of memory was this? Where was Raeann? I had done exactly what I did last time, hadn't I? So why did it feel so different? What went wrong?

"Why don't you sit down?" Ryder said quietly, his voice flat and cold.

Oh shit! I'm so busted.

Defeated, I dropped down in the vacant seat next to him. The heat from the fire seared my skin, forcing me to lean back as far away from the fire as I could.

Okay, something had gone wrong, very wrong. I was supposed to be seeing a memory, not having an uncomfortable confrontation with him in the middle of nowhere.

"Where are we," I asked.

"Somewhere in my mind, I can only assume, but I didn't bring us here. You did. The question is why? What is it you were trying to see? What were you looking for?"

107

Ryder's tone and expression were so cold, not at all like the guy who had just knocked my socks off. He was definitely pissed.

Thinking quickly, I asked, "Is it so wrong to want to kiss you? I wasn't trying to see anything. I have no idea what's going on."

The second part was true. I was pretty sure my theory of thinking a question and going into his memories was correct. I had caught him off guard last time, but this time he must have been prepared for it. If he really knew how to do it, he might have seen my memories instead, so I was relieved it was still my secret.

"Ryder, will you look at me?" I shifted uncomfortably in my seat. He turned his liquid silver eyes on me. There was a spark of anger in them along with a bit of something else. Regret? Oh no!

"Obviously we have an issue with the kiss. I'm sorry I got . . . a little carried away." He rubbed his hands over his face as if he was trying to wipe away his actions. His face was unreadable when he finally looked up at me.

"I'm not sorry," I said quietly. "It was one of the best kisses in my life, and I'm not about to be sorry for it."

Did I really just say that! Why can't the ground just swallow me up now?

I looked away into the darkness. When he knelt in front of me, I turned my attention back to him.

"What is it you're looking for?" he asked, his voice low and husky.

"Nothing." Nervous, I fidgeted in my seat. Was he talking about the kiss or why we were in no man's land?

"Oh really," he said, smirking. His eyes sparkled as if he was laughing at me.

I looked away self-consciously. "Let's go back. I'm exhausted and this little trip was a surprise, to say the least."

I tried to sound sincere, still trying to play the I-don't-know-what-happened card. It was partly true that nothing about this trip was what I had expected. I wasn't entirely sure if he bought it or if he was still a little suspicious. He was smart, so I went with suspicious.

"All right. If you haven't found what you're looking for," he said, watching me carefully.

I just shook my head. "I don't know what you're talking about."

"Okay, let's go back." His expression closed up, and he suddenly sounded tired.

Ryder took my hand to pull me up and I shut my eyes, bracing myself for the electric shock of feeling his warm skin. I stepped a bit closer, feeling his warm body against mine. I longed for another kiss, but the dizziness soon overcame my mind, pushing the thought from my head.

. . .

When the dizziness faded, I was weak, weaker than any other time before. This last trip had apparently been too much, too soon. Blackness closed in on me, swallowing my body.

I opened my eyes and felt the rise and fall of Ryder's slow, steady breathing. He was lying on his back on my bedroom floor, my head on his chest. When I pulled away, he slowly sat up, shaking his head.

"So you weren't trying to find anything out?"

"No, but I don't feel so good," I said, changing the subject. Exhausted, I leaned against my bed for support.

Ryder peered at me like he wasn't buying it. "Do you want to know what I think?" he said, watching me carefully. "I think that you were trying to see another memory, trying to get an insight into my past."

I ignored him. He was dead-on, though. I played with the strands of the floor rug, rubbing my fingers through them again and again.

"Listen, Ryder, you need to go before my brother and his friends finish their game in the basement. I can't have him find you up here," I said quickly.

He stared at me for a moment, then rose to collect the book. "All right."

"Do you mind if I look at it? I won't let anything happen to it. I promise," I said, holding out my hand in the hope he would let me keep it.

"Not a chance." He smiled as he put it back in his bag. "If I loaned it to you, there wouldn't be a reason for us to get together tomorrow."

I couldn't help but return his smile. Despite his moodiness, I found myself looking forward to seeing him again.

"I'll let myself out. You rest," he said.

"Okay. G'night, Ryder."

"Good night," he said as he disappeared out my door.

Chapter 11

Guilt haunted me as I walked into the school building. Yesterday I was kissing Adam after school, and then I got the kiss of my life from Ryder last night. I didn't think that kissing two guys in one day qualified a girl as a slut, but I definitely wasn't planning to push my luck. Once again, I found myself wishing my mom were still here so I could talk to her about it.

Callie showed up at my locker. "Hey, girl. How are ya today?"

She was dressed in a dressy green top and khakis. I had pulled on my new silver hoodie and a pair of jeans, and matching sunglasses topped off my ensemble.

Callie just shook her head and smiled when she got a good look at me. "Nice touch, Violet. Only you could ruin a sexy shirt like that." She laughed and I frowned at her. "I'm just teasing. You look amazing as always even with *your* wardrobe."

Ryder walked up to us. "Morning, Vi."

Callie laughed and I narrowed my eyes at him.

"Hi, Ryder," I said, feeling a little disgruntled. "Don't make me frown, you're going to give me premature wrinkles."

"Since when do you care about your appearance," he asked me, stepping closer to invade my personal bubble again, although I'd been minding less and less lately.

"I don't. I'm just stating a fact," I said.

"Nice shirt." His gaze traveled over me. "It must be new."

"Yes, but that's beside the point," I said.

"Well, correct me if I'm wrong, Callie, but most girls who buy new shirts are usually trying to impress someone," he said, taking a hold of my sunglasses on either side and pulling them off.

My barrier was gone and his icy eyes seemed to see right through me. Butterflies invaded my stomach, giving me a nervous tickle, and I couldn't move. He tucked the stem of the glasses into my jeans pocket so they were hanging on my side, and his hand lingered there a second, causing my skin to tingle just below the surface.

When he removed his hand I was able to move once more, free from Ryder's pull. Callie gave me a knowing, you've-got-it-bad smile, and I automatically rolled my eyes at her.

"No, you're definitely right," Callie said with a giggle, confirming Ryder's thoughts. She couldn't help herself, letting her matchmaker side come out again.

"I can assure you, Ryder, that the shopping was strictly therapeutic," I said, taking a step back.

"Hmm, my mistake then," he said, his silver eyes gleaming playfully.

Adam and Olivia walked by arm in arm, and I felt a twinge in my gut. Guilt?

Adam stared at me, the sight of my new shirt obviously throwing him off guard. Both Callie and Ryder seemed to notice Adam observe me. Olivia waved in her friendly way, snuggling a little closer to her boyfriend as they went by. I waved back politely.

"I have to meet Henry before class." Callie's words drew my attention back to her. "See you two at lunch." She gave me a sly smile and turned the other way.

"I can't believe we match again," I complained halfheartedly. "It's like you have ESP."

"Let me walk you to your class," Ryder suggested, giving me a sidelong glance as he fell into step with me.

I reluctantly agreed, although I was still a little embarrassed by the kiss he didn't bring up.

"Why don't you come to my house after school?" he said. "You don't have to work, do you?"

I gave him a shy smile. "No, I don't."

"Sounds good."

We had just arrived at the classroom door when Mr. Johnston, my English teacher, interrupted our conversation.

"Ms. Vancourt, you're wanted in the principal's office."

"What?" Panic gripped me, and I looked at Ryder for support.

112

"Don't worry," he said quietly. "I'll go with you."

"Too bad we didn't see this coming," I grumbled. "That would've been way more helpful. I wonder what she wants."

"Yes, I know," he said, looking so self-confident and sure of himself. "There isn't much I'm going to be able to do. The only thing I can do is make my presence known by walking you there."

He ran a hand through his golden-blond hair, in frustration no doubt. He put his hand on the small of my back as we walked to the principal's office. It was weird and uncomfortable to have him guide me like a child, although I was sure he didn't mean it in that way. I wasn't really sure how he meant it.

"I know there isn't much you can do," I finally said. We stopped just outside the open principal's office door. She looked up from a stack of paperwork and saw me with Ryder. He narrowed his eyes but gave a nod of acknowledgment to her, which Principal Margaret returned.

"Text me when the meeting is done." He started to walk away. "Oh, and Vi, don't say anything stupid," he called to me.

"Okay," I said. I watched Ryder till he rounded the corner, then inhaled a deep breath and stepped over the threshold. Easier said than done, I thought. Okay, nothing stupid, I chanted silently.

"Please come in and sit, Violet. You'll have to forgive me for staring at you yesterday. It's just that aside from my daughter and Ryder Essen, I didn't know another one of you existed at this school."

Yeah, right.

"But leave it to Ryder to find a quick replacement for Raeann," she said as she watched me carefully.

Rather than react to her jibe, I kept my mouth shut. *This lady is kind of crazy.*

Principal Margaret raised a thin eyebrow at me. "He did tell you about their relationship, didn't he?"

"I don't understand why he would? We aren't dating." *Although I wish we were.* "We're just friends," I added.

The woman stared at me, a challenge in her eyes. "You don't feel it's important to know that there was another one of you with silver eyes?"

Why would I?

I shrugged. "It's just an eye color, I don't understand what the big deal is. And you're making me late for class."

Maybe I overdid it a little, trying to be too nonchalant. Plus, it was hard to keep the irritation out of my voice. I tapped my fingers on the chair arm, needing to occupy my hands.

She eyed my hand pointedly, as if she was annoyed she didn't have my full attention. "You weren't too concerned about class yesterday afternoon, now were you?"

I stiffened at her comment. Damn, I played right into that.

"I wasn't feeling well," I lied, which I hate to do because it causes nothing but trouble, but I didn't see a way around it.

Trying to calm my nerves, which were zinging like ping-pong balls throughout my body, I studied the woman, noting that her eyes were a little wide for her face. Narrowing my eyes a little, I started to picture her with a frog's tongue. My lips began to twitch as I tried to stifle a smile.

"When you leave school because of an illness, do you always take a friend with you," she asked, her expression smug.

"What are you getting at?" I said, narrowing my eyes at her.

She gave me a triumphant smile that looked anything but warm. "I want you to show Raeann around the building. Introduce her to your friends and so forth. Make her feel welcome."

"No way!" I spat out.

"If you agree to this, I won't give out a week of detention to your friend Callie for skipping class." She looked down and made a notation in some sort of notebook with long, curving strokes.

I sat there tapping my foot, furious that a principal would blackmail me to show her daughter around the school. My blood ran hot through my body. That couldn't be the real reason; it just didn't make sense. Why on earth would she want me to get to know her daughter?

"Fine," I mumbled. Callie shouldn't have to pay for my mistake; it was my fault she left to begin with.

Margaret gave me a catlike smile and handed me a piece of paper.

"What's this," I asked, looking at the tiny slip.

"Your detention slip." She smiled. "I never said anything about letting *you* off the hook."

"Whatever!" I said, and crumpled it up.

Her smile faded quickly as I threw it on her desk. It gave a nice fluffy bounce, landing in the neckline of her top and falling into her bra. Her face grew red and her mouth fell open.

"Bitch," I mumbled under my breath as I made haste for the exit and slammed the door behind me.

So I lost my cool and did exactly what Ryder warned me not to do. Oh well, I couldn't take it back now.

I texted Ryder on my way to first period, then stuffed the phone back in my pocket.

Me: We need to talk about Raeann.

Moments later my phone buzzed. I whipped it back out.

Ryder: OK.

I assumed we would talk more after school at his house. Maybe she was harmless . . . maybe she and her mom both were, but the sinking feeling in my gut told me otherwise.

When I arrived at my first period class, sitting next to my empty chair was a smiling Raeann. Her blond hair was curled into little ringlets, and her platinum eyes gleamed triumphantly. Her obnoxiously pretty looks were enough to make me want to turn around and skip the rest of the day. But I just gritted my teeth.

"Sorry, it took a little longer than expected, Mr. Johnston," I called out to the teacher, and he motioned impatiently for me to take my seat.

I gave Raeann a pointed look as I took my seat next to her in the back.

"I guess you had a nice meeting with my mom," she said quietly.

"As if any meeting with your mom would be nice," I shot back in a low voice, angry all over again.

"It took a while to track down where Slade had moved, but we eventually found him," she said smugly. "What I didn't count on was Slade finding *you*." Her blond brows were furrowed, and her angelic face seemed displeased.

"Why do you call him Slade? His name is Ryder," I hissed.

"His name is Ryder Slade Essen," she shot back. "I call him by his middle name. It's what he used to go by."

"Girls!" Mr. Johnston snapped. "This isn't social hour."

Raeann's chin jutted out in defiance but she kept her mouth shut, her pretty silver eyes trained on the teacher.

At least his interjection allowed me to ignore her comment, but it was going to be a very long day. The day got worse when Mr. Johnston handed out a pop quiz on American writers in the 1900s. I did the best I could, but without actually reading the material I was supposed to read, I was struggling. At least I had paid attention in class and when I finished, I was somewhat certain I had at least passed and my grade wouldn't suffer too much, because I was currently carrying an *A*.

All morning Raeann stuck to me like gum on the bottom of my shoe. No, wait, that would be tolerable. She was more like a leech on my skin. I made a face just thinking about it.

Ryder avoided me as much as possible whenever she was around, I noticed. I missed his annoying banter. Her mother had made sure that Raeann was in all my classes, probably in hopes that we would become good friends, but I sincerely doubted that would ever happen.

By the time lunch rolled around, I was exhausted from listening to Raeann's chatter. I don't know how the girl could have had many friends. It was all about how popular she was at her old school, the name-brand items she owned, what she drove; she was turning out to be quite a materialistic person, which meant she'd fit right in with

116

the popular kids. Didn't anyone ever tell her that money couldn't buy happiness? My guess was probably not.

When we arrived at the lunch table, I made quick introductions. Everyone took Raeann in with a smile, except for Adam, who just looked skeptical. JP was more than interested as he ushered her to a seat right next to him and then struck up a conversation, which freed me to sit next to Callie. I never thought I'd be grateful to JP, but at that moment I was.

Callie gave me a pointed look.

"She's in every single class I have," I complained under my breath.

"Where's Ryder?"

I shrugged. He had skipped out on last period and seemed to have skipped lunch as well.

"Not sure, and at the moment I have enough to deal with than to worry about him. I'll catch up with him later," I assured her, although I was definitely curious why he was avoiding us. I could only assume it was because of Raeann.

After school, it looked like I'd be heading to Ryder's house.

Chapter 12

"Hi, Xavier!" I said brightly as I stood on Ryder's front porch. "Is Ryder home?"

"Hello . . ." The man paused as he smoothed his tie and averted his gaze.

"Violet," I offered, raising my eyebrows a little. Wasn't it part of his job to remember who people were?

"Yes, of course. Violet," he repeated, then said carefully, "He's a little busy at the moment. I can show you into the study, if you like."

I shifted uneasily under the butler's scrutiny. "Sure."

When he ushered me into the foyer, I noticed there was a pair of girl's heels in the entryway. Xavier maneuvered me past them, then led me down the now-familiar corridor.

"This way then, miss."

Instead of going to the den, he took me to what looked like a modern study, with a large desk that dominated the center of the room. I strolled around, taking in the bookshelves that lined the walls, completely filled from floor to ceiling. It was an impressive collection.

"He will be with you in a little while," Xavier said, then shut the door behind him as he left.

I walked over to the books and scanned the titles. There were a ton of classics like *The Scarlet Letter* and *To Kill a Mockingbird*, books I wouldn't have pegged Ryder to read. Running my finger along their spines, I noted a lot of books on eclipses and astronomy.

After looking through a telescope in the corner of the room, I walked over to the desk and sat down, then swiveled back in forth in the comfy chair. A laptop rested in the center of the desk, and an iPad and a wireless printer sat to the side.

I tapped my foot, tired of being kept waiting. It couldn't hurt to look around for a bit, could it?

I smiled to myself as I pulled open the top middle drawer and found pencils, pens, and notebooks inside. They were organized and stacked, the smallest pencil to the biggest pencil, largest notebook on the bottom to the smallest on top.

Neat freak.

I brushed some of the things aside, purposely disorganizing them. My fingers brushed against something round that protruded from the back of the drawer, and I pulled it open a little farther to check it out.

There seemed to be a button on the side. *Interesting.* I let my fingers graze over the top and heard a click from somewhere underneath.

I searched around and underneath the desk. A small compartment with a latch appeared; had I not pressed the button, I would have thought the face of it was part of the design of the desk. I unhooked the little latch and the door dropped open. It was clean, no dust, as if whatever was hidden inside had just been placed there very recently.

My heart raced with excitement. I knew I shouldn't be poking around like this; it was an invasion of Ryder's privacy and he would definitely be pissed. But I couldn't help myself; I had a million questions about my father and the clans and our powers, and had only gotten a few answers. I deserved to know the truth, right? Besides, the inside of the hidden drawer was calling my name.

I stuck my hand inside, barely containing my excitement, and grabbed hold of something hard, pulling it out. It was a journal, and after flipping to the first page, I confirmed it was Ryder's journal. Who even kept a journal anymore? It seemed so old-school.

Frowning, I set it quickly on the desk and reached inside to empty the rest of the contents. My fingers brushed something smooth—like a picture?—and pulled it out, then smiled at my guessing skills. I was right on the money.

When I turned it over to look at it, my fingers began to tremble and I dropped the photo to the floor. The picture was of *me*! Icy tendrils worked their way up my spine. I recognized the outfit I was wearing and the setting . . . it was Callie's birthday party at the diner's outside patio this past year, which meant the picture was taken before I met Ryder. But why?

My heart raced, both from worry over getting caught snooping, and with confusion and anger over the photo.

I snatched the picture off the floor and looked at the back for any notes. Nothing. Thrusting my hand inside the drawer again, I searched to see if there was anything else. At the very back I found something small, and pulled out a key with a fancy embossed *S* on it.

What did the *S* stand for, and what did the key open? My mind raced while I scanned the room for something that the key might open, but I saw nothing that looked promising.

Voices in the hallway outside the door made me freeze, and panic twisted my stomach. Quickly I stuffed the key, picture, and journal back into the compartment and shut the little door, latching it and then pushing up to make sure it blended back into the woodwork of the desk. My fingers worked as quickly as my heart raced.

When I was done I sat back, letting out the breath I'd been holding as Ryder opened the door. I looked down to see my hands were shaking.

That was close. Way too close.

"Xavier said you were in here," Ryder said as he stepped in and shut the door. He sounded tired.

He was dressed in dark blue jeans and a dark blue button-down shirt that wasn't tucked in, the top three buttons left undone. My heart did a little skip and a hop as I took in how his hair and eyes contrasted with the dark colors he wore.

I tried to relax, but my mind kept wandering back to why there was a picture of me hidden in his desk.

Ryder glanced at me and asked, "What's wrong, Vi?"

Whoa. I was obviously not wearing my best poker face.

"Nothing," I said as I shook my head, reassuring myself and trying to clear my mind. I took a deep breath to calm my nerves, but my hands were still a little shaky so I clasped them together under the desk, hiding them.

If only I had brought my backpack, I could have stuffed his journal into it. Normally I wouldn't be one to pry or to "borrow," but since Ryder had a picture of me hidden away, it seemed to justify my doing a little snooping. Even though had I not been snooping, I never would have found out about the picture. Regardless, the photo certainly made me feel better about my decision to get to the bottom of it.

"I hope you weren't waiting too long," he said.

Deciding the best defense was a good offense, I jumped right in. "Ryder, who's the girl?"

In response, he folded his arms across his chest and stared at me, narrowing his eyes. "What girl?"

I said nothing, giving him the chance to explain while we stared each other down, our eyes locked in a battle of wills. As I waited him out, my heart started to race again.

His face was full of firm resolve. He wasn't going to tell me.

"Would you believe me if I said it was my aunt?" Relaxing his posture, he gave me a tired half smile, then uncrossed his arms and ran a hand through his hair.

"Nope." I pushed back in the chair, rose, and walked over to him.

Ryder shrugged and gestured to the door. "Come with me."

I let out a long breath and followed him across the hall to the den. I took a seat on one of the stools and watched as he walked behind the bar, his posture tense.

"I'm beginning to sense a pattern here." I gestured to the empty glasses and noted that one of them had a pink lip print smudged on one side.

"You are, huh?" he said, pulling out two fresh glasses and filling them with ice and Coke. He set one in front of me.

"Thanks." I hesitated, playing with the straw, then glanced up to find him watching me, his brow furrowed. "Ryder, Raeann's mother put her in every single one of my classes. And where were you all day? I felt abandoned."

His expression was thoughtful. "I know—"

121

He was interrupted as the door opened and Raeann's blond head popped in. "Ryder, I forgot my purse—"

My mouth fell open in shock, and she narrowed her eyes angrily when she saw me.

"What's she doing here?" She frowned, then her lips formed a pout.

"We're just visiting," I told her as calmly as I could, and looked at Ryder for confirmation. The smirk on his face told me that he clearly thought the whole thing was comical, which thoroughly ticked me off.

My temper rising, I jumped off the stool and said, "I don't need to be in the middle of whatever you two have going on, so I'm outta here." Avoiding looking at either of them, I made a beeline for the door.

Raeann stalked over to Ryder and jabbed a finger at his chest. "Slade, what in the hell do you think you're doing?"

She could have him for all I cared, but deep down I did care. A little.

I reached the door and walked through it without looking back.

"Vi, wait!" Ryder called to me, but I kept going, picking up the pace and half jogging through the house to get to the foyer.

Ryder caught my waist with one arm and stopped me abruptly when I had just reached the front door. I spun on my heel, hastily facing him. He gripped my elbow gently, but firmly enough to keep me from walking out.

Leaning close to my face, he pleaded, "Will you give me a chance to get rid of her so we can talk?"

He actually sounded sincere, which surprised me. This was the Ryder I really enjoyed being around, but he was only like this about two percent of the time.

I shook my head disbelievingly. "Are you serious?"

His steady gaze met mine. "Of course I am."

Not sure what I wanted to do, I stared at him, watching a succession of micro-emotions cross his face. They were subtle and fleeting, and I wished I could decipher them. I sighed and relaxed my stance a little.

Seeing I was no longer ready to bolt, he released his hold on my arm and said, "Wait in the study. Please. I promise I won't be long."

I returned to the study and settled on the couch, trying to relax, but I was still a bundle of nerves. A picture hanging above the fireplace caught my eye, and I stood up to take a closer look. Up close, I could see it was of Ryder when he was very young, and a boy who resembled him quite a bit. They both had the same build and similar facial features. The only difference was this boy looked several years older and had intense olive-green eyes, higher cheekbones, a little more defined chin, and curly dark hair.

I started pacing; patience wasn't really my strong suit. Knowing it was wrong but dying to know why Ryder had a photo of me, I decided to investigate the upstairs to occupy my time, curiosity trumping the other emotions I was feeling.

After poking my head out into the hallway to ensure the coast was clear, I scooted up the stairs quickly. When I reached the top, I found a hallway with three doors leading off it. I peeked in the first room on the left, a bathroom. It was simply decorated with just the bare essentials, so I assumed it was Ryder's bathroom.

The next door I opened revealed a bedroom, with a familiar jacket draped over the chair at the desk. Ryder's bedroom. I was only going to peek, but found myself walking in. I knew I should be getting back downstairs, surely he would be finishing up soon, but something lying on the desk caught my eye. It was the Essen family book. I walked over and picked it up, skimming to the end because I'd only seen the first few pages.

"Find what you're looking for?"

Chapter 13

I nearly jumped out of my skin at the sound of Ryder's voice, even icier than usual, coming from behind me.

Shit.

Slowly, I set the book down and turned around. Forcing a smile on my face, I said, "I was just being nosy. I always wondered what your room looked like."

Something flickered in his eyes, then he seemed to relax as he walked over to the bed and sat down.

God, he was perfect. A lock of his hair fell onto his forehead, and I wanted to brush it aside, maybe run my hands through the rest of it. Kiss those attractive lips.

Wait! What am I thinking?

I shook my head a little, clearing my thoughts, then asked, "Is Raeann gone? What did she want? Do you know what she's up to?"

Ryder chuckled. "Whoa! Slow down, Vi. One at a time. Come sit." He patted the spot next to him.

"I don't want to be that close to you," I said softly, thinking back to the picture he had hidden away, then firmed up my resolve. "So, back to the real reason of why Raeann was here visiting you today."

He reached over and snagged my sleeve, then pulled me to sit down next to him. "Why do you care?" he said playfully. "You jealous, Vi?"

That tug I always experienced when I was near him was back, but I ignored it. "You know I'm not jealous." Trying to lighten the mood, I gave him a playful nudge in the side.

"You don't sound too sure, though," he said with a smirk.

I glanced away, at a loss for words for a second. I wasn't sure if I just didn't like Raeann being here because she and I got off to the wrong start, or if it was because I was beginning to have feelings for Ryder. There was a definite attraction between us, but I still had strong feelings for Adam. It was hard to let someone else in, even though Adam and I weren't together anymore. I also worried that my attraction to Ryder wasn't real, that maybe it was just the special connection with our silver eyes and the mysterious visions we saw when we touched.

"So quiet," he teased, smiling at me.

"I just have so many questions," I said hesitantly, then came to a decision. Since he had let his guard down, I figured I'd take advantage of it and have a heart-to-heart.

"For me?" he asked, and I nodded. He glanced at my lips for a second, then lifted his gaze to my eyes. "Okay, shoot."

"How long ago did you find out about me," I began.

"I've known about you for as long as I can remember," he said quietly.

His admission surprised me, and my eyes widened. "Did you ever come to find me?"

His gaze locked on mine and didn't waver. "Once I did. You just looked so happy in your life that I didn't want to be the one to mess it up. My aunt said fate would eventually bring us together, and that I'd just have to be patient. I actually have a memento from that day." He smiled. "A picture I took of you. Just so I could remember what you looked like, but as it turns out, I didn't really need that."

Okay, I'd buy that. That explained the photo I found, but I still had to find out about the key. "Why was Raeann really here?"

Ryder shrugged. "We used to date, but it was pointless. I didn't feel anything for her, so I broke it off. She wanted to know if we were dating or if I was attracted to you." He motioned with his hand between us and I froze.

Are you?

My heartbeat picked up and I inhaled sharply. "What did you say?" I breathed out, then held my breath. I was dying to know the truth, and since he was being so forthcoming, this was my best chance to find out for sure.

"Not yet, and yes," he said, answering both my questions.

I slowly released my breath. My hands rested on the bed's comforter, and he slid his over to mine but stopped just millimeters away. I looked down, and my gaze lingered on our hands. It was impossible for us to touch without having a vision, which made things difficult, because at that moment I wanted nothing more than to touch his skin, to feel the warmth of his fingers closing on mine.

When I looked up, he was staring at me, the smoky gray of his gaze reflected back at me. Somehow I knew that he was thinking the same thing.

He cocked his head to the side. "The real question is . . . do you have feelings for me?" His eyes were intense with curiosity, and my cheeks burned under his watchful gaze.

"You don't get to ask the questions yet," I said, teasing my way out of answering. I wasn't ready to answer, and if he couldn't tell from the way that I kissed him last night, then he deserved to wait.

"Well then, fire away. Ask me whatever you want." He leaned lazily onto one elbow.

My phone beeped, signaling that I had a text message, and I slipped it from my pocket for a second. When I saw the text was from Adam, I frowned. Couldn't he just leave me be?

Ryder watched me carefully. "I'd ask who it was from, but judging from your expression, it's not from Callie, which leaves only one other person I've seen you talk to."

His assumption was right, of course, there was no use in denying it. "It's from Adam. I'll look at it later," I said with a shrug.

"Go ahead and look now. It could be important."

I rolled my eyes. "Nothing he says is important."

He laughed. "Is that what you say when I send you a text?"

"No way!" My cheeks flamed when I realized I'd responded much too quickly.

Ryder chuckled. "Sure. You're just saying that because I'm sitting right in front of you."

"No, I'm saying it because it's the truth. Now, let's get back on track."

126

"All right, we were talking about you having feelings for me," he said, looking at me mischievously.

"No, we weren't." I smiled at him. "I was just about to ask you where you were all day."

"I went to Marquette to see my aunt. I wanted to talk to her about Raeann and Margaret Norman moving here."

Now my interest was piqued. "What did she say?"

"I told her about your new talent about seeing my memories, and she suggested you trying it on Raeann to see what we can learn that way."

"That's a great idea! Do you think it will work?" I had to admit I was curious.

"It's worth a shot."

"Okay, I'll try," I said and he smiled at my enthusiasm, his silver eyes shining.

My phone beeped again, disrupting our happy little moment. I glanced down to where I'd set it on the bed. It was another text from Adam. Inside, I was screaming with annoyance. On the outside, I just frowned.

"I guess I better see what he wants," I said. "He's persistent."

Ryder looked thoughtful but didn't respond.

I picked up my phone and opened the first message.

Adam: Violet, can we talk? Will you please call me?

His messages still gave me butterflies. I could almost hear his tone of voice as I read the words. He sounded desperate. How was I supposed to move on if he kept sending me texts like these? I sighed and flipped to the second message.

Adam: I really need to talk to you. Are you going to the bonfire?

Hmm. Interesting.

"What does it say?" Ryder asked, leaning forward slightly as if he was trying to peek. If I didn't know better, I'd think he was jealous.

"He wants to talk," I said, and gave him a reassuring smile. "Not an emergency or anything."

"I see." He looked away from me, his face impassive, and I could almost see his wall building back up.

Impulsively, I leaned over and kissed those gorgeous lips. I couldn't help myself, kissing him seemed like the only way to keep him from putting his wall back up. His lips were soft and hesitant as he kissed me back, and he reached up to cup my cheek gently. His breath feathered my cheek as his tongue parted my lips, his kiss growing more insistent, more passionate.

The familiar tingles coursed through my body, and I shut my eyes as the blindingly bright colors flashed around us. The dizzying feeling overcame me as I succumbed to the rush of wind whipping around us as we traveled. To where—or when—I wasn't sure. My emotions swirled as well, frustration mixed with anger at myself for allowing this to happen again.

Then the dizzy feeling faded away.

• • •

Nothing but blackness surrounded me. A stone wall was cool against my back.

"Ryder," I called out, hoping to hear him. I felt around and realized I had my phone in my pocket so I grabbed for it, using it as a flashlight. The dim illumination revealed that I was in some kind of cave. Was this the night of the bonfire? Why would I leave to go to some cave if it was?

Two shadows walked toward me. As they drew closer, I recognized Adam and JP.

"Listen," JP said, "I'll distract Olivia for you so you can talk to Violet here alone, in private. No one will come this way." He smiled. "You two can get back together and it will be just as it was."

JP seemed convincing, even to me. But then I recalled what Raeann had wanted JP to do so she could get Ryder alone.

"Thanks, JP!" Adam gave his best friend a smile.

It broke my heart to see how happy just the thought of us two being alone made him. It was a shame, because I wouldn't let that happen. I couldn't be alone with him.

128

Strangely, the scene before me started to fade, which hadn't happened before, and it scared me. Where was Ryder? I hadn't touched him, so I knew we weren't traveling back to our present time yet. Off balance, I swayed, and everything became a little distorted. I shut my eyes.

When the world had righted itself, I opened my eyes to find myself outside in the fresh night air. I searched the faces of the kids from school milling unknowingly around me, and noted they were all in costume except for me, and probably Ryder, I assumed.

A moment later, I found Ryder leaning against a tree, observing the activities around us. He looked over at me and frowned. "What took you so long to get here?"

"I'm not really sure. I ended up in some cave where I overheard JP telling Adam that he'll distract Olivia so Adam can be alone with me. That's how Raeann will get you alone during the costume party. We just won't let anything separate us, and whatever she's planning isn't going to work."

Ryder nodded. "Just one question first. Why would Adam want to be alone with you?"

My cheeks burned with an unwelcome blush. Thank goodness, it was night. I didn't think Ryder would notice.

"Is there something more to your relationship than you let on?" Ryder asked, his wall definitely back up based on the coldness of his voice.

I shrugged and looked away as I spoke. "There used to be more to it, but I ended it not that long ago. He's with Olivia. Always has been. They have an arrangement between their families, so you can't repeat any of this, okay?" It surprised me that I trusted Ryder with my deepest secret. Had it really been only a week or so? It seemed like I'd known him forever.

"You still care about him, though," he said uneasily. "Do you love him?" He frowned and folded his arms over his chest.

I decided to be honest. "Yes, I care about him. No, I don't love him. I could have easily fallen in love with him given the right circumstances, but he's in a relationship. He's pretty much pre-engaged to Olivia. I didn't let myself get that close."

129

"What about the kisses we shared?" Ryder's silver gaze bore into me, demanding the truth.

"I have feelings—" My heart leaped in my throat. I wasn't really ready to completely admit my feelings for him, so I stopped myself. If I didn't say it, then it wasn't real yet.

Ryder reached out and wrapped his arms around me, drawing me to him. He pressed his soft, full lips to mine hungrily as our mouths molded together. I didn't mind traveling back like this . . . melting into his warm embrace while his kisses fueled my blood. When it occurred to me this was the first time he had kissed me on his own, the realization made me giddy like a little girl.

I closed my eyes as the wind whipped around us, my hair flying in loose curls. The bright-colored lights intruded on our private moment. I didn't care that we were in the midst of chaos as the dizzying feeling touched my mind and made my muscles numb. The moment seemed right as Ryder and I clung to each other, his hand fervently tangled in my hair, our breathing heavy.

● ● ●

When the onset of wind died and the lights stopped flashing, the numbness gave way to tingling and my mind became clearer. I opened my eyes to find us standing in his bedroom, and realized our lips were still molded together. I sighed and began to pull away, but Ryder gave me one more kiss before we parted. I stepped back and looked at him warily.

"I care about you too," he said, his expression neutral. "You don't have to say it."

His words made my heart stop beating. Just hearing them made me want to stay longer, but I knew I should leave. There was too much emotion swirling around us, and he was too intoxicating. I took a couple of steps back, drawing in a fresh breath so his scent wasn't nearly as strong. "I should be going."

"Okay. See you tomorrow," he said.

I looked back at Ryder before I walked out his bedroom door. He was leaning over, straightening the comforter on the bed, and my breath hitched at the sight of him. He paused and looked up, and our eyes met one last time.

I had to bite my tongue to keep from saying *Not if I see you first*, like I always did with Adam. Letting out a little sigh, I said, "See ya tomorrow." Then I smiled and left, heading for home.

•　•　•

I walked through the front door of our house and was greeted by the aroma of Italian spices wafting in the air. When my stomach growled in response, I realized I was starving. Following the sound of voices, I made my way to the kitchen and found Vick there with a couple of his buddies.

"Want some pizza, Vi?" Vick asked as he placed a slice onto a paper plate and offered it to me.

"Yes, please!" I snatched the plate greedily; I always was a sucker for Italian.

Vick's friend Randy lifted his slice in greeting, and mumbled, "Hi, Violet," between bites.

"Hey, Randy."

"You didn't tell me your sister was hot, Vick."

I turned around to see an unfamiliar face. He was a good-looking guy, but so not my type. Any guy that hung out with Vick was strictly off-limits, per my stepbrother.

"Watch it, Jase, that's my sister!" Vick said in a sharp tone.

"I didn't mean any offense." The new guy looked at Vick apologetically, but it seemed insincere. "You know my mouth kind of runs away with me," he said with smirk.

I ignored the new guy. Chances were it was the first and last time he would be invited to the Williams household, just because of his runaway mouth. Vick was seriously protective of me.

Waving good-bye to the guys, I grabbed a Coke and headed to the living room, happy to see my stepdad was home for a change.

"Hey, Dad." I sat down next to him on the couch.

His schedule at the hospital was brutal so I hadn't seen him in a while, but I had to know if he knew that my real dad was alive or not. I just wasn't sure on how to bring up such a subject, or whether to admit where I'd heard it from.

Dad glanced over at me, pausing from flipping through the sports channels. "Hi, honey. How is everything?" He sipped from the cup of coffee he'd been holding.

I stalled for a second, placing my pizza and Coke on the coffee table. Gathering my courage, I asked softly, "Did you know that my real dad is alive?"

Dad practically choked on his coffee and looked over to me, his eyebrows raised. "Violet, where did you hear something like that?"

Not wanting to answer, I simply shrugged and twisted my hands in my lap.

He frowned for a moment, then an emotion that looked like regret flitted over his face. "Yes, Violet, he is."

Tears filled my eyes as he confirmed my worst fears. I'd been in denial, trying to convince myself that he didn't know, but I was wrong. "How on earth could you and Mom have lied to me all these years!" I yelled. "I don't understand."

"Violet, there's so much you don't know. Since she died, it's been weighing on me. I've wanted so much to talk to you about it, but—"

I couldn't take it anymore; the lies and betrayal were too much. Without a word, I grabbed my dinner from the coffee table and sprinted up the stairs to my room, my heart breaking.

Chapter 14

It was a tough few days emotionally for me after my aborted chat with my stepdad. He left to return to the hospital shortly after I ran upstairs, and I had been avoiding him ever since, which was pretty easy considering he was never home anyway.

Determined to put it behind me, when Friday night finally rolled around, I was practically bouncing with anticipation. Ryder was picking me up at seven, and we were going to the bonfire together. Excited about our first outing together—I wasn't sure if it could be considered a date—I spent an hour in my closet finding something to wear. I finally settled on jeans and a white fitted sweater with a hood, and of course, matching white sunglasses. When the sun went down the bonfire would be pretty bright, I reasoned. Ryder wouldn't like the shades, though, and I smiled just thinking about it.

The doorbell rang and I hurried out of my room. Vick was sitting on the couch with a couple of his friends watching basketball, and was quicker about getting to the door.

"I'm here to pick up Violet," I heard Ryder say to Vick as I descended the stairs.

"I'm Vi's brother, Vick. Nice to meet you." The two of them shook hands.

"Ryder Essen," he said as he gave me a once-over when I reached the door. I noticed Vick giving him a thoughtful gaze. "Vi, you look gorgeous but you're going to have to lose the sunglasses."

I smiled, knowing he was going to say that. Deciding to play nice, I took them off and put them in Vick's hands.

"See you later," I said to Vick.

"I'll be here when you get back," Vick called out, but I was already shutting the door.

Ryder's black Tahoe was parked in the drive. He opened the door for me, which was a nice surprise. Guys our age never did that kind of thing. And he looked really good. He was wearing jeans and a black-and-red jacket he had zipped partway up with a black T-shirt of some kind underneath.

Callie texted me earlier in the day to tell me she was going to ride with Henry and meet us at Ardent's Field. On the outskirts of town, it was more of a small clearing in the middle of the woods than a field, so I had no idea why it was called that.

We slowed down in a forested area and parked along the side of the road with a ton of other cars. When we got out of the truck, the smell of burning hit us, and gray curls of smoke rose slowly in the air above the trees ahead. We had a little bit of a trek through the woods before we would arrive to the clearing, so I was glad the sun was still out, making it easy to find the path the rest of our classmates had taken.

I sucked in a deep breath as we started through the woods, pushing branches out of the way and breaking some as we went. The scent of the woods mixed with smoke smelled great. Parties with bonfires were the best.

Ryder glanced my way as we headed down the path. "What's up, Vi? You don't seem like yourself tonight. You're too quiet."

"Sorry, just thinking," I said. "Actually, I was worrying about what was going to go down tonight, and wondering if this was our first date. Even though you didn't officially ask me, I was still hoping it was. Overthinking things again, my specialty." I gave him a small smile, a little embarrassed I'd just said all that aloud.

Not paying as much attention as I should have, I tripped over a root in the path. Ryder had quick reflexes and quickly caught my arm, steadying me.

"Careful now," he said. His hand slid down to grasp mine, and I was surprised to see he had put on a thin pair of black gloves.

I smiled at him, thinking how nice it was to be holding hands, but he kept his eyes straight ahead. My stomach clenched at the thought that maybe he was simply being nice and I was reading into it, but then I remembered our kiss and told myself to relax.

The woods began to thin out when we were just about to reach the clearing. A big bonfire was blazing in the center, and a lot of students were gathered around drinking and socializing already. A stream of kids lined up near one keg off to the right. Several smaller fires with big logs placed around them for seats were scattered around the edge of the clearing.

The popular kids were circled near a smaller fire on the far side of Ardent's Field. Among them were Raeann and JP, Adam and Olivia, and my bestie with Henry. I tried to let go of Ryder's hand, but he was firm about hanging on to mine. I just felt a little awkward as we approached the group, worried how Adam and Raeann might react. My concern was justified when Raeann shot me a dirty look.

"Hi!" Callie exclaimed, jumping up to give me a huge hug. I hugged her back, forcing Ryder to break his hold on me.

"Hi," I said, laughing at her enthusiasm. I took a seat on her left since Henry occupied the right. Ryder took a seat next to me, and rested his hand on my thigh.

"Hi, guys," I said to Adam and Olivia simultaneously. I only met Adam's eyes for the briefest of seconds and could tell he wasn't happy. Instead I focused my attention on Olivia, who was cheerfully smiling at me.

"It was great you guys could make it," Olivia said politely.

"Yeah, well, I wouldn't be here if it wasn't for this one," I said, nudging Callie in the arm.

"What are besties for," she said, smiling at me.

"True," I said.

"What's with the gloves, Ryder?" Callie asked, looking at him curiously.

Ryder hesitated a moment as everyone's heads turned toward him, and he shrugged. "I get cold," he said. "Low blood pressure."

A few minutes later, Callie and Olivia were chatting as Raeann and JP made their excuses and wandered off into the woods. Assuming they were going to talk about what Ryder and I already knew, I stood up and said, "I need a drink."

Adam started to stand, but Ryder cut him off.

"I'll go with you," Ryder offered quickly, his serious gaze on me.

"Sure." I smiled at him, almost able to see myself in the liquid mirror of his eyes. But Ryder's emotions were shuttered, and I knew that I wasn't going to get a smile in return. In fact, it looked like he wasn't really enjoying himself. He had more fun on the walk through the woods to get here than he was right now.

Ryder took my hand and we walked over to the kids lining up to get a drink from one of the kegs. I chuckled inside, knowing Vick and my stepdad would have a cow if they knew I was at a party where there was drinking.

"Vi, are you having a good time?"

We were waiting in line, with me standing in front of Ryder. I could feel the warmth of his body against my back and his warm breath against my ear. He massaged my shoulders gently, and I leaned into the soothing feeling.

"I am now," I said quietly. Every nerve in my body was attuned to his touch, and I felt sick with the butterflies that invaded my stomach. The line was moving forward and I took a step, mimicking the person in front of me so I wasn't in Ryder's grasp anymore.

He trailed his hand down my back until he reached the curve of my hip, and then let go. "Are you?"

The last thing I wanted to do was turn around and face him right now. My stupid cheeks were on fire again, this time just from his touch. Frustrated with the effect Ryder had on me, I said nothing. Instead I concentrated on moving with the line and watched as the setting sun left a mosaic of colors in its wake. It wouldn't be long till there wouldn't be any light left in the sky and the moon rose.

"I enjoy being around you," he said. "I probably would have picked a better location for a first date, but this will have to do."

Sensing the teasing in his tone, I whipped around. Ryder was wearing a half smile, his eyes warm in the dim light.

"So this is a *date*?" I said, surprised that my thoughts were so close to his.

He shrugged and the smile disappeared. "If you want it to be, it is."

"Okay, that sounds great." I grinned at him, then turned around to get a cup. We had come to the head of the line and I noticed instead of a keg it was a "wop," which meant hard liquor and juice. It will probably be better than beer anyway, I thought.

Ryder filled my cup. I took a drink of the shiny red liquid and it was surprisingly good. Not even a hint of the alcohol I was sure it contained. Ryder filled his cup next.

"Cheers," I said happily, clanking my plastic cup with his. "Here's to our first date." He returned my smile and we headed back to our group, hand in hand.

When we reached the fire, we found some of the others spearing marshmallows with long sticks, and sat down right where we'd been sitting before. Callie was leaning against Henry, his arm around her as she held a marshmallow over the fire. As usual, he was looking at her with adoration.

After I settled in beside her, she nudged my shoulder and said, "Raeann was telling us before you got here that she's going to have a party. With costumes and all."

"Really?" I said, trying to sound surprised. Of course I already knew that.

"Yes," Olivia piped in, smiling enthusiastically. "I want to be Padme from *Star Wars*, and Adam can be Anakin." She put her hand on Adam's knee at the mention of his name.

Adam glanced down at her hand lingering there and looked completely repelled by it. I wasn't the only one who seemed to notice. Ryder cleared his throat, and Adam looked at me guiltily.

"Wouldn't that be fun to make it a couples theme," she went on, seemingly oblivious to what had just happened.

"That's a great idea!" Callie chimed in. "We could go as Romeo and Juliet." She looked at Henry, and he shrugged.

"Whatever you want, babe," he responded unenthusiastically. "As long as there's beer," he said, tipping back his cup for a long drink.

It sounded like fun, so I turned to Ryder and suggested, "We could go as Guinevere and Lancelot."

"If I get a sword, why not?" He smiled and my heart melted. When he smiled, which was a little more often now than when we first met, he was devastatingly handsome, and it seemed like that smile was meant just for me.

From the corner of my eye, I saw JP and Raeann coming out of the woods and heading our way. JP was staring at me, then his gaze drifted to Adam, but I pretended not to notice.

"We decided we're going to do a couples costume theme for your party," Olivia announced to Raeann as she sat down, and started filling her in on all the details on who was wearing what.

Raeann looked at JP. "We could go as Maid Marian and Robin Hood."

"Or we could go as the Queen of Hearts and the Mad Hatter," he countered, making a crazy face.

I thought the latter suited them, and surprisingly she did too. "That sounds great," Raeann said happily.

"Hey, Adam, let's go get a beer," JP said to him, and both boys stood up and headed toward the increasingly long beer line.

"Do you want a s'more?" Callie asked.

"Some more of what?" I asked, laughing out loud at my lame joke.

Callie cracked up, laughing as she pulled her toasted marshmallow from her stick. I contemplated the sticky, gooey sweetness and opted against it.

I shook my head. "No, that's okay."

"Suit yourself," she said as she took a big bite of her toasted marshmallow-and-chocolate sandwich. Henry wasted no time in scooping one off her plate. She gave him a dirty look and I laughed again.

"What?" He wrinkled up his freckled nose. "They look so delicious." Callie shook her head and gave him a wry smile.

Ryder leaned over so close that his lips almost touched my ear. His warm breath tickled me when he asked, "Hey, Vi, do you want to dance?"

Surprised that he would ask, I glanced over to the makeshift dance floor on the other side of the clearing. Someone's iPod docking station was playing, and several kids from our school were fast dancing in the area.

I didn't hesitate at all. "I'd love to." I didn't think I'd ever been so happy. My face hurt from all the laughing and smiling I was doing tonight; not even Raeann could ruin my good mood. I took his gloved hand and we headed off in that direction. It was so nice actually being able to spend time with a guy out in the open instead of constantly hiding from everyone.

We started to move to the beat of the music, and every now and then Ryder would grab my hips and pull me closer, running his hands along my sides, flowing with my natural curves. His touch warmed my insides and sent an energy humming throughout my body, making me totally aware of his body in relation to mine.

When the next song started, Ryder pulled off some smooth, sexy moves that made me pause with a *wow*. The boy could dance. Soon there were people stopping all around us just to watch him, nodding their heads with the beat. It was great, because even though everyone was focused on him, Ryder's only focus was on me, and it made me feel special. After a few songs had passed, I was starting to sweat, but it appeared I was the only one.

"Hey, can we call it quits for a while?" I asked, nearly panting. "I need a breather."

Ryder wrapped his arms around my waist, pulling me closer, then leaned his face inches from mine. I held my breath, waiting for his answer.

"How about a slow song first? You can cool off in my arms."

"More like heat up," I said under my breath.

"What was that?" He cocked his head to the side curiously.

"Nothing," I said innocently, thankful he hadn't heard what I'd said.

The music had slowed down to something more romantic, and the sweet melody filled my ears. A shiver ran down my back and I trembled in his embrace, partly because my feelings were a wreck, and the chill in the fall air didn't help. Ryder looked at me with concern, his brow furrowed and his lips pressed into a contemplative line. I resisted the urge to shiver again as my nerves danced at the little shocks I received everywhere his hands touched me.

Snuggling in, I rested my head on his shoulder, enjoying being so close to Ryder. A low murmur surrounded us as other couples chatted as they danced, but Ryder and I swayed in peaceful silence, each of us attuned to the other's breathing and heartbeat. I reveled in his warm embrace, enjoying the comfort of just being in his arms, and wondered if he felt the same way.

The song ended way too soon.

"You ready for a breather, Vi?"

When I nodded, he tucked my hand in his gloved one and led me back to the fire, where our new little circle were still hanging out.

"You were really great out there!" Olivia gushed at Ryder, and Callie nodded her agreement.

"Thanks," he said, shooting them an easy smile. "I had a really good dance partner."

Instead of looking at Ryder, I concentrated on the blazing fire, not wanting the attention his words directed at me, and silently wished for my sunglasses. Adam's gaze practically burned a hole through me, and it was hard not to notice the death glare Raeann shot my way. At least JP didn't make any smart-ass comments; he just watched me.

I finished my drink and looked at Ryder. His gray eyes flashed silver in the firelight, making a warmth spread through me.

Raeann straightened up and stuck her chin out a little farther, making it look way too pointy. She turned her haughty eyes on me, then slid her gaze to Ryder. "Ryder, can you get me a drink?"

He glanced at me hesitantly, and when I said nothing, he stood up. "Sure, Raeann."

As I watched him make his way toward the long line again, I crossed my arms over my chest to dull the stabbing sensation that gripped my stomach. Ryder was only trying to be nice, but Raeann goaded me from across the fire pit with her smug smile.

Looking away, I was surprised when a warm hand took mine and pulled me off the log. I glanced up to find Adam staring down at me with those deep blue eyes.

"Take a walk with me, Violet," he said quietly, tugging me toward the woods. Callie just shrugged and Raeann looked pleased. I hesitated, but reluctantly let him lead me away.

"I can't be gone long, Adam." The woods were dark and it was hard to see where we were stepping. I tripped slightly when my foot snagged a root. It was colder out here and I rubbed my arms. "Where did Olivia go?"

"Bathroom," he muttered.

"Adam, let's be quick about this. Ryder will be back soon."

I stopped, refusing to go any farther into the woods, pulling him to a halt about twenty feet in. He turned around quickly and caught me completely off guard when he locked lips with me. His hand went behind my head, tangling in my hair and holding me in place. His other arm wrapped around me, pulling me flush with his body, and I squirmed against him. My rapid heartbeat threatened to fly out of my chest, not because it was an exciting kiss, but because I was worried that Ryder would see us.

I placed my hands on his chest and pushed him hard, turning my face away from his. "What are you doing?" I cried out angrily. "Adam, are you crazy?"

"Only about you," he said. "Listen, Violet, I love you. I can't stand to see you with Ryder. You belong with me," he said earnestly. His hands were still on my hips, still trying to grab me firmly and pull me back to him.

"You belong with Olivia," I said quietly, feeling my heart break a little. I still had feelings for Adam, and his pain felt like my own. I hated hurting him. Tears filled my eyes.

"Shit," he murmured and dropped his hold on me, then moved back to give me some space. "I'm sorry."

Embarrassed, I brushed the tears away and said, "I can't talk about this any more with you. It's too exhausting." I stepped back to peek through the trees and saw that Ryder was still in line, and Olivia still wasn't back yet. Taking in Adam's contrite expression, I said, "It's okay, really. We can be friends." But I honestly wasn't sure if Adam could handle being just my friend.

"Friends?" He shook his head. "I don't understand why we still can't be together. Are you coming to work at my house on Sunday?"

"Yes, I'm working at your house on Sunday," I said absently as I peeked through the trees again. When I saw Ryder starting to head back to the fire, I said, "Look, I've got to go. Ryder is heading back this way."

"Why do you care so much about what he thinks?" Adam said angrily. "After all, you said you were just friends with him."

"I have feelings for Ryder," I snapped. "It's nice hanging out with someone and not having to hide that fact." I'd been careful not to use the word *relationship*. I knew what I said was harsh and that it hurt Adam to hear it, but the guy was really pushing my buttons.

Adam's shoulders slumped, and his blue eyes dimmed somewhat.

I started to head out of the woods with Adam on my heels. I'd hoped to beat Ryder back to the fire, but when I stepped back into the clearing, he was just handing Raeann her drink. His eyes were clearly focused on me, and they looked cold and unhappy. The chill from them ran through my body, and I wrapped my arms around myself, wishing I hadn't left my sunglasses at home. I missed the way they hid me from the world, and could use a little protection from Ryder's glare at the moment.

Ignoring Ryder's bad mood, I sat down next to him and listened as he asked Raeann about some old friends from where they used to live. She was very animated as they chatted, drinking and smiling a lot. But when I glanced over at JP, I noticed he seemed a little put off by the turn of events.

"Let's play Truth or Dare," JP said loudly, waggling his eyebrows as he looked around the circle.

"Sounds like fun!" Raeann exclaimed.

Adam and I looked at each other apprehensively. I wasn't keen on the idea, and I had an inkling he wasn't either.

JP tapped his chin as he glanced around, then said, "Henry, truth or dare."

"Dare," Henry said, all eyes turning on him.

"Moon everyone," JP demanded with a laugh.

"Are you serious?" Henry asked, his eyes wide as Callie giggled loudly.

"Drop your drawers and moon everyone," JP said. "That's the dare, take it or leave it."

Henry let out a sigh and said, "All right," then turned away and pulled down his pants, revealing a pair of pale butt cheeks.

"And what a nice ass that is," Callie exclaimed, slapping it hard.

"Hey, let's not get frisky in front of everyone, okay," he said to Callie, smiling as he sat back down.

When the laughter died down, Henry said, "I pick Adam. Truth or dare, Adam."

"Truth," Adam said, watching me thoughtfully as Olivia leaned her shoulder against him.

Henry looked up at the dark sky for a moment, then asked, "Do you like football?"

"Yes," Adam said with a smirk.

JP shook his head and called out, "That's way too easy. We already know Adam likes football. After all, he *is* captain of the football team. How about this—Adam, tell us one secret you've never told anyone."

Without hesitating, Adam said simply, "I'm in love."

I froze and Ryder stiffened next to me, then turned to glare at me for second.

Shit. JP knew what Adam meant. Callie knew what he meant. I knew what he meant. And I was pretty sure Ryder knew what he meant. Olivia thought Adam was referring to *their* relationship and she hugged him ecstatically, kissing his cheeks numerous times and leaving pink lipstick marks on his face.

"I love you too," she said, bubbling over with excitement. Adam looked down at the ground and then gave her a tight smile.

Raeann frowned, not looking the least bit happy. She must have realized that Adam distracting me wasn't going to happen.

"Adam, it's your turn to pick someone," JP said.

Adam looked straight at Ryder and narrowed his eyes. "Ryder, truth or dare."

143

When Ryder returned the glare, I practically shivered at the tension in the air and wondered if anyone else could feel it too.

Ryder's icy wall was back in place as he said, "Truth."

"Are you in love with Violet?" Adam asked point-blank.

I wasn't sure what Adam was trying to prove . . . that he loved me and that Ryder didn't? There was no way Ryder could be in love with me; after all, we just met a week or so ago. Sure, we had a strong connection, but we weren't even in a relationship.

I stiffened uncomfortably at the silence surrounding us. Raeann looked eager, awaiting Ryder's reply. JP seemed mildly curious as well.

"I can honestly say I've never been in love before," Ryder said quietly, and I let out the breath I was holding, relief washing through me.

"Liar!" Raeann cried out with all the bitterness of an ex still in love.

"Your turn, Raeann." Ryder gave her his movie-star smile, ignoring her outburst. "Truth or dare?"

"Dare," she said with a hard edge, obviously still angry about his admission.

"I dare you to go out into the woods alone with Violet for fifteen minutes."

Ryder gave her a fierce look; he had her cornered and she knew it. He pinned her with those silver eyes, and she opened her mouth to speak but nothing came out, so she closed it. She fiddled with her hair and straightened her shirt, then she glanced around, obviously flustered.

I put my hand on Ryder's knee and squeezed it, and he gave me the briefest of smiles. The others started to fidget as everyone awaited a response.

"Fine," Raeann spat out. "If Violet wants to talk privately, that works for me. She may just learn something she doesn't want to know."

She got up and stalked toward the woods, lighting the way with a small flashlight she pulled from her pocket. I followed her, my

144

thoughts plagued with suspicion and worry as I avoided hanging branches and roots. She stopped when we were a good distance away from the fire, and tilted her head as she glared at me, obviously waiting for me to speak first.

"What's your deal?" I asked Raeann. "What do you want from me?"

She kicked her shoe into the dirt, avoiding my eyes as she said, "Violet, you have to be careful of Ryder. You don't know what he's capable of. I do. I've known him for a long time, and we used to be good friends." She sat down on a log and toyed with her flashlight, then looked up at me. "Fifteen minutes is going to be a long time." She blew out a long breath. "You better take a seat because I don't have much else to say to you."

"Did you and Ryder experiment together?"

She looked up at me and gave a quick nod.

A cool breeze whipped down the path and I hugged myself, trying to keep warm. Resigned to having to wait, I sat down next to her, and she gave me a suspicious glare.

What does Raeann want with me? I repeated this thought over and over and then reached out to grab her hand. *Please work*, I added.

Then I shut my eyes, determined to ignore the repercussions of time traveling into a memory.

• • •

When everything was still and quiet again, I opened my eyes to see Raeann and her mother sitting and talking with a man I didn't recognize.

"Margaret," the man said with authority. "She's my daughter too. You may not like it, but the fact remains that she belongs here with us. Raeann, how do you feel about this?"

"I've always wanted a sister," Raeann said, but from her voice I couldn't tell if she was being sincere or not. I stepped a little closer, fear and dread building in the pit of my stomach as I peered over Margaret's shoulder.

145

"It's settled then. You'll be moving to where her stepfather lives." The man tossed a picture of me on the desk toward Raeann and her mother, and my heart seized with shock.

Glancing at Raeann, I touched her hand and gave it a soft squeeze, and was instantly transported back to the present.

. . .

Lying on the ground, I sat up to find Raeann glaring at me.

"You've been passed out for ten minutes. What the hell happened?" she demanded.

Raeann is my sister. How could I not know? The knowledge hit me hard and I grabbed my stomach, praying I wouldn't lose my lunch.

She stood over me, waiting for me to respond, but I said nothing as I stood up and brushed off my butt. I couldn't tell her what I saw; I didn't know her agenda yet.

I could only hope that blood really was thicker than water.

Chapter 15

Around midnight, Ryder and I said our good-byes and left. The mood was somber on the way back to the truck. We didn't hold hands and we didn't speak, both of us lost in our own thoughts.

My mind was spinning, wondering if Ryder was still upset about the whole woods incident with Adam, and I hadn't even explained what had happened yet. Maybe I won't have to, I thought, trying to look at the positive side. After all, I tended to be a glass half-full, not half-empty kind of girl.

It wasn't until we were well on our way to my house that he first spoke.

"Tell me what happened in the woods," he demanded, his eyes deviating from the road for a second.

"She told me not to trust you, and she wouldn't let me get close enough to even try seeing a memory," I lied as I pushed up my sleeves, a little too warm with the heater on. Was he trying to roast me? "Can I roll down the window?" I shifted uncomfortably.

He nodded and glanced at me. "Are you hot?"

"Yes," I said, not sure if I was hot because it was warm in the car, or because I was starting to get worked up. In either case, I desperately needed the window down.

Ryder rolled down the window partway, allowing the cool breeze to blow my hair out of my face. I shut my eyes, savoring the moment.

"Violet," Ryder said quietly.

Uh-oh. I knew that tone of voice. I looked out the window, waiting for the question I dreaded.

"Uh-huh?" I said casually as I could manage. My heart raced and my throat was tight as I twisted my hands in my lap and waited for the inevitable.

Ryder scorched me under his intense gaze, biding his time until he finally he asked, "What happened in the woods with Adam?"

His tone was as cold as his expression, and that was what I'd been dreading. Although his grip on the steering wheel was tighter than it should have been, otherwise he seemed calm but distant, and that was nothing new. When I didn't answer right away, he glanced at me again, frowning this time.

If I wanted any kind of relationship with him, I had to be honest. But I didn't have to look at him while I was being honest.

Staring at my hands as I picked at a torn fingernail, I said, "Adam wanted to talk to me alone, and he ended up surprising me with a kiss."

I looked up just in time to see Ryder's jaw tighten. He was mad, and I couldn't really blame him there. Here we were on our first date, and I kissed another guy.

"I'm sorry, Ryder. I shoved him away as fast as I could," I said, then sighed. "I shouldn't have gone out there with him to begin with. I know that now."

I sighed. I had a feeling that this incident was going to douse any romantic spark that had ignited between us. But just the fact that he was angry meant that he did actually care. Showing even that emotion was all I needed.

I put on a brave face. "Are you going to say something?"

His gaze stayed fixed on the road as he shot back, "What would you like me to say?"

Yes, he was definitely pissed. Sometimes guys were so impossible! Wait, that wasn't true. Adam was simple. Ryder, on the other hand, was way more complex. At this rate we would reach my house before we had anything resolved, which worried me, but then I realized he wouldn't get over this tonight. He needed time alone.

A few moments later, Ryder pulled to a screeching halt in front of my driveway. Saying nothing, he just glared straight ahead, refusing to look at me.

"I would say I had a great time, but that would be a lie," I said quietly.

His gaze flicked to mine, his distant and cold expression softening for just an instant.

148

"Okay, have a good one." I had just put my hand on the door handle when he spoke up.

"Violet."

Ryder saying my full name in that way drew my full attention to him. I let my hand drop from the handle and rest in my lap while I waited for him to finish.

"I'm not used to opening up to anyone," he said. "But I can clearly see that Adam is the type of guy you're into. After all, he said he loved you in front of everyone at the bonfire."

I shook my head and said, "That was for Olivia," but even I could hear how lame it sounded.

"He let her think that," Ryder said, nodding his head once in agreement. "But I know it was for you. I'm not angry with *you*, just in general. I wish I could have been the one to grab you and kiss you unexpectedly in the woods. How romantic would that be? But that isn't something I'll ever be able to do because one touch . . ."

He trailed off and looked into my eyes, not having to continue. We both knew what would happen with one touch.

Reaching out, I touched his sleeve. "I won't let Adam get me alone anymore. Raeann didn't try to get you alone either, so it has to be at her costume party that it will happen. That's next Friday, right?"

"I think so."

"We need to find out what Raeann's doing here."

Ryder looked away from me, seeming lost in thought. He wasn't pushing that issue, which made me wonder why. As I pondered that, he surprised me by pulling me into an unexpected embrace that made my insides warm up and my heart beat a little faster. As I rested my head on his shoulder, I felt a gentle pressure as his lips kissed the top of my head, my hair protecting us from the reaction of skin-on-skin contact.

Oh, how I longed for those lips to touch mine.

"Have a good night, Violet."

Ryder's warm breath in my hair sent shivers throughout my body. I was beginning to love the way my name rolled off his tongue. Then he slowly released his hold on me.

I was smiling the whole way into the house.

• • •

Vick was asleep on the couch when I tiptoed inside. My brother looked peaceful there, but I figured I'd better wake him to let him know I made it home safe and sound.

"Vick, I'm home," I said, gently shaking his shoulder.

"Hey, Vi." His voice was sleepy as he squinted at the wall clock. "I must have dozed off. Dad's sleeping. He has surgery early tomorrow morning."

"Okay, I'll be quiet," I said. "I need to go to bed." Suddenly feeling tired, I was headed to the stairs when Vick spoke up again.

"Vi, Dad said you guys had a fight."

As I paused on the staircase and looked down at him, he said, "You found out about your father. I'm sorry you found out that way." Vick studied me, his eyes filled with warmth and compassion.

"Yeah, I'm going to find my real father someday," I said, then shrugged. "I probably wouldn't know what to do if he was actually around, though."

Before he could try to defend my stepdad, I went up to my room to get ready for bed. I changed into a tank and pajama bottoms, then decided to send a quick text to Callie.

Me: Hey, I had fun tonight! It was great hanging with you and everyone.

My phone buzzed just as I finished brushing my teeth. *That was quick.* She must have been awake.

Callie: I had fun too! I can't believe Adam! That takes guts, and in front of Ryder too!

I grimaced, my stomach in knots at the memory.

Adam had been the center of my universe all summer, so it felt strange to be thinking less about him as Ryder consumed more and more of my thoughts. Everything about Ryder was a mystery. The

150

fact that he was a very private person made me more curious, and I kind of enjoyed the challenge of getting him to open up. He seldom expressed his feelings but when he did, something magical seemed to awaken in me. It was hard to explain. It was like connecting with someone on a completely different level, as if we were on one frequency and everyone else was on another.

I turned in for the night, pushing all thoughts of guys from my mind. Otherwise, I wouldn't get a wink of sleep.

• • •

The next morning, I awoke to the sound of the doorbell ringing over and over. Annoyed, I pulled on my robe and went down the stairs, rubbing my hands over my face to wipe the sleep from my eyes. I called out, but Vick was nowhere to be found.

When I opened the door, there was no one there, just an embarrassingly large display of flowers. My mouth dropped open. Five floral arrangements in beautiful vases sat on our front porch— dozens of crimson roses and delicate forget-me-nots interspersed with baby's breath and ferns.

I stepped out on the porch and shielded my eyes from the morning sunshine as I looked for whoever rang the bell, but there was no one around. Not sure if I was more excited or embarrassed, I picked up the arrangements one by one and put them in the entryway, then looked at them closer.

There was a white card on each arrangement, but instead of a being addressed with a name, each white card was labeled one through five. Assuming the flowers were for me—after all, I was the only girl in the house—I opened the first one.

I hope the roses make you feel the way I feel when you're around me.

How sweet, I thought. I plucked the second card from the flowers and opened it.

I love the way you sing when you dance.

Did I sing last night when I was dancing with Ryder? I must have. Then I slipped the third card from the tiny envelope.

151

In my eyes you can't do anything wrong.

A sinking feeling developed in the pit of my stomach as I pulled the fourth card from its holder.

I will love you forever!

I dreaded looking at the fifth card, but I had to know for sure. My hands trembling, I pulled out the last card.

Yours always, Adam

I closed my eyes and clutched my stomach, feeling sick. What was I going to do with all of these?

The doorbell rang again and I startled, dropping the cards to the floor.

"Oh God," I whispered. Adam just wasn't giving up. The flowers were flattering, but too much. Thank God Vick wasn't home. If he were, I would never hear the end of this.

I turned around and opened the door. My mouth dropped open when I saw Ryder standing there, especially with the embarrassing display of flowers right behind me. The cards lay scattered on the floor.

"What's all this?" Ryder raised an eyebrow.

The last person I expected to see right now was Ryder, and I was speechless. Not sure what to say, I said nothing.

"Let me guess," Ryder said with a sarcastic edge. "Prince Charming is at it again?" He narrowed his eyes, definitely irritated by the grand gesture.

Finally coming to my senses, I snapped, "Help me get these out of here." Without another word, I left the door open and grabbed the closest vase, then began hauling it up the stairs, hoping he would follow.

"You want me to help carry another guy's flowers to your room?" he yelled up to me.

I paused and glanced behind me over my shoulder. "Look, I really don't want my brother to see these. He'll get the wrong idea."

Ryder stooped to pick up the cards off the floor, and I instantly regretted not grabbing those first. But my hands were full now, and

152

there was nothing I could do about it. Without looking at the cards, he grabbed a vase and followed me up the stairs. I let out a little sigh of relief.

"Just set them over there." I pointed to the corner of my room where I had already placed the one I'd brought up. He set down the vase he'd carried, then quickly flipped through the cards before dumping them in the wastepaper basket I had next to my desk. I had to suppress a chuckle; I didn't really want to keep the cards anyway.

When we were done hauling the rest of the flowers, Ryder sat down on my bed and I took the desk chair, not wanting to be that close to him. He was too damn gorgeous.

"So, what brings you by?" I asked, and held my breath as I waited for his answer.

He didn't say anything at first, just stared at me, which made me feel self-conscious. I was still in my pajama bottoms and tank, and my auburn curls were a little wilder than usual, since I hadn't showered yet or even brushed my hair.

"I wanted to see if you'd like to get a bite to eat," he said in that icy tone I hated. "But I can see you've been busy."

I hated when he shut me out, so I got up and sat on the bed next to him, so close my thighs brushed against his khakis. My body instantly upgraded to high-alert status, delicious nerves running through my body, wildly heating my face. Ryder gave me an arrogant look and didn't budge an inch.

"Ryder," I said, my voice dripping with disapproval. "One of these days I'm not going to be able to breach that wall of yours."

Surprise wavered in his eyes, but only for a second. If I had blinked, I would have missed it.

"You're hard to resist." His voice was husky and his gaze softened as he pulled me to him in a warm embrace.

It was a careful dance as he rested his hands on the fabric covering my back, his long-sleeved T-shirt shielding most of our skin from touching. I closed my eyes and relaxed my cheek against his chest, enjoying the sound of his rapid heartbeat, knowing mine beat just as quickly. The longer I remained in his arms, the louder and faster my heart thudded, and my chest constricted, making it hard to breathe. I so wanted to kiss him, my lips aching for his touch.

"Ryder." I hesitated for a moment, hoping he wouldn't take this the wrong way. "I think I'd better take a rain check on lunch."

It wasn't that I didn't want to go with him. I was just unsure about going to Price's Stop-and-Shop, since it was the only restaurant that kids our age went to eat. Since Adam's dad owned it, I felt like I would be rubbing it in Adam's face if Ryder and I ate there.

"Is it because of last night?" Ryder asked quietly, and I pulled away to look at him, putting unwanted space between us.

"No! Of course not," I reassured him. Ryder and I weren't officially a couple, and I wasn't sure I was ready for anything like that. But Adam was definitely making it hard to move on.

"Can I kiss you?" Ryder said as his lips twisted into a smile.

"Yes," I whispered, my body instantly melting inside at the thought of those gorgeous lips touching me.

Ryder didn't hesitate, immediately molding his lips over mine. He teased my mouth with his tongue, willing me to open up to him, and I did. The blinding colors swirled around us as he tugged me closer to him. My hair whipped about our faces, my wild curls shielding us from the bright lights. His lips pressed more intensely, demanding more of me as the dizziness swept over me, Ryder's touch doing a little magic of its own.

When the chaos subsided, I opened my eyes to find myself alone. The warm glow from Ryder's touch faded, leaving me feeling bereft. A chill swept over me as I tried to move and realized that my hands were bound in front of me. Terrified, I sat up, peering out into the blackness as I desperately searched for Ryder.

Chapter 16

A fire blazed in the distance, and I squinted as I tried to make out the people who were gathered around it. I sucked in a breath when I recognized Ryder; there was no mistaking that perfectly tousled blond hair.

What did Ryder have to do with this?

I scanned the other faces, trying to find someone else I might know. My body filled with dread when my eyes landed on Principal Margaret. Why on earth was I tied up, and why wasn't Ryder with me? And how the heck did I get out of here?

"Ryder!" I screamed.

It drew his attention immediately, and he walked over to where I was.

"Let me loose!" I said frantically.

Ryder's face was blank, his expression cold and unreadable. He inched closer to me and opened his mouth as if he was going to say something, but then seemed to change his mind.

Why would I be tied up, yet he wasn't? And who were those people? Ryder was wearing a costume, so it was definitely the night of the costume party.

Overwhelmed by fear and confusion, I reached for his arm. I didn't want to stay there another second. Ryder's impassive expression while I was bound and helpless haunted me.

"Get me out of here!" I shrieked as I desperately grabbed his hand, and my world began to spin.

• • •

What the hell was that about?

I opened my eyes to find myself still clinging to Ryder's chest as I lay on top of him. I jumped off immediately, cringing away from him, unsure what to believe. It looked like he was on their side, and my heart ached at the confusion of it all.

155

"What was that?" I shrieked, but Ryder only looked at me with that same placid expression. "Why was I the only one tied up? What were you doing with Raeann's mother?"

I was furious, so sure Ryder was holding something back. He obviously didn't want me to see what was coming. But then why risk it? Why kiss me at all? I was confused, to say the least, and his silence wasn't helping matters.

"Calm down," he said quietly. "I'm not quite sure what exactly was happening, but I'll try to figure out what's going on."

His words rang surprisingly true. I almost believed him.

"But the people? You knew them, right?"

His eyes didn't waver for a second as he said, "No." He actually seemed bored, as if he was answering a question in class, not dealing with something as life-changing as this.

Liar. I crossed my arms in front of my chest.

"Listen, some things are better left unsaid—" he started, but I cut him off.

"You need to leave, Ryder," I said forcefully. "I'll talk to you later after I've had time to cool off. If you know something about what's going to happen the night of the party, then you need to tell me."

Ryder rose from the bed and walked over to me, stepping inside my personal space. "Don't forget how it felt when we kissed," he said with a warm smile. His fingers trailed the side of my waist, forcing me to inhale sharply and stiffen at his touch.

"All right," I said hesitantly.

With absolute certainty, I knew I needed to get back to his house and look in his journal. I had to know what it contained, and I desperately wanted to know what that key with the fancy embossed *S* was for. But if I was going to get any of that accomplished, Ryder couldn't know that I was suspicious.

"Ryder," I said, stalling and biting my lip. He paused at my door and turned around. "I know you can figure out why I was their prisoner, and I know that you'll do everything in your power to try to prevent it from happening. I'm sorry I snapped at you."

A shadow of doubt crossed his face, so I went to him and put my arms around his waist. He hesitated slightly before wrapping his arms around me.

I let out a sigh of relief. Step one, complete. Ryder was no longer on the alert.

He gave me a heartfelt kiss on the top of my head. "I'll see you later, Vi," he said quietly, and then I was left alone.

• • •

I decided to pass the afternoon doing homework, which I really hadn't any time for recently. When I was done, I was starved, so I scavenged the fridge to make a turkey sandwich.

My phone rang as I lounged on my bed with my plate. "Hey, Callie."

"Come to the movies with me!" she exclaimed with a little more enthusiasm than normal.

"Now? Why, what's up?" I said warily. What usually excited Callie was matchmaking, and I wasn't in the mood for it.

"It'll be a good movie," she said. "Honestly, you won't regret it."

"I don't know . . ."

"Trust me!"

"All right," I said reluctantly, even though my gut instinct told me I shouldn't go.

So I wolfed down my sandwich and went to meet Callie outside Price's Cinema Plaza, another local business that Adam's dad owned. She was alone when I got there.

"Here's your ticket." She shoved a small piece of paper into my hand and pushed me toward the double doors of one of the theaters.

She led the way as we fumbled through the darkness, then stepped aside and nudged me into a row. I stopped suddenly and Callie ran into me. There sitting in the row was Henry and Adam, with two seats saved in between the guys.

I turned around to Callie. "Are you nuts? I'm not supposed to be seen with Adam."

157

"No one will know, Violet. Adam brought a friend too."

"Well, hello, Violet," JP said as he grinned at me.

Oh, this was just great. I rolled my eyes as Callie pushed me into the seat next to Adam. I slumped down and crossed my arms unhappily. I should have known better. Hopefully word about this didn't get out. I really didn't want to explain this to Ryder.

Adam leaned over and whispered, "Violet, I told you I had to talk to you."

Ignoring him, I kept my eyes on the previews.

"Listen, JP told me what he did. I know that it was the reason behind your decision to not see me anymore." His voice cracked a little. "JP's sorry," he said earnestly.

I turned my head, meeting Adam's gaze. His eyes radiated sincerity, so I glanced over to JP, who was watching the screen until Adam elbowed him.

"I'm very sorry," JP said too sweetly with a grin I wanted to slap off his pretty-boy face.

Then it hit me. This was all part of JP's elaborate plan to separate Ryder from me at the costume party. I wasn't falling for it. I didn't want to hurt Adam, but I wasn't about to let anything happen to Ryder either.

I shrugged. "Whatever," I said, directing my attention to JP because looking into Adam's eyes would hurt too much.

"Violet, it means we can still be together," Adam said, and took my hand. I could hear the desperation in his voice. His hand was warm to the touch and it still felt familiar in my own, but it didn't hold the slightest bit of tingle that it used to.

"I'm sorry, Adam. No, we can't." I pulled my hand from him gently.

"It's because of Ryder, isn't it?" Adam asked me in a low voice, but I could tell JP was listening in with how far he was leaning over. Everyone in the theater seemed to be enjoying the movie. I didn't even know how it began, I was too distracted by Adam.

"No, Adam," I whispered back. "It's about Olivia. It's over. I'm sorry."

The truth was I had a lot of shit to sort out right now, and I really didn't need anything complicating it more. Thoughts of my real father flowed through my mind.

I stared straight ahead, unable to concentrate on the movie. Adam's gaze kept drifting over to me, making me uncomfortable, and I finally couldn't take it anymore. I got up without saying another word and left the theater. I was halfway to my car when I heard rapid footsteps heading my way, and glanced back to see JP sprinting toward me.

"Violet, you bitch!" he exclaimed, his eyes narrowed.

"Me? Are you for real? You're the one who got what you wanted, JP. You made sure of that!"

I reached my car door and pulled it open, but he pushed it shut and leaned against it, then crossed his arms and glared down at me.

"We aren't done talking yet. You hurt Adam," he said, his threatening tone reminding me of our altercation in the boys' restroom.

"JP, Adam is with Olivia. The whole thing between us is over. There's nothing to talk about. The only reason you care is because Raeann wants you to have Adam distract me, otherwise you wouldn't even want me to even look at him."

Shit. I covered my mouth, frustrated with myself for revealing so much. I made the worst spy ever.

"What have you heard?" He narrowed his eyes at me.

My mind reeled as I tried to come up with a way out of this mess, then decided that the best defense was a good offense.

"JP, are you really that dense? Can't you see that Raeann has it bad for Ryder? She's using you!"

Shock crossed his face for a second, and I waited, letting what I'd said sink in. Then he moved quietly aside, giving me access to my car. I felt a pinch of sadness for him, but only a pinch.

"See ya," I said sharply, then got into my car and drove away.

I made a detour to the mall to pick up a card for Ryder, and then continued on to his house. Ryder's Tahoe wasn't there. Now would be as good a time as any to borrow his journal. In case I got caught, the card I'd bought would be a good excuse for sneaking into his office. I could always say I was going to surprise him. It should work; I had it all planned out.

I smiled at my own cleverness. Nothing was going to get in the way of discovering the truth.

Chapter 17

I paused on Ryder's front porch and took a deep breath, hoping the house would be unlocked. Lucky for me, when I tried the handle, it turned. My heart pounding, I opened the door and peeked inside; it was eerily quiet.

Knowing I'd better hurry up so I didn't get caught, I walked through the house as quickly as I could. Outside Ryder's office, I turned the handle and pushed the door open, then walked in and shut the door behind me with a trembling hand. Snooping was one thing, but breaking and entering was on a whole different level, even if the house was unlocked and I didn't technically break in.

The office was quiet and the shades were halfway drawn, so the room was somewhat dim. I took a step toward the desk and froze as the office chair swiveled slowly.

I sucked in a deep breath when Ryder's keen eyes fixed on me. My heart rate sped up, both at the sight of his heartbreakingly gorgeous face, and at the fact that he looked perturbed.

"Violet."

My heart fell. It was never good when Ryder used my full name.

He narrowed his eyes, his wall firmly in place. "What are you doing here? Xavier didn't tell me I had company."

Putting on a thin smile, I waved the card at my side. "I was going to surprise you," I said, keeping my tone as casual as possible, but even I could hear the quiver in my voice.

Where the heck is his truck?

"I didn't think you were home," I added.

Ryder frowned. "The truck needed an oil change. Xavier had someone pick it up."

"Oh." Obviously a life of crime wasn't for me. I was so rattled that I sounded stupid, and I mentally cursed myself.

"So, let's see it?" he said, motioning for the card, but I put it behind my back.

"Some other time," I teased. "It wouldn't be a surprise if I handed it to you."

His eyes narrowed again. "All right then. What seems to be bothering you?" When I only shrugged, he leaned forward and said, "I know that look, Violet. What gives?"

Crap. Rather than admit I was snooping again, I decided for door number two. "Callie invited me to the movies . . . and it turned out that Adam was there too. I didn't know he was going to be there, I swear. Apparently, JP set it up."

Ryder's eyes flashed with anger. "Is that so?"

"As far as I know."

"Is there anything else you want to tell me?"

"No, nothing else happened. Except . . ." I paused, debating whether to come clean about my slipup. "I kind of let JP know that I knew Raeann was using him."

"Hmm." Ryder seemed lost in thought as he twirled a pen in his hand.

"I don't think JP will tell her what I said," I said hopefully. "I think he has too much pride for that."

"Hmm." He leaned forward, placing his elbows on the desk as he stared me down.

Feeling awkward, I shifted from foot to foot as if I'd been called in front of the principal again. If I couldn't snoop, there was no reason for me to stay. I wasn't sure if I trusted Ryder anymore, and I definitely didn't trust myself alone with him. He was just too freaking attractive.

I turned toward the door and said, "Sorry, but I have to go. Vick will be expecting me home soon, and I have to work tomorrow."

Ryder rose from his chair and walked around the desk, coming to a stop much too close to me. I was minding less and less about him invading my personal space, almost welcoming it, even though I should probably keep him at arm's length.

With him standing so close, I had to look up to meet his eyes. I couldn't read any mistrust in them, just determination.

Could Ryder possibly be my knight his aunt spoke of in the cards? Could he be the one to save me from being Principal Margaret's prisoner, or was he a . . . *traitor*? I didn't want my thoughts to go there, but couldn't help myself. What if he was pretending to care when he actually didn't feel anything for me? What if he and Raeann were laughing behind my back?

My conflicting emotions must have played across my face because Ryder's eyes suddenly softened. I didn't want to be coddled, so I pushed the last few thoughts from my mind.

"What's wrong?" he asked quietly.

"Nothing," I said automatically, just like every girl when something was wrong but they didn't want to come out and say what the trouble really was.

"I don't think you're being honest with me," he said quietly. "The last visit to the future bothers you."

Of course it bothers me, I screamed inside. *I was tied up and you didn't help me!* But it wouldn't help my plans to admit that, so I looked away.

Ryder put both his hands on my shoulders and shook me gently. "Vi, I won't let anything happen to you. I don't know how you got tied up."

He sounded sincere, but he'd already proven he could lie—pretty easily, actually. I wanted to trust him, wanted to let him hold me and comfort me, but I couldn't. My judgment was definitely iffy when it came to Ryder because of the powers we shared, not to mention the attraction I felt for him. But I wanted more information, and to get that I had to keep a cool head.

Needing some distance, I stepped back. "I'm fine, really," I said as convincingly as possible. "I know you won't let anything happen to me if you can help it." *Wow, that sounded good. I almost believe myself.*

Ryder's posture relaxed a fraction. "Stay for dinner, at least."

I opened my mouth to say no, then realized this might be my only opportunity to get into his desk and grab that journal. Especially since my burgling skills went to waste.

163

"Okay." I gave him a winning smile. "Just let me grab my purse and put this card away."

"All right. Hurry back, though," he said with a half smile.

Relieved that he believed me, I hurried down the hall and out to my car, grabbed my purse, then came back inside. I was pretty sure Ryder would be waiting in the den, and almost positive I would have enough time to sneak back into his office and grab the journal.

I tiptoed back down the hall and instead of veering off into the den, I rushed into his office and made a beeline for his desk. Frantically, I went through the steps to open the secret drawer. Relieved to find the journal where I'd seen it last, I grabbed it and quickly tossed it into my purse. I hesitated a second, considered taking the key as well, but decided against it and locked the drawer.

Thinking back to my tarot card reading, I grabbed the card that I originally brought in case I got caught and used Ryder's pen to write:

Thanks for being my knight in shining armor. ~Vi

I couldn't forget what the rest of the tarot cards meant. With that thought, I tucked the card into the envelope and laid it on the desk, then hurried to the den. Before I walked in, I took a deep breath to calm myself. The journal was burning a hole in my purse; I was dying to get out of there and read it. But instead of bolting for home, I put a smile on my face and walked over to the bar.

Ryder looked up when I walked in. "Xavier should be back soon with my truck. I thought he had someone pick it up, but it I guess he decided to take it himself. Looks like we'll have to order in. Anything in particular you feel like eating?"

"Can we order Italian?" My mouth watered at the thought of the delicious dishes our local Italian restaurant carried. Since it was my favorite, I already knew what I wanted.

"Anything you want." He brought out his iPad and after conferring with me, ordered lasagna for himself and chicken parmesan for me, then arranged for our dinner to be delivered.

"So, what time do you work tomorrow?" he asked, his tone casual.

Obviously Ryder was asking because he was uncomfortable with my working at Adam's house, especially after Adam proclaimed his love for me in front of our friends at the bonfire, even if most everyone thought he meant Olivia. I realized that if Ryder worked at Raeann's house that it would bother me too, so I tried to be considerate.

"I can go in anytime really, but I'm aiming for around eleven. I think Adam's mom will be home," I added, "so there won't be any way for him to sneak off to see me."

Why did I say that? I wanted to stuff a sock in my mouth. Now Ryder knew that Adam and I used to sneak off and see each other while I was working. Ryder was already hard enough to get through to; I didn't need to make it worse.

"It's not that we *do* that all the time, I mean *did* all the time. Past tense," I explained. "I was trying to be there at work when he couldn't bother me, since he seems to keep showing up everywhere I go."

Ryder stared at me thoughtfully. "Save it, I don't need you to explain."

Embarrassed by my rambling, I shifted in my chair and brushed against my purse strap, dislodging it from the chair back where it had been hanging. It clunked heavily to the floor, and I hurried to grab it.

"What do you have in that thing?" he asked.

I cringed but forced my face to stay neutral as I replaced the strap. "Makeup and stuff," I said casually, and then sent up a silent prayer of thanks when the doorbell rang.

Ryder stood up. "That must be the food. Be right back, Vi."

The familiar nickname put me at ease, that and the fact that we weren't going to be talking about my purse anymore.

The aroma of Italian spices drifted to the den even before he walked back in with the food, and I realized I was famished. Ryder set out our dinner on the bar, and we enjoyed each other's company, eating in silence and giving each other the occasional smile. He tried to make small talk, but my mind was on the journal hidden away in my purse.

165

After yet another vague response from me, Ryder laid his fork down and said coldly, "Violet, what's going on? You don't seem like yourself."

"I'm sorry, my mind is elsewhere," I said, looking down at my food as I tried to come up with an excuse for being so distant. "Um, I was thinking that we need to order our costumes and expedite shipment if we're going to have them in time for Friday's party."

Ryder frowned, then seemed to relax. "Is that what this is about?"

I nodded, relieved that he seemed to buy it.

"I already ordered them this morning," he said. "They should be here Tuesday."

"Oh." I couldn't hide the fact that I was surprised. Usually guys weren't good planners, but then again this was Ryder, so I shouldn't have been so surprised. "Guinevere and Lancelot?" I asked, checking to be sure he ordered the right costumes.

"Yeah, it was easy. I just went online and ordered them. It's not rocket science," he said sarcastically.

I laughed out loud. Ryder was funny when he wanted to be. "Yes, I know it's not rocket science."

I glanced at his clock. It was nearing seven. Vick wouldn't be wondering where I was yet; after all, it was a Saturday. Inside I was dying to take the journal and go curl up in bed with it.

Ryder pushed his plate aside and stood up to stretch, his shirt riding up to reveal his contoured abs.

Wow.

"That was a good idea," he said, then cocked his head at me when he noticed I was checking him out and gave me a smug grin.

My cheeks burned, and I cursed my fair skin as I nodded my head in agreement. He leaned toward me, invading my personal space, and I held my breath.

"You have a little bit of sauce right here," he said, his voice husky as he touched the corner of his own lip.

I grabbed my napkin, now even more embarrassed.

"What I wouldn't give to lick it off," he continued in a low voice, his gaze smoldering as it focused on me.

My eyes grew wide at his forward comment. It excited me in a way that made my body tingle, my blood pump faster, and brought heat to my face. The worst part was that I suddenly wished he could too. We both knew what would happen if we touched . . . but would it be worth it?

I finished wiping my mouth and set the napkin down, not breaking eye contact with him. Frozen in place, I was unsure of what the next move would be.

The truth was that I completely adored everything about Ryder. I loved his sexy, mysterious side when we were alone, and his charming side like when he befriended the popular group. I even respected his cold side, when he tried to shut his feelings off to the world, because I knew what he was really like underneath. I was completely, one hundred percent a Ryder Essen fan, and I only hoped and prayed that whatever I would read later in his journal wouldn't destroy those feelings growing inside me.

I also wondered if he found out, would he forgive the invasion of his privacy?

A little rattled, I was the first to break eye contact. "What should we do now?"

Ryder raised his eyebrows at my question. "I know what I'd like to do," he said with a mischievous smile. "But I need to behave."

Instead of kissing me, he wrapped me in his arms. It was so easy to let my head fall to his chest. I snuggled in, listening to his heartbeat and enjoying the rhythmic rise and fall of his chest; it made me feel safe. It felt like I belonged here with him.

Eventually I leaned back, and he looked down on me with what looked like longing. I felt the same way, but we hadn't discussed our feelings for each other, or even established that we were really dating yet.

To me, this seemed like the perfect time to broach the subject.

"So . . . ," I said, letting the word hang there.

"What's up, Vi?" he said playfully. "You look like you're going to say something important." His lips curved into a beautiful smile, which made me want to kiss him.

I had never approached a guy about something like this before. The relationship with Adam just happened, and he was always the one talking how he felt about me. The way I felt for Ryder made me nervous, and to bring it up made that even worse, but I was dying to know where I stood with him.

"So," I started again, looking up at him through my eyelashes. "This thing between us, is it a serious thing from your viewpoint?" As I stumbled through the last sentence, he smiled and my stomach clenched.

Thing? I silently scolded myself. I could have picked a better word.

"I was just curious," I added as I pushed my plate away. "You know, with Raeann and Adam hanging in the mix."

Ryder leaned one arm against the bar top, resting his right foot on the lowest rung of my stool. My knees brushed against his inner thigh, and I steeled myself not to move.

"It's time for a serious conversation, is it?" he said, giving me a teasing smile, thoroughly enjoying my uneasiness.

I shrugged. "Just curious," I repeated.

"Well, I'd like to call you my girlfriend, but I think you need to sort out your feelings for Adam first." His expression grew serious. "Let's just say that it wouldn't be good if you and I were dating, and Adam Price kissed you secretly in the woods."

There was a dangerous glint in his eyes that caused my heart to speed up. I believed every word that came out of his mouth. He wasn't bluffing.

"I don't want to be with Adam," I said quickly. "What I want more than anything right now is to be with you." Feeling empowered, I held my head high, standing my ground. I'd finally had said how I truly felt about Ryder, and I wasn't taking it back. The ball was in his court now.

He gave me a warm smile. "All right, Vi, let's make it official then. Okay with you?"

Thrilled inside, I grinned back and nodded.

"Come sit with me," he said and went over to sit on the couch, then patted the spot next to him.

I walked over to him and sat down comfortably in his arms.

Once I'd settled in, he asked, "Vi, are you happy now?"

What kind of question was that? Was he referring to the fact that our relationship was now official?

"Yes," I said simply. I wasn't lying; it was partly the truth. I was happy to finally know where we stood. Although I still felt wary because of the last vision we experienced, and shivered unexpectedly just thinking about it.

Ryder nodded, then flipped on the TV and reached for my hand, sliding his fingers between mine. My hand fit perfectly in his gloved one, and we relaxed for the next couple of hours. Most couples our age would probably spend time like this making out, but we weren't a normal couple.

At that thought, I sighed, and he responded by pulling me a little closer. I wished it could be more.

The time with Ryder flew by, and I startled when my phone rang. I pulled it from my pocket and answered with a quick hello.

"Vi."

"Vick." I sat up, pulling out of Ryder's arms as I glanced at the wall clock, my heart sinking when I realized how late it was. My stepbrother was going to kill me.

"Do you have any idea what time it is," Vick demanded.

Shit. "Vick, I'm sorry I lost track of time. I'll see you soon."

"Vi, don't hang—"

I pressed the END button, cutting Vick off.

"I have to go." I glanced at Ryder, whose attention was focused on his phone as he read a text. His brow was crinkled as he scrolled through the message.

"I'll walk you out," he said, slipping his phone into his pocket. "It's hard to text with these gloves on."

But he didn't take them off. Instead he untangled his legs from mine and got up, then turned and pulled me swiftly from the couch

169

and flush with his body, surprising me with the full-on contact. He wrapped me in his arms and held me tightly for a moment, then sighed before dropping several kisses on my hair.

I smiled at the warm feeling flooding my chest. Then I reluctantly pulled away and went to retrieve my purse from where it was hanging on the back of the barstool, and followed him to the door.

"What are your plans for tomorrow?" I asked, and Ryder looked at me a little oddly but said nothing at first.

As we walked toward the front door, my mind whirled. Here we go again, I thought. I was his girlfriend now, right? Then it shouldn't have been thought of as a strange question. Maybe he just wasn't used to how things worked when you were a couple.

"Aren't you working?" he finally asked.

"Yeah, I am. But not for the whole day."

"Text me when you're done," he said as we reached his front door and he pulled me close for another lingering kiss on the top of my head.

I wrapped my arms around him, enjoying the warmth of his body. Then I pushed thoughts of his body right out of my head.

"Good night, Ryder."

"'Night, Vi."

• • •

After leaving Ryder's, I drove home as fast as I could, even speeding a little. When I got home, I found Vick sitting on the couch with one of his friends.

I was surprised to see the new guy that Vick had called out for saying I was hot. His eyes were clearly focused on me as I kicked off my shoes. I wasn't sure why, but my eyes kept going back to him, taking in his sandy hair cropped short on the sides and curls on the top that were a little longer. He was good-looking, I had to admit.

"Vi, where were you?" Vick's eyes glimmered with anger.

"I was hanging with Ryder. I didn't realize that it was one o'clock already."

At the mention of Ryder's name, the new guy narrowed his eyes, clearly unhappy. Or maybe I was just imagining it.

"Who's your friend?" I said to Vick, changing the subject and catching him off guard.

Vick glanced next to him. "Jase," he said quietly.

I glared at the guy; he just rubbed me the wrong way for some reason.

"Good night, Vick," I said before Vick could grill me any further, and heading up to my room.

"We'll talk tomorrow then," he called up after me.

Determined not to let my little run-in with Vick spoil my mood, I plopped down on my bed and pulled out my phone to text Callie. It was too late to call her.

Me: Guess what? Ryder and I are officially a couple! I'm so happy!

It didn't take long for her to respond. Knowing Callie, she was probably still talking to Henry.

Callie: Wow, that is so exciting! I knew you two would eventually end up together. Adam is going to be disappointed.

I frowned at her concern for Adam. He was the one who was breaking the rules.

Me: I know.

Dealing with Adam tomorrow would be hard. I needed to tell him that I was dating Ryder now, and hoped that would give him the incentive he needed to leave me alone.

I decided to put that thought out of my mind and pulled the journal out of my purse. I held it to my chest, anxious at the thought of what I was really going to do. Opening this book was going to change everything, but I had to know what Ryder was hiding from me.

Chapter 18

I lay down on my stomach, setting the book in front of me, and opened the cover to the first page.

July 7th – I had a meeting with the Richtenburgs today. They've asked me to keep an eye on a girl located an hour from where I live. They said everything had to be carefully documented, but nothing digital, since it could be hacked. I'm not one for longhand or even journals, but I don't have a choice in the matter. So I'll keep this journal, then send them reports via snail mail later. Apparently the girl has the characteristic they're looking for. I'm on my way to find her now.

I wondered if he was still with Raeann at this point. It was over the summer, so the girl he referred to must be me.

July 9th – I found the girl. She isn't at all what I expected. I watch from a distance and observe her daily routines as well as the activities of her family members. I'm not sure why the Richtenburgs wanted all this information, but I know enough not to ask questions. I wanted to find a reason to talk to the girl, to see if I can figure out why they're so interested in her, but I'm under strict orders not to allow her to see me.

My heart sped up but I turned the page, hoping to get more insight.

July 10th – I'm back in my hometown. I had to report my findings to the Richtenburgs and confirm the girl's whereabouts. I also handed in my logs on her daily routines and her family's. The only thing I kept to myself was a picture I took of her. I couldn't bring myself to let go of the only thing I had as a reminder. I asked them when I could see her again or if I would get to meet her. They told me that it would all come in time. I'm not good at being patient, so they'd better hurry up. Raeann is getting jealous since I've been talking about the girl lately. I guess I just can't get her out of my head.

The next entry didn't pick up again until six weeks later.

August 31st – I went to see my aunt today; she's helping me out. She told me that the girl will seek us out soon and I'll get a chance to meet her. I'm anxious for the day to come. I finally broke up with Raeann. She's a selfish, psychotic bitch and is trying to make my life a living hell. Who wants a relationship with someone you can't physically touch without repercussions? The Richtenburgs are still biding their time about the girl. I've learned that her father is part of the Silvercrest Clan. So her joining us will be inevitable, but as of right now she remains unclaimed.

Unclaimed? My mind was spinning. What the heck did that mean? And who were the Richtenburgs?

I turned the page again, having to squint to decipher Ryder's sloppy handwriting. He did say in the beginning that he wasn't much for writing longhand, though.

September 15th – The girl came into the store today for a reading about some guy. I'm not sure how I missed the guy with all my research. It must have really been kept on the down low. I'm afraid I was a little rude to her. I'm not sure why I act the way I do sometimes. I suppose it's just easier hiding the real me from the world.

My chest felt tight. He *was* talking about me. It unnerved me to think that Ryder had been spying on me and my family. Curious, I flipped the page and found the rest of the journal blank, except for a log of my comings and goings for the last several weeks. *Creepy.*

Who are the Richtenburgs? The question kept repeating in my head. Frustrated, I slammed the book shut and tossed it into the drawer of my nightstand, then glanced at the clock. It was almost two.

Exhausted, I snuggled up under my covers and closed my eyes. Even though I was tired, I couldn't sleep. All night long I just tossed and turned until my sheets were a tangled mess.

• • •

Hours later, I finally gave up and looked at the clock again. It was almost six in the morning, so I decided to get into the bath and soak in some lavender. Once the tub was full and steaming, I squeezed my eyes shut as I submerged my body until nothing but my head was above the water. I let out a sigh of relief. The water felt good, but my stomach was still in knots.

I was thoroughly confused. I cared about Ryder and I cared about Adam. A confrontation with Adam was inevitable today, and I didn't want to have to deal with it just yet. And I was worried about Ryder. He would eventually discover that the journal was missing, and if he didn't guess who took it right away, he would soon enough.

Letting out a deep sigh, I washed up slowly, taking my time to relax and let go of my worries. When I finished, I toweled off and walked back into my room, feeling free and refreshed. My hair fell in a tangle of wet ringlets, even though I had wrung them out as best as I could. They clung to my bare back, making tiny rivulets run down my moist skin.

I had just shut the bathroom door and taken a few steps toward my closet when a gloved hand covered my mouth, and I was yanked back against a warm body so I was flush with every inch of him. Pinned tightly, I could neither scream nor move. I felt vulnerable, not only because I couldn't defend myself, but because I didn't have a scrap of clothing on me.

He bent his head forward, his breath tickling my ear. "Don't scream," Ryder said in a low voice.

I was angry as hell but I wouldn't scream, so I nodded my head. When he let go, I kept my promise, but I ignored him and went straight to my closet. Furious, I pulled out my clothes, trying to ignore the fact that his gaze roamed my naked body freely, scorching my backside as I dressed quickly.

"You've got some nerve," I said as I tied my sneakers. "Ryder, I wasn't even dressed." I finally turned to look at him.

He stood a few feet away, his arms crossed over his chest, his eyes narrowed, mirroring my own anger.

"Where is it?" he demanded.

I rolled my eyes, not bothering to deny it, then shot back, "If you answer my questions, I'll tell you."

He shook his head and said in a low, dangerous voice, "Violet, you're in no position to negotiate," as he stepped closer to me.

Ryder was right; I couldn't force him to talk, and the journal wasn't mine. He stood in front of me, staring me down with barely controlled anger.

Defiant, I glared back at him. "I didn't ask for a boyfriend that was going to keep secrets from me."

Yet that was part of Ryder's allure. I knew he wasn't like Adam, and that was probably part of the reason I fell for him—because the two were so different. Adam would have begged for forgiveness at this point, and Ryder would never; he was too proud to do something like that.

"Violet, hand over the journal. I need it," he said through clenched teeth.

I grabbed the front of his T-shirt between my hands and tugged. "What does being claimed have to do with anything? Who are the Richtenburgs?" I pleaded.

Ryder hesitated and looked away, once again refusing to let me in.

"Forget it." I sidestepped around him, then reached into the nightstand drawer and grabbed the book, chucking it at him as hard as I could.

He had good reflexes and caught it easily. Even though it was unreasonable, it made me that much more angry at him. I left the room and went downstairs quickly, Ryder right on my heels as I ran through the front door and out into the rain.

I stood for a moment, barely noting the awful weather. My clothes were immediately soaked and I still didn't care; my hair was already wet from my shower anyway. The clouds were an angry dark gray, matching my mood. It was cold out, and I wasn't sure what I was doing, but my emotions had taken over. I felt angry, frustrated, and alone.

Ryder's hands grasped my shoulders. When I turned around, I saw that he was soaked as well. He scowled at me, his lips a hard, tight line as he tossed the book into the Tahoe and motioned for me to get in.

"No," I yelled over the rain that pelted us. Unleashing my fury, I shoved him away from me and shouted, "Go home," then took off running down the sidewalk.

"Vi, don't be stupid! You're going to catch a cold!" Ryder yelled after me.

I ignored him, irrationally wishing he would chase after me. It was something that Adam would have done, but Ryder was nothing like him. Behind me, I heard Ryder slam his door shut and the squeal of his tires on the wet pavement as he sped away from me, and I pumped my arms, lengthening my stride so I could put as much distance between him and me as possible.

I tried running my sorrow, heartache, and pain out of me. My muscles in my legs were aching and burning with every step I forced myself to take. I ran until I was exhausted, then turned and walked home, still as lonely and confused.

• • •

By the time I finally made it home the rain had stopped, but I was soaked, cold, and starving. I tried to be quiet when re-entering the house, but my shoes were wet and simultaneously squeaked and squished as I walked.

An early riser, Vick was already up and about. He met me in the foyer, leaning against the wall as he watched me tug off my wet shoes. "Vi, why were you outside in this kind of weather?" When I simply shrugged, he studied me for a moment, then said, "Come on. I'll make you some breakfast."

"Just let me get changed and I'll be right down." I went up to my room and stripped, then put on a clean pair of jeans and light blue hoodie.

Vick was pulling together ingredients when I met him in the kitchen, and from the looks of things, homemade pancakes were on the menu for breakfast. Cooking was Vick's passion; he was going to culinary school to be a chef.

176

After helping myself to a glass of orange juice, I took a seat on a stool and watched him make the pancake batter. Trying to sound casual, I asked, "Have you talked to Dad?"

Vick glanced up as he stirred. "Yeah, he had to go in early this morning for rounds, and I saw him before he left." He stopped and checked the temperature on the griddle, then asked, "Why were you outside walking in the middle of the storm?"

"Because, dear brother, this is my life." I waved my hand in the air. "Nothing but one big storm cloud. It seemed appropriate to walk around in one. Or run in it, for that matter," I said sadly, not caring if he thought his sister was losing it.

Vick paused for a second but didn't turn around. Focusing on the stove, he poured perfectly round circles onto the hot griddle and said over his shoulder, "You know what they say? For every storm cloud there's always—"

"A silver lining," I finished for him in a weary voice. I'd heard the saying many times before from his father, and it only made me sad to hear it now. Everything was so confusing for me right now, and I was beginning to feel that my storm cloud intended to make itself a permanent fixture in my life.

"It can't be that bad," Vick said. He flipped a pancake higher than I would have dared, then punched his fist in the air as it landed perfectly. Glancing up to be sure I appreciated his pancake-flipping prowess, he grinned at me and said, "Surely nothing a little butter and syrup can't fix."

I laughed at him, smiling for the first time that morning. Vick always knew how to make my bad days better. And three buttery, syrupy pancakes later, I did feel like the day wouldn't be all that bad.

Today was Sunday, my last free day before I had to return to school and deal with JP, Raeann, and Ryder . . . none of whom I really wanted to see. Wondering what was going to happen this Friday was also in the back of my mind.

It was going to be a long week.

* * *

When I pulled up in the Prices' drive that afternoon, the garage was wide open and empty. The only car there was Adam's, which meant

177

his mom wasn't home to run interference and keep him from pestering me. As if on cue, he came out of his house just as I got out of my car.

Crap.

Not wanting to be rude, I waved but didn't stop, heading straight for the shed. The weather was still overcast but it wasn't raining anymore. I figured I'd pull weeds in the garden or clip the hedges.

"Hi, Violet," Adam called out as he walked over to me. He was wearing dark jeans and a white undershirt with a black unzipped sweatshirt. "How are things with Ryder?" he asked with an edge in his voice.

I kept walking and Adam fell in step with me. "Um, he's probably pretty angry with me right now."

Just because Adam and I weren't seeing each other anymore didn't mean that he wasn't still one of my best friends. After all, I'd shared everything with him before, and it felt natural to confide in him now. Although I was pretty sure that Ryder would disapprove.

Adam slid his hands into his jeans pockets and glanced my way. "Why, what seems to be the trouble?"

"I kind of borrowed his journal, and he was pretty mad when he found out," I said, thinking back to how he'd shut me out again.

Adam chuckled and shook his head. "Really? People still write in those things?"

I shrugged. "Yeah. Nothing I can do about it now."

As we reached the shed, he glanced at me, apparently gauging my mood because he changed the subject. "So, what's on the agenda for you today?"

"Weeding and clipping," I said as I unlocked the shed. "Where are your parents?"

"Out of town until tonight." He grasped my arm, his expression hopeful as he asked, "Want some help? I feel like we haven't really spent any time together and, well, you said we could be friends. If that's the only thing I can have, I'll take it."

"Thanks for understanding, Adam."

When I grinned up at him, he caught my hand in his and gave it a little squeeze. He looked down at me, his blue eyes so familiar and his affection so genuine, it pinched at my heart. I dropped his hand and said, "I think I can handle it myself, though. You should go do whatever it is you had planned today."

"Olivia and I were going to go down to the lake to check on the Stop and Shop."

I forced a smile on my face. "Sounds like fun," I said a little too brightly.

Adam rested a hand on my shoulder. "You know, Olivia wouldn't mind if you wanted to come hang with us."

"No, that's okay. I have plenty to keep my mind busy. Thanks, though," I added quickly.

He gave me another one of his gorgeous smiles. "Catch you later," he called as he jogged away across the lawn.

When I was done pulling weeds, I drove by Callie's house but her car wasn't there. So I decided to drive by the Stop and Shop, and sure enough, her car was in the parking lot. It looked like a few kids were hanging out there, but I didn't feel like being social.

With a sigh, I turned my car around and headed home. Maybe some studying would take my mind off my problems.

• • •

Vick and his friend Jase were in the living room when I walked in the door.

In a bitchy mood, I said, "Jase, I didn't think you'd be back," as I kicked off my shoes. I couldn't understand why Vick kept having him over; the guy seemed like a real jerk.

"Vi!" Vick said sharply, giving me a warning look.

Jase smirked and raised an eyebrow at me as he said, "Vick said I'm welcome here anytime."

Frowning, I looked to my brother for confirmation, but Vick just shrugged his shoulders. Before I could say anything else, Jase surprised me by asking, "How about a game of pool?"

179

He was the last person I wanted to hang out with; the guy made me uneasy. But then I remembered the odd look on his face when I'd mentioned Ryder's name before, and my curiosity won out.

"All right," I said hesitantly. "I'm breaking, though."

As Jase followed me down to the basement, Vick called out to us, "I'll make us some popcorn. Then I've got the winner!"

"Sounds good!" I yelled back to him.

"How do you know my brother?" I asked casually, giving Jase a once-over as he selected a pool cue from the holder.

He gave me a crooked smile as he chalked the tip. "From the court." Vick frequently played basketball at the neighborhood court, and since he made friends easily, it didn't surprise me in the least.

After racking the balls, I chalked my cue and took aim to break. Jase's constant scrutiny unnerved me, and I felt stiff as I took my shot. I'd had a lot of practice, though, and the balls broke beautifully, landing me two solids. Inside, I was jumping for joy, but I just gave Jase a smug look I had to eat when I missed my next shot that bounced off the corner pocket.

"Nice. Looks like you've had some practice." He leaned over to eye his first shot, his muscles flexing underneath his black T-shirt.

"Thanks," I said as he sank a stripe in the corner pocket. As he lined up his next shot, I racked my brain to come up with a natural way to bring up Ryder in the conversation.

"The game of pool takes strategic finesse." He bounced the cue ball off the sidewall and sank a stripe into the middle pocket, then took aim for his third shot.

Quickly, before I lost my nerve, I blurted out, "Do you know Slade Essen?"

Jase flinched, scratching the cue ball. He glanced up at me, a glimmer of anger in his eyes, and I wasn't sure if it was because I mentioned Ryder's name or because he screwed up.

"Yes," he said calmly, then gestured toward the table. "Your shot."

180

"What do you know about him?" I asked, leaning against the table. "When I mentioned his name before, you looked like you might know him."

He narrowed his eyes at me, his voice tight as he said, "Violet, I'm not from around here but I practically grew up with him, and I know he shouldn't be here." Seeming agitated, he tossed his pool stick from hand to hand as he waited for me to take my shot.

"Is that why you're here? Because he is?" I asked innocently, then bent over and placed the cue ball before I took aim.

"Aren't you a curious little thing." He closed the space between us, studying me intently, which sent a little chill down my spine.

I took a deep breath to steady myself, then deliberately sank the eight ball to end the game.

"Game over. You win," I said, giving him what I hoped looked like a natural smile as I put my cue stick back in the holder.

"You're quite the challenge." Jase cocked his head to one side, eyeing me as he laid his pool cue on the table and I turned to head back upstairs.

Before I could move, his hand shot out and he grabbed my arm firmly. "Don't get me wrong, I like to win," he said with a dangerous smile. "But not like that." I glanced down pointedly at his tight grip, but he didn't release me, just pulled me an inch closer as he said in a low voice, "Are you sure I can't interest you in another game?"

Annoyed, I yanked my arm from his grip, and grimaced when I saw the white impressions his fingers had left. Although he didn't really hurt me, Jase was definitely making me uncomfortable. Sure, Ryder liked to invade my personal space, but Jase's behavior was downright creepy.

"Come on," he whispered. "Why don't we make a little wager?"

Although I didn't have any more answers about how Jase knew Ryder, I had to assume he was part of a clan. His interest in me was strange, not to mention inappropriate, and I didn't feel safe around him.

Enough is enough.

181

As he reached out to brush his fingers along my cheekbone, I jerked away from him and said tightly, "I'm not interested in playing any games with you," then turned on my heel and ran up the stairs.

"You're up, Vick!" I yelled as I passed the kitchen, the smell of popcorn wafting through the hallway.

There was no sense in saying anything to Vick about Jase's weird behavior; he'd just think I was overreacting to normal teasing. So I went upstairs to my room, shut the door, and locked it. Just to be sure, I also locked the door between Vick's room and our shared bathroom.

Feeling a little better, I flopped on my bed and called Callie.

"Hey!" she said as she answered on the second ring. "What's up?"

"Not a whole lot. What are you doing?" I turned over on my back.

"Just hanging with Henry at the Stop and Shop. Why don't you come down?"

"Nah, not in the mood," I said glumly.

"Too bad. Ryder's here," she said in a singsong voice.

"What's he doing?" I asked cautiously.

"Oh, he's talking with some girls from school."

Throwing an arm over my eyes, I said, "Not my problem anymore."

"What?" she shrieked. "I thought you were a couple now."

"We've had a fight," I said unhappily.

"Violet, if you like him, you should make an effort."

I heaved a sigh. "I'm just too tired to deal with boy drama. I'll see you tomorrow."

Then I hung up before Callie could argue with me. I was a confused wreck. Ryder hadn't explained anything to me, and I wasn't sure where we stood. Jase had something against Ryder, and apparently something against me as well. And then there was Raeann, her awful mother, and JP.

Suddenly tired, I closed my eyes, giving in to the temptation of drowning out my thoughts. Tomorrow was soon enough to address the Jase thing with Ryder.

Chapter 19

The next morning I put on my armor—a black hoodie and black jeans with matching sunglasses. I looked like I was attending a funeral, and felt like it was my own.

Inside my locker was a package wrapped in pretty purple paper and tied with a cream-colored ribbon. Inside I found a carefully folded silver dress, my costume for Friday night, but no card. Ryder must have wrapped it.

I tossed the box back into the bottom of my locker, grateful for Ryder's thoughtfulness, but not wanting a reminder of what would happen to me Friday night at the party. And I didn't want to think about how Ryder was able to get into my locker.

"Well, hello, Violet."

I rolled my eyes before turning around to see JP standing behind me. "What do you want, JP? You only talk to me when you're up to something."

JP held up his hands, palms out, and said urgently, "Listen, Violet, just hear me out. I know we don't like each other. But I really like Raeann, and I know you said she was using me, but I really want to try to win her over. And since you're in all of her classes, I was hoping you could help me out." He paused, his expression serious. "I know you have no reason to want to help me, since I totally screwed everything up with you and Adam. But if you could look past all that, I'd really appreciate it."

I peered up at him, taking in his puppy-dog eyes and his pleading expression. He actually seemed sincere, something I'd never seen before since he was usually either picking on me or otherwise making my life miserable. Maybe if I helped JP, it would lessen the animosity between us.

"All right," I said with a sigh. "What do you want me to do?"

"Yes!" he exclaimed, making a fist and happily thrusting it in the air.

Embarrassed, I pulled his arm down. "Careful, people will wonder what's going on." But I couldn't help but smile as well.

"Okay, so here's what I was thinking." He pulled out a little white box and opened it carefully. Inside was a necklace with a small teardrop diamond pendant.

I let out a soft whistle. "Is that real?"

"What do you think?" he asked, frowning.

"Okay, I get it," I said sarcastically. "You don't buy cheap jewelry."

"Not if you want to impress someone like Raeann," JP said as he handed the box to me. "So if you could just hand it to her and make polite conversation, I'd really appreciate it."

"Hey, guys!" Adam popped up out of nowhere and draped an arm around both of us. "It's weird to see you two talking and not yelling," he said with a raised eyebrow. "What's up?"

JP gave him a smirk. "Would you believe that Violet and I have put aside our differences for once and are trying to get along?"

"No," Adam and I said in unison.

JP laughed. "All right, fine," he said, then filled Adam in as we made our way to my first class.

I spotted Ryder walking toward us down the hall, and nearly tripped over my own feet. Everything around me faded away as I focused on the hard look he leveled on me, which made my stomach flip. He took in Adam's arm draped over my shoulders, and his eyes turned even colder.

When I stiffened and took a steadying breath, Adam stopped listening to JP and gave me a long sideways glance.

"See you in third period," I said, then veered down the hallway to my first class.

I took my seat and it wasn't long before Raeann joined me. She was all decked out in pink today, wearing a pink vest, white tank, pink skirt, and pink heels. I rolled my eyes, and then remembered I had to be nice. She was my sister, after all, even though she had no idea I knew this.

Catching her eye, I smiled and said, "I'm excited about your costume party." The funny thing was, I didn't have to fake the smile because I was actually excited.

"I am too," she said, but the odd look in her eyes gave me pause.

"Oh, I almost forgot." I pulled the little box from my backpack and handed it to her.

"What's this?" She looked at it curiously.

"It's from JP," I said. "He asked me to give it to you."

"Really?" After opening it, she squealed, "This is beautiful!" and beamed with pleasure. "I'll have to thank him."

"Girls!" Mr. Johnston called to us and gave us a disapproving glare. "I may have to separate you two."

Raeann and I both sat up straight and paid attention, but I silently prayed that he would. It would at least save me from making small talk.

Instead I tuned him out, doodling little circles in my notebook as I thought about the two guys who were making my life difficult. I felt better about the situation with Adam. I still cared for him a lot, but he was making it easier on me instead of harder on me now, which proved how much he really did care.

Ryder, on the other hand, was a different story. I was nervous about seeing him in third period. I still didn't know what the odd key was for, and that was bugging me big-time. I thought for sure it would have been mentioned in his journal, but it wasn't.

And then there was Raeann. I still couldn't figure out her angle in all this. Surely she wouldn't just move here for some guy she used to date? Or maybe she moved here because we were sisters, but since she hadn't let on that we were related yet, maybe not.

I adjusted my sunglasses and frowned. I might not have all the pieces to the puzzle yet, but I soon would.

186

Chapter 20

My worrying continued through the morning. By the time third period rolled around, I was a wreck.

I was one of the first in the classroom, and Adam was right behind me. After dropping his backpack at his own desk, he perched himself on the edge of mine. It was nice that everyone knew we were friends now, that it wasn't weird for people to see us talking anymore. With an internal sigh, I remembered I had Ryder to thank for my acceptance into the "in crowd."

"Are you sure you're okay?" He leaned toward me, pinning me with that mesmerizing blue gaze of his, trying to see my eyes, but I knew he couldn't see anything behind my shades.

"I'm fine," I said, sinking a little lower into my chair.

"Hey, Olivia," I said as she walked up to us and gave Adam a hug.

"Hi, Violet," she said with a huge grin. "All set for Friday? Are you and Ryder getting excited?"

At the mention of Ryder's name, I got queasy again. Olivia had no idea we were having a falling-out right now, and Adam only had a hint of what was going on. Before I could respond, I was interrupted.

"We sure are," Ryder said as he walked past us. There was a slight edge to his voice, although nobody else would probably pick up on it. He took his seat next to me and let his book fall heavily to the desk.

When did he get here?

"That's great! We're excited too," Olivia exclaimed. "Come on, Adam. Let's take our seats, class is going to start soon." She gave him a tug and he stood up, but gave my hand a little squeeze before he went.

I stared at my hand long after his touch was gone. Then I glanced at Ryder to find I wasn't the only one who had taken notice.

187

I shouldn't have to justify my friendship with Adam; a friend could squeeze another friend's hand, couldn't they? It probably just bugged Ryder because he knew how Adam really felt about me. If I were in Ryder's position, it would probably bother me too if he were still close friends with Raeann. Feeling bad for him, I felt I should speak up.

"Ryder, it didn't mean anything," I said quietly, even though the teacher still hadn't shown up yet.

"I need to talk with you. Get your shit and follow me." His voice was hard with anger, and I could tell that he was barely able to rein in his rage, barely in control.

My stomach knotted up as I picked up my backpack and stiffly followed Ryder out of the room. I didn't know where we were going; I just kept following in the wake of his silence. It felt like a heavy curtain had fallen around us, while butterflies swarmed my stomach. When he headed outside the school and toward the student parking lot, I realized he was leading me to his Tahoe.

Ryder was dressed in black today too. His blond hair was a nice contrast with the dark clothing. His button-down shirt was undone at the top and looked extremely sexy, but I couldn't let myself get distracted by this. His normally full, sensual lips were firmly pressed into a menacing straight line. He really was pissed.

When we reached the Tahoe, he didn't open the door for me like he'd done before. Instead, he climbed in on his side and waited with his hands on the steering wheel. For a second, I contemplated bolting for my car, but then decided it might just make things worse for me in the end. So I reluctantly opened the passenger door and climbed in.

I shot Ryder a sideways glance when I finally managed to shut the door. He was tense, angry; he wouldn't even look at me. We sat in silence for a moment as I wondered what he was going to say. My cheeks burned, and I wasn't sure if it was anticipation of our impending conversation or from the warmth of the truck, but I rolled my sleeves of my sweatshirt up to my elbows. Any little relief was welcome at this point.

"Violet, how did you find my secret compartment?" His voice was coldly in check. The depths of the coldness emanating from him sent shivers through me. It unnerved me how his tone could affect me in such a way.

When I answered, my voice was small. "I found it when I was waiting for you to finish up with Raeann." Then I slowly looked up from my fidgeting hands.

"Take the damn sunglasses off!" he yelled.

I was dumbfounded. Before I could reach up, his hand shot out and ripped the shades off my face, then he tossed them angrily into the backseat.

"Ryder, I'm sorry," I said, feeling exposed without the protection of my sunglasses. "I shouldn't have taken the journal, but you haven't been exactly generous with information either. This is my life we're talking about, and you have information I need."

He kept his mouth shut, conceding my point, then ran his hand through his hair in frustration. "Listen, Violet." He turned and our eyes locked. His voice was still angry and sharp, but the coldness in his icy silver eyes had dissipated a little. "I don't do well with sharing. So if you're going to keep Adam as a friend, you'd better make sure he knows to keep his hands to himself."

A whisper of relief washed through me. He was at least talking to me, so that was progress. Deciding to take advantage of it, I asked, "Ryder, who are the Richtenburgs?"

His eyes widened and his face grew serious. "They're the ruling family of the Manipulators, and have been for generations. They try to keep the other clans in check, because having special powers is seductive. Sometimes people go crazy with it, drawing attention to us, and they try to make sure that doesn't happen. What they say goes." His voice gentled. "Look, I'm not the bad guy here, okay? I'll do whatever I can to protect you, but I need you to trust me and leave this be. Please, for me, don't go pushing for answers yet."

Trust you? Yeah, right.

He suddenly reached over and grabbed my hand. My heart sped up, and I flinched anxiously at his touch. Even when he wore gloves, I still had a strong reaction. How wonderful it would be to be touched by him, and not have to endure the visions that came along with it.

"What's this?" Ryder stared at my arm, then held it up. Upon closer inspection I saw faint blue marks of three fingers, and it dawned on me that it was from when Jase grabbed my arm.

"Oh . . . it's nothing really." I shrugged, and his eyes looked on with dismay. Ryder was so complicated; furious at me one second, and worried about me the next. I was hoping he would let it go, but the stubborn look on his face suggested otherwise.

"Who did that, Violet?" he demanded, still holding my arm.

"My brother's friend Jase was trying to keep me from leaving, I think. I'm sure he didn't do it on purpose. He wanted to play pool, but I didn't want to play with him anymore, so I sank the eight ball and he wasn't happy with me."

"Jase?" Ryder's voice was quiet and low as he squinted at me. He slowly released my arm. "Jase has been in your house?"

"Yep, he said he knew you, and that you practically grew up together."

"Yeah, I know him. We both go to school together in New York." He leaned closer, an edge in his tone as he added, "He's a multi, Violet."

Thinking back, I couldn't remember what color eyes Jase had. "A multi? What's that again?"

"Multis belong to a clan that tries to claim unclaimed members of other clans. They're renegades, and they're dangerous. They don't follow the rules." He gave me an impatient look, then said emphatically, "You can't stay at your house anymore. It's not safe for you there."

"Are you crazy? Ryder, my stepbrother would worry, not to mention my stepdad. You can't tell me what to do. This has nothing to do with you," I insisted, my voice rising.

"Everything you do involves me, especially where your safety is concerned. You're unclaimed, don't you see?" He wiped a hand over his eyes. "Shit. I've already said too much."

I sat back in my seat and crossed my arms stubbornly. "Dad won't notice, but I won't worry my brother."

Ryder glared at me. "Tell him you have a big project to work on, and that you're going to stay at a friend's house for the next few days. Just until I can get something figured out."

"Screw you, Ryder."

I jerked open the truck door and jumped down, leaving my sunglasses in my hurry. There was no way I'd let him dictate how I was going to spend my time. Thoroughly pissed off, I slung my backpack over my shoulder and stomped toward my car on the other side of the parking lot.

Ryder had definitely crossed the line this time. It was nice that he wanted to protect me, but this was way overboard. My stepbrother would flip if he knew Ryder wanted me to stay with him, even for just a few days.

I heard the truck before I saw it. From the corner of my eye, I could see Ryder inching his truck along beside me with the window down. "Vi, please be reasonable," he begged.

"I am being reasonable," I huffed. "You're the one who isn't. You want me to stay with you just because my brother's friend is a multi? To top it off, you won't explain why? Just leave me alone. I'll see you Friday, and not sooner."

My mind was made up. I needed a break from the overbearing, sexy, and secretive Ryder Essen. Ignoring him as he idled nearby, I jumped into my car and stepped on the gas.

At home I turned my phone on silent, locked the door, then curled up in my bed and cried myself to sleep.

In that moment, I knew I was a goner. No matter what foolish things Ryder did . . . my heart would never belong to anyone else.

Chapter 21

Feeling like a spectator in my own body, I made small talk with Callie. Small talk! That just wasn't me. I didn't speak to Ryder at all, and my heart was in anguish over this dilemma. Worse, he had withdrawn from me and didn't even try to speak to me, no doubt super pissed about me blowing him off.

All week, I took each day one step at a time. I went to class and pretended to listen while I doodled. Took a bathroom break. More lecturing, lunch, and so on. I put on a fake smile and made nice with everybody. I could be an actress.

It was Thursday night before the worry about what might happen to me at the party really set in. While I was in the shower, I began trembling, but I told myself that as long as I stuck by Ryder, everything would be okay. Wouldn't it?

Once I was out of the shower and dressed for bed, the need for some reassurance became overwhelming. I grabbed my phone and sent Ryder a quick text.

Me: Are we still on for tomorrow? Or are you still not talking to me? Your Guinevere

I got a kick out of my signature line, and smiled to myself as I hoped he would too. My phone buzzed, signaling an awaiting message. I opened up his text and my stomach fluttered in anticipation.

Ryder: Guinevere, yes and no. Your Lancelot

Although I could practically hear his response, knowing his tone would be all clipped and to the point, the only problem was I didn't really understand his point. No, as in he still wasn't talking to me? Or no, he was? Surely it was a good thing the way he signed off.

Me: Lancelot, no, you're not talking to me? Or no, you are? Please be a little more specific. Your Guinevere

Me: P.S. I made it through the week with no harm coming to me . . . what a shocker!

It didn't take him long to reply.

Ryder: Guinevere, don't push my buttons with sarcasm! No, I am talking to you. You were the one who just wouldn't listen, and so far I guess you've been lucky. Lancelot

He was so exasperating sometimes. All joking aside, I really needed to ask him something. I could only hope he was more willing to share info now than the last time we talked.

Me: Why did the Richtenburgs have you keep tabs on me? Please tell me. I'm on my knees begging . . .

Maybe the imagery would help my case. I was grinning like a fool while I waited for his reply. Of course, watching my phone wasn't going to make him reply any sooner. When the familiar buzzing sound came, I fumbled with the phone, trying to hurry to read his message.

*Ryder: *Smiling and shaking my head at you!* You aren't going to distract me with that visual! No, and this is the final time I'll tell you. Leave this alone!*

Okay, Mr. Charmer himself was back. Oh, how I loved him. It was too bad I could never tell him how I really felt. Someone who was that closed off surely would be against the idea of me loving him. It made me kind of sad in a way. Did I dare rile him up at all just for fun? I entertained the idea for a minute before replying.

Me: What happened to my Lancelot? Well . . . Jase is downstairs, maybe he wouldn't mind filling the shoes?

I waited impatiently for his reply. Maybe he wouldn't think it was funny. I mean, I was only kidding. I wasn't serious, and of course Jase wasn't downstairs tonight. I was about to text him and tell him I was just joking around when my phone buzzed.

*Ryder: I don't think Jase's shoes are big enough . . . and you know what they say about big feet! *Wink* I'll talk to you tomorrow. Go to bed NOW!*

Thank God he knew I wasn't serious. He was smart, funny, and yet sometimes distant and cold, confusing as hell and dangerously sexy. Ryder was my night and day, and I loved him, all of him.

Me: Good night!

I snuggled into bed, a little disappointed I didn't hear from him again the rest of the night.

Chapter 22

Friday I woke up early, giving myself extra time to get ready for school. Today I wanted to look spectacular. I wasn't going to wear my usual hoodie, but definitely wanted the sunglasses; they were still my shield against the world.

I chose a pale blue skirt and white button-down blouse, leaving the buttons undone just enough to draw attention to myself. Going for the sexy schoolgirl look, I chose killer white sunglasses and white high-heeled boots that went up to my knees to complete the outfit. I wanted Ryder to want me the way I wanted him, and if this outfit didn't get his attention, nothing would.

After brushing out my auburn curls, I pulled some up in a clip, away from my face. The rest of my hair cascaded down my back in sweeping loose curls. Then I actually put on some makeup for a change, including a touch of light pink lip gloss that made my lips shimmer.

Once done, I glanced in the mirror one last time and was happy with the result. I pounded down the stairs excitedly, in a hurry to get to the Mustang and to school.

"Whoa, Vi."

I paused at the front door and turned to see my brother making himself a fruit smoothie for breakfast. A little self-conscious, I stopped and stammered, "Vick. I didn't see you there."

"Where's the stampede?" His eyes widened as he took in my outfit, then he grinned at me. "Just kidding. You look great, by the way."

"Thanks, Vick," I said with a smile. "See you later. Oh, I have a costume party tonight. I won't be home because I'm staying at Callie's later, so don't worry."

"All right, Vi, see you tomorrow. I'll let Dad know." He stepped over to give me a swift hug, and then I rushed out the door.

I shoved my sunglasses on and headed out into the early morning light. The sun was bright and the sky was clear; it was going to be a gorgeous fall day. A glimmer of anxiety threatened and I chided myself. Hoping I had nothing to worry about tonight, I pushed the thought out of my mind.

When I got to school, it was still a little early; the first bell hadn't rung yet. I found Callie, Henry, Adam, and Olivia sitting at a picnic table in the courtyard.

"Hi, Violet. Meow," Callie said, laughing. "You look gorgeous!"

"Thanks!" I gave her a hug.

Henry was talking on his phone, but he gave me a welcoming smile. Adam eyed my barely legal short skirt, then averted his eyes and mumbled a greeting.

"Hi," Olivia said with a warm smile. As Adam draped his arm casually around her shoulders, she asked, "Where's Ryder?"

"I don't know. I was hoping you'd seen him."

Ryder pulled into the parking lot, his bass thumping so loudly it drew everyone's attention before he shut it off and hopped out of his truck. Spotting me immediately, he headed in our direction, taking off his jacket as he made his way over.

I searched his face for some trace of his mood today, but his expression was shuttered. His blond hair shone in the early morning light, giving him a golden-boy appearance in his pale yellow button-down and cream khaki pants. Oh my God, he was hot! Focused entirely on me, his gaze practically scorched me, and I held my breath as he closed the now short gap between us.

"Hello, Vi." His voice seemed to caress my name in a low, seductive way as he draped his jacket around me, wrapping his arms around me and holding me close to him.

I wasn't expecting that. I leaned back against him and let myself relax. Nothing could go wrong as long as I had Ryder with me.

"Isn't this skirt a little short?" he whispered just for me to hear.

I peeked up at him through my eyelashes. "Is it grabbing your attention?"

196

"Yes," he murmured.

"Then my mission is accomplished," I said sweetly back to him, unable to hold back the smile that was trying to break free.

"You're in a playful mood," he mused.

"That I am, Lancelot," I said teasingly.

"Why, Guinevere, a mood like that can get you into a lot of trouble," he said, tickling my side and causing me to giggle out loud.

My laughter drew Adam's attention. He glared at us, his brow creased and his eyes narrowed.

Uh-oh, I knew that look. I grabbed Ryder's gloved hand and pulled him away.

I turned back and waved at our friends, calling out, "See you guys later," as we headed inside for classes.

"Ryder, are we good?" I said more seriously as we walked. "I mean, are we still, uh, you know . . ." I waved a finger between the two of us.

His silver eyes focused on me momentarily before he looked away. "Listen, Violet. Let's not have this conversation right now, okay? Everything is more complicated than I ever thought it would be, and it's best . . ." He paused, and I couldn't help but think it wasn't a good sign that he wouldn't even look at me.

"I just don't think we should discuss anything right now," he said finally.

My heart splintered at his words. It sounded like he was going to break up with me but either changed his mind or chickened out at the last minute. The happiness I'd just enjoyed disintegrated, and it took all my strength just to walk with him at my side and pretend nothing was wrong, that his words didn't mean a thing to me.

"Take it easy, Ryder," I said coolly. "You're off the hook. I didn't mean anything by it."

I stopped outside my first class and simply looked up at him, watching his expression change from perplexed to wary as he studied me. My cheeks warmed up under his intense gaze. "I better get to class. If I don't see you later, I'll see you tonight. Are you picking me up?"

"Yes, I'll be there at eight." He leaned forward slightly as if he was going to say something else, then merely shook his head and walked away.

I had a hard time concentrating for my first two class periods, a little embarrassed that I assumed Ryder and I were still a couple. My thoughts kept going round and round.

He was probably still pissed about the invasion of his privacy, and I couldn't really blame him. I knew the risk I was taking when I took his journal. How could I possibly tell him that I love him now? He practically jumped out of his skin when I just asked if we were still a couple. But he was no angel himself. He was keeping big secrets from me, resisting every opportunity to come clean and spill them.

I passed Callie in the hall just outside my third period class. She was wearing a big grin that took up a good portion of her face. "I'm so stoked for the costume party, I can hardly wait!"

"So I've noticed." Her good mood was contagious, and for a moment I forgot all about Ryder and the awkward moment we had earlier.

Adam and Olivia walked up, but he paused outside the door while she continued to her seat. He glanced at Callie and asked, "Can I steal Violet from you for a minute?"

He ran his hand through his dark hair, his blue eyes tense as they fixed on me. When Adam requested private time these days, it was never a good thing. My heart began beating rapidly as I wondered what he wanted with me. Flustered, I looked away, and noticed that Callie was frowning.

"Um, sure," she said slowly. "See you at lunch, Violet." Then she waved at me and as she walked away, shot me a look that clearly said *you'd better spill the beans later*.

When I leaned with my back against the lockers, Adam stepped close, placing one hand on the locker next to my shoulder. Uncomfortable that he was standing so close, I stiffened and glanced down the hall, hoping Ryder wasn't nearby, but the bell would ring soon and he would be along any minute.

Adam leaned forward, bringing his mouth a whisper away from my ear. His breath warmed my cheek and I tilted my head away, nervously tucking my hair behind my ear.

"What?" I said with an awkward laugh. "Are we telling secrets now?" I stepped to the side, pushing his chest slightly to give me more room. Adam's sudden seriousness was strange, and I hoped to lighten the mood.

"Listen, Violet," he said in a low voice.

"What?" I breathed out and pulled my backpack up to my chest, desperately needing a barrier.

Adam sighed. "I like being friends, don't get me wrong. I've told you that I love you and that's still true," he said, stumbling a little over the three big words.

My stomach lurched. Where was he going with this?

"I've been seriously thinking about this for some time now, even before you broke up with me." He frowned, and the sadness in his eyes cut me. "If I'd acted sooner, you'd still be mine."

"I don't understand what—" I started, but he cut me off.

"I'd give it up, Violet. Everything I have and am entitled to, just to be with you. I'd go against my parents for you."

Stunned, I gasped, then pressed my hand to my mouth as I stared at Adam. When he reached up to take my hand and held on to it, I glanced down at his lingering fingers.

"No, you can't!" I shook my head and tugged my hand from his. "I'm in love with Ryder," I blurted out, then pleaded, "Don't ruin your life because of me."

I looked up and Ryder was at standstill a few feet away from us. His eyes flashed with anger as he took in the sight of Adam and me.

No, no, no, this can't be happening to me. As if I didn't have enough problems. *God, did he hear what I said?* Mortified, I covered my face with my hands.

"Adam, please go inside," I mumbled through my fingers, then pulled my hands away from my face.

Adam frowned at me, his eyes cold with disappointment. "I'm sorry to hear that. Well, I can be patient." He shrugged and stepped past me into the classroom.

Relieved that Ryder had gone inside as well, I sucked in a deep breath. Since I couldn't dig a hole in the ground and hide inside it, I took my sunglasses out of my backpack and put them on, grateful for the instant privacy they gave me. The barrier they provided made it that much easier to be in the same room with the two guys who were making my life difficult.

I took my seat at my desk, trying to ignore the irritating noise Ryder was making behind me as he rolled a pen back and forth on his desktop. It was really annoying, but I was going to keep my mouth shut. The last thing I wanted to do was start a conversation that might lead to discussing what had happened just outside the classroom.

A moment later my phone buzzed in my pocket. When the teacher wasn't looking, I pulled it out and saw I had a text from Ryder. I held my breath as I opened the message.

> *Ryder: Violet, take off your shades! You know I hate when you wear them. I'm being blocked from seeing the real you.*

Oh, he was insufferable. When was he going to get it?

> *Me: What you see IS what you get. You should remember that.*

> *Ryder: Are you sure you want to play it that way? Because I saw quite a bit a little while ago . . .*

> *Me: Did you just see or did you hear too?*

> *Ryder: Wouldn't you like to know? ;)*

As a matter of fact, I did want to know. I glanced back at him to see he had a smirk on his face. So he was in a playful mood now. Well, at least I didn't have to worry about him being angry about what happened earlier. I shoved the phone back into my pocket and did my best to pay attention to the teacher.

A little worried, I glanced at Adam. I still cared for him and hated to hurt him, but he needed to know how I felt about Ryder. It was time Adam let me go and worked on his relationship with Olivia.

Even though I'd only known Ryder a couple of weeks, it was as if I'd known him forever. On the other hand, I knew so little about him.

The only thing I did know for sure was that I was in love with the sexy, smart, sometimes cold and distant Ryder Slade Essen more than I ever thought possible. And it felt good saying it out loud.

• • •

When third period was done, I took my time packing up my stuff. I wanted to let Adam and Olivia get a head start to our lunch table so I could be sure to sit a distance away from them. The last thing I wanted to do was to rub my feelings for Ryder in his face.

Throughout the class, Raeann had been discreetly watching us from her seat at the front of the classroom, near the door. She was always so quiet and observant in this class, which was odd. As I watched her gather her things and walk out, I let out a little sigh of relief, then picked up my backpack and headed out. I was the last one to leave.

I found Ryder leaning against the lockers just outside the classroom, waiting for me. He fell in step with me as I walked.

"You didn't have to wait for me," I told him. "I do know where the lunchroom is."

"I'm sure you do. But what kind of date would I be if I didn't walk you to lunch?"

"That's sweet of you." I glanced at him, giving him a warm smile.

"Why wouldn't I want to walk with you?" Ryder came to a sudden stop, grabbing my arm and halting me. Without a word, he pulled me a little closer, gazing down at me as if he cared . . . a lot.

I swallowed a lump in my throat. *Here goes nothing.*

"I'm just confused," I said, looking away from his handsome face.

"About what?"

"Us," I said meekly, a little embarrassed that I wasn't sure if there was even an "us" anymore.

"Vi . . ." He shook his head, then averted his eyes as he said, "I know I haven't told you much, and I can't really explain why."

"Can't? Or won't?" I said quietly.

"Both." His gaze met mine again, and his eyes were sad. "But it doesn't change the fact that I want you."

"You do?" I felt like singing. This handsome guy wanted me the way I wanted him!

"Of course I do."

"So you're still mine?" I asked hopefully.

He sighed. "For as long as you want me."

For the first time in what seemed like days, I felt a little more confident in us. But still, his words hit me hard. *For as long as you want me*. I had a bad feeling that Ryder was still holding back, hiding something important, something I wouldn't like.

As we walked, my mind churned. Why couldn't our relationship be more simple and straightforward? After all, we were just juniors in high school. Why was it always so complicated with him?

Then it occurred to me—what if his secret had something to do with Raeann? My stomach twisted at the thought.

Trying to relax, I took his gloved hand as we neared the cafeteria and changed the subject. There was still so much I didn't know about him, so I decided to try an easy question. "Ryder, do you have any hobbies?"

"Actually, I do. At one point, stalking you was a hobby of mine." He chuckled, apparently amused at his own joke.

I frowned; that wasn't funny. I remembered the picture he had taken of me this past summer, and the spying he had done for the Richtenburgs.

"Come on, for real?" I poked him on the shoulder and he brushed his shoulder flirtatiously against mine as we walked.

I sucked in a quick breath, suddenly wanting a lot more touching from Ryder than a light shoulder bump. I suppressed a hint of a smile at the thought, but Ryder noticed.

"What are you thinking right now?" he asked, slanting his eyes at me with an amused look.

God, he's gorgeous! My heart began beating wildly, and I forgot what I was going to say.

When he raised an eyebrow at me, I scrambled, trying to come up with a response. "Um, you can't change it around on me right now. You're supposed to be answering the question, not me."

Ryder looked up at the ceiling, deep in thought, then glanced my way and said, "I like to snowboard."

That was all it took for my imagination to scream into high gear. In my mind's eye, I could see Ryder wearing hot snowboarding gear and slaloming wickedly down a steep snow-covered mountain with the wind blowing his perfectly tousled golden hair.

I sucked in a breath, trying to calm myself. What was it with guys who snowboard that was so hot? I could picture Ryder sweeping me off my feet at the end of his run, then giving me a perfect kiss that would melt the cold from our lips while I wriggled impatiently in his arms for him to put me down. The smell of fresh air and evergreen trees would linger around us.

"Vi," Ryder said as he tugged at my hand. "Hello . . . earth to Vi."

"Huh?" I said guiltily. My cheeks grew hot as my daydream slipped away.

"What were you thinking?"

"Wouldn't you like to know?" I said with a mischievous smile as we entered the cafeteria.

Ryder and I fell in line with everyone else waiting to get lunch. As we built salads at the salad bar, he leaned over and whispered, "Yes, I would."

Anxious about the party tonight, I wasn't sure how much lunch I would be able to get down. I declined everything else but the salad, and watched with amazement as Ryder filled his plate with several pieces of pizza. He gave my nearly empty tray a curious look but didn't comment, for which I was grateful.

When we got to our table, Raeann was gushing about her party. "Okay, so the party starts at my house and then moves to the backyard for dancing and drinking." She smiled happily. JP had his arm around her shoulders, hanging on her every word.

I couldn't help but roll my eyes, which Callie reacted to by giving me a swift kick in the shin under the table, catching me a little harder than she intended. When I sucked in a sharp breath and pressed my lips together to keep from yelping, she widened her eyes and shrugged in apology.

Ryder rested his hand on my knee as I picked at my salad, not in the mood to eat. I glanced across the table and noticed that Adam and Olivia seemed to be getting along well. He was actually paying attention to her for a change, which I was glad to see. He was a great friend and I wanted him to be happy. I took a bite or two, listening to the lively chatter as everyone compared notes on their costumes.

"What's the matter?" Ryder asked me quietly.

"Huh? Oh. Nothing," I said and looked up.

His silver eyes seemed to smolder when I met his gaze, causing me to completely lose my train of thought. When his walls were down, his good looks and charming personality took my breath away.

"You're not hungry," he said, gesturing at my plate, and I shook my head.

Ryder wrapped his arms around me, pulling me against his chest. I relaxed into him, breathing in the scent of his cologne and crisp smell of his clean clothes. He smelled heavenly. Snuggling closer, I closed my eyes, imagining it was just the two of us at the table.

• • •

"Lunch is almost over," Ryder whispered.

Startled, I looked up to see the lunchroom nearly empty. Ryder's tray was empty, and the remains of my salad looked a bit limp.

Whoa, did I fall asleep?

I gave him a panicked look. "Where is everyone?"

"You fell asleep and I didn't have the heart to wake you," he replied softly.

My eyes widened in horror. "Oh no! That is so embarrassing," I said as I covered my face with my hands.

"It really wasn't that bad," Ryder insisted, pulling my hands down. He was gazing at me with the burning intensity of a boyfriend who longed to kiss the girlfriend he hadn't seen in months.

I held still, locked in his gaze and unable to breathe as he leaned closer, bringing his mouth close to my mine. When his lips were just a breath away, I closed my eyes, bracing for the whirlwind that would come when we touched.

Instead he took in a sharp breath, and when I looked up, his expression was almost pained as he gazed at me warily. "I'm sorry," he said quietly. "I wish there weren't repercussions to this."

Disappointment shot through me, and my face probably showed it. Then I thought back to the sentence in his journal, *Who wants a relationship with someone you can't physically touch without repercussions.* I shut my eyes tight.

"Believe me when I tell you I'd like to kiss you for hours and then some." Ryder trailed off, leaving his meaning to my imagination. "Come on, let's get going or you'll be late for class."

I didn't believe him, though, and grudgingly got up and followed him out of the cafeteria. The rest of my classes couldn't go by soon enough.

• • •

Hours later, I was pacing the living room, anxiously waiting for Ryder to come and pick me up for Raeann's costume party. As usual, Dad was at the hospital. Vick wasn't home, apparently out for the night with his friends, and for that I was grateful. If he were here, he'd tease me mercilessly.

I checked my reflection in the mirror in the hall for the millionth time. The long silver dress Ryder had ordered for me had a deep neckline that showed enough cleavage to make any guy swoon, and the back dipped low as well. The sleeves were a transparent silver material, puffy at the top and cinched at the wrist, and a long slit up the side of the dress revealed peeks of my leg when I walked. Diamond earrings and a matching necklace that had belonged to my mother added some sparkle, complementing the slim diamond clip of hers I'd used to pull back my hair. My soft auburn curls cascaded down my back, tickling my bare shoulder blades.

For the first time ever, I felt girly and very pretty. Tonight my armor was my costume, and although I missed my sunglasses a little, I felt confident enough to go without them.

Ryder's black Tahoe pulled up right at eight o'clock. I was so excited to see him that I didn't wait for him to come to the door, I just picked up my beaded evening purse and ran out the door. My silver heels slowed me down a bit as I tottered down the walkway, and I stumbled once but caught myself. I definitely wasn't cut out to be a runway model.

His expression seemed troubled as he started to exit the truck, but a smile crossed his face when he spotted me already heading his way. "Anxious much?" He walked around and opened the door for me, his voice husky as he offered, "Let me give you a boost."

I nodded and smoothed a damp palm against my dress. "I am."

Ryder put his hands on my waist and gave me a little boost into the truck. I tucked my dress under my legs as he shut the door.

"You look gorgeous, Guinevere," he said as he climbed into his side. He shifted the truck into reverse and turned to glance behind him as he backed the truck out of the driveway.

"Thank you."

I took in his outfit, appraising him appreciatively. He always looked good, but tonight he was especially attractive. His costume was simple: an expensive black suit that was cut slim against his body, a silvery-gray dress shirt open at the neck, and black dress shoes. A medieval-looking sword sheath hung from a loop on his belt, decorated with red, blue, and gold gemstones that almost looked real, matching the hilt of the sword within it.

My heart skipped a beat; I was completely and utterly infatuated. Tonight Ryder was my own modern-day Lancelot.

"Is there a real sword in there?" I asked, eyeing him cautiously.

Ryder gave me a smirk. "No, but it would have been fun if there was," he said in his cocky voice. "I doubt I'd be allowed at the party if that was the case," he added.

Chapter 23

Raeann's family's house was nestled on a large parcel in an evergreen forest outside of town. The house itself was massive with three stories faced in a cream-colored brick. Red pavers led from the driveway to the wide porch that showcased oversized oak double doors.

Several cars were already parked around the large circular drive, and Ryder angled his Tahoe in line with the rest. The driveway surrounded an expanse of lush green grass bordered with azaleas, circling a stone fountain with a series of shooting jets. A professional photographer was set up by the fountain, taking photos of couples sitting on a bench in front of it.

"Wow! This is amazing," I said, happy I hadn't opted to miss this event.

He scowled as he pulled his key from the ignition. "It's her usual. Raeann always has to go all out on everything."

Sometimes I let myself forget that Ryder and Raeann used to date. He obviously knew her well. The thought made me frown, putting a momentary damper on my mood.

"Would you like to get a picture taken?" he asked as he helped me out of the Tahoe.

"I'd love to."

His hands were warm on my hips, and his touch sent little shivers throughout my body. I sighed happily as we walked toward the fountain with his arm looped around my back, his hand resting lightly on my hip.

The photographer smiled warmly at us as we walked up. Brisk and efficient, she positioned us on the bench in front of the fountain. As she directed us to turn this way or that, Ryder's fingers pressed against the fabric of my dress, seemingly innocent, but sending tingles through my body just the same.

"Now if you could look at each other and pretend it is just the two of you," she said as she focused her camera.

I didn't need any help getting lost in Ryder's eyes, nor did he. Our eyes locked, each of us fascinated with the other. I wanted so badly to run my fingers through his hair, to put my hands around his neck and kiss him without the side effect of our cursed silver eyes.

As the photographer clicked away, my thoughts whirled. Was I enough for him? I worried I wasn't. Ryder and I hadn't talked too deeply about what we would be missing out on should we stay together. Obviously the physical limitations of our relationship would be a problem. although I feared it would be more of an issue on his end than it would be on mine. He was enough for me and I loved him.

"All right, lovebirds." The photographer's cheerful voice startled us, then she added, "Your photo has been sent to the printer and will be available as you walk in the front door."

Wow, this was really a first-class setup. Ryder touched his hand to the small of my back as we continued up the pavers to the front doors, which now stood open.

When we walked in, a man wearing a Robin Hood costume greeted us and presented us with our photo, which I slipped it into my purse.

The foyer was designed to impress, and I craned my neck to take in the massive chandelier, brightly lit and sparkling, hanging from the soaring ceiling. The decor was elegant and obviously very expensive, set off by an elaborate mosaic floor.

A sitting area off the foyer featured a cream-colored leather sectional facing abstract paintings above a fireplace. Dark blue drapes were tied back revealing a large picture window, and the last rays of the setting sun cast the room in a golden glow.

"I thought the foyer was impressive," I whispered to Ryder. "The blue room is even better."

Ryder laughed out loud, and I looked up to find him gazing down at me, a warm expression softening his normally cool eyes.

A banner hung over another doorway with glittery gold letters that read FOLLOW THE YELLOW BRICK ROAD. How clever. We stepped under it into a hall with gold carpeting, lined with large painted canvas murals hung on both walls. The mural depicted a jungle, and it felt like you were walking on a golden road surrounded by lush forest.

"Geez, maybe I should have come as Dorothy," I said with a laugh.

"With me as the Tin Man?" Ryder gave me his dreamy smile. "Do you know how much I want to kiss you right now," he whispered, burning me with his intense gaze.

"No," I squeaked out softly.

"Trust me, it's taking all my willpower to hold off," he said, rolling his eyes and pulling me a little closer as we walked. "Especially with you in this dress." His sly smile thrilled me, and I grinned back.

The hallway ended and branched off with doors to the left and right. We peeked in the left door first and found a dining area, the tables set with candelabras that illuminated the cobweb and spider decorations. Apparently Raeann had decided to go with the Halloween theme after all, calendar be damned. A skull displayed on a bale of hay in the corner caught my eye. It looked so real.

"Wow!" I walked in and eyed it closer.

"That's my great-uncle Pete, God rest his soul. My mother takes him everywhere," Raeann said jokingly. When I whirled around, startled, a smile played on her lips as she said, "You look like you've just seen a ghost."

Raeann walked toward us wearing a short skirt decorated with little black hearts, a skintight black lace bodysuit cut way too low, and a black feather fascinator. She looked like she was auditioning for a men's magazine instead of hostessing a party for teenagers. Her blond hair was pulled up, leaving wispy tendrils around her face, and she looked gorgeous.

Ryder tightened his hand around my waist and gave her a wary look.

"I'm just playing," she said, giving him a teasing swat across his chest.

Something flashed across my vision as she reached past me, a delicate silver bracelet hanging from her wrist. The inscription made me hold my breath. On it was engraved R & R FOREVER.

Did it really mean what I thought it meant? Did it stand for Raeann and Ryder? I knew deep down in my gut that it did, and that she was wearing it to taunt me and rub it in his face.

I glanced at Ryder, and his horrified expression told me he noticed it too. I had to get out of there.

Needing a minute to myself, I pushed between them as I stammered, "Excuse me." As I walked away, I could hear an edge to Ryder's tone as he spoke with Raeann, but I no longer cared to hear what he had to say. Not sure where to go, I decided to check out the other room.

I walked inside, too upset about Raeann and Ryder to pay attention to my surroundings, and the door pulled shut behind me. My heart seized when I heard the little click of the lock. I was surrounded by nothing but blackness. Blindly, I reached out for the wall, searching for a light switch, but felt something cold and hard. A little off balance in the darkness, I leaned back against it for stability, and realized it felt like stone.

"Ryder?" I called out, hoping he might hear me on the other side of the door.

This was ridiculous. I unzipped my purse and pulled out my phone, then switched on the flashlight app. The tiny illumination revealed that I was in a room that had been renovated to resemble a cave. Two of the walls were lined with shelving holding bottles, and the air was cool. Apparently I'd walked into a wine cellar.

"Oh my God." I covered my mouth.

This was it! This was the vision I'd had, but I had mistaken the dates. Ryder was alone with Raeann. When I realized she had succeeded in separating us, I felt sick. She'd deliberately flashed the bracelet in front of me, knowing it would upset me and I'd run off, and I fell for it.

Stupid, stupid girl!

Two shadows moved toward me in the darkness. As they drew closer, I could see one was Adam, which was no huge surprise. JP was with him, and my temper flared just at the sight of him, our truce long forgotten.

Before they could say anything to me, I interrupted, knowing exactly what JP was going to say. "Of all the lowlife things to pull!" I shouted at him, then turned to Adam. "I don't want to hear it, Adam."

I turned back around and felt for the handle. I had to find Ryder, and fast.

"Wait!" Adam said frantically.

Ignoring him, I held out my phone and was relieved to find the door handle. But no matter how hard I tried to turn it, the handle wouldn't budge. It was locked!

JP laughed at me, a sneer in his voice as he said, "Hear him out and maybe I'll let you out of here."

Suddenly a band began to play elsewhere in the house, the music so loud it was hard to hear anything else. JP turned on a flashlight he was holding, and the room lit up in a soft glow. I couldn't believe that the walls looked so much like a cave, the texture was so real. In my vision, I actually did think it was a cave. This must have cost a fortune. Who spends that kind of money for a wine cellar?

JP grinned, apparently pleased with himself, and in his Mad Hatter costume, he looked convincingly crazy. His top hat was perched at a jaunty angle on his head, and his vest had little black hearts on it that matched Raeann's skirt. He was wearing blood-red gloves, and a matching handkerchief peeked out of his front pocket.

He clapped Adam on the shoulder. "Go get her, tiger!"

I glanced at Adam, who stood there awkwardly with his hands in his pockets, looking sexy with his hair spiked with a little gel. He was dressed all in black, with black gloves and matching cape. A light saber hung from his belt, making him look like he'd just walked off the *Star Wars* set.

Tired of playing games, I glared at Adam. "Look, I don't have time for this. We'll talk later."

He opened his mouth, but closed it again, his blue eyes so sad in the dim light.

211

"Say something!" JP insisted.

Wheeling on JP, Adam threw his hands in the air. "I've already been over this with her time and time again," he said angrily. "It's no use!"

As they glared at each other, I took advantage of the distraction and skirted around them quickly before JP could stop me. I found the door they must have used and rushed through it, shutting it behind me and finding myself in a stairwell.

Shit. Now what?

With no other choice, I climbed the stairs, trying not to trip on the hem of my dress. At the top, the landing opened into what looked like a ballroom, and I walked in, searching through the crowd for my friends.

I let out a sigh of relief when I recognized Callie and Henry; the star-crossed lovers were talking animatedly by a punch bowl. She was wearing a floor-length pink gown with pink roses in her hair. Henry wore a black suit with a renaissance black velvet tunic and waist sash, with touches of pink trim that coordinated with Callie's dress.

"Callie!" I rushed at her, giving her a big hug. "You guys look great. Nice color," I teased Henry.

He smiled back good-naturedly. "Hi, Shades!"

I had never been so happy to see my bestie. I released her and took a step back, surveying the room.

"Great party, huh," she asked, taking a sip of her punch.

Glancing around, I noted there was a mermaid and merman by the door making out. There were also some dwarfs and a Snow White—group date?—talking animatedly in the other corner. Adam and JP walked into the ballroom, but kept their distance from me.

"Yeah, it's been great!" I forced a playful tone. "How did you guys get up here?"

She laughed. "Oh yeah, you must have chosen the wrong door. The one on the right leads up here. The rest of the party is outside, though." She grabbed my hand and pulled me to a balcony that overlooked the back of the property.

212

Looking down, I saw a bonfire in the middle of the enormous backyard, with fake grave markers and severed body parts scattered about. It looked eerie now that the sun had set, with all the evergreens and shrubs on the edge of the property making the darkness seem gloomier. A lot of our classmates dressed in costumes milled around, drinking and having fun. On one side, a refreshment table was set up, a long line of thirsty guests keeping the bartender busy.

"I'm going to head outside," I told her. I had to find Ryder.

"I'll come with you if you want," she offered.

"You don't have to. After all, you can't leave Romeo unattended. Someone is likely to pounce all over him," I joked.

"Yeah, yeah," she said with a giggle. "Suit yourself. The stairs are over there." Then she walked back into the room in search of Henry, who probably hadn't left the punch bowl.

I took the stairs she pointed out and stepped outside, scanning the crowd in search of Ryder. He needed to know the reason I left so suddenly. And I wanted to tell him I was sorry for being so stupid. Like a fool, I'd played right into Raeann's hand and had done exactly what she expected me to do.

• • •

Where is Ryder?

After wandering through the guests for a while, searching for Ryder, I stopped several feet away from the bonfire, enjoying its warmth for a moment as I wondered where he could be. Uninvited, an arm circled my shoulders, and I stiffened.

"Hi, Vi."

At the sound of Ryder's voice, I turned and said, "Oh my God! I was so worried. I just—" Surprised at his appearance, I took a step back. "Why did you change clothes?"

Ryder now wore a Grim Reaper costume, dressed head to toe in black with a large cloak over his shoulders, black gloves, and a black mesh mask for his face.

Confused, I peered at him for a moment. Here I was worried about him, and he was just changing clothes. For what reason, I had

213

no idea, but we had more important things to talk about, so I brushed off my irritation.

"Listen, Ryder, I'm sorry that I took off. I needed some time to think. It occurred to me that Raeann just wanted to get you alone, and I let that stupid bracelet upset me."

I looked up at him but couldn't see his eyes through the black mesh, and it dawned on me that this was how he must feel when I wore my sunglasses. No wonder it annoyed him so much.

Without a word, he took my hand and led me away from the fire. We worked our way through fairies, goblins, and assortment of monsters, then he steered me to the edge of the yard and into the woods, down a narrow path. The brush was thick on either side of the narrow trail, and I had to lag a little behind in order for us to fit.

It was full dark now, but I felt comfortable and safe with Ryder leading the way. The silence between us wasn't awkward. Thinking he was wanting to be romantic, to pull me away into the woods like Adam had at the bonfire, I just ambled along behind him, enjoying the sounds of our footsteps crunching in the leaves and crickets chirping. Although the sun had set, the moon wasn't yet high enough to lend us much light. Before long, the sounds of the party faded and the hum of insects was the only music we heard.

"Where are we going?" I asked, but he didn't answer. "All right, Mr. Mysterious." I yanked hard on his hand, pulling him to a stop, and he turned toward me. "I know you're trying to be romantic, but I don't think it's a good idea that we venture too far off." I tilted my head to the side, trying to see past his mask as I added, "For all we know, Raeann could still be planning something."

He stepped closer and pulled up the bottom half of his mask. As he dipped his head, bringing his mouth toward mine, I closed my eyes tightly. My blood singing with excitement, I leaned forward, feeling his warm breath on my lips.

When his lips touched mine roughly, I nearly jerked back in surprise. They were hot and moist and . . . *different*. He invaded me with his tongue and pulled me to him tightly, trapping my arms at my sides.

I braced myself for the sudden rush that always happened when Ryder and I touched. Yet the kiss continued and I kept waiting, not enjoying it very much and distracted, because it usually didn't take this long for us to be swept away.

A moment later he pulled away abruptly. His bottom of his mask fell back down, covering the lower half of his face, and my eyes flew open in surprise.

"You're not Ryder," I whispered, horrified that this guy had kissed me. "But I heard you talk," I accused him. "It was Ryder's voice."

"A recording. Worked pretty well, didn't it?" he said smugly in a voice that was clearly not Ryder's. The stranger sounded familiar, but I couldn't place his voice.

He grabbed my hand and started pulling me forward again. "Now I don't have to pretend I'm that arrogant kid anymore."

Kid?

"You're not much older," I snapped at him.

"Not much," he conceded. "But enough." He yanked at my hand, pulling me faster down the path.

Not knowing how far we'd come from the party, or what this guy had in mind, fear turned my blood to ice. If I wanted to get away, I'd need to be able to run, so I kicked off one high heel when he was looking away from me. Careful not to let him see, I waited for another opportunity, then lost the other.

A few yards later I pulled back on his hand, then planted my feet. "I'm not going anywhere with you."

Ignoring me, he dragged me a little farther as I struggled against him. I glanced around for anything I could use against him as a weapon, but didn't see anything that might help. My best defense would be my own two legs.

Desperate to distract him, I asked, "Why did you kiss me?"

He came to a stop and turned around, his posture stiff and angry. "Because I wanted to," he gritted out. "And I always do what I want."

"Do I get to know who my mysterious kisser is?" I asked, my voice a little shaky. I needed to get a head start on him somehow, or else I'd never make it back to the party.

215

"We aren't far from where we're going. You'll just have to wait to find out," he said roughly, stepping back and pulling me forward again.

"I'm not the kind of girl that waits for anything," I said in my most seductive voice.

God, I hope this works.

Once again, he stopped and turned my way, keeping a firm grip on my arm as I reached up and pulled the mask off.

When I saw his face, I forced a smile to my lips and tried to act pleased.

Jase smiled back at me triumphantly, as if I were some trophy he'd just won. "And here I thought you had a thing for Ryder."

He was a good-looking guy, but definitely not my type. And his caveman tactics definitely didn't earn any points with me. I wasn't sure what the bad blood was between him and Ryder, but I'd find out in due time.

"Can I tell you something?" I said quietly.

He leaned forward and I put my hands on his shoulders, pulling him toward me. He took another step closer, and . . .

Bingo!

I brought my knee up hard into his groin, and his breath came out in a whoosh. When he grunted in pain, I pushed him with all the strength I could muster and bolted. I ran as fast as I could, my bare feet sinking into some soft areas of the path that were nothing but muck and leaves. Without the height of my heels, the hem of my dress dragged on the ground, catching on bare roots here and there that I had to tug against to be free of. But I was grateful for the slit in the dress that allowed me to move so freely.

Much too quickly, heavy footsteps pounded through the leaves behind me. Jase had apparently recovered and was gaining on me.

I didn't look back, remembering advice my stepfather had given me before my first track meet in seventh grade. *Never look behind you*, he'd told me. *You lose time trying to gauge how close someone is to you.*

Jase's ragged breathing was behind me, much too close for comfort. I was getting winded, and my legs burned with the effort as I struggled to put as much distance between us as possible.

His fingers brushed my back as he made a grab for me.

Oh God. I swung my arms harder, trying to gain momentum and push ahead, but it was too late.

It happened in such a rush. I was shoved hard from behind, losing my footing as my legs tangled in the thin fabric of my gown. I went down hard, landing face-first on the mucky trail, and turned my head to the side so my cheek and chest took the brunt of the impact. My cheek burned and tears instantly sprouted to my eyes from the pain shooting throughout my body. A second later, I felt a crushing sensation as Jase fell on top of me and knocked the wind out of me.

I couldn't move, no matter how much I wanted to. I willed my body to get up, throw a punch, anything to get away, but my limbs weren't taking instructions from my brain.

Jase turned me over onto my back and straddled me across my stomach. My vision was a little blurry and my head hurt, but I thought he took a small vial from a pocket of his costume. He shook the contents onto a white cloth.

"Sweet dreams, baby." His handsome features looked sinister as he grinned down at me, then covered my mouth and nose with the cloth.

Outraged, I struggled for a moment, then everything went black.

217

Chapter 24

When I came to, I heard voices and music. I tried to sit up, but my arms and legs still wouldn't cooperate. Frustrated, I opened my eyes for a second, but everything was blurry, and dizziness forced me to shut them again.

"How long will she be out?"

A familiar voice. Ryder?

"It shouldn't be too much longer." A woman's voice. "But you failed us, you let your feelings for the girl get in the way." Her voice rose as she commanded, "Take him away."

"Don't hurt her," Ryder called out, his voice strained.

I tried to lift my head, tried to call out to him, but it was useless. Warm fabric pressed against my face, and blackness overtook me once more.

. . .

Sometime later I came around to find myself on my side, my injured cheek pressed against the cold ground. I opened my eyes, and when the light from the fire made me feel dizzy, I quickly shut them again.

Someone was speaking, but was interrupted by a now-familiar voice. Jase. "I think she's coming around."

There was silence, then someone said, "Let me finish!"

Oh my God! It was Principal Margaret. Even in my dazed state, I knew it had to be her. Where was Raeann?

The dizziness faded a little, and I rolled over to my back.

"With this brand she'll be ours!" Principal Margaret yelled.

My thoughts raced as my muddled mind tried to make sense of what I was hearing. *Is she talking about me? And what the hell does she mean by* brand?

Startling me, a man's voice boomed. "Margaret Norman, what on earth do you think you're doing with my daughter!"

Carefully, I sat up and looked through bleary eyes to see it was still nighttime. My hands were tied together with rope in front of me, and I was sitting on the ground in the middle of a clearing in the forest. A group of people I didn't know that were gathered around a small bonfire started to scatter and run away. Confused at what was happening, I froze, and my eyes grew wide as I saw Margaret cowering before a large man.

He pulled out a pistol and waved it in the air as he shouted at her. "This isn't how we treat our kids. She won't be claimed until she chooses to be, and most certainly not with the multis. I'm taking this up with the Richtenburgs, and I'll see you punished for this. How dare you betray me and our people! You'll never see Raeann again."

Margaret let out an ugly laugh. "Oh, Richard, go ahead and do your worst. The girl's not safe until she's claimed, and I know what kind of power she holds."

My head was still fuzzy, and I strained to focus as I stared at the man. He looked so familiar . . .

I tried to lift myself from the ground but fell back again, my head hurt so much and my legs were tangled in my long dress. The last thing I remembered was being at the costume party and trying to find Ryder, then being led away by Jase.

My face hurt. I touched on the cheek I'd injured and found it tender and swollen; it was probably a pretty shade of bluish purple by now. My muscles aching, I pulled myself into a sitting position.

"Ryder," Richard said, "thank you for calling me. I'm so thankful I could get here in time."

I glanced around, feeling broken and violated, furious that my free will had been torn away from me. Apparently Principal Margaret was the ringleader of this kidnapping plot and Jase was in on it. Was Raeann a part of this? If she didn't know what her mother was up to, she would be upset by all this. Did Ryder have anything to do with it? I thought I remembered hearing his voice. My mind was spinning with unanswered questions.

I heard movement behind me and turned my head toward it a little too fast, causing a sharp pain to shoot through my neck. Ryder stood nearby, watching me. He looked as handsome as ever, even with the traces of a new bruise under one eye.

His silver eyes met mine warily. "Vi, are you okay? I was so scared."

Numb, I couldn't speak and just gazed at him in a daze.

"Ryder." The man named Richard addressed him with authority.

"Yes, Rich," Ryder responded instantly.

"Please take Violet somewhere safe. I'll contact you later."

"Yes, sir. Will do."

Ryder then untied my hands and gathered me up in his arms, where I felt safe and secure. I took one more look at Richard before Ryder walked away with me. He looked so familiar, yet I was sure I'd never seen him before. Tears of frustration filled my eyes.

"Ryder," I said on a sob, trying to get my breath. "Who was that man who saved me?"

Ryder pressed his lips against my hair. "That was your father," he said softly. "I'll explain what I can when we get somewhere safe."

Shocked, I struggled against him, trying to get down. "Let me go! I need to talk to him!"

Holding me tighter, Ryder shook his head. "It's not safe. You have no idea how badly they want you. I'll answer your questions once we have some distance from here. And he'll talk to you when he can."

Frustrated, I buried my face against his shirt and sobbed quietly. He made steady progress down the forest path back to Raeann's party, but by the time we finally reached the clearing with the bonfire, I was shivering. Whether from shock or from the cold, I had no idea.

At the edge of the clearing, Ryder set me on my feet, which were unfortunately still bare. I tried to smile at him, but I was pretty sure I looked a mess. My makeup was probably smeared all over my face, and when I reached up to my hair, I found a few twigs that had lodged in it from the chase.

Together we walked toward the bonfire and joined Callie and Henry, who were standing nearby with drinks in their hands.

"What the hell happened to your face?" Callie exclaimed when she saw me. "Henry and I have been looking all over." She frowned at the rumpled state of our costumes, then smiled with a gleam in her eye. "What were you two doing in the woods?"

"You won't believe who I just met," I said, then started giggling hysterically and couldn't stop.

Ryder looked down at me. Concern flickered over his face, then he wiped his expression and shrugged at Callie. "I think she's had a little too much punch," he mumbled. "Callie, I have to get her home. I'll have her call you tomorrow."

He took my hand and hurried around the front of the house. The beautifully landscaped lawn was heaven on my battered and bruised feet. My heartbeat was erratic and my breathing was heavy. Sweat was starting to drip down my back, and my dress clung to me from it. I didn't feel like myself, as if I were a different person. Someone tried to take my free will tonight, and my father and Ryder saved me. *My father.*

Ryder led me to his Tahoe and opened the door, then placed me gently on the seat and buckled me in like a child. His eyes were lit with anger as he settled in the driver's seat, making them practically glow. God, he was good-looking. I watched him, noting how his jaw was tense as he maneuvered the truck around the drive and headed off the property. When he turned onto the road he accelerated quickly, throwing me back against the seat.

"Are you okay?" he said as he glanced quickly at me.

I nodded and turned to watch the trees zip past us as we sped on. Once on the highway, we picked up the pace even more. Nervous, I glanced at the speedometer, and wiped my sweaty palms on my dress but decided to keep my mouth shut. Ryder probably had good reason for speeding like he was.

"I don't think we've been followed," he finally said, his face relaxing a little.

"Good," I said, "because I need a shower. Please take me home now."

221

I'd had enough of feeling like a pawn in somebody else's game for one night. I was sore and tired, and filthy to boot. My head was spinning with all the unanswered questions, and I was reeling from having seen my real dad in the flesh for the first time. All I wanted was to go home and get myself clean, then crawl into my bed and pull the covers over my head.

Ryder looked at me with raised eyebrows, then narrowed his eyes as if I'd said the dumbest thing ever. "Are you out of your mind? We don't have time for you to shower. You aren't safe! We're going to swing by your house so you can pack a bag real quick. Then we're going to get the hell out of town until I know it's safe to bring you back."

He took his eyes off the road a moment to glare at me, clearly exasperated. Returning his attention to the road ahead, he shook his head and swore under his breath.

Chastened, I tried to make myself smaller in the seat and mumbled, "I understand." My eyes burned with tears. I looked out the window and clenched my fists, furious at myself for being such a crybaby tonight.

"I'm sorry," Ryder said in a low voice. "When we get to the cabin, where it's safe, I'll draw you a bath then."

I glanced over to see a pained expression on his face, but he didn't take his eyes off the road.

The car was tense and silent until we pulled to a stop in front of my house. I glanced at the time; it was midnight.

Please let Vick be out. Please let Vick be out. The last thing I needed was to explain to an overprotective brother why I was showing up at home with Ryder to pick up clothes when I was supposed to be spending the night at Callie's. There were no lights on, so it was probably a safe bet that he was still out with his friends.

I opened the door hesitantly and poked my head inside, listening. Nope, he wasn't home. *Thank God.*

Ryder pushed me inside and impatiently circled a hand in the air, indicating I should hurry up. "Come on," he said tersely. "Grab some clean clothes."

"Okay, Mr. Bossy Pants," I mumbled as I hurried up the stairs.

"We don't have time for your cute little remarks," he said as he pushed past me into my bedroom. "Where's a suitcase?"

"Duffel bag. Closet," I said absentmindedly as I rifled through my dresser, pausing just for a second to daydream about how nice it would be to escape with Ryder under normal circumstances. He would help me pack, but without the attitude, and would steal a few kisses and give me sexy I-want-you-now looks. If we were normal, that is, but we would never be normal.

"What's the holdup?" he said impatiently, trying without much success to rein in his temper.

I had pulled out fresh socks and underwear, and I childishly threw them at him. My eyes were welling up again with a fresh bout of tears, and overwhelmed, I sat down on my bed, covered my eyes, and cried. As I hung my head and sobbed, I could hear Ryder stuff my things in the bag.

Trying to get a hold of myself, I wiped my wet cheeks, sniffling as I looked down and saw Ryder's feet appear in front of me. He stood still for a moment, as if he wasn't sure how he should react to my mental breakdown. I peeked up at him from between my fingers, and he looked lost. Then as if he'd made a decision, he pulled me to him and let me cry on his shoulder.

"I'm so sorry," he whispered against my hair. "I know you didn't ask for any of this. I should have left you alone. Raeann's mother would have never found you if it weren't for me." He kissed the top of my head, then tilted my chin up with his gloved fingers so he could look in my eyes. "We have to hurry, though. Can you finish packing, or do you want me to?"

"It's not your fault, Ryder. She probably would have found me anyway," I whispered as I pulled away from the comfort of his arms, and immediately felt cold.

Hurrying, I pulled out some jeans, a couple of hoodies, and a pair of sunglasses that would go with anything, then grabbed a brush and my toothbrush from the bathroom. Since I was still barefoot, I pulled on some socks and put on my running shoes.

"All set?" He seemed to relax a little, his expression softer now that I was ready.

223

I nodded and followed him back out to his truck.

When we got to Ryder's house, he led me to the den and said, "Wait here."

As I took a seat on a barstool, I heard him speaking in a low voice to someone. Xavier came in and went behind the bar.

"Mr. Essen has asked that I keep you company while he gathers some things for your stay."

I rolled my eyes. "In other words, you were told to make sure I don't run?"

A surprised look crossed his face, then he asked politely, "Would you care for a drink?"

"I'll take a Coke and an aspirin," I muttered, wishing I could drown out the events of tonight and numb the pain I felt.

When Xavier placed a tall glass of Coke in front of me, I downed it quickly. I'd just finished it when Ryder stepped back into the room.

"I'm ready, let's go."

I followed him back out to the truck. "Do we have to stop for gas?" I asked.

"No, I always keep the tank topped off."

"That's good," I mumbled.

"Are you in shock?"

"No, just exhausted." And mentally drained, I added silently.

"Try to get some sleep."

As we merged into light late-night traffic and headed north, I closed my eyes and passed out.

• • •

I was sluggish when I opened my eyes from Ryder's insistent tugging.

"We're here," he said as he unbuckled my seat belt.

"Where's here?" I asked, my head still fuzzy from sleep. Outside the truck it was very dark, the moon dimly illuminating the forest that surrounded us.

"My dad has a cabin on the other side of the lake. We'll stay here for the rest of the night."

I let out a yawn, then asked, "Ryder, why can't I talk to my father?"

He got out of the Tahoe and opened the hatch to get our stuff. Not meeting my eyes, he slung my duffel's strap over his shoulder and picked up his own bag, then sighed and said, "Let's get you inside first, and then I'll explain."

Frowning, I followed him as he walked up to a compact lodge-style home that was much nicer than what I'd call a "cabin." I stopped for a moment, taking in what little I could see of the A-frame in the night. It was like something out of a magazine.

Ryder unlocked the front door and turned around to see me gawking. "Come on," he urged.

I shrugged and followed him up the wooden stairs and through the front door. The entry opened into a large great room with a soaring ceiling, but he didn't turn on a light. He grabbed me with a gloved hand and tugged me inside.

A mirror on the wall caught my reflection and I almost died there on the spot. "Kill me now," I whined. "I look awful!"

Ryder glanced at me and shook his head. "What did you expect after what you've been through?"

We passed through the living area so quickly, I didn't get to see much. He stopped at the end of a hallway and opened a door. I followed him in, curious.

"This is where we'll stay," he said as he turned on a light, then pointed to another door. "The shower is through there."

I surveyed the bedroom. It was large, and much nicer than you'd expect from a cabin at the lake. The decor was rustic, not like cheesy talking-fish-on-the-wall rustic, but more with a very understated we-have-lots-of-money woodsy feel.

Then I realized what he'd said. *This is where we'll stay.* We. As in the two of us.

I took in the lone queen-sized bed in the room and crossed my arms over my chest. No, absolutely not. There was no way I sleeping with him.

225

"I hate to break it to you," I said to Ryder as he dropped our bags on the bed, "but this arrangement just isn't going to work."

I loved Ryder, but I'd never slept with a guy before, even just to sleep. There was no way I could do this; I'd be too nervous of something happening that shouldn't. Either of the sexual variety, or of our skin touching and having to suffer through the side effects of an unwanted shared vision.

Ryder huffed out a sigh and ran a hand roughly through his hair. "Listen. I'm not taking the risk of sleeping away from you. Besides, the cabin only has one bedroom, so you don't have a choice. I promise I'll behave." His eyes were stormy with emotion, anger and frustration and something else I couldn't define turning them into molten silver, and I felt myself shrink away a little.

I didn't bother to respond; there was no point and I was too exhausted from the long night to argue with him. Resigned to sharing a room with him, I went to my duffel bag and looked for my pajamas, then groaned in frustration.

"What's the matter?" Ryder walked over to where I stood at the end of the bed. His gloved hand went to my shoulder, caressing me gently.

"I forgot my pajamas," I muttered.

An amused gleam lit his eyes as he said matter-of-factly, "I've already seen you naked, you know."

When I narrowed my eyes at him, he chuckled a little.

"I can lend you some boxers and a T-shirt, if you want." His silver eyes were wide and sincere, and there was no trace of humor in his voice. Ryder could be so sweet when he wanted to be.

"Thank you," I murmured, caught off guard by how serious he was suddenly. He handed me a pair of boxer shorts and a tank, and I headed to the shower.

The water was hot, just the way I liked it. Still feeling a little numb, I washed the dirt and sweat away. Mesmerized, I watched the water swirl toward the drain, then started sobbing as the cumulative effects of the night's events hit me, letting my tears mix with the stream of water pouring over me.

"Vi!" There was pounding on the door. "Are you okay?"

226

Instantly I froze and called out, "I'm okay," my voice husky with emotion. Embarrassed to be caught crying yet again, I stepped out of the shower and wrapped a towel around me. When I walked out into the bedroom, Ryder was sitting on the bed.

"Vi," he said softly. "I'm so sorry. Come on, let's get you taken care of."

He took another fluffy towel and wrapped it around my head, rubbing vigorously at my wet hair. I was shivering now, and whether it was nerves or just my system crashing on me, I didn't know. Not knowing what to say, I just sat there like a doll, letting him take care of me as I tried to still my spinning thoughts.

When my hair was no longer dripping, Ryder patted the towel against my shoulders and arms to dry them. He inspected my face, then stepped into the bathroom for a moment and came back with a tube of ointment, tipping my head back before applying some to my cheek. He bit his lip, his face tense as he tended my scrapes. His touch was so caring and so gentle, it made me fall for him a little bit more.

"I can handle it from here," I said softly.

"Okay. I'll see you in a minute." He handed me the extra towel and left me alone.

When I walked into the bathroom and looked in the mirror, a stranger gazed back at me. I didn't recognize her, even though she mimicked everything that I did. My auburn curls were in a tangled mess, and I finished brushing them out slowly, every stroke taking great effort. I was exhausted. I felt sad and hollow, somehow. And confused, as if I didn't know who I was anymore.

When I emerged from the bathroom, all clean and sporting his boxers and tank, I found him lying on the bed, propped up by a couple of pillows as he talked on his cell phone. His mouth was set in a tense, grim line, and he was listening to whomever he was talking to.

He glanced at me warily. "Okay, call me when we can return," he snapped. Then he ended the call and threw the phone aside.

I stilled, unsure if I really wanted to go over to him.

227

Glancing up at me, his expression gentled as he said in a tired voice, "Come here."

I walked over to him and carefully scooted onto the bed, making sure not to come too close to him.

"I love the way your hair frames your face," he murmured so quietly I had to pay close attention to hear him.

"Thank you." *I think.*

"We need to talk," he said quietly.

"I know," I murmured, feeling all the fight and exasperation leave my body. His eyes were too intense.

"What would you like to know?"

Ryder's silver eyes were burning into me with the intensity of all the fire and passion I felt in my love for him. Could he possibly feel the same way? I didn't think so. He said he'd never been in love, but maybe he would never let himself be. After all, how could you fall in love if you were dead set against it?

"What are you thinking?" he asked, interrupting my train of thought.

"Um, nothing." I blushed, a little embarrassed. How could I say, *I was wondering if you loved me back?*

"When will I get to see my father again?"

"Sometime soon, okay? I'm sure of it. Now that he's seen you, he won't let you go, especially since you're not claimed yet."

"I don't understand what being claimed means." I moved a little closer to him and rested my head on the pillow right next to his head.

He sighed, averting his eyes as he said, "Being claimed is a ritual where you get branded with the symbol of your clan. Once you're branded, you belong to that clan forever, unless you're exiled."

"Okay," I said slowly, my mind spinning with questions. "Why are there different clans?"

"Each clan's members have a specific color of eyes, and they have special powers. Our clan with our silver eyes can see the future. You're special, the only one who can also see memories. That makes

228

you important, and valuable to people who would want to take advantage of your power for profit. Like the multis."

Ryder stroked my arm with his gloved fingers and shut his eyes for a moment. "The multis are a bunch of renegades, a group of misfits that don't want to follow the rules. They're trying to gather unclaimed teens of many clans to form a superior one." He opened his eyes and looked down at me, his expression solemn. "They were trying to brand you against your will to make you a part of their clan."

"Oh my God." I felt sick. This whole thing was way over my head. "You're claimed?"

"Since I was eight."

My mind immediately pictured a young Ryder with blond hair and wide, serious silver eyes. "Oh." I couldn't hide the shock I felt.

Ryder's eyes darkened as he stared at me, becoming intense. "What I wouldn't give to kiss you," he murmured.

I jerked my head toward him, my eyes wide as my stomach did little flips. How did he do this to me? "Ryder, I—"

"Look," he said quickly, interrupting me. "I didn't know what they were planning. I figured it had something to do with me. When you took off after Raeann flashed that stupid bracelet in your face, I tried to go after you, but two of the older guys in the multi clan jumped me. They said that I had to go see Jase, but when I got to the meeting spot, he wasn't there, and I had a bad feeling that something had happened to you."

He cupped my cheek with his gloved hand, forcing me to look at him, and whispered, "Please forgive me."

Breathe, just breathe.

"It's not your fault, Ryder."

He wrapped his arm around me, pulling me to him, and buried his nose in my hair, breathing deeply. "I'm going to keep you safe. No worries. Okay?"

I snuggled a little closer, but said nothing.

"What's wrong? Talk to me."

229

I turned in his arms so I could face him. The earnest look in his eyes and the warmth of his body gave me the courage I needed to speak my mind truthfully. Whether he was ready or not, I needed to get this off my chest.

I took a deep breath. This was it. "I love you," I said, hoping he would take it well.

He flinched slightly, his eyes wide, as if he didn't believe what he had just heard. When he didn't say anything, I felt my heart sink.

"Let go of me," I murmured, pushing against his chest.

He tightened his hold. "Wait, that was . . ." He paused, seeming to be searching for the right words, and hope flared back to life inside me. "It was just the wrong thing to say."

I gasped as hope died within me. "Telling you how I feel was the wrong thing to say?"

I had to ask, just to be sure, because I'd believed with all my heart that Ryder was my knight from the tarot cards. But he had to be open for love in order for it to happen, and he wasn't open to that. Apparently it was too much of a risk for him to open himself up that much to one person, too much of an emotional investment for him.

"I'm sorry." He looked contrite, his eyes searching mine, and I could see my pain reflected in them.

"Me too," I whispered, and then took a deep breath to calm myself. "Now, please let go of me. I need to sleep."

Seeming reluctant, he released me, and I immediately felt chilled without his arms around me. I moved as far away from him as I could, turning my back on him as I pulled the covers over me and burrowed down. It took forever to get comfortable, but eventually I drifted off to sleep, dreaming of knights and cards.

Chapter 25

When I woke up, I was in Ryder's arms. I stiffened for a moment, worried about slipping into a vision, but he was still wearing his gloves and a long-sleeved T-shirt so our skin wouldn't touch. My cheek rested against his warm chest, and I could feel every rise and fall as he breathed, and the steady beat of his heart. I shifted and peeked up warily at him to find him still asleep.

Needing to pee, I slipped carefully out of his arms and went to the bathroom. While I was there I changed my clothes and brushed my teeth, so I felt refreshed as I stepped back into his room.

Ryder was standing next to the bed, zipping up a fresh pair of jeans, and his upper torso was naked. I sucked in a little breath as I watched him pull on a baby blue T-shirt, his muscles rippling as he did. He didn't take his eyes off me, and I didn't dare speak.

"Are you taking me home now?" I asked.

He nodded. "I got a phone call. It's safe now."

I let out a sigh of relief. "Okay."

"I don't want to take you home," he said suddenly, his silver eyes searching mine. "I want just one more day of you and me."

Uncomfortable under his gaze, I shifted from one foot to the other. "I can't," I said, nervously brushing my hair away from my shoulder with my hand. "The only thing I want right now is to be home in a warm bath with my iPod, drowning out the world with my music. The last twenty-four hours have been crazy, and I just want to be away from you." My eyes blurred with unshed tears, and I blinked them rapidly. "I don't want to have to look into your face knowing that you'll never feel the same way about me as I do about you."

Hurt flashed in his eyes, just for a moment, but then slipped away as he regarded me warily.

"I told you one day I wouldn't be able to breach your wall," I said, then turned to leave.

231

"Wait," he said, and I turned back, not daring to allow myself to hope. "I've never been in love, Vi. It's not something I'm used to—"

I raised a hand to stop him. Back to square one. "It's okay, Ryder. You don't have to explain. I get it. I just . . . I need out before I get too emotionally involved." As if being in love wasn't already too involved. My hands trembled and I clasped them together to keep them from shaking.

He walked toward me and I felt myself wanting to run into those strong arms. Instead I forced myself to turn and pick up my duffel, then headed out the door.

Chapter 26

The storm clouds were a deep bluish-gray, but it wasn't raining yet. How fitting to have another day that matched my dark and bleak mood. I was already settled into the Tahoe by the time Ryder came outside. After locking up the cabin, he climbed into the driver's seat and threw his bag into the backseat, then sat there for a moment, merely staring out the windshield.

"Damn it," he yelled as he slammed his palms against the steering wheel.

Startled, I glanced over at him. He was definitely distraught. I must have royally pissed him off.

He slammed the steering wheel, then turned to me quickly, unfastened my seat belt, and threw it aside.

"Hey!" I protested as he grabbed me forcefully by my arms and pulled me over the console to straddle him. My cheeks burned at the intimate position.

Ryder's hands caressed my back, pulling me down closer so our faces were an inch apart. "Vi, I do have strong feelings for you," he whispered.

My heartbeat picked up at the feel of his warm breath on my lips, and my blood heated under his hot gaze. When his silver eyes locked on mine, I forgot to breathe. I barely had a chance to gasp before his warm lips touched mine in a tender kiss. My lips parted, and I slipped my hands around his neck and wove my fingers through his hair. It felt so good to touch his skin, to stroke him and play with his hair as if we were normal people.

As our lips moved together, I braced myself, knowing what was coming. When the wind began to whip around us, he wrapped his arms around me in a tight hold that barely allowed me to breathe, and his gloved fingertips stroked my back, making me shiver. I shut my eyes as his lips moved to my neck, my feelings whirling in the chaos that was inside me as well as all around me.

233

After a moment the wind died down, and my brain began to clear.

. . .

Luckily I didn't pass out this time. When the whirling stopped, Ryder's lips still moved along my neck in featherlike kisses. I was no longer straddling him in the front seat of the Tahoe, but was instead standing with him on my front porch, firmly wrapped in his embrace.

"Ryder? How is it that we can still be touching and not be sent back to the truck?"

"I don't know and I don't care," he said putting his lips back to mine, and I instantly melted into him. His lips moved against me hungrily, and I returned the kiss with just as much passion.

Moments passed before logic broke through our lust-filled haze, reminding me that we were here for a reason, and I needed to find out what that reason was.

"Ryder," I whispered against his lips.

His kisses slowed slightly, and he let out a low moan of frustration as he forced himself to part from me. I was breathing heavily, drained from that extraordinary kiss.

"As far as kisses go, that one is at the top of my list," he said with a crooked grin.

Elated at first, I suddenly wondered how high that list was, but pushed the thought from my brain. We had more important things to figure out.

He grasped my hand and tugged. "Come on, let's go in."

I pulled back then gave in, pouting a little as I said, "I'm afraid if I let go I won't be able to hold you again. This has been the longest I've been able to touch you."

When we walked inside, I looked around the living room. My stepfather was sitting on the couch and my brother was pacing. Something in my gut told me this was what I was going to walk into.

My stepdad's expression surprised me. It wasn't worry I saw in his eyes; it was the look of an impending punishment. Vick, on the other hand, was frantic and worried. His jaw was tense and his mouth constricted in a grim line.

"Oh my gosh, my stepdad is home. I have a bad feeling about this." Before the words were completely out of my mouth, the phone rang.

My brother jumped for it, but before he could reach it my stepdad picked it up. "Hello," he said coldly.

The anger in his voice made my stomach turn. I feared coming home, hating it when Dad was mad at me, but the look on my Vick's face pulled at my heart and I knew I had to.

"You found her!" He narrowed his eyes, his jaw clenched. "Call me when she's on her way," he said brusquely, then hung up the phone.

Turning to Ryder, I said, "We need to get back," and he nodded.

He released my hand, then wrapped his arms around me and pulled me to him quickly, his lips seeking mine. "My favorite way to travel," he murmured between each kiss.

The swirling colors closed in on us, and for a moment we were just lips and warm breath and colors and wind.

• • •

When I opened my eyes, silver met silver, and I could see a flash of wonder quickly replaced by doubt. I was still straddling Ryder in the front of his Tahoe. He shook his head, causing a golden sun-kissed lock to fall on his forehead. I gently put the strand back in place with my fingertips as my other hand rested on his neck.

"What did you think of what happened?" I said. "Who do you think my stepfather was talking to?"

Ryder lifted me and slid my body back onto the seat next to me.

"I'm not sure. Your real dad, maybe?" he said, watching me carefully. He leaned one elbow on the steering wheel as he angled himself toward me. "I'm going to be in trouble with the clan regardless." He shrugged, but the worried look in his eyes said there was more to it than he was telling me.

235

"Is your dad going to be angry?" I slanted a glance at him as I wrapped one of my auburn curls around my finger, unconsciously twirling and un-twirling and twirling.

"Probably." His lips tightened. "His big thing has always been to do what you're told and don't cause a ruckus. This just reflects badly on my family, and the Richtenburgs aren't people you want to piss off."

"We should get going."

Ryder looked back at me as if he wanted to say something, but then his expression shuttered. I could practically see the wall going up behind those icy silver eyes, and I sighed. He did everything on autopilot as he backed out of the driveway and headed toward the highway.

"How long till we get there?" I asked.

"It's about 160 miles, so I'd guess three hours and fifteen minutes."

Realizing I was stuck in the truck with him for three hours, I smiled to myself. When I glanced over to him, he was watching me intently, his expression serious.

"What's with the smile?"

"Does a girl need a reason to be happy?" I asked smugly.

"In your current situation," he said, then frowned. "Yes, you do because you should be anything but happy right now."

There he goes again, telling me how I should feel like he knows everything.

His phone rang and he lifted it to his ear. "Yeah," he said, then listened for a moment. "Yes. Okay." There was a pause as he listened some more. "Good. See you then." Another long pause. "I understand." When he disconnected the call and tossed his phone into the console, he looked grim.

"What? Who was it? What did they say? Should we still go home?" My words ran together because I was frantic. Ryder didn't look happy, and it made my stomach twist in a foreboding way.

He held his palm out toward me, patting the air. "Whoa, slow down, Vi."

236

"Tell me who that was and what they said," I demanded.

He sighed, his eyes troubled again. "That was your dad. Richard."

What now? My stomach twisted painfully at the worry I could sense radiating from him.

"I'm to take you home to your stepfather's. A plan of action will be decided at a later time." His jaw tightened and he averted his eyes.

"What is it you're *not* telling me?" I asked, and saw the flicker of surprise flash in his eyes when he realized I caught him trying to deceive me.

He cleared his throat. "You're not going to like this," he said, his voice low.

"I can handle the truth," I said firmly, my gaze unwavering from his face.

Despite his tight control, micro-expressions flitted over Ryder's face as he slightly increased the truck's speed, changing lanes to pass a slower driver as he put miles between the cabin and us.

"I can't be around you," he said abruptly and his gaze flicked to mine, as if he were judging my reaction.

Can't be around me, can't be around me? My mind took in his words and put them on repeat until realization dawned on me. *Oh no!*

"You're breaking up with me?" I gasped. Tears instantly pooled in my eyes and spilled over my lashes, cascading down my cheeks. "No. You can't," I whispered.

"Vi," he said softly.

Stunned, I sat there and twisted my hands, focusing on just clasping and unclasping rather than dealing with the blow he'd just dealt me.

"I'm sorry," he said, "but if I can't see you, how do you suppose this thing between us will even work?"

This thing? His eyes were once again icy. Couldn't he see how much I was hurting? Couldn't he see his words were like a knife

237

twisting in my soul, damaging the very essence of my being? Couldn't he see how much I loved him?

I wrapped my arms around my stomach, trying to console myself, offering myself a little warmth, but it didn't keep the cold from invading my body as an icy river flowed through my veins. My tears stopped abruptly as my feelings were soon numbed with cold acceptance. So this was what it felt like . . . acceptance of a doomed fate. Would the storm in my life never end?

"I'm sorry, Vi. I really am. If there was a way around this, I'd gladly take it. But right now I have to follow their rules."

I was so sick of not having any control over my own life. First I lost my father when I was too young to even remember him, then this summer I lost my mom. Then I fell for Adam but couldn't actually be with him because of his arranged marriage, and now Ryder and the Richtenburgs and the whole mess with my real father. I wasn't sure how much more of this I'd be able to take. I felt helpless, as if I were a pawn in someone's twisted game.

"It's part of my punishment for not following their rules to begin with. You're supposed to go to the academy, to learn how to use your powers in a controlled environment. My experimenting with you was unsanctioned, and breaks one of the most basic rules of being a Manipulator, one of the first we learn. I'm sorry." He paused for moment, then added, "For the record . . . the time I've spent with you has been the best time in my life."

I thought back to how angry he was over me having read his journal. Yeah, we definitely had our ups and downs, but I was in love with him. Those feelings weren't going to go away.

I knew one thing was for sure; I couldn't let the clan know that I was in love with Ryder. In my heart, I knew they would use him against me if they ever discovered the truth. Apparently I was important to them, and they'd do whatever was necessary to bend me to their will.

"I won't stop loving you," I warned him, and he gave me a small, sad smile.

"For your own sake, I hope you do."

When I swung my head toward him, hurt at his harsh words, he kept his expression impassive, his walls firmly in place. I nodded, acknowledging what he'd said but not wanting to speak for fear of breaking down into tears. An uncomfortable silence hung between us until he finally reached over and turned on the radio, and we spent the rest of the ride sharing only occasional glances, keeping our thoughts to ourselves.

When we pulled up in front of my house, butterflies fluttered inside my stomach. I sat there for a moment, clutching my door handle with a white-knuckled grip, dreading what might happen inside. Sure, my stepdad might be mad at me for not coming home last night and lying about where I'd been, but somehow the anger I saw in our vision seemed much deeper than that.

When I finally got the courage to open my door, Ryder said, "I'll walk you up." He grabbed my duffel from the backseat and got out of the Tahoe, then joined me on the sidewalk, his hand resting in the small of my back as we walked to the front door.

I felt sluggish, wanting to put this off as long as I could. We didn't even make it to the porch before the front door flew open and Vick came running out.

"Vi!" His face was pale and his expression frantic. "What happened? Dad's home and—fair warning—super angry that you weren't home last night." He eyed Ryder accusingly.

"Settle down," I said, and pulled him into a hug. It so felt good to be wrapped in his arms. I opened my mouth to speak, but the words wouldn't come out. I wanted so badly to tell him what happened, to tell him the truth, but I couldn't. The words wouldn't form.

"I went to a party and decided to do the responsible thing and not drink and drive," I said, settling on telling a little white lie. I recalled Dad saying once that white lies were okay if you were saving someone from having hurt feelings. Not that my stepdad would believe any of it to begin with. I let go of Vick and he nodded, seeming satisfied with my answer. He shook Ryder's hand.

"Nice to see you again. I'm sure I'll see you around," he said to Ryder.

239

I didn't bother correcting Vick that he probably wouldn't be seeing Ryder again. As soon as that thought entered my brain, though, I pushed it away. It was too awful to think about.

"You don't have to walk me to the door," I said to Ryder. "It'll be all right." Looking up into Ryder's face, I could see the uncertainty that lurked in his silver eyes; he looked so lost. Without a word, he simply handed me my duffel bag.

I waited for him to say something, but the moment stretched out as he merely looked at me, opening and then closing his mouth again without saying anything. The silence grew heavy between us until Vick's head turned back and forth back and forth as he studied us, his eyes narrowing. With a sigh, I grabbed Vick's arm and tugged him toward the front door before he asked more questions.

"Vi," Ryder called from behind me, and I stopped and turned back.

"Yeah?"

His brows drew together as he asked in an uncertain voice, "Will you be okay?"

"I will," I assured him, trying to sound as confident as I could, but my voice was too high and squeaked in the end. I was too chipper and unlike myself, I wasn't sure if I even believed myself. Then I turned away and followed Vick into the house.

Inside, my stepdad jumped off of the couch with that look in his eye. Momentary relief crossed his face when he saw me walk in with Vick and drop my bag in the entryway.

"You stayed out with a boy," my stepdad started, and before I could even answer, he narrowed his eyes and said, "Out of all the boys in this town, you have to pick some guy from the wrong side of the tracks?"

I was totally confused. "Ryder? He's not from the wrong side of the tracks. He's not even from around here!" Furious at his assumptions, I demanded, "How do you even know who he is?" I crossed my arms in front of my chest and stood my ground, glaring at my stepfather.

"Oh, I have my sources." Dad stood there with his hands on his hips as he glared back at me. "You're grounded. I haven't decided your punishment yet, I have some things that need to be addressed first. I'll give you my decision at the end of the night."

With the conclusion of that argument, I grabbed my bag and ran upstairs, exaggerating each stomp as I went, then slammed my door childishly. If he was going to treat me like a child, I might as well act like one. I tossed my duffel in the corner and flopped down on my bed, staring up at the ceiling as my eyes burned with tears.

Vick entered my room from the bathroom door and sat on the end of my bed.

"What do you want?" I asked sulkily.

"Listen, Vi, Dad's really angry. He spent over an hour talking to Richard, to your real father."

"What?" Shocked, I sat straight up. "What did they say?"

"I don't know, Vi, I just know that it was him because I answered the phone and gave it to him."

"This isn't good." We'd always been so close; I wanted to tell Vick everything. I wished I knew what my father and stepdad had to discuss. "Thanks, Vick, but I'm exhausted and just need to sleep."

"Did Ryder hurt you in any way?"

Vick's question caught me off guard. I frowned, then realized he must have noticed the bruise on my face. "Not unless you consider a broken heart in the same sense," I said quietly.

"I'm sorry, Vi." He squeezed my leg gently and then left the same way he came in, shutting the door to the bathroom quietly behind him as he went.

I pulled out my phone to look for any missed messages. None. Geez, I felt unimportant today. So I curled up in my bed and closed my eyes.

• • •

My stepdad woke me when he came into my room. He stood in my doorway, looking all businesslike in his suit and tie.

To hell with him! I wasn't one of his patients; I was his kid. I might not be his blood, but he did raise me. I pulled myself up to a sitting position and narrowed my eyes, waiting for him to say something.

He cleared his throat, as if a little uncomfortable. "Listen, I know that as a father figure I haven't been around much."

Wow, understatement of the year!

"I learned about a month ago that your real dad was going to get custody of you and take you away. I've just been trying to come to grips with this myself, because you're my little girl." Dad looked away for a second, then cleared his throat. "I've come to a very difficult decision, because I know your mother would agree with it, God rest her soul. But I don't have much choice."

Oh no, he brought up my mother. This can't be good. I took a deep breath, bracing myself for what was about to come.

With a pained expression, Dad looked me in the eye and said, "I'm conceding to your father's wishes and sending you to the Richtenburg Academy."

My heart shuddered to a stop, and my mouth fell open as every bit of moisture evaporated. I couldn't say anything. I wanted to scream *What the hell are you thinking!* but I knew irrational outbursts would get me nowhere.

Scrambling mentally, I tried to be logical. "What about my job?"

"I'll talk to Alex, and maybe when you come home for the summer you can pick up where you left off."

Thank God! At least it wasn't a year-round private academy.

"Where is this academy?" I asked, trying to stay calm, but my stomach twisted in a way that only allowed me to take short gasps of air.

"It's on the eastern edge of Lake Ontario in New York." His blue eyes softened, then pleaded with me. "Please calm down. There's no use getting worked up over this."

Realizing I didn't have much of a choice, short of running away from home, I shrugged.

Dad stood up to leave. "Your father's going to let you be a part of my life if I agree, so I don't have a choice," he mumbled. "It's for your safety, Violet."

"Are you kidding me?" Vick blurted from the bathroom doorway.

I startled, not realizing he'd eased into the room. Vick walked over to the bed and sat down, then put his arms around me and pulled me into a hug. Sighing, I snuggled into his embrace, grateful to have someone on my side. I loved my stepbrother dearly.

"You're going to send her away," Vick spat out, "just because her biological father that she doesn't even know thinks it's best for her?" He waved his hand angrily, slicing it through the air.

"She'll be back for the summer," Dad said, his voice resigned, "and then we'll re-evaluate her status. If she earns good grades, then maybe she can come back for her senior year and graduate with her class."

The finality in his voice told us that the subject was closed. From past experience, I knew it would do no good to argue, so I gave Vick a tentative smile and I mouthed *Thanks*.

I pulled away from Vick and watched my stepdad leave, listening to his heavy footsteps descend the stairs to the living room. Vick stood up and followed, giving me one last look before he shut my bedroom door, his face masked with concern.

A moment later I could hear the argument pick up downstairs where it had left off. Vick wouldn't give up easily, but he knew as well as I did that his dad wasn't going to change his mind.

Resigned to my fate, I decided to text Callie first.

> *Me: Hey! I hate to just spring this on you and there really isn't any good way to put this, so I'm just going to come out and say it, I'm moving to New York to attend a private boarding school. I don't have a choice. We'll still talk all the time, I PROMISE!! I'm so sad about this. I'm going to miss you.*

My eyes blurry with tears, I hit the SEND button. I knew the first thing Callie would worry about was not having her BFF around, or that I might make a new one, so it seemed smart to reassure her that we wouldn't lose touch.

I decided to text Ryder next.

Me: Hi. I know we aren't together or anything, but you're the only one I can talk to about this sort of thing. My father talked to my stepdad. I'm now officially enrolled in the Richtenburg Academy in New York. I'm not happy about this. I have to quit my job and leave all my friends. I guess I just wanted to say good-bye.

I hit the SEND button, then wiped my nose on my sleeve. There was only one other person that I needed to text, but my phone chimed before I could start.

Callie: What!!! How can your dad do this? What am I going to do without you? This is awful! What about the prom? I figured that we were all going to go together, and now we won't be able to! :(

Wow, and my dad thought I was dramatic? It didn't surprise me that she would flip out; after all, I'd do the same if I were in her shoes.

Me: Listen, it will be fine. You know I'm not really into the whole prom thing anyway. It's something normal people do, and we both know I don't like to be normal. I'll hopefully be home for Christmas break. We'll hang then, and I'll text you all the time. No worries!

I decided I'd better go to Mr. Price's house, and made my way down the stairs. Even though Dad said he'd call Adam's father, I wanted to be the one to tell him I'd be moving and that he needed to hire someone new.

Having to leave my friends was horrible, but at least there was something for me to look forward to. I was really hoping that I'd finally be able to meet my real father and hopefully have some sort of relationship with him. After all, he did save me from the multi clan.

"Violet." My stepdad's stern voice stopped me in my tracks.

"Yeah." I paused with my hand on the doorknob, not wanting to turn around.

"Your flight leaves tomorrow, so you'll need to pack tonight. I have surgery scheduled for early tomorrow morning, so Vick will be taking you to the airport."

What else is new, I thought sarcastically. It figured that he wouldn't be taking me himself; Dad hadn't been there for me much lately.

"Your father arranged for your academic records to be sent to the academy today, so they should have them already. Where are you going?"

"I'm going to talk to Mr. Price and say good-bye to Adam," I said harshly, clutching the doorknob tightly. I was angry and knew that my voice showed it, but my stepdad didn't seem to care.

"Good," he said, and before he could say anything else, I rushed out and slammed the door behind me.

My phone beeped just as I was pulling into Adam's driveway, signaling a text. It was probably either Ryder or Callie. When I glanced down and saw that it was from Callie, I frowned, a little irritated that I hadn't heard back from Ryder. He was the only one I could talk to about this, and he didn't even have the decency to respond? Okay, I was more than just a *little* irritated.

I got out, reluctant to leave the safety of my car, and put on my black shades. It was a perfect color for my foul mood. I didn't really need them because the sun wasn't shining, but I wanted them. They made me feel safe.

I wasn't surprised when Adam came out of his house as I was on my way up the walkway.

"To what do I owe the pleasure of seeing you today, Miss Vancourt?" He pulled me into his arms, and I immediately melted against him. He was just so familiar and comforting that I let myself relax into his embrace.

"Geez, you smell wonderful," he said, then his tone became serious as he pulled away. "What *are* you doing here? You aren't scheduled to work."

I felt my tears coming. It was hard saying good-bye. After all, despite our doomed romance, Adam was the best guy friend I had.

He tilted my chin up. "Sunglasses?" he chided.

I shrugged, and my eyes focused on his through my protective wall.

"Okay, Violet, what's wrong? You're starting to scare me." His voice was tentative, his eyes wary.

"Adam, I . . ." I wanted to tell him everything about Ryder and Principal Margaret and the multi clan and my real dad, but none of it would come. I couldn't bring myself to speak of it. I wasn't myself anymore, and that was the worst part of all. I wasn't me.

"Adam . . ." I tried again, taking a calming deep breath. "I came to say good-bye." My voice cracked. When a frown appeared on his face, I rushed on. "My stepdad is transferring me to a boarding school in New York, and I wanted to come say good-bye in person. After all, you have played a big role in my life for so long, and I felt I owed you that at the very least."

His face fell as my meaning sank in. "Shit, that's the worst news I've ever gotten."

"Oh, come on." I gave him a playful shove in the chest, but his hand quickly went up and covered mine, holding it in place. "It's true. At least when you broke up with me, I could still see you every day, and the possibility to make amends later was still there. With you in another state, that possibility is gone."

"I'm sorry, Adam." His name rolled off my tongue so easily, but the thrill I used to feel when saying it had died a long time ago.

"When do you leave?" he asked, his blue eyes scanning my face.

"Tomorrow."

"So soon?" He shook his head and looked away. "When will you be back?"

"Christmas break. And summer. I was hoping your dad would let me come back to work in the summer."

For the first time, he smiled. "Yeah, for sure. I'll insist on it."

I pulled my hand out of his grasp and backed up a step. "Will you let your dad know? Since he's not home, I mean."

"Sure. Are you still going to have your phone on you?"

"Of course." I gave him a bright smile, trying hard to be upbeat. "Text me anytime. Please, I'll need it to keep my sanity."

"I will. You may get sick of me, though." Adam's tone was playful, causing me to giggle.

"Whatever! See you later," I said.

Adam's expression fell a little, then he said softly, "Not if I see you first."

As I headed back to my car, I sobered too, realizing as Adam had that I wouldn't see him later. It would be a long time before I ever saw Adam Price again.

● ● ●

On my way home, I found myself pulling to a stop in front of Ryder's. It bugged me that he hadn't responded to my text. His Tahoe wasn't out front of the grand white house, but I decided to try my luck anyway. I knocked on the door and looked up at the brilliant blue sky, trying to enjoy the gorgeous fall day while I waited. The leaves from the trees were starting to change colors, and the sun was hot. It was my favorite time of year, and despite this being one of the worst days of my life, I wanted badly to shake off my sense of impending doom.

When no one came to the door, I decided to try it and found it unlocked. Pushing the door open, I peeked inside, but all was quiet. With a shrug, I walked in. After all, it wasn't the first time I had sneaked into Ryder's house uninvited.

All the lights were off. I flicked the switch and found there was no power. *Weird.* I made my way to the office and the door creaked as I pushed it open. There was nothing in there. The desk was covered with a throw cover, as if it would be a long time before someone came back. I shut the door and went to the den. All the furniture there was covered as well.

"He's gone," I said in disbelief, and my voice echoed in the empty room.

I leaned against the door and slid to the floor, burying my face in my hands, and let my tears flow freely. Devastated, I wallowed in the realization that I had no one to turn to, no one to talk to. I was alone in this.

Alone in the empty house, I sobbed until I was cried out. When the tears finally stopped flowing, I wiped my face and looked around, sniffling as I got to my feet.

I was nearly out the front door before I changed my mind and turned around, deciding to check Ryder's desk drawer to see if the key and picture were gone. Back in his office, I sat down in the old desk and opened the top drawer, seeking the little button that would make the latch underneath the desk appear. When my finger brushed over it, I pressed it, and the door fell open to reveal the secret compartment underneath.

Reaching inside, I felt around. The key and photo were both gone, but I found a small piece of paper and pulled it out, then opened it with shaky hands.

Hello Vi,

I knew you would end up here eventually and scope out my secret hiding place, because I know you and you just can't help yourself. A little advice: Quit trying to be so nosy all the time. I'm sorry for all the trouble my involvement with the Richtenburgs has caused you, and I'm sorry for hurting you. I do care a lot for you . . . more than you'll ever know. Please stay safe. Have a nice life.

—Ryder Slade Essen

"Asshole," I muttered, and crumpled up the note and threw it back into the compartment. With a newfound determination, I left his vacant house and went home. Fueled by my anger with everything that had happened to me, I packed diligently, not leaving anything out. I cranked up some Avril Lavigne to drown out my thoughts, and sang along with the lyrics while I threw everything that was important to me in my duffel bag.

When I was finished, I checked my phone. Still no word from Ryder.

He was definitely ignoring me, and I was mad at him.

• • •

That night I lay awake as the moonlight filtered in through my bedroom window. I tossed and turned, restlessness tangling me up in the sheets as my mind churned.

My bags were packed, and in the morning my brother would take me to the airport. I would be starting over—alone for the first time—and it scared the hell out of me. The only silver lining I could find in this whole mess was that I would eventually get to meet my real dad.

As I lay there thinking, someone opened the door to my room and crept in quietly. He was bathed in shadows, and didn't say anything as he walked closer.

"Vick, what are you doing?"

"Shhh," was his only response, and it put me on alert. I instantly sat straight up in bed, tugging the sheet higher around me.

Ryder's face came into focus in the darkness, and I didn't know whether to be angry or afraid or happy. My emotions surged, swirling together all at once. I was angry that he hadn't returned my text, afraid because of who he was, and happy because I thought he was gone and that I would never lay eyes on him again.

Deciding to play it cool, I whispered, "What are you doing here?"

"I got your message and decided to drop by and see you."

"A text back would have been fine," I huffed out, "but no, you come here and scare the bejeezus out of me in the middle of the night."

Ryder said nothing, just sat down on the edge of my bed and stared at me with his silver eyes. A little uncomfortable at the intensity of his gaze, I propped my pillow against my headboard and leaned back against it.

"So now that you're here, what is it you wanted to tell me?" I asked.

Ryder's eyes were full of emotion, yet he wouldn't speak the words. Did he reciprocate my feelings for him? Part of me hoped so.

Finally, he said softly, "I wanted you to have this."

He handed me a picture, the one taken of us the night of the costume party. We both looked so happy and carefree, and my heart pinched just looking at it.

Then he set my purse down on my nightstand and said, "And you left this at the party."

"Where did you get these?" My voice cracked as I struggled to keep my emotions in check.

"Raeann gave them to me," he said in a low voice. "She claims she didn't know what her mother was up to."

"Do you believe her?" I asked, watching him closely for any sign of hesitation.

"Yes. I believe her."

"Do you still care about her?"

"For the last time, no!"

A glint of anger flashed in his eyes, and I cast my gaze down and worried the edge of my blanket with my fingers.

"When do you leave for the academy?"

A little relieved at the change of subject, I looked up at him and said sadly, "Tomorrow. I went and said good-bye to Adam today. He was pretty upset."

Ryder rolled his eyes. I knew he couldn't care less about Adam; I was just hoping to make him a little jealous. It would be nice if he admitted how deep his feelings ran for me instead of pretending that he didn't care all that much.

"Will I ever see you again?" I asked cautiously.

"Vi, I'm in deep shit with the Richtenburgs right now. The best thing for you would be to make a clean break with me."

"I don't want a clean break," I said, trying not to whine. "I want to experiment and do all the things we used to do, but only with *you*."

"Please don't make this any harder on yourself." His lips quirked up slightly, then he leaned forward, as if to kiss me.

Instinctively I pulled back, regretting it when I realized my reaction hurt him. "I'm sorry."

He moved to stand up, and without thinking I grabbed hold of his face, one hand on either side of his beautiful mouth, then pulled him to me, my lips pressed to his. I didn't care that we would travel to a shared vision together; I just wanted to get lost in this kiss. I loved this guy, and I wasn't going to let him go without making sure he knew it.

Ignoring the dizziness, I kissed Ryder with abandon, telling him with my passion that he was all I needed, all I wanted.

• • •

When I opened my eyes, we were somewhere I didn't recognize. I pulled away, but Ryder's fingers were twined in my hair, and he pulled me back to his mouth insistently. His tongue parted my lips and I opened for him, loving every taste of him. The feeling of his lips on mine sent adrenaline coursing through me, making my blood sing. I was breathless when we parted, and there was a look of awe in his eyes.

"It's so hard to stop," he whispered.

"I know."

"So, what now?" he said as he glanced around.

I took in our surroundings for the first time. We were standing in what looked like a dorm room with cream-colored walls. There were two twin beds, one on each side of the room, covered with quilts in a traditional pattern of dark and light red squares.

"I wonder if this is my room or yours," I teased.

"Hmm." He gave me a smile. "You know what this means, don't you?"

"No." I shook my head, still feeling flushed from the kiss I gave him. The way he made me feel was so surreal, it felt like a fantasy.

"It means we'll be at the academy together. Otherwise, I wouldn't be here with you now, seeing this." He swept his hand around at the room.

Excitement flooded through me and I beamed at him. "This is great! They won't be able to keep us apart after all!"

"Slow down," he said quietly. "You and I both know that I can't do this. I need to lay low for a while and be on my best behavior. It

251

would be smart for you to do the same. I'm just glad that I'll be able to see you, if only from a distance."

At the realization that Ryder still didn't want to be with me because of the Richtenburgs, my heart sank. Needing a moment to regroup, I got up and looked out the window to see where we were.

The landscaping below the window was beautiful with a large fountain in the center of plush grass, and sporadically placed maple trees, rosebushes, and carefully trimmed shrubbery. A wrought-iron fence encompassed the grounds, and beyond the fence to the sides of us, the trees grew denser. In the distance was what I assumed was Lake Ontario. I could see big-city skyscrapers on the opposite side of the lake, the enormous span of water separating bustling city life from the more serene scene here. It was beautiful . . . maybe it wouldn't be so bad at the academy.

"The view is gorgeous," I said, admiring the surroundings one last time.

"You're right," Ryder said from behind me. "The view *is* gorgeous."

The longing in his voice made me turn around, and I found his silver eyes taking in every inch of me. When I realized he was talking about me, I blushed.

"Come here."

I moved forward as if compelled, not taking my eyes off his, silver to silver. I stopped just inches from him, close enough to feel the warmth of his body.

"Are you ready to go back?" he asked.

"Yes," I whispered.

I thought for a moment that he was going to kiss me, but instead his fingers barely touched me, a feather-light caress along my jawline and down my neck, then slipping behind my head and entangling in my hair.

Ryder pulled me close to him, cradling my head against his chest. The only sound I could hear was the thudding of our hearts, then the onset of a rush of wind. The colored lights performed their magical dance as I shut my eyes, allowing myself to feel safe and secure in his embrace as the dizziness overcame me.

. . .

When I opened my eyes, Ryder was still holding me on my bed. I started to pull away.

"No, not yet," he said. "Just a little bit longer, then I'll go."

His lips brushed my forehead in a soft kiss, and then he pulled back. I gazed at him, unsure of what to say next, the knowledge that this was the last time I'd be able to speak to him for a while weighing heavy on my heart.

The silence between us grew, and before I could stop them, the words flew from my lips. "I love you!"

He shut his eyes tightly, as if the words hurt him in some way, and my heart ached at his reaction.

"I know," I said quickly, a tremor in my voice. "I remember what you said."

When he opened his eyes, they looked at me with indifference. His wall was back firmly in place. I really didn't understand how he did that so well, burying his feelings behind a steel shield.

When he still didn't say anything, I knew it was time to finally give up. "Good-bye, Ryder," I said softly, and for just a second, I saw the hesitation flash in his eyes.

"Good-bye, Violet."

I watched him leave my room quietly, shutting the door behind him. Then I curled up in my bed and cried myself to sleep.

. . .

My alarm blared at five in the morning. I trudged into the bathroom and slowly showered away my sleepiness and ill will, determined to sweep away the storm I'd been living in and look at the bright side for once.

Just concentrate on your grades, I told myself, and then you can come home.

My mind spun as I readied myself for the day, but each train of thought kept circling back to the same place—every cloud has a silver lining.

253

Refusing to wallow in the pain of losing myself, I went through the motions of getting ready without dwelling on any one thing for too long. When I left my room with my luggage to head downstairs, I was smiling from my pep talk.

"Violet." My brother looked miserable as he took the duffel from me and wrapped me in his warm embrace.

"Hey, Vick." I gave him the smile I had been forcing myself to wear since I woke up.

"I'm not happy about this," he said softly as I handed him my keys and followed him outside to my car. God, I was going to miss my Mustang.

"I know." My shoulders sagged when I settled in the passenger seat. "Take good care of her for me, will you?" I said, patting the console of my most prized possession.

Vick rolled his eyes at me, then used his bossy big-brother voice as he said, "Violet, if you need anything you call me, you hear?"

The most time I had ever spent away from my stepbrother was in fourth grade. My stepdad sent me to a basketball camp for a week, and I cried almost every day. Vick was a big part of my life, and I loved him dearly. He always looked out for me, especially after our mom passed, and I was going to miss him like crazy.

"I'll always have my phone on me," he added, "so you can text me whenever you want."

"Vick, I'll be fine," I reassured him, wishing I was sure of myself as I sounded.

Chapter 27

At the airport, I gave Vick a hard hug good-bye. I was a bundle of nerves, never having flown before, and prayed that I didn't mess up and miss my connecting flight in Detroit. Aside from a crying infant on the first leg, a delay before the second leg left, and a little unexpected motion sickness, my trip was pretty uneventful, thank goodness.

After exiting the plane in New York and waiting for my luggage at baggage claim, I slung my duffel over my shoulder and looked around to see there were countless drivers waiting for their clients. I didn't know who would be there to pick me up, but then I spotted a guy in his early twenties holding a sign that read MISS VANCOURT.

I couldn't help but roll my eyes at the formality of it, and walked over to him, taking him in. Well dressed, he was wearing a gray suit, white cotton shirt, and a tie. He had curly dark hair and intense olive-green eyes that seemed surprised when he saw me, but only for a second. He quickly recovered and gave me a professional once-over.

"I'm Violet Vancourt," I said.

He nodded curtly. "I have a private helicopter waiting to fly us to the academy. It's a very short flight. If you will follow me," he instructed, all business. He purposefully took my shoulder bag and threw the sign into the first garbage can we passed. He had a smooth but rapid gait, and my legs had to move double-time to keep up. My stomach still wasn't feeling the greatest, and the rapid pace just upset it more.

"Can you take it easy?" I asked, slowing my pace deliberately.

He cocked his head to one side as he frowned slightly. "We're on a time crunch, Miss Vancourt."

"You can call me Violet," I offered.

"Fine," he said, then slowed his pace to even it out with mine. "Turn this way." He gently guided my shoulders, angling me toward a long corridor.

I gave him a fleeting look. *Okay, Mr. Business.*

As we walked, I studied him surreptitiously, thinking he looked familiar somehow. Despite his unfriendliness, he was undeniably handsome. He had high cheekbones, a defined jawline and chin, a straight nose, and full lips that curved up in a polite smile that didn't quite reach his eyes. In fact, he seemed pretty indifferent to my presence.

When we exited the building, he laid his arm gently across my shoulders, guiding me to the helicopter that was already running and waiting on standby. He ushered me onboard and pointed to the seat next to the pilot's.

"Sit there," he instructed, making me feel like I was in school.

I sat down and buckled up as he stowed my bag, thinking that it was appalling that they would waste money on a helicopter for just two people. He took the seat next to me and carefully checked my seat belt. Once he was positive I was secure, he buckled his and started his flight pre-check.

"What's your name?" I asked.

Looking up from his clipboard, he blinked at me. "I'm sorry, that was rude of me not to introduce myself. My name is Rowan." Then he reached forward and flipped several switches. The engine roared to life, and the helicopter's huge blades began to slowly rotate.

My eyes grew wide and I pressed a hand to my stomach, praying it would behave during this flight. If it was upset on a large airliner, I could only imagine how it would react to going up in this death trap. Maybe if I diverted my attention, my stomach would stay calm, so I decided to see if I could get some answers to some questions.

"Rowan, what do you do for the Richtenburgs?" I asked, purposefully referred to the family themselves instead of the academy to get a reaction from him.

"I head up the academy's security detail," he said.

Security?

As the helicopter lifted off, I was suddenly pressed into my seat. When we had leveled off, I studied him for a moment, then asked,

"Why would they send their head of security to pick up someone like me?"

Rowan cocked his head to one side as he glanced at me, a glint of amusement in those olive-green eyes before he faced forward again.

"Jase wanted to ensure you arrived safely."

His words sent a cold chill coursing through my body, freezing my blood.

Sneak Peek: *Silver Bound*

(Book Two of the Manipulator Series)

The roar of the helicopter's engine filled my ears as I sat stiffly in the co-pilot's seat, feeling a cold spike of fear seep into my bones. The Richtenburg Academy had sent their head of security to pick me up at the airport, an unwanted escort to a private boarding school that I definitely didn't want to attend.

As the helicopter lifted off, I was suddenly pressed into my seat. When we had leveled off, I studied the pilot for a moment, then asked, "Why would they send their head of security to pick up someone like me?"

Rowan cocked his head to one side as he glanced at me, a glint of amusement in those olive-green eyes before he faced forward again.

"Jase wanted to ensure you arrived safely."

His words sent a cold chill coursing through my body, freezing my blood. It stunned me to learn that Jase was associated with the academy. Just a couple of days ago, Jase had defied the Richtenburgs and had tried to kidnap me, wanting to brand me against my will, to force me to become a part of their renegade clan. It had been a close call, and I'd barely escaped.

My expression turned arctic. "You don't say. How kind of him?" I said sarcastically. "He's a multi, isn't he? Are they punishing him from trying to take me?"

Rowan raised his eyebrows slightly, amused by my snarky comment, and ignored my question. "You're feisty." He chuckled. "No wonder he likes you," he mused out loud.

His comment caught me off guard. "Who?"

"Jase, of course," he said with a smirk. "Who did you think?"

"He's a pompous ass. He's your friend, I take it. You know what they say about 'like company.'"

1

He shot me a bewildered glance. "Did you just call me a pompous ass?"

"If the shoe fits. That's all I'm saying." I shrugged and gave him an innocent look.

"Listen here, kid." Rowan leaned toward me, intruding in my personal space. "I may be arrogant but I've worked my ass off to get to where I am today, so I have every right to be. As far as being an ass, we can agree to disagree."

When he settled back in his seat, I let out the breath I'd been holding. I still thought he was an arrogant jerk, but kept my comments to myself.

When we landed a little while later, I shut my eyes tightly. How did I get from point A to point B? This whole mess started when Ryder made his grand entrance into my life and my heart. I couldn't shake my feelings for him, even though I was never able to completely melt his icy exterior. I knew he cared about me, but he wouldn't admit to it or wouldn't allow us to be together.

What was it with me and secret relationships? Did I have issues? Why was I always attracted to the guys who weren't truly available?

God, I missed Ryder. I hoped that he'd arrived already, since we'd learned that he'd be attending the academy too, but my gut feeling told me he hadn't. I sighed aloud and shoved my sunglasses on my face, needing the reassurance of my armor against the world.

I opened my eyes to find Rowan staring at me intently. "What?" I snapped at him, but he didn't reply.

He quickly undid my seat belt as well as his, then rose to collect my bag. He held out his hand to help me up from the seat, and I took it grudgingly, uncomfortable with the proximity between us.

When we exited the helicopter, he made me wait so he could go first, and then took my elbow in an adamant way to make sure I didn't trip on the way down. He didn't bother to let go of my hand as we made our way across the private airport to the waiting limo.

I frowned. God, this organization was rich.

He held the door open for me and I climbed in.

"Thank you," I replied, not forgetting my manners, no matter how perturbed I was with this whole ordeal.

2

He raised his eyebrows, miming a look of shock, and I rolled my eyes and shut the door.

He put my bag in the back holding area and climbed in the other side. "Thirsty?" he asked as he settled next to me. I noticed there was an ice bucket built into the side of the limo, and two glasses hung on a small rack on either side. A freshly chilled bottle of water rested in the container. "Sure, that would be awesome." He unscrewed the top and poured a glass, handing it over to me.

Parched from the flight, I took a tentative sip, then a longer swig. The limo's windows were tinted, giving its interior a calming dimness. I settled back into my seat and tried to relax as we sped along toward the academy, studying Rowan as he poured himself a glass of water and took a long drink.

My gaze traced the high curve of his cheekbones down to his strong chin. He seemed familiar somehow; the sensation that I'd seen him before was so strong. Once he'd had his fill, he leaned back and stretched out. A little embarrassed that I was staring, I was glad my eyes were hidden behind my shades.

"Do you really need those things on in here?" He gestured to the sunglasses, his tone irritated.

Wow, does he sound like Ryder!

"As a matter of fact, I do," I said, going on the defense.

He raised his eyebrows. "And why would that be?"

"For peace of mind. My shield to the world." Or rather *you*, I thought.

He chuckled quietly. "If you insist. I guess I'll allow you to keep them on."

"Don't kid yourself," I said. "It's not like you have a choice in the matter." I rolled my eyes, but knew he couldn't see.

The trees thinned out as we approached the entrance to the academy. There was actually a security guard standing post in a little building. He motioned us through with a wave of his hand, and we pulled up to a huge wrought-iron fence with a gate. The limo driver rolled down his window, entered a security code, and swiped a card, causing the big gates to open slowly. The Richtenburg Academy had

3

quite the security system, considering it was in the middle of nowhere.

The gravel drive crunched as we traveled along it slowly, lined with flowers on either side. The sprawling lawn was beautifully manicured with the occasional evergreen and maple trees. A redwood gazebo was situated in the distance near a pond with a fountain and what looked like a porch swing.

The first building we approached was a stylish sandstone brick building with big double doors. An elaborate emblem of an *S* was displayed prominently above the name painted in elegant letters on the sign above the door—THE HOUSE OF SILVERCREST.

"This will be your dorm," Rowan said, his eyes on my face.

I leaned close to the window, peering up at the building. "How many live in this house?"

"It has thirty rooms, two per room."

The limo pulled to a slow stop, but Rowan made no attempt to get out just yet. He swirled his drink and then tossed the rest of it back. I felt like I should hurry and drink mine as well. I took a long swallow, but couldn't finish it all. He patiently waited for me to finish.

"Is it a full dorm?" I took another sip while I waited for him to explain.

"No. You'll see."

"Okay."

I took the last sip of water and handed him the glass. He put it away and then we both stepped into the warm fall weather. The limo driver took my bag from the holding compartment in the back and followed Rowan and me up the marble steps to the front door.

"Here's your key."

He handed me a key just like the one I'd found in Ryder's desk, and my heart sank. Ryder knew about this school. He owned a key just like the one I'd just been given. Then realization hit me and I wanted to slap my forehead with frustration.

This is the school Ryder goes to, the one in New York he told me about. I'm such an idiot.

4

I put the key into the door to make sure that it worked, then slid it into my pocket.

Rowan frowned at me. "Curfew is at one during the weekends and eleven on weekdays."

I rolled my eyes at the rules. There wouldn't be anything to do here anyway.

"This is a coed dorm, but no girls are allowed to room with guys," he added.

We stepped through the threshold onto a rug situated on gleaming hardwood floors. Stairs led upstairs to our left, and a closet was to the right. Movie-theater type seating crowded the living room, and I was pretty sure that was supposed to discourage cuddling between the opposite sexes. No sofa, no loveseat. The large flat-screen TV mounted to the wall was a plus, and the surround sound looked like it was good quality.

Rowan gestured toward the TV. "There's a movie night every Sunday at seven. It's always pretty busy, and the movies that are picked are pretty decent."

We walked past the living area into the kitchen area.

"The fridge is always stocked for snacks and such," he said. "We have a cleaning crew readily available. The two maids live in a house at the far corner of the campus."

"What, you couldn't find any men to do the dirty work?" I shot at him.

Sensing my hostility, he raised his palms in surrender. "I wasn't in charge of hiring the help," he said defensively, then his lips curled up slightly. Apparently he was amused by me yet again.

I didn't really know what he expected me to say. Oooh, I like the marble countertop? Whatever.

"Can we move on to the bedroom?" I blurted.

Wow, did I just stay that out loud? The way I said it came out as an innuendo rather than a legitimate question. I looked away, suddenly embarrassed.

He smirked, catching on quickly and surprising me by playing along. "If you insist. You do know that we would have to keep this quiet. You could get me fired." He chuckled quietly, and my cheeks burned.

Forgetting myself, I laughed and playfully hit him in the stomach. "Ryder, stop!"

The smile on Rowan's face vanished.

Shit. Did I really just call him Ryder? Yep, I did. I was mortified.

The silence was deafening. "I-I'm sorry," I said, stumbling over my words. As he just stood there staring at me, assessing me, I rambled on. "It's just that, I was close with someone . . ."

I took a deep breath and held it, my anxiety riding high. "With Ryder." I breathed out in a huge whoosh. "The names are so close, and you remind me of him."

I looked at the floor, again feeling the impact of the loss. Every time I spoke Ryder's name, something hit me in the gut. A heart-wrenching desire to be near him consumed me, and I felt like I was dying inside. I craved him near me. He made my heart race, and took my breath away. He was my other half; I knew that now. Yet our situation kept us apart, and it was driving me crazy. Even though these emotions left me feeling unhinged, I still couldn't get past the fact that he was the reason my life had been turned upside down, in both a good and a bad way.

"Let me show you to your room," Rowan said coldly, all business again.

No one liked being called by the wrong name, but what was it to him anyway? I apologized and that should have been enough. There was an undercurrent of anger radiating from him; I could feel it roll off him in waves. My dark mood growing even darker, I followed, deciding not to speak any more than necessary.

I followed him down the hall of the first floor. Rowan stalked by an open door, and I saw a couple of guys tossing a football back and forth. I barely even caught a glimpse because it seemed that Rowan was on the warpath.

"Hey, Essen!" a male voice called to us.

I nearly tripped over my own feet as Rowan suddenly stopped, pivoting so quickly that I ran into his chest. He put his hands my

6

shoulders, pushing me away from him roughly, but waited until I had my balance to release me as he directed his attention past me to the boy.

I could only stare at Rowan. How had I not seen the resemblance? They were both heart-stopping in their looks, with the same hot-then-cold split personalities.

"Yeah," he called down the hall.

"Are we on for football tonight?"

"Yes," he said as he stared into my eyes, as if he were answering us both at the same time.

Yes, he is Ryder's brother! Shit.

I couldn't find the words to speak. I opened my mouth and it felt as dry as cotton. Rowan turned and took a sharp left onto yet another staircase. I tried to wet my lips as I followed. I had no idea he had a brother; Ryder never spoke of him. Although the reality of it was that I hadn't really known Ryder all that long. He kept secrets from me, and those secrets burned inside me and scarred me.

Finally working up the nerve, I spoke to him forcefully, trying to grab his attention. "Rowan, is Ryder here? I didn't realize he had a brother," I said, trying to provoke an answer. Any answer.

We passed several more doors in silence before Rowan suddenly stopped, causing me to run into him yet again. He grabbed me and roughly pushed me up against the wall with one hand. Holding me there, his eyes burned with anger.

"Violet," he said, his tone deathly cold. "Don't speak to me of my brother. You . . ." He paused as if to collect himself, and took a deep breath, trembling with emotion. "You're the one who has caused him so much trouble."

I gasped as my eyes began to sting. *I won't cry. I won't cry.* But I could feel the tears starting to come and tried to calm down, but found my temper rising. Rowan was dangerously on the edge of losing it, and yet I couldn't help myself.

"I thought security guards were supposed to be able to control themselves?" I raised an eyebrow at him. "I was wrong. You and Ryder are nothing alike!"

7

"Damn it!" he yelled, punching the wall next to me. His fist went through the drywall and little bits fell onto my shoulder, hair, and floor.

I jerked in his grip, freezing with the realization that I might have gone too far.

He spun away from me and took a couple steps, then turned. "You're going to your room now," he said, pulling me from the wall.

My heart dropped. I guess I wouldn't have it in good with security. That was too bad; I could have used that to my advantage. Now Rowan would do his best to get me into trouble, and would be watching me like a hawk. I'd have to tread carefully around him.

We took a sharp right and followed the staircase up to the third floor. He stopped at the second door and knocked quietly. A pretty brown-haired girl answered the door, and she smiled warmly at Rowan.

"Hi, Rowan."

Her eyes were silver, which shouldn't have been a surprise since this was the House of Silvercrest. I felt like an idiot for not expecting it, but immediately felt a grudge against the unsuspecting girl. The only other girl with silver eyes I'd ever met was my half sister, Raeann. At the thought of her, I found myself wishing I knew that she was okay.

The girl turned her gaze on me, giving me a sweet smile.

"Serene, this is Violet," Rowan said, his tone still cold.

"Hey," I said casually, and offered my hand. She took it without hesitation. As soon as I touched her, I gasped.

What was I thinking? She had silver eyes, which meant that when we touched we would travel into the future together. *Dumbass*.

My head pounded and my vision blurred as brightly colored lights began whirling around me. Wind picked up my hair, whipping it around my face, and I felt like I was falling. When the familiar spinning began, I closed my eyes. My muscles relaxed as my will left my body, and I let the dizziness consume me.

• • •

8

The sound of music blaring much too loudly made my headache worse as I opened my eyes to see Serene sitting in some kind of lab. Everything was white, cold, and sterile. I glanced around to see Rowan standing guard at the door. Jase was there too, speaking with Serene and . . . Ryder?

My body warmed and tingled at the sight of him; I missed him already. Then the pieces fell into place as I realized this was one of Serene's memories.

"She knows Ryder," I muttered to no one in particular.

"It doesn't work with her, Jase. I don't know why," Ryder was saying, sounding frustrated.

Jase looked at Ryder pointedly. "There has got to be a way to figure out how to make her work!"

Ryder shrugged. "Jase, these are people we're talking about. Not—"

Jase waved a dismissive hand at him and Ryder shut his mouth, but his jaw was clenched. I knew that look well; Ryder was pissed.

What's going on?

Serene's face was blotchy, and her brow pinched. "Why can't I do it?" she said, then dropped her face into her hands as she started to cry.

I drew closer, wanting to try something, and stopped right in front of Ryder. He leaned back casually in his chair, brushing his hands through his hair.

Would I return from this memory if I touched him?

I reached out a tentative hand toward him and stopped inches from his forehead. My heart raced and I held my breath as I let my fingers trace his hairline along his forehead. Closing my eyes, I braced for the unexpected, then opened them slowly, but nothing happened. I must only be able to end the memory by touching the person who owned it.

I looked at Ryder wistfully, longing to touch him more, but not wanting to interfere with the memory itself. I jumped back as Ryder suddenly leaned forward.

9

"Let's try something more personal," he said with a suggestive smile.

His words turned my stomach into a volatile storm. *No.* I shook my head. I couldn't watch this. Not if he meant what I thought he did. I took a tentative step back, but couldn't pull my gaze away from him.

Ryder's perfect lips were smirking at Serene. Her silver eyes went wide with surprise, then desire.

"No!" I screamed, knowing that no one could hear me. I wrapped my arms around my stomach, trying to protect myself, to calm down, but I couldn't look away.

I watched him lean forward, drawing her face toward him with his strong hands. Her eyes slowly closed as his lips covered hers.

Ick. Despite my disgust, I found myself stepping closer to them, curious to see if they would have a reaction similar to the one that I experienced with him.

Ryder deepened the kiss, then suddenly pulled away. "Nothing," he said, his voice dispassionate and cold, flipping the switch on his humanity. This was the Ryder I knew so well—calm, collected, and devoid of emotion.

"Shit," Jase said. "You." He pointed to a nurse. "Take two vials of blood from each of them."

I walked over to Serene. I had seen enough, and all I wanted to do is curl up and go to sleep, so I touched her arm.

The dizzying feeling instantly invaded me, fogging my brain. I shut my eyes, trying to brace myself. As the colored lights started flashing, I felt sick. My stomach was doing somersaults.

Oh God. How could I room with her now? How could I pretend that I didn't see anything? Obviously, I couldn't, and my temper flared.

• • •

I whispered Ryder's name as tears rolled down my cheeks. Sadness swept through me as I began to come to, but I kept my eyes closed.

10

A dispassionate voice called my name, and I slowly opened my eyes to find myself lying on something soft. I gasped and abruptly sat up.

"I'm not rooming with her," I blurted, my eyes wide.

Rowan narrowed his eyes at me and spoke into a communication device, fancier than a walkie-talkie. "Jase, I need you at the House of Silvercrest, third floor, and stat." He set aside the device, then asked me, "What happened to you when you touched her? Nothing happened to her."

He was so much like his brother, which made me miss Ryder more.

"Is Ryder here?" I pleaded as I pulled my knees up to my chest and wrapped my arms around them. I felt exposed, like I was a specimen on display.

"He's not here," Rowan said coldly, "and it's your fault. All the trouble he's in is because of you."

We glared at each other until the sound of quickly approaching footsteps drew my attention toward the door. Jase appeared in the doorway, his hair unruly and wet, and his amber eyes intense. I had forgotten how good-looking he was.

He released his breath with an audible whoosh. "Out of the way, Rowan," he said sternly as he advanced on me, taking a seat on the bed in front of me.

"What happened?" he asked, speaking to me, but Rowan was the one who answered.

"She passed out when she shook Serene's hand."

"You didn't have a vision," he asked me, his voice low and hypnotic.

"No, I . . ." I shook my head. "Never mind."

"Tell me," he said. "I need to know what's going on."

"Where is Ryder, and why are you not being punished?" I asked, using what happened to me as leverage to get some answers.

"Ryder's being punished. I was just following orders, so technically I did nothing wrong." His voice was patronizing, as if he were talking to a small child.

11

Pointedly, I nodded toward Serene and then asked him, "Can we speak alone?"

Jase nodded and glanced around. "Give us the room," he commanded.

Serene practically jumped for the door. Rowan, on the other hand, hesitated slightly before leaving.

Once we were alone, I said, "I can't room with her. I want a room to myself." He opened his mouth to respond, but I cut him off. "If you give me that much, I'll tell you what happened. Do we have a deal?" I asked, offering my right hand.

"Deal," he said, taking my hand in his and giving it a quick shake before releasing it.

I took a deep breath. "Sometimes when I touch someone else who has silver eyes like mine, I get drawn in and witness a memory. I don't know why it happens."

Jase remained composed, but curiosity brightened his eyes. "What did you see?"

"I saw Ryder and Serene in a sterile room with you and a nurse. Ryder was touching Serene, trying to have a vision, but there's something wrong with her. When she touches someone with silver eyes, there's no reaction."

At the memory of what came next, I swallowed. "Ryder kissed her to see if that would make a difference. It didn't." My voice grew weaker. "It takes a lot out of me to see a memory rather than having a vision. I can only think it's because I'm alone in the memory, but in the visions I've had, I had Ryder with me."

"That's interesting," he said, sounding genuinely intrigued. "Do you think you can control what memory you see?"

"I don't know." I thought hard. "It's possible, I guess. I just don't have enough experience yet. Ryder and I didn't get a chance to practice a whole lot."

Jase frowned when I mentioned Ryder's name. "You've earned your own room. You're so unique, I don't think that you should be alone, though. So this is a dilemma for me."

"Geez, what do you think I'm going to do? We're on an island, for crying out loud."

He stared at me for a moment, considering what I had said. An emotion I couldn't decipher flashed over his face, making me wonder if he wasn't telling me something, which seemed to be happening a lot lately, and a shiver of apprehension ran through me.

"I guess I have no choice," he said reluctantly. "Follow me." He grabbed my duffel that was on the end of the bed and led me down to the end of the hall. "You can have this room."

"What's so special about this room?" I glanced around, thinking it was pretty much like the other dorm rooms I'd seen here, and watched him while he set my duffel near the familiar red-checkered bed.

"Well, you won't have a roommate, but Rowan's room is right through there. You'll be safe with him this close."

I glanced through the door that led to a bathroom and another room beyond. *We're sharing a bathroom, just like Vick and I did. Well, that's just great!*

"Are you kidding me? He hates me. I won't be safe."

Jase cocked his head to the side as he studied me. "He might dislike you, but his job is his first priority. He won't fail me."

I sighed aloud and shrugged. "Fine." I finally crossed my arms, not knowing what else to do with them.

Jase walked over to the window and glanced out, but I didn't bother joining him. I knew what he would see, having seen it before in a vision. "The view is quite beautiful. I think you'll like it." He stepped back to look at me.

"I do like it. I've seen it before in a vision."

He raised his eyebrows. "Have you now?"

"Yes." I clamped my lips together, refusing to give him any detail. He'd just have to think about what that meant. Changing the subject, I said, "So, can you tell me how many students with silver eyes have the same ability that I do?"

Jase ambled toward me. "This is a private school, and there are no regular kids that attend this school. Many of our students have certain powers, but you're the only one who can see memories." His eyes narrowed and his voice cut through me as he said, "It makes me wonder what else you can do."

13

I backed up a step, thinking I seriously needed to learn self-defense. *I wonder if they offer a class in krav maga, or something like that.*

His expression cleared, then he reached into his shirt pocket for a piece of paper, which he handed me. "Here's your class schedule. Since it's Sunday, you can take today for yourself, but tomorrow I expect you to be in class. No one from your dorm is in any of your regular classes. The only time you'll see them is your last period each day, when you'll try some supervised experiments with them."

His gaze was so intense, I had to look away. "And if I refuse?" I asked quietly.

"You fail. I doubt your dad will be happy about that. Then there's always the possibility of summer school. You're unclaimed right now, but soon you'll have to make the right decision and join your clan."

I was horrified. My mouth dropped open, but then I quickly composed myself. "Is Ryder here yet? Please just give me that much."

Jase frowned at me. "He really has his hooks into you, doesn't he?"

What? I'm no one's pawn.

"No," I said as I shook my head. "He's just the one I'm familiar with. If I have to experiment, I'd rather it be with him."

Jase walked toward the door, then turned back. "I'm sorry, Violet. Ryder is too close to this. When his punishment is up, then he'll be free to come back to class." He gave me a sympathetic smile. "He never should have disobeyed his orders. He should have stayed away from you. You should remember that."

Then he smiled at me, a smug smirk that made me want to slap it off his face, but I settled for squeezing my fists tightly at my sides.

I wonder what they're doing to Ryder?

The thought of something bad happening to Ryder made me sick to my stomach, but I had more immediate worries. Jase's parting shot sounded almost like a threat. I would have to watch my step here at the academy, or I might learn firsthand exactly what kind of punishment they meted out.

14

Acknowledgments

Few writers work completely alone, and I'm no exception. Many people deserve my sincere thanks and appreciation for their help along this journey.

First, a huge thank-you goes out to my parents, Brian and Margaret LaCrosse, for always encouraging me to pursue my dreams, and for helping me make this one come true. I love you!

Thanks to both my sisters for all their support during this journey. To Dr. Amber Lynn Lacrosse for countless reading and discussion hours – You are my biggest cheerleader and my biggest fan. To Deanna Fryczynski – For our special lunch visits when I just need to clear my head and someone to listen to me ramble.

To my wonderful husband and the father of our two girls – I love the life we have together. Thank you for your continued love and support.

To Pam Berehulke, editor extraordinaire – I'm so lucky to have someone like you in my corner. You are extremely talented, and I'm learning so much from you along the way. I can't thank you enough.

To the talented Collin McWebb of McWebb Designs – Thanks for creating a beautiful cover for me. You, my friend, are truly appreciated.

To Amy Swanson my WBFF (Work Best Friend Forever) – Thank you for always dropping everything to read anything I put in front of you, and for your valuable feedback.

In no particular order, a huge thank-you goes out to these wonderful authors who helped in some way along this journey – Cat Miller, Lori Brighton, and Molly McLain. You are all so wonderful and talented.

Finally, to my special friends for your love and support – Jesse Griffin, Emily Noblet, and Brooke Buckley. You ladies rock!

To my readers – Thank you for taking a chance on a new author. Please leave a review where you purchased this book to help other readers make an informed buying decision. Authors love reviews!

About the Author

Crystal Martin resides in Michigan with her husband, Brent, her daughters Riley and Rayne, a boxer named Razer, and two cute bearded dragon lizards.

An outdoorsy sort of girl, she enjoys horseback riding and camping. When she's not spending time with family and friends, Crystal is usually found writing or reading. *Silver Lining* is her debut novel.

Crystal can be found on Facebook at www.facebook.com/CrystalAnnMartin. She loves chatting with readers, and invites you to connect with her there.

Silver Lining is her first book.

Made in the USA
Columbia, SC
19 September 2022

67303925R00154